CW01653917

DOUGLAS BADER

DOUGLAS BADER

A biography of the legendary World War II Fighter Pilot

JOHN FRAYN TURNER

WRENS PARK

ACKNOWLEDGEMENTS

Some of the material for this biography comes from the two years of talks I had with Douglas Bader. I also talked to Thelma Bader and all the people listed below. I shall always feel indebted to them for their generous help:

John Addison
Max Aitken
Dermot Boyle
Paul Brickhill
Harry Broadhurst
Peter Brothers
David Butler
Peter Cadbury
William Carr
Ian Collins
Denis Crowley-Milling
Alan Deere
Hugh Dundas
Randel Ferraiolli
Alan Garrow
Margaret Garrow
Sue Goodhew
Victor Goodhew
Joan Hargreaves
Louis Jackets
Johnnie Johnson
John Loudon
Jill Lucas
Laddie Lucas
Kenneth More
John Perkins
Frederick Richmond
Alf Robens
Walter Seabrook
Hartley Shawcross
Roy Snodgrass
Iain Stewart
John Stuart
Peter Townsend
Gus Walker
Roy Welensky
David Westmorland
Frank White

Copyright © 1995 John Frayn Turner

First published in the UK in 1995
by Airlife Publishing Ltd

This edition published 2001
by Wrens Park Publishing, an imprint of W. J. Williams & Son Ltd

British Library Cataloguing-in-Publication Data
A catalogue record for this book
is available from the British Library

ISBN 0905 778 75 8

All rights reserved. No part of this book may be reproduced or transmitted in any form or by any means, electronic or mechanical including photocopying, recording or by any information storage and retrieval system, without permission from the Publisher in writing.

Printed in Great Britain by Biddles Ltd, *www.biddles.co.uk*

Chapter 1

Ever since the time when he lost his legs, Douglas Bader's life was bound to be a struggle. But fortunately he found it funny too – that helped him survive. He called the rest of his life 'The Further Adventures of the Legless Ass'.

On the serious side, he always saw issues as good or bad, black or white. In a world of increasing compromise, this strong simple outlook was not necessarily appreciated, and he might have been considered as a complex amalgam of human qualities, often with apparently paradoxical views. Sometimes he could be dogmatic, intransigent, even rude; but always he was infinitely courageous and caring. He was positive, decisive, affirmatory, and he believed in people, not places or things.

He was called one of the greatest Christians alive – even though he rarely went to church. And he had an ambience of greatness. Perhaps he was destined for it . . .

His story began in India. Jessie Bader was living with her parents in the present Pakistan. At the local club for the British, seventeen-year-old Jessie met Frederick Bader, a civil engineer twenty years her senior. They married when she was only eighteen and their first son arrived about a year later. He was named after the father but referred to as Derick to distinguish him from Frederick Senior. Within a year, Jessie expected another child, and they decided it would be best for both of them to return to England for Jessie to give birth. They stayed in the select area of St John's Wood, London, before and after the confinement, Douglas Robert Steuart arriving safely on 21 February 1910.

Not too long afterwards, they despatched Douglas to the Isle of Man, where he lived with relatives for the first year or two of his life.

Then he was escorted out to join his parents in India. The plan had been for them to stay out there indefinitely, but after another year or so they all set sail for England again, where Frederick started to study law. As might be imagined, the family were less well-off than abroad, where they had enjoyed servants and some style. Living more modestly at Kew in Surrey, they had to exercise some care over finances.

World War I then intervened and Frederick received a commission in the Royal Engineers. Soon posted to France, he saw little of his family thereafter, so Douglas's memories of him remained, at the best, scanty. At five or six, Douglas was already a spirited character. They sent him to a prep school called Colet Court, already attended by his older brother Derick.

Douglas stood up for himself staunchly against bigger boys and could fight well even at that tender age. Derick moved on to another school in Sussex as a boarder, and in the holidays Douglas tended to take a junior place to Derick in their mother's attention. In due course, Douglas went on to the same Sussex prep school. He knocked out an older boy in an affair of honour; he started to play rugger and he was soon selected for senior teams with larger boys.

Meanwhile in 1917 shrapnel hit Frederick in the head while fighting on the Western Front, but he did not come home from France. As soon as he had more or less recovered, he returned to the Front – with some of the metal still embedded. He suffered pain from these remnants. Next year the Armistice arrived with Douglas nearly eight and three quarters. Frederick had to remain on duty in France, but did not seem to mind this very much.

Peace did not mean much change in the prep school routine. From the age of only nine or ten, Douglas was learning Latin and Greek, languages that stayed with him throughout the rest of his life. Three years after the end of the war, his father was still in France, working with the War Graves Commission there. Then in 1922 came the shocking news for the family that he had died in St Omer as a result of his war wounds of five years earlier. The significance of the location does not become apparent until much later in Douglas's life.

Douglas had not seen much of his father and so survived the blow. Children of his age have always been resilient. He reached his last year at the prep school. In the time since he joined it, he had graduated to captain of the three main games played there – rugger, soccer and cricket. He was also a star runner. In view of the family's rather reduced money situation, it was fortuitous that he also did enough work to win a scholarship. This would take him on to St Edward's School in Oxford.

Jessie Bader was then thirty-two; still darkly, vitally attractive and still the wilful woman she had always been. Her first marriage had been less than idyllic. Now she married for the second time. Her choice was the Reverend Ernest Hobbs, a vicar in Yorkshire. So they all had to move up there into a capacious rectory provided with the step-father's calling.

In the school holidays of summer 1923, when Douglas was thirteen, his mother sent him for a short break with his aunt Hazel, who was married to an RAF flight lieutenant, Cyril Burge. Cyril was the adjutant at the RAF College, Cranwell, in Lincolnshire. He showed Douglas an Avro 504, the current training aeroplane and the boy sat in a cockpit for the first time. Douglas loved everything about that holiday at Cranwell, but it went into his memory along with many other youthful fancies at an impressionable phase. It could not be said that he at once fell in love with the idea of aeroplanes and flying.

Douglas joined St Edward's School in September 1923, wearing a regulation blue suit – and a bowler hat! He started to kick it from the first day there. The bowler could have symbolised imposed discipline – never Douglas's favourite form of control. He then kicked a soccer ball for the first term, but really preferred rugger, which came in the second term, after Christmas. Douglas had been a 'mercurial' (Paul Brickhill's adjective!) fly-half at his Sussex school. Now they put him in his House first fifteen almost at once.

1924: games took precedence over work, with cricket and rugger both especially time-consuming.

1925: Douglas was still working less than he should have been in class, and only doing well because of his intrinsically agile brain. That summer he got his cricket 'cap' for the school when only fifteen-years-old and actually came top of both bowling and batting averages for the team.

While still under sixteen, Douglas got a place in the first fifteen rugger team, again in his favourite position of fly-half. As in the cricket XI, he was the youngest member of the team, and he managed to score a try in his first match representing the school. In another one later on he scored *seven* tries!

At sixteen or so he became a school prefect. That summer, though, he contracted rheumatic fever and nearly died. With the prayers of the whole school directed at his recovery, he survived this serious illness and regained strength. By the return of the rugger season, he was back to normal and elected captain of the first fifteen. He felt that the responsibility was good for him and he responded to the challenge and the honour. He was always best when his energies could be harnessed and channelled in some such way and not be let to run wild. Which they did on occasion throughout his life!

What would he do when he left school? In December 1927, a chance visit to the school by someone then at Cranwell reminded Douglas of the College and that summer week there. He thought of the flying, but first of all he pondered longingly on all the games they played there. It seemed rather like heaven to him.

Douglas wrote on that same day to Cyril Burge to enquire about his being accepted as an RAF cadet. Jessie was against it and said they could not afford it anyway. They could not find the fees, she insisted. Only then did it transpire to Douglas that for the last year or two some of his school fees had been met by a Mr Dingwall, a master at St Edward's. Douglas was staggered and embarrassed and thanked him profusely for his generosity.

Cyril Burge wrote to tell Douglas that the RAF gave six prize cadetships to Cranwell each year. Douglas was determined to get one of these – although the candidates would number perhaps some hundreds. The odds were heavily against him, but that was always how he liked it.

Douglas really had to swot for the first time in his short life! In the early summer of 1928 he was made captain of cricket and then in June he was summoned to an RAF examination. He did the written paper well enough and then excelled in the crucial interviews for character and aptitude. The medical disclosed his record of rheumatic fever, but they passed him medically all the same. Now he just had to wait for the results.

Finally the letter arrived from the Air Ministry. He opened it. He had come fifth and won a cadetship. As a reward, Mr Dingwall bought him a second-hand motor-cycle: appropriately bearing the makers' name Douglas!

So he left St Edward's at the age of eighteen and in mid-September rode to Cranwell proudly on his new motor-bike. The cadets all wore bowler hats. Douglas could not seem to get away from them, even in the Royal Air Force.

He flew for the very first time that late-September. It was just to acclimatise him to the act of being in the air. Douglas was strapped into the rear open cockpit and then he had his baptism of hearing a propeller at close quarters. They took off. Douglas peered over at the fields of Lincolnshire. He was thrilled with every moment of those thirty minutes. One of many first-time thrills in his adventurous life.

Only a day later, he was allowed to handle the control column while actually airborne. He soon acquired the feel plus the co-ordination of mind and muscle. Early on his instructor, Flying Officer Pearson, instilled into him always to call the machine an aeroplane or an aircraft. Thereafter Douglas always adhered to one or other of these respectful nouns.

By the next month, Douglas had registered six and a half hours' training with dual controls. Out of the blue one day, Pearson asked him:

'Could you take it around on your own?'

Douglas answered affirmatively at once. And with a few final words of advice from his instructor, he was up and away. Pearson watched the Avro anxiously, although he knew Douglas was an exceptional student. DB did not disappoint him, coming in for a smooth three-point landing after the first solo of his life. So he chalked up another first that day.

Douglas now had two loves – his original passion for rugger and also flying. As young men have always done, he tried smoking and drinking while at Cranwell, but actively disliked both of them. So he ignored the habits for the rest of his life. The Bader decisiveness asserted itself at a relatively early age.

Before long, Douglas had the thrill of being selected for Cranwell's rugger first fifteen. But flying had already begun to overtake even rugger as the love of his life. He fully intended to apply to be a fighter pilot and was introduced to aerobatics by the tireless Pearson. So at this phase his activities tended to be, first flying, followed by rugger, cricket, hockey and boxing. Somehow he just found time for theoretical studies, but they came below games in his list of priorities.

To harness the impersonal discipline imposed from somewhere above, Douglas still needed the sense of responsibility or challenge. In the absence of being a prefect or equivalent official, as at school, he found outlets for his temperament in beating some of the 'pettier' Cranwell rules, like being back in College by midnight. This wayward, boisterous behaviour, allied to coming nineteenth from twenty-one in his annual exams, brought him up before his squadron commander. Despite Douglas's undoubted abilities in the air and on the sports field, the officer told him:

'I'm fed up with you.'

Then he had to go in front of the Air Vice-Marshal for a further severe admonition. This proved in retrospect to be a turning point for Douglas, when he decided that he must cease being a boy and start to behave more like a man. But it could not happen completely and all at once. However, he did try.

Douglas devoted more time to his studies and less to fooling around. He got his Cranwell 'colours' for all his four principal pursuits in sport: rugger, cricket, boxing, hockey. He had about a score of boxing bouts at Cranwell altogether and ended them all with a knock-out – except one. Only in his final fight was he himself K.O'ed!

1930: Douglas's better behaviour justified his being made an under-officer of a training squadron. He reacted to this positively in every way. He buckled down to his studies and went from strength to still greater glory in games.

The final examinations came round in June 1930 and Douglas took them with a relatively easy mind. Then before the results were posted on the board, he took part in a memorable internal cricket match, captaining his training squadron against the other one. The bare figures hardly tell the whole story. Their opponents scored 238 all out, Douglas capturing half the wickets. Then his squadron collapsed to twenty-three for four wickets, before Bader reached the crease. The rest was rather like a boys' story – though minus the happy ending.

Douglas was still there at 135 for nine wickets. None of the other batsmen had reached double figures. The last man partnering Douglas hardly had to face a single ball from opposing bowlers. Douglas hit boundaries of both sorts, singles, or threes, to keep the bowling. Amazingly this last pair put on a further ninety-two runs. At that point, they needed only a couple of sixes to win the match. Douglas was 194 not out, the other man naught not out! But then Douglas attempted a tremendous hit for one of those sixes – and was caught out. Quite a match.

Douglas came second in the exams and his report on leaving Cranwell read simply: 'Plucky, capable, headstrong' with a high grading for his flying. The ideal qualifications for a responsible, individualist, potential fighter-pilot.

Douglas was commissioned Pilot Officer Bader and posted to No 23 Squadron, RAF Kenley, in Surrey. To celebrate, he swapped his motor-bike for an Austin Seven car, vintage 1920s, and drove it to his new station. On the morning after arrival there, his flight commander unravelled to him the mysteries of the Gloster Gamecock – the fighters then flown by the squadron. Douglas took to the sky in one of them that same day. He soon got to know that two of these fighters would be displaying aerobatics at the famous annual Hendon Air Show. Douglas made a mental note of his intention to be one of the two Gamecock pilots the following year.

But it was still August 1930 and the latter end of the cricket season. Almost as soon as he joined Kenley, he was selected to be one of the few in the RAF Cricket XI. In the autumn, the celebrated rugger team, the Harlequins, invited him for a trial. He passed this well, becoming their newest centre three-quarter. Then his cup was complete by being chosen as fly-half for the RAF fifteen. He began to get his name in the quality newspapers that covered rugger extensively.

February 1931: to celebrate his twenty-first birthday and transition to man's estate, Douglas changed the homely Baby Austin for an MG sports car – more appropriate both to his image and his character. Self-willed, dynamic, still sometimes wayward. All the Gamecock pilots started to train madly for the 1931 Hendon Air Show. The leader was already chosen, so that only left two possible places, numbers two and three, the reserve. Already someone had been killed trying a manoeuvre, so supreme skill was needed.

They had strict instructions to keep above 500 feet at all times during their aerobatic training, but Bader liked to knock off the last nought and fly at fifty feet. In April, the three aerobatic pilots were named as No 1, Day, the leader; No 2, Bader; and No 3, Stephenson, the reserve. Both Bader and Stephenson liked to try slow rolls at fifty feet and on one of these, Stephenson stalled and nearly crashed. That would have meant a court-martial if he had been seen, but luckily he got away with it.

Douglas still tended to be wild, confident almost to conceit, yet brilliant at everything he essayed. He batted for the RAF at the famous London Oval cricket ground, making sixty-five runs in half as many minutes. Then came the news he had awaited above all else: confirmation of the Hendon Air Show personnel. Day and Bader would definitely be the two Gamecock pilots that summer. The afternoon of the show came and went. Quarter-of-a-million spectators saw the two fighter-pilots give a quite superlative exhibition.

Then the idyllic life went on. Douglas magnetised girl friends. Three or four of them he had, in series or in parallel. He was never sure which. He got press publicity and flew on more displays. And the inevitable games continued, too. He heard that the RAF might defer the normal overseas posting due for him soon, in case he were selected to play rugger for England. That would, of course, be an honour both for Bader and the Service.

But Douglas still had that dare-devil in him – that actual element essential to be a fighter-pilot in the first place. Two pilots had crashed and been killed while ignoring advice – and orders – never to attempt aerobatics under 2,000 feet. The height had been raised to try to avoid further tragedies. Bader again ignored the edict and was reprimanded for showing off in this manner.

November 1931. Douglas was selected as fly-half for the Combined Services team to play the visiting Springboks fifteen from South Africa. He was in the wars during this match and broke his nose. Not fully better from the ordeal, he played indifferently for the Harlequins in the following week. So, psychologically perhaps, Douglas was feeling that he had to prove himself somehow to compensate for these two slight failures. Knowing the quicksilver personality of Douglas Bader, it is a possible theory for what ensued in December.

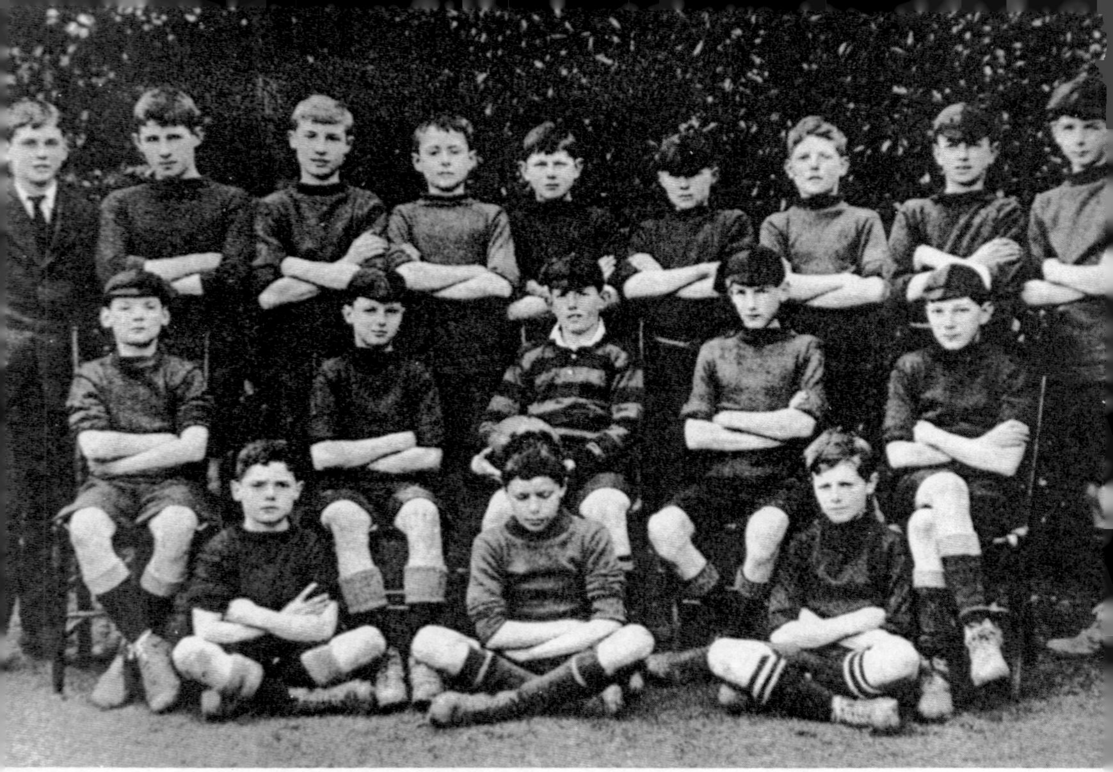

Temple Grove Preparatory School, Eastbourne. Douglas Bader front row, left. *(Harper Collins)*

The prefects with the Headmaster, St Edward's School, Oxford 1928. Douglas Bader front row, second from right. *(Harper Collins)*

The Gamecock, 23 Squadron, Kenley, 1930, *(Harper Collins)*

The aerobatics team for the Hendon Air Display, 1931. Bader, Day, Stephenson (reserve). Ten years later they were to meet in prison camp in Germany. *(Harper Collins)*

Chapter 2

On 14 December 1931 Douglas flew over to Woodley Aerodrome, Reading, with a couple of other pilots, Phillips and Richardson, to see Phillips' brother there. They had coffee and chatted to some of the chaps in the flying club at Woodley. One or two of them had been trying to needle Douglas into showing them some aerobatics, but the RAF pilots were as usual under orders not to do so. Douglas had proved himself at the Hendon Air Show.

The RAF trio took off in their aircraft to fly back to Kenley. Phillips and Richardson went first, while Douglas brought up the rear. He was still smarting from the needling in the clubhouse and decided to show them what he could do. He turned, dived low over the Woodley field and did a slow roll just a few feet off the ground. He made a slight mistake and the aeroplane crashed on to the grass somewhere in the middle of the airfield. Douglas finished up with the whole machine wrapped around him.

He was not dead. He was not even unconscious. But he had hurt himself very badly. His right leg had the rudder bar right through the knee and was very nearly severed from his body. His left leg was broken between the knee and the ankle where the seat had been forced forward, and he was still sort of sitting on it. The strange thing was that he did not seem to be feeling any particular pain in this messy lower part of his crushed body.

Douglas was of course wearing his usual flying overalls and uniform, so the evidence of the crash was not yet apparent. The pain that he did in fact feel came from his back. The fighting harness had held him when the aeroplane hit the ground and his body had tried to lurch forward. This harness saved his life and he felt the pain from the wrench to prove it. At that first minute after impact, Douglas simply sensed a kind of buzzing in both legs, rather like the feeling you get when hitting your funny-bone. Only this was in his legs.

Douglas and the aeroplane finally landed upright and it did not catch fire. A man called Cruttenden got to the scene first, undid the straps, somehow dragged Douglas out of the cockpit, and transferred him to an ambulance that had arrived with commendable speed. Cruttenden sat with him in the ambulance and saw that he was bleeding dangerously from his right leg. Douglas had severed the artery and so Cruttenden stuck a large hand tightly over the bit of overall and leg where the blood was coming from. Douglas was always convinced that Cruttenden saved his life by that action alone.

They hurried him to the Royal Berkshire Hospital at Reading, where the next thing he remembered was lying on or near the operating table, with the face of the splendid anaesthetist, Commander Parry Price, gazing down at him. Price was about to put the nozzle over Douglas's face, when Bader protested as vehemently as he could:

'Don't give me an anaesthetic – I can't stand those things.'

The reason for this outburst was because Douglas had been taken to a nursing home in Manchester Square, London, by his mother when he was only about five and a half. Here he had been pushed on to an operating table, preparatory to having his tonsils or adenoids out. They told him he had been dressed in a red nightshirt so that he would not see the blood. Then someone thrust a great nozzle over his face. This had stuck in Douglas's mind for sixteen years and was why he tried to push the nozzle away then.

That was all Douglas recalled for a day or two.

Eventually the world filtered back into his consciousness. He opened his eyes and made out the figure of a sister, with her back towards him. She was standing in front of a window and looking out at a blue sky and scraps of clouds fluffing across the sun. Douglas could not remember anything, neither his name nor what had happened. His head lay against the inner wall and his feet pointed towards that window. Then looking again, he saw a cradle over his legs. He looked beyond that to the end of the bed, to the nurse, to the sky beyond.

'What am I doing here?' he asked softly.

'You're awake, are you? Well, you've had an accident in an aeroplane and you've hurt yourself. We're looking after you.'

'Thanks awfully.'

The sister left the room and returned with a man wearing a grey herringbone suit. He had slightly grey, wavy hair and looked rather like a don or something else academic.

'I'm afraid you've had a bit of an accident, old son, and we've had to take your right leg off', he said.

Douglas was extremely weak, too much so to care. This initial statement made no real impact on him at all. He said:

'I'm sorry, doctor, I'm being such a nuisance.'

The doctor was in fact the surgeon, Leonard Joyce, who had performed this first operation. Douglas was not too weak, however, to have a look underneath the bedclothes as soon as he was left alone again. He wanted to see what a 'leg off' looked like. He lifted up the bedding slightly and saw that his right leg appeared to be just what he would have expected: a little bit of stump with a bloody bandage around it. Yet it had no effect on him. He did not feel any emotion at all. Perhaps this was nature helping him over the first shock. He was really too weak to care. Then nature came to the rescue again.

An hour or two after awakening, he started to feel the pain. His left leg began to hurt like hell, but his right leg or the remains of it did not trouble him at all. He learned later that there must have been pain in both, but in such cases the major pain always prevails over the lesser one. Douglas found it hard to tell why this left leg was hurting, because as far as he knew then, it was simply broken and they had set it. When he saw that it was still apparently whole, he could not think why the pain was so strong. What he did not realise was that it had become badly poisoned.

Not long afterwards, the surgeon came back and said:

'Look, we've got to reset that left leg. It's going to hurt a bit, so we're going to give you an anaesthetic.' Another bloody anaesthetic, thought Bader.

In due course a nurse appeared with a phial of evil-looking pink fluid. She inserted it in his backside and before he had hardly time to say, 'That's never going to do anything', he had passed out again.

He woke up feeling very drowsy, but not at all sick and with no other ill effects. His left leg was still hurting like hell, though. Just as it had been before. He actually started to think 'I don't know why they don't cut this one off as well.' He went on lying there in this frame of mind, when the leader of 23 Squadron came in to see him. Douglas realised later that he had probably been sent in for the job. They talked for a bit in general terms.

'You know,' Douglas said, 'this bloody left leg hurts like hell. I can't think why they don't cut it off. Because the other one doesn't hurt me at all.'

'Do you really want it to be cut off?' the squadron leader asked.

'Yes – I just can't wait.'

'Well – as a matter of fact, they have cut it off.'

Douglas only paused for a second.

'Then why the hell does it hurt so much? Surely it shouldn't do now?'

He did not even bother to look at it to check up. He was primarily concerned at the fact that it still hurt him. Fortunately there is nothing so effective as pain to make someone concentrate their attention. At least the pain occupied Douglas's mind to the exclusion of everything else. So perhaps it was a good thing just at that time.

During this twilight period after he had lost his second leg, Douglas touched bottom. The pain went on and on and on. He felt weaker instead of stronger. He got to the stage of being slightly lightheaded and not really aware of what was going on around him. Shadowy figures came and went and did things. Douglas felt dimly aware of them. Then the pain started to subside. But so did he. At one time he just remembered lying on his back and feeling no pain of any kind. He did not know if it were night or day even. He was barely conscious of touching or feeling the bed; in fact, he was barely conscious at all. But he did vaguely feel that this was marvellous. No pain, no effort, very cosy, very agreeable. Peaceful. Then he heard a slight sound, a murmur, followed by somebody saying:

'Sh! There's a boy dying in there.'

It reached his brain with a clarity and an intensity, as though someone had spoken the words right beside his bed. He suddenly got a jerk in his system and he reacted.

'So that's why it's so cosy. So that's what they think. Well, they're bloody well wrong. I'm going to do something about this.'

Douglas dragged himself into clear consciousness, back came the pain, and he knew he was fighting it. He started slowly to get better. One of many turning points.

Later on this left him with a complete indifference to death. He was unafraid of it, because after that, it did not occur to him that it was anything other than rather agreeable. But this did not alter his resolve to avoid it at that time of his life. At twenty-one he had a lot left to do.

People often asked Douglas, 'Wasn't it terrible when you realised you had lost both your legs?' The answer was 'No, because I never had any shock.' He had been cushioned against any idea of shock by the persistent repetition of hearing that he had had his legs off. It ceased to have any impact and he became rather bored by the whole thing. Strangely enough, Douglas derived strength and mental balance from the very knowledge that it had been his own fault.

As he recovered after that critical point, Douglas began to spend a lot of his time in reading. He had always loved poetry and he re-read Swinburne while in hospital:

> 'The glass of the years is brittle
> wherein we gaze for a span.'

Only a short while earlier, he had been a healthy, athletic young man without any cares. Suddenly the brittle glass had shattered and he was lying in bed minus his legs and reading Swinburne. He went on combating the pain, which lessened the impact of the loss of legs. By the time he could eventually assimilate the significance of his accident, its importance had diminished. The pain plus the repetition of the facts did this. The result was that the absence of psychological impact had a considerable effect on his mental attitude to the whole affair and his own future. So when the pain did end, and he began to mend physically, the mind was not agitated by the loss of legs. This was also because Douglas had no idea of life without legs, could not assess the future, so left it alone. Each day was enough. Later on, in fact, when he was recuperating, Douglas used to dream he had artificial legs, but they worked in exactly the same way as his ordinary legs. This was because he had never known artificial legs or being without his real ones, so that anything in his subconscious was automatically associated with what he could do before the loss.

On Christmas Eve 1931 they moved him across to the nursing home called Greenlands. It was only ten days since the crash. He was well looked after here and thoroughly spoiled. In general he had a splendid time in this early convalescence. A man came over from Oxford to fit him with a peg-leg. The way they fitted him was to wrap some wet plaster of Paris bandage around his leg, let it set, and then rip it off. Douglas's leg was pretty sore still, because the stump had not healed completely. What they seemed to have forgotten was that when the plaster of Paris came off so did all the hairs.

The man returned with a peg-leg incorporating a hinge to look after the bend and stretch of the knee. He also brought a corset. The peg-leg had a rubber heel stop on the bottom. Douglas put on the peg-leg and tried to get up on some crutches. He was still very feeble after what was by then a couple of months' complete inactivity – apart from the major shock to the system of losing the legs. He did not do well in supporting himself and the crutches kept flying out in all angles. The nurse, Dorothy Brace, was wonderful with him, but said, 'Take it easy – and I do wish you wouldn't use that appalling language!' But after a couple of days, Douglas managed to get upright on the peg leg, with the aid of the crutches, and he staggered about for a few steps. Soon he improved and was hopping around freely on this leg.

So Douglas had quite a bit of fun walking about successfully on his peg-leg progressing from the high crutches down to elbow crutches. Then the surgeon, Leonard Joyce, told him:

'I've got to have another go at both your legs, because they were both what we call guillotine operations and I haven't had a chance to trim them properly, so that the artificial leg people can make a decent job.'

The bone on Douglas's right leg was almost sticking through the flesh, while the fibula on his left leg was too long.

'I'll have to do you again,' Joyce told Douglas, 'but I'll do them both together. Then you'll be in good condition to go to the artificial leg place.' He gave Douglas the greatest confidence and was a remarkable surgeon for those earlier days. So Douglas had his legs trimmed up, which was followed by yet another period of pain and inconvenience. Then came the time to leave Greenlands. It was a wrench for Douglas, but he kissed all the nurses, got into a Royal Air Force car, and was taken to the RAF Hospital at Uxbridge. They had all minded so much at Greenlands. Douglas would not forget them.

At Uxbridge he felt he was back in an atmosphere he really understood and where he belonged. There were rules and regulations, yet they seemed reasonable ones. Douglas was in a ward with other officers. Legend has it that one of them had his ear drop off during a guest night at RAF Martlesham! He was at Uxbridge to have it riveted back on again! Victor Streatfield had broken his arm. John Peel had a broken leg. The whole RAF atmosphere had a bracing effect on Douglas. He used to go around on his peg leg or sometimes early on with his wheelchair. They would push him fast down a slope in the wheelchair, and he would end up in a flower bed with the chair on top of him. This all helped to restore his sense of humour. One of the many RAF traditions has always been to make light of whatever happens: to minimise it whether good or bad.

It was during Douglas's stay at Uxbridge that he first met Thelma. The patients who were inmates of Uxbridge were not supposed to have cars, but John Peel did keep an open, four-seater Humber in a garage down the road from the hospital. One day in May 1932 and still a mere five months since the crash, he and Victor Streatfield and Douglas decided to get it out, take a drive, and stop somewhere for tea. So they all rolled down the road, rather like naughty boys. Victor had his arm in a sling and supported on a metal frame in front. John had his broken leg. And for some obscure reason, Douglas decided to drive. He was wearing his peg leg. He reckoned that as long as John Peel would prod the clutch at the start, he could drive it once they got going.

It was a fine day and they had the hood down. After more than a slight contretemps in Slough, they left fists shaking at them. Then they drove into Windsor Park, which was easy without any traffic. Then on to Ascot and towards Bagshot. It was getting near teatime, so just after passing the Cricketers' Inn, they spotted a place called The Pantiles. On the left-hand side, this was one of those roadhouse innovations from America of the early 1930s. 'That looks just right.'

They drove in over the gravel and pulled up. People at tables in the garden stopped eating and drinking tea to watch this motley trio in such a state of physical disrepair disgorging from the Humber. Victor was sitting in the back with all his metalwork. John hobbled out. And Douglas followed on his crutches. They moved across to a table and sat down. Then the most beautiful girl that Douglas had ever seen walked up to serve them.

'Would you like tea?'

Douglas gazed at her.

'We'd like three teas,' John said.

'Do you want cream or plain?'

'Cream,' they all decided.

As she walked away, Victor said in a stage whisper, 'Do you think she has got a sister?' That was the meeting of Thelma and Douglas.

They all vowed they would go back there as soon as they could. When they arrived on one or two later visits, the other girls always said, 'Go on Thelma, there are your boy friends!' Two of the girls were good friends of hers. She always managed to serve the RAF trio and after a few visits Douglas discovered that her father had been in the Royal Flying Corps and she had cousins in the RAF.

Meanwhile, with the natural optimism of youth allied to Douglas's own very individual *joie de vivre*, he had the feeling that if someone would just give him some proper artificial legs, he would be running around on them in no time flat. But in this context, the operative word was in fact – flat. He went to Roehampton, where he was fitted with proper legs. These had a foot on them below the knee and an artificial articulated leg above the knee. But there was no physiotherapy in those days. He had a terrible job trying to manipulate the upper leg. Douglas got this pair of legs and took them back to Uxbridge. For the first time since his accident, he received its full impact. He found himself utterly unable to move. To walk on these things seemed totally impossible. This was no moment for a philosophical approach to the problem. It became a straight physical battle. Douglas refused to accept this unexpected setback. He decided he was not going to be a nuisance or a burden to his friends: he would become independent of the assistance of other people. That was his immediate and only goal. All else could follow.

He tried to walk up the ward. He fell down. Needless to say, it was a linoleum floor and a highly polished one at that. Douglas picked himself up and tried again. He fell again. He kept on falling. The chaps in the ward encouraged, lifted him off the ground, or else just laughed at him. They were in fact behaving naturally and characteristically, and nothing could have been calculated to help him more. They made rude remarks about his efforts, but they picked him up. Gradually he got better at standing and walking. They noticed and commented and praised.

Now it was high summer. Douglas could walk. He had not been down to The Pantiles for a while, because he wanted to surprise Thelma by arriving walking upright and unaided. He did it. He had got his MG and had the pedals changed round so that he could drive it. He had also passed his medical and received his notice of posting to RAF Wittering for testing to see if he could fly, and he had been down to friends at Lympne, where he flew an Avro 504 without any problems. So things were looking better than at any time since 14 December 1931.

Douglas drove down to Bagshot and got Thelma alone for a few minutes. She saw him and was suitably impressed at his walking. He told her he was going to Wittering and could he ask her out soon. She said she would be back in London by October. So Douglas set off for Wittering happily.

One day in October, he drove the eighty-eight miles from Wittering to London to see Thelma. That was really the beginning and it proceeded rapidly from there. He took her out to the Monseigneur Club, on the corner of Lower Regent Street and Piccadilly. Then they used to go to the Café de Paris. Another favourite place was the new Ace of Spades on the Kingston-by-Pass. They did a lot of dancing and canoodling. Thelma was very good at dancing and used to lead Douglas. In the latter, he led her.

CHAPTER 3

At RAF Wittering they let Douglas fly Bulldogs again, but because of his disability they insisted on an instructor being present in the second trainer seat. Douglas flew to his usual high level of professionalism and there seemed to be no reason why he should be failed as fit for the full flying duties of a pilot officer. The Chief Flying Instructor at Wittering soon realised the absurdity of the situation and told Douglas:

'There's nothing more we can teach you about flying and there's no point in your mucking about not able to go solo.'

So the CFI gave the medical board his opinion as to the flying ability of Bader minus legs. Still an outstanding pilot . . .

Douglas was summoned to London for yet another of the string of medicals he had endured since his accident. He discovered that this time he did not need a medical at all, but was scheduled to see the Wing Commander. Douglas reasonably expected to hear that he would be passed as fit for a flying squadron. But instead he heard the worst news. The Wing Commander started to speak, but Douglas could scarcely take in the meaning:

'The Central Flying School say you can still fly pretty well.' Pause. 'Unfortunately, we can't pass you fit for flying because there's nothing in King's Regulations which covers your case.'

Douglas was shocked and retorted rather insolently:

'Well, why the hell did you send me there to be tested?'

He stormed out to go and tell Thelma the bad news. Nearly a year after the accident, he was posted to RAF Duxford in Cambridgeshire – again, another irony in view of later events. His job there was officer in charge of motor transport – a simple duty if not actually a sinecure. This was the last thing Douglas needed at any time.

One day near the anniversary of his crash, one of the flying instructors at Duxford took him up in an Atlas biplane and let Douglas handle the controls most of the time. Another morning, this instructor, Flying Officer Joe Cox, let Douglas tackle a solo landing, watched by other pilots. Unluckily they were also watched by the authoritarian Wing Commander of the station. He told both men off but at least took no further action.

Finally in late-April, Douglas heard that the Air Council had decided to put him on the retired list due to 'ill health'. Soon afterwards a letter from the Air Ministry informed him that he would be granted £100 a year disability pension plus £99 10s a year retired pay. Quite a generous gesture for those days. Nearly four pounds a week. Douglas could not starve, but nor could he live as he would want to on such a sum.

Thelma proved a consolation to him, but it was clearly going to be a traumatic time for him – and thus for them both. At once he met the slump conditions of the world in the early 1930s outside the shelter of the Service. He tried the Officers' Employment Bureau – without success. Little work existed for fully fit men. He went right through that first week thrashing about looking for non-existent jobs.

The Bureau suggested he tried the Asiatic Petroleum Co, so he arranged an appointment to be seen. They told him that they had a small but expanding aviation section, which might be able to offer him a job. The manager of aviation did indeed have an office vacancy for someone to assist in the sales of aeroplane fuel abroad. He offered Douglas £200 a year. Douglas was not used to the business world and wanted to avoid sounding too eager to accept. He said he would ring them back shortly – although he had really already decided he must take the job.

He drove hurriedly to tell Thelma and they went to their favourite roadhouse, the Ace of Spades, to celebrate. He is quoted as proposing to her that evening over curry with the words:

'I suppose we can start thinking about getting married now.'

Thelma implied that she would agree but suggested they keep their engagement secret at present to forestall any objection from her parents. Douglas survived the first two weeks at work, but eventually had to dictate his first letter – to be signed by a senior man in the section. This gentleman told Douglas that the letter read more like a telegram, adding:

'You want to wrap it up a bit to the chaps out there.'

So Douglas and the shorthand-typist together constructed a long letter which softened the immediate meaning of the words. But it seemed to be what the senior man liked, so that minor crisis was over. But with Douglas there would always be more.

He had updated his original MG sports car, which now symbolised the standard of living he insisted on preserving. One Saturday they were travelling fast on the Great West Road in outer London when Douglas tried to squeeze between a lorry and a large car – and just failed. The MG lost the two wheels on his side and also the driver's actual door. Neither Thelma nor Douglas was hurt but the accident cost them a lot – in money and pride and sheer physical effort. By a coincidence, Thelma knew the occupants of the car.

Douglas had to travel by public transport for several weeks while the garage repaired the MG And when he went to see Thelma after using the Underground or buses, he still had to climb those darned ninety-six stairs to her flat. The two bills for the other car and his own arrived – £10 plus £68. The garage told him he could settle the big one by instalments of a pound per week. The money situation seemed to mean their wedding plans being postponed, but Douglas decided differently:

'Why don't we get married anyway, *now*?'

Thelma raised the twin questions of the money and her parents' consent. 'We'll manage somehow,' he insisted. And as to her parents, he had the idea of not telling anyone about the marriage!

They had to wait three weeks for a special licence, due on 5 October, and then Douglas was due for two weeks' leave from his boring job. The wedding day arrived at last. Douglas collected Thelma in her very special dress at 11 am. He drove to Hampstead Registry Office, where they were duly married. Afterwards, Thelma hid the wedding ring and Douglas drove her home.

The flat where she lived was part of the house owned by her mother and stepfather, Lt.-Col and Mrs Addison. The Baders told the Addisons that they were engaged. Later that night, Thelma's mother gave her an old diamond ring that had belonged to Thelma's grandmother, so the problem of buying an engagement ring was solved – after the wedding! No-one suspected the couple were married, then or later.

Thelma's uncle had recommended to them a guest-house at Porthleven in Cornwall, so they had arranged this for the secret honeymoon, booking separate rooms as an engaged pair. They were awoken in their own rooms each morning by the landlord of the guest-house, who never imagined that they were really on their honeymoon. It had rained much of the way driving down to Cornwall and for the fortnight they were there, but nothing mattered. They were wed.

Back in London again, Douglas dropped Thelma at her mother's house in Avonmore Mansions, while he went home to his bed-sitter. From south-west to north-west London. Despite a pound a week rise in his salary, Douglas got fed up with his job and the difficulties created by being parted from Thelma – though he saw her most evenings and at the weekends. It was a strange arrangement.

But life went on. One weekend, two friends, Adrian Stoop and Tinny Dean, suggested that Douglas and Thelma drive down to a golf course at Hartley Wintney, where the two men were going to have a game. After the two men had left the first tee, Douglas said he would like to try with a club and ball. This was the start of something . . .

He swung the iron but did not connect with the accursed little ball. Worse than that, he fell on his back. As he had done many times before. He got up. He fell three more times. It got to the twelfth time until the club struck the ball. Douglas watched it fly through the air – from the vantage point where he had fallen once more! Another dozen shots and he hit it again, but still fell. Forty times that day.

They stayed overnight at the Stoops' home and next morning Douglas was up early with his golf club and ball in the garden. The same sequence happened over and over. He managed to hit the ball, but always fell down after the stroke. Twenty or more times. At last he tried a shorter, slower swing and remained on his metal legs.

'Now perhaps you'll be satisfied,' Thelma called to him.

But Douglas was never satisfied with less than perfection, so continued. Successfully now, with several hits and fewer falls. The next weekend they went down there again and Douglas only fell occasionally, and by one further weekend he had mastered that first hurdle of hitting the ball and keeping on his legs. As with so much else he did, this symbolised more than simply hitting a golf ball.

By the time another fortnight had elapsed, Douglas was ready and raring to try on the actual golf course. The first tee is always an ordeal when there are onlookers, but luckily Douglas struck the ball well and it traversed a hundred yards or so. More important than that, Douglas was still upright. He told Tinny Dean to go on ahead while he practised on the first two holes. The exertion caused him a lot of pain, the stumps of his legs rubbing sore spots with the unaccustomed twisting of the golf swing.

Douglas began to anticipate the weekends for these golf outings. He and Dean played at Fleet in Hampshire and he fell only once over two complete holes. He was driving further than his original hundred yards. The effort put a lot of strain on his arms and body, but he concentrated and improved. From two holes, his sorties increased to four holes. Thelma accompanied him to Fleet frequently and he told her:

'This could be a game I might play on level terms with anyone.'

The energy that Douglas had put into all those other games before the crash now went into golf. They let him join the club down there for a small sum and he bought half-a-dozen clubs and a bag at a Railway Lost Property Office. Progress continued. Thelma caddied for him and before long he had managed nine holes in one session. He used zinc ointment to stop his stumps feeling so sore, but he still got very tired. But the tally rose to twelve holes at a time and only six months after that first day at Hartley Wintney, Douglas went a full round of eighteen holes and professed not to feel tired at the end of it. Moreoever, he had doubled the length of his drives to 200 yards: good for any golfer.

Douglas being Douglas, that was not enough. One day that December, he played two rounds. An effort for any able-bodied individual, this was a superhuman achievement for him. He used to sweat profusely at the strain necessary to walk and swing the clubs. Golf saved his sanity, because the boredom of his job drove him almost to distraction. He tried for a flying vacancy with the firm as aviation manager in Egypt, but they refused to consider him. So golf continued to be his outlet, his safety-valve, and through it he got to know a lifelong friend, Henry Longhurst. Together they played regularly, often two rounds a day even in the teeth of winter weather. Douglas returned one round of 81. Henry himself was a golf journalist, enthusiast and expert – with a scratch handicap – so he was the ideal playing partner for Douglas.

When someone is fitted with a pair of articificial legs, there is a tendency to spinal curvature, particularly if one leg is slightly shorter than the other. And when they get in a permanent physical condition suited to wearing the legs, this state affects other parts of the body.

When Douglas crashed, he was not unconscious and he recalled sitting in that Bulldog single seater, or what was left of it, and looking at the one of his legs which had the rudder bar through it. That was the right leg. The left leg was broken between the knee and ankle. The foot and ankle were somewhere underneath the seat and he was sitting on that bit. He had felt no pain from his legs at that first shock stage, but he had a hell of a pain in his back. Then much later all the pain seemed to have transferred to his legs from his back – which he forgot about for a long time. In view of what had happened to his legs, it did not occur to the doctors to consider his back.

About the mid-1930s, Douglas started to become very susceptible to stiff necks. Everyone has had these at times, either from sitting in a draught or some such cause. Douglas found that he used to get it on one side of his neck, after he had washed his hair and was rubbing his head rather violently. Suddenly he would feel a click and he got a sharp pain from his neck down to his shoulder. The neck became quite rigid. By the following year this grew rather frequent, so Thelma said one day:

'You must go and see Auntie Audrey's man.'

'Who on earth is he?' asked Douglas.

'He's a bone setter.'

In the late 1920s and early 1930s, there had been two pioneers in this field, called Barker and Blake. These were the original bone setters who burst on the medical scene. Instead of cutting out displaced cartilage of rugby footballers, they used to put them back. They also treated tennis elbows. Barker and Blake persevered to win the eventual distinction of being accepted by the medical profession. Herbert Barker was in fact knighted for his services. Blake had an assistant called Harold Langley, who subsequently started up on his own and became Auntie Audrey's man!

Douglas went to see him first in his open two-seater MG sports car. Langley told him to take off his clothes and sit on a couch. Then he said to Douglas:

'Did anyone tell you that when you had your accident, you damaged your spine? Not badly, but you've got a slight compression.'

Langley went on:

'All I've done is just to free it. There's no problem.'

He gave Douglas exercises to do for the neck, and explained the general physiology:

'When you walk with your artificial legs, you lead with your head. In other words, your balance is done entirely by your head, and your neck remains rigid. Your neck and head go the same side as your feet when you walk. You don't turn your neck on your head, so you are getting this solid neck. Do these exercises to help keep it free.'

Douglas followed the advice and the neck gradually got better. He visited Langley once or twice a year and said to him on one occasion:

'If I come every two or three months, can't you do something to stop me getting these things at all?'

Langley said: 'No – I can't do anything for you until it goes wrong and then I can put it right. But if you do these exercises, you'll find it won't go wrong as much as it has been doing lately.'

The neck did improve, but later on Douglas found that he began to get a nerve spasm in the leg. The limb jumped about and hurt as though someone were forcing a knife or scalpel into him every few seconds. After a time this agonising effect became very wearisome. He had it on several separate occasions and, needless to say, it stopped him sleeping. So Douglas went back to Harold Langley for help, and as usual the bone setter came to the rescue.

'Good Lord, yes, I can do that without any trouble at all.'

He removed the cause of the nerve spasm, and Douglas was without pain instantly. Again he gave Douglas exercises to do, and these were carried out faithfully. But he was bound to get this occasionally.

Four years after their original wedding, they remarried in St Mary Abbott's Church, Kensington, this time with the blessing of friends and relations – who would probably have given their approval all the time. The secret of their previous years remained right until after the war. For once in his life, Douglas drank liquor – champagne, of course. And half-a-dozen glasses of it! Or they might have been tumblers! Never one to do things by halves or in less than due style for the occasion. Then they drove to Cornwall for the second time after getting married. A unique achievement, probably, in the annals of matrimony.

Back in London, they shared a new flat for the first time, in West Kensington and not far from Thelma's previous home. Douglas had tried tennis in country gardens with Thelma during the 1930s, and now he launched on a new game – squash. His golf handicap plunged from sixteen to nine. Single figures.

Douglas could not have gone on indefinitely at Shell (as the company had now become) but his life would take a fresh turn soon. They had remarried in 1937. Munich came in 1938. Czechoslovakia in 1939. In the spring of that year Douglas wrote to Air Marshal Sir Charles Portal asking if he could now be considered for flying duties. He received the anticipated refusal, exactly as he had done on one or two previous requests made during that decade. But this time Portal added a more hopeful note for Douglas: 'You can rest assured that if war came we would almost certainly be only too glad of your services in a flying capacity after a short time, if the doctors agreed.'

The day before war was actually declared, Douglas persuaded Thelma to go into the country for a while until they saw how things would turn out. Her family had taken over part of a bungalow beside The Pantiles – that original Bagshot meeting place of Thelma and Douglas. On the Sunday morning when the war started, Douglas wrote to Sir Charles Portal once more. Despite Douglas pestering the Air Ministry regularly, an interminable month passed before he finally ripped open a telegram asking him to attend an Air Ministry selection board at Adastral House in Kingsway.

Douglas waited with a dozen-or-so other men all eagerly wanting to be selected for RAF officer service. When his turn came to be called, he was shown into an office where he found Air Vice-Marshal Halahan – the Commandant at RAF Cranwell in Douglas's days there. Halahan asked him what job he wanted.

'General Duties, of course, sir.'

In RAF parlance, that meant flying. But Douglas was disappointed to hear that Halahan was only handling ground jobs, not the flying branch. Then the air marshal wrote a note, slid it into an envelope, and handed it to Douglas.

'Take this across to the medical people – and good luck,' he said.

Douglas made his limping way over Kingsway to the medical unit where he had been invalided out seven years earlier. Not a propitious omen. However, he handed the note to the warrant officer at reception there. Douglas sat and waited. At length the warrant officer returned and made out a new file in his name. A more promising sign, perhaps?

'Come along, sir, we'll get you done as quickly as possible.'

The next minutes of his life proved to be so crucial to Douglas that he wrote them down later so that he would always remember them:

> 'I didn't know any of the doctors this time, but everything went perfectly except for the chap with the rubber hammer who tests your reflexes by knocking you on the knee and seeing how quickly your foot and shin jerk. I'd been stripped except for my trousers, and he said: 'Just pull your trouser leg up and cross your knees.' I said 'I can't and it's no good.' I explained the position and we both had a good laugh. He had a look at them while I walked and professionally was very interested. He tested my reflexes by hammering the inside of my elbows instead. Seemed much the same.
>
> 'I visited the various rooms in turn; eyes, ears, nose and throat; blood pressure, heart and lungs – never a shadow of doubt. I asked the last doctor, "Am I all right for flying?" and he gave a short laugh as though I had been joking. Finally, my file was complete and the Wing Commander sent for me. He also was a different chap, slightly bald but with quite a pleasant face. I sat down. I could see he was looking at my file as though he were thinking, not reading. Then he looked up and said: "Apart from your legs you're a hundred per cent." He pushed a bit of paper across to me, and said: "Have you seen this?" It was Halahan's note. I said: "No, sir." I looked at it and as far as I remember it read:
>
> "I have known this officer since he was a cadet at Cranwell under my command. He's the type we want. If he is fit, apart from his legs, I suggest you give him A.1.B. category and leave it to the Central Flying School to assess his flying capabilities."

> 'I handed the note back without a word. I looked at him. I had the feeling of being tremendously alert at a terribly important cross-road. I think I stopped breathing. I remembered 1932 – the same scene, – different circumstances, different man behind the desk saying there was nothing in King's Regulations to let me through. The silence seemed to go on. I don't know whether it was a second or ten seconds. I had the feeling the doctor wanted to look away, but I was not going to let him. I was looking directly at him, willing him to think my way. He said, "I agree with Air Vice-Marshal Halahan. We're giving you A.l.B. and it's up to the flying chaps. I'll recommend they give you a test at C.F.S."

Douglas felt thrilled and hardly knew how to get through the days until he heard from the RAF again. Then on 14 October 1939 a telegram from the Central Flying School at Upavon read:

'Suggest you report for test 18th October.'

He did not wait for the date proposed but drove down to Wiltshire the next day. He met two former colleagues there – Joe Cox and Rupert Leigh, the latter being the officer who would test him. That afternoon he led Douglas out to a Harvard monoplane trainer, which was more complex than the old Bulldog, the last type of aeroplane flown by Bader. Leigh piloted and did a circuit and landing before offering Douglas the controls:

'Right. She's yours.'

He took off all right and after ten or fifteen minutes he felt at home again in the air. They spent an hour altogether with Douglas practising take-off and landing. Leigh was fully satisfied and told Douglas that he would recommend him to be posted for a refresher course.

Yet another month or more passed until the RAF finally wrote to offer him a regular commission in his former rank and seniority. The letter arrived on a Friday. He replied at once, saying he would be back at Upavon on Sunday. Douglas had a final day with Thelma at The Pantiles on the Saturday. And then on the Sunday morning, Thelma cried for the first time as he swung a leg into the car to drive down to Upavon. Douglas felt in two moods – sad at parting from Thelma, but relieved to be back in the RAF.

CHAPTER 4

Douglas did not waste any more time. On the Monday morning, he got all his new flying gear. That afternoon an officer he knew, Christopher Clarkson, accompanied him on a first official refresher flight in an Avro Tutor biplane. After making a couple of landings with Clarkson in the rear seat, Douglas was allowed to go solo. He recalled it vividly:

> 'This, then, was the moment. At last I was alone with an aeroplane – 27th November 1939 – almost exactly eight years after my crash.
>
> I turned Tutor K3242 into wind and took-off. I remember the afternoon as clearly as today. It was 3.30, a grey sky with clouds at 1,500 feet and a south-west wind. A number of aeroplanes were flying around. I went a little way from the crowd.
>
> I had a new flying log-book then. I look at it today and read: 1939. November 27th. Tutor K3242. Self. F/Lt Clarkson. 25 minutes. Tutor K3242. Self – 25 minutes. These are the two entries . . .'

When he was finally able to put on his RAF uniform, he felt a complete sense of rightness in being where he was at that particular time. The days crowded in on him and he loved it. After a few more sorties in the Tutor, he graduated to a two-seater Fairey Battle. At the time this represented a modern daytime bomber. Only one week had really elapsed. The camaraderie of the mess always attracted Douglas, especially in wartime, and it was soon enhanced and enlivened by the arrival of Thelma for a week – staying nearby with Joe Cox and his wife. Her role took shape as following Douglas to a number of RAF stations over the coming months. But much more than that.

January 1940: the start of an historic year. A further graduation of aircraft took Douglas on to the Miles Master, the final rung before being allowed to pilot a coveted Spitfire or Hurricane. Douglas did not mind which it would be, and it turned out to be a Hurricane first. No dual controls now, only solo. On his second flight in this new generation of fighter, Douglas decided it was time to try aerobatics, to see how the aeroplane would respond. It exceeded even his hopes. He knew that aerial fighting would involve aerobatics.

January passed and the 'phoney' war period continued a little longer. Joe Cox felt more than happy for Douglas to head for an operational squadron.

Cox contacted an old chum, Geoffrey Stephenson, then the leader of No. 19 Squadron at RAF Duxford. Geoffrey set the wheels moving and Douglas was soon on his way to the same station that had marked his farewell from the Service. They classified Douglas as 'exceptional' on leaving Upavon, Joe Cox adding the very true words: 'He lives for flying.' So despite the long interim years, Douglas had retained his lightning-flash reflexes – both mental and physical.

He had just four days' leave with Thelma at The Pantiles. They were ninety-six bitter-sweet hours for them both. Thelma naturally worried about what would be in store for him. For his part, Douglas was really straining to be on active service. Once more, she put on a brave front, helped him pack, and waved him off. As before, Douglas could not help being pleased, but dare not show it too much.

From this moment on, for as long as it took to win the war, the life of Douglas Bader meant flying. Virtually nothing else mattered. Flying and flyers. Time was relative. He might live for hours, days, weeks or months – or if he were lucky, years. He did not think about the future. Instinctively he knew that an air battle must be coming sooner or later.

RAF Duxford formed part of 12 Group, Fighter Command, covering an area from somewhere north of the River Thames to East Anglia – and a little beyond. Mainly south of the Thames flew the fighter force of 11 Group in south-east England, while 10 Group were responsible for the region further west.

The various commanders were as follows:- Air Chief Marshal Hugh C. T. Dowding was the Air Officer Commanding-in-Chief, Fighter Command, with headquarters at Bentley Priory, Stanmore, Middlesex, just north of London; Air Vice-Marshal K. R. Park was AOC 11 Group; Air Vice-Marshal T. L. Leigh-Mallory, AOC 12 Group; and Air Vice-Marshal Sir C. J. G. Brand AOC 10 Group. The first three of these four commanders figured vitally in Douglas's life in the near future.

Meanwhile, it was February 1940, as Douglas approached his thirtieth birthday: old by comparison to most of the other pilots. That first evening at Duxford, he met Tubby Mermagen, the leader of the second squadron at Duxford, No 222, flying Blenheims. Geoffrey Stephenson would be Douglas's squadron leader and their aircraft would be the legendary Spitfire.

Stephenson was away for a day or two, but almost as soon as the two men met again Douglas got his first chance to fly a Spitfire. A pilot a decade younger than Douglas showed him the basics and he was soon up and away. Then he got airborne again to practise flying a Spitfire in formation. And the next stage was an actual dawn patrol to protect a sea convoy. Douglas's initial operational sortie. Eight machine-guns could fire at a split-second's notice, but no enemy presented themselves to warrant pressing the fire button.

In between practise and active sorties, they discussed fighter tactics. Douglas had studied the history of air fighting and was a staunch proponent in favour of getting 'height and sun' as the aces used to do in World War 1. This was not really official Air Ministry thinking. Furthermore, the official orders still told them to fly 'line astern' and attack singly – utterly opposite to Douglas's conception. And the methods advocated from above also eschewed dog-fights as being rather outmoded and inappropriate for modern aircraft.

Douglas disagreed violently but obeyed orders, more or less. His flying skill soon earned him promotion to section leader of three Spitfires. Meanwhile, Tubby Mermagen and his fellow pilots were exchanging their Blenheims for Spitfires. That must be a good bargain. Some of 222 Squadron had been posted elsewhere, and Mermagen was seeking reliable replacements.

'I want a new flight commander. Would you come?' he asked Bader.

Before the move was made, however, Douglas chalked up several slight aeronautical incidents! Already he had hit a hut and the branches of a tree on two previous flights. Now he made a mistake to prove he was not superhuman after all. Taxying in a Spitfire one day, he failed to take-off properly and smashed into a nearby field at some 80 mph. He hit his head quite severely, but walked away on his tin legs without further mishap. He cursed himself for an elementary error of failing to change from coarse to fine pitch. An artificer straightened out his bent legs, he got into another Spitfire, caught up the rest of them, and flew over a convoy as detailed in orders. No enemy aircraft came in sight that day.

Despite this lapse, Leigh-Mallory saw him at Duxford a week or so later. Douglas offered no excuses for having wrecked a precious Spitfire – Leigh-Mallory liked that. Then he announced:

'You're going to 222 Squadron as a flight commander.'

This meant promotion from flying officer to flight lieutenant. Challenge and responsibility again. Dog-fight practice; formation aerobatics; 'height and sun' flying; firing practice; and solo low aerobatics when he was all alone. They would never cure him of that.

Thelma stayed a lot of the time at the local Duxford pub and became resigned to the hazards. At least there seemed to be little actual combat yet. May. Blossom time. Sunshine. Rupert Leigh joined Duxford to take command of a new squadron, No 66. Hitler moved his troops towards the coast. No 222 Squadron was posted north to Kirton-in-Lindsey, near Grimsby, for easier convoy patrolling. This went on throughout most of a fateful week, and then they were rudely awakened – literally – and ordered to take-off at 0400 for Martlesham – due south again – not far from Felixstowe. No gear, just pilots and Spitfires.

Tubby Mermagen came over the grass of Martlesham and told Douglas and the others:

'Patrol Dunkirk, 12,000 feet. Take-off as soon as we're refuelled.'

It was late-May and they still did not know about any impending evacuation from the Continent. The name Dunkirk conveyed no special significance at all.

As squadron leader, Mermagen led them in the climb to 12,000 feet. Assembled and heading for the goal, they sighted black smoke through their screens. A lot of activity went on in the sky above the smoky area, but they had to keep to their orders of patrolling at 12,000 feet. An hour or more later, they all returned. Orders en route for landing were changed from Martlesham to Manston to Duxford to Hornchurch in Essex. They actually reached the skies over Duxford before flying back to Hornchurch, where they all landed. Not an auspicious debut for Dunkirk.

'Take-off at 0430, sir' Douglas's batman said in his ear.

Soon they were flying out over the sea towards Dunkirk once more. Below they suddenly saw some of the 'little ships' – spreadeagled across from the coast of south-east England to the Continent. This marked the squadron's first real introduction to the war at close quarters. The Spitfires were there to try to protect the Allied Expeditionary Force in its desperate evacuation from the beaches around Dunkirk.

'Aircraft ahead.'

A squadron of Messerschmitt 110s. But they banked away from a fight and aimed for cloud-cover, which they found. Douglas had now at least seen the Luftwaffe; they existed.

The 0330 routine continued for another couple of days or so. Take-off at 0430. The black smoke spread ever wider, ever denser. Now they flew much lower than the original 12,000 feet; more like 3,000. But too soon their fuel forced them to leave the skies over Dunkirk, and enemy aircraft were free to return to attack the Allied ground force still there.

One more morning. Actually over the Dunkirk beaches, Douglas and others spotted Me 110 fighter-bombers, but again the Luftwaffe pilots turned away. Douglas and his whole flight went after them and suddenly saw Me 109s. The enemy fired at the Spitfires. Close enough, the Me's were, for their black crosses to be clearly seen even at over 300 mph. One enemy fighter was on fire, and perhaps destroyed. On landing, Douglas discovered that two of the squadron's pilots and aeroplanes were missing . . . That was all they knew at that stage. They might be safe, they might not.

June now and the patrols went on from Hornchurch. From less than a mile overhead, they watched the ever-changing epic of Dunkirk. Most of the ground forces had now got away. Only the valiant rear troops remained. By 3–4 June Dunkirk was over. Douglas flew on the very last patrol over the beaches on 4 June. The remnants of material and craters and wrecks could not fully convey what had happened there. Then he headed for home and a brief rest. They had all been on duty non-stop for over a week. Douglas slept the clock around almost twice. He got a weekend pass and saw Thelma, once more installed at The Pantiles. It seemed a long time since their first meeting there.

Within forty-eight hours of the end of Dunkirk, during the night of 5–6 June, the Germans started air activity over Britain. By a coincidence, the date of 6 June was precisely four years before D-Day. On this particular night, the enemy attacked East Coast aerodromes and ports in 12 Group area.

A week later nearing midnight on 13 June, Douglas found himself high above the Humber in response to the report of an aircraft believed flying inland. He looked around but saw nothing in the night gloom. The weather was foul, too, and the ground controller told him over the radio-telephone 'Return to base.' Easier said than accomplished. The black-out below made the ground virtually invisible; the rain was increasing; and he could scarcely make out his home flare-path. He overshot the runway, braked hard, but ended up with a jolt and a jar having broken the under-carriage. This could be getting to be a habit. As on a previous occasion involving a smashed Spitfire, Douglas was summoned to Leigh-Mallory – for promotion!

'I'm giving you a squadron, No 242.'

Douglas pointed out that this had now happened twice: two pranged Spitfires, two promotions. Leigh-Mallory replied straight-faced:

'Don't worry. Your new squadron has Hurricanes!'

Then came the more serious note. The squadron was the only Canadian one in the entire RAF. Most of its pilots came from Canada, naturally; they had been flying in France, and they had suffered pretty badly. Leigh-Mallory felt rightly that they needed someone tough to pull them together again and he thought of Douglas. They didn't come any tougher.

242 was then at RAF Coltishall. Douglas drove back to collect his gear, and then headed straight for his new station. Promoted from flying officer to flight lieutenant to squadron leader – all in two months! A little more rapid than in peacetime.

At breakfast next day, Douglas ran into Rupert Leigh, whose 66 Squadron was also at Coltishall. Then Wing Commander Beisiegel briefed Bader on the personnel of 242 Squadron – about four were English and the remainder Canadian as expected. Douglas heard that the squadron had sustained casualties in France and finally had to fly back to England minus their squadron commander and both flight commanders.

Douglas discussed the squadron with his newly-appointed adjutant, Flight Lieutenant Peter Macdonald. Together they made their way to meet the pilots for the first time. No point in putting off the moment. 'A' Flight hut stood at the edge of the airfield, so that the pilots could be ready at once for any scramble call. The squadron knew he would be arriving at some time, but he burst in without warning, Macdonald bringing up the rear. They were all relaxing in chairs or lying on their emergency bunks. None of them got up.

'Who's in charge here?' Douglas asked in an even voice. Silence.

'Isn't anyone in charge?'

'I guess not,' someone said at length.

Douglas left and went to 'B' Flight nearby.

'Who's in charge here?' he asked again.

Silence and then a Canadian said:

'I guess I am.'

He was a flying officer, so Douglas asked:

'Isn't there a flight commander?'

'There's one somewhere, but he isn't here,' came the voice again.

'What's your name?'

'Turner . . . Sir.'

When the squadron had heard about Douglas, one of them voiced their sentiments: 'That's all we need – a leader with no legs.'

Now the air felt tense. Douglas sensed the situation. He was always a sensitive man, despite a few other failings! Again, he did not speak but went out of the hut. They were all very near their respective aircraft, on maximum readiness. So only yards away stood a Hurricane. Douglas clambered on to the monoplane wing, and lifted a leg into the cockpit in his inimitable style. Flying gear was there ready for instant use; he jerked on a helmet; he knew the Hurricane would be fuelled; and so he switched on the engine. There was only one way to prove himself to these pilots – and he took it.

He had to win their respect. For half an hour he took the fighter through a series of expert aerobatics – loops, rolls, stalls, spins. He did not climb once during all these manoeuvres. He landed, taxied to a stop, climbed out unaided, got in his car, found his office, and summoned the squadron warrant officer, Bernard West. Douglas was aware, however, that every one of the pilots had been watching because they were outside the hut when he left the Hurricane.

He got on well with West at once, but did not like the news that the warrant officer had in store for him. Using the phrase 'in store' advisedly. They had neither spares nor tools to keep the eighteen Hurricanes flying long, despite requests for replacements. Douglas decided to take immediate action again.

But, first, the pilots. He summoned all the squadron to his office. He told them off for not looking smart, only to discover that they had lost all their stuff in France, along with most of the spares and tools. Turner told him how they had to fend for themselves desperately over there – and how they had lost seven men killed. Douglas apologised for not knowing the full story and then sent them to Norwich to order all the uniforms and kit they needed. He guaranteed that the costs would be covered.

He also talked to each one of them singly. With one exception, he passed them suitable for his squadron. He acquired two flight commanders, Eric Ball and George Powell-Sheddon. An Me 109 had nearly got Ball over Dunkirk with another squadron, so he had been blooded. Powell-Sheddon had a slight stutter but was a pilot trained at Cranwell, good enough for Douglas. So he had got a squadron – on paper. Now all he had to do was get them back to fighter standard and morale as soon as possible. There might not be much time.

First, however, they would need those spares and tools. While the squadron began to smarten itself up all round, Douglas sent a signal to 12 Group:

> '242 Squadron now operational as regards pilots but non-operational repeat non-operational as regards equipment.'

Wing Commander Beisiegel was annoyed with Bader for not clearing such a signal with him first, but it was too late to cancel it then. Warrant Officer West warned Douglas that 12 Group would not like the signal. So Douglas broke it to him that a copy of the signal had gone to Fighter Command as well! West made a classic response to this extra news:

'Well, sir, we'll either be getting our tools or a new CO!'

The Squadron Leader (Equipment) at Fighter Command Headquarters phoned Douglas that evening to tell him off about the signal. After a heated exchange between the two level officers, the equipment man ended up saying:

'The Commander-in-Chief is furious about it.'

Leigh-Mallory 'happened' to land at Coltishall the following morning, ostensibly to take a look at the squadron. Later he broached the subject of the signal, revealing to Douglas that it had provoked 'a mild sensation' at 12 Group. But Leigh-Mallory was very reasonable about it and merely warned Douglas that he would be summoned to HQ by the C-in-C Fighter Command.

Coltishall to Hendon to Bentley Priory. Dowding sat at his desk and asked Douglas at once:

'What's all this about equipment and that signal of yours, Bader?'

Douglas explained the facts. The equipment officer had already given a written report to Dowding about his phone exchange with Bader. Pressed by Dowding, Douglas said:

'He tried to shake me by saying you were furious about my signal and that annoyed me.'

Dowding buzzed for the officer and told him that he would not tolerate any officer taking his name in vain or predicting his emotions. He ended by dismissing the squadron leader from the Headquarters within twenty-four hours. After that it was all plain sailing between Dowding, his air vice marshal on equipment, and Douglas – a raw squadron leader! The time: next day. The scene: Coltishall. Lorries arrived there with crates of spares. Douglas and West supervised the hundreds of items being unloaded and then Bader felt finally justified in sending another signal to 12 Group:

'242 Squadron now fully operational.'

In a matter of days the squadron had regained its self-respect, self-esteem, under the unerring example of Douglas's leadership. That first aerobatic display had done its work. He used every day to train them in preparedness for the anticipated air attack. He also got to know them all well, and Thelma came up to Coltishall to stay in a nearby house. Douglas made Stan Turner one of his section leaders and soon they were as ready as they would be for the Luftwaffe. The waiting proved frustrating, though, and even when it was nearly over, the fight only started slowly, a little at a time. But at least it did start.

Night-time, early-July. Some seventy enemy aircraft were plotted, with East Anglian aerodromes and Midland industrial areas the main recipients of the raids. For the first time since spasmodic raids had started, one or two bigger towns and cities began to be mentioned among the places visited: Derby, Coventry, Debden, Duxford, Coltishall, Bircham Newton, Finningley, Swinderby, Stamford, Lowestoft, Cromer, Wittering and Sutton Bridge.

242 Squadron had to wait a fortnight before their first real encounters. Then on 10 July, marking the official start of the Battle of Britain, part of the squadron went into action. Green Section were up early that morning. While patrolling at 8,000 feet over a convoy ten miles off Lowestoft, they sighted two Heinkels. P/O Latta spotted one, put on speed, and closed with the German. After an exchange of fire, he got to within fifty yards, when the enemy darted into a cloud layer at 4,000 feet, with its starboard engine smoking. Latta followed through the cloud-veil but did not spot the Heinkel again. He himself received one hit on the wing of his Hurricane.

Sub Lt Gardner had the most decisive combat of the trio of Green Section. He glimpsed a Heinkel vanish into clouds at 17,000 feet, but was told to return to the convoy. Back above the ships, he noticed another aircraft four miles south-east of the ships. Catching it up, he established it as an enemy – always an important rule to observe even under stress. Then he dived to the attack in direct line astern. For the second attack he came in fast at angle of twenty-five degrees on the port side. He hit both the port engine and undercarriage. After a third attack, the Heinkel either crashed or pancaked into the sea. In the two or three minutes before it sank, one of the crew climbed on to a wing . . .

The section leader, P/O Eckford, actually saw two bombs plop close to the convoy and then spotted a Heinkel climbing north into the nearest available cloud cover. On emerging from the temporary shelter, the enemy met a burst from Eckford which silenced the tracer which had been patterning from the top gun of the bomber. Both aircraft sank into cloud and re-emerged, the Heinkel with a wake of white smoke. So much for 242 Squadron on Day 1 of the Battle of Britain.

Next day, 11 July, meant a memorable date for Douglas Bader. It marked the morning when he shot down his first enemy aircraft. There would be a score or so confirmed successes to come in the next year and a month, but this was the first.

Throughout the whole period from midnight to 0830 on 11 July, the weather remained wretched and any interception most difficult. Flying was bad enough. Fighting out of the question. So how did he do it?

At dawn the report reached 12 Group that a bomber was attacking Cromer and also machine-gunning searchlights. Group asked 242 to send up a section, but Bader decided he would have just as good a chance on his own. Despite appalling visibility and with heavy rain precipitating from low clouds, he took off at about 0600 and somehow sighted the bomber, a Dornier 17, a couple of miles off the Norfolk coast from Cromer.

At an altitude of only 1,500 feet, he made two attacks. The first from 100 yards or so was head-on for two seconds, turning into a second burst of six seconds from a stern attack made at 150 yards. Through the rain spattering the screen, Bader saw his tracer hitting the Dornier. One brief burst from the enemy rear-gunner lit up the late-dawn gloom. Bader did not see anything more, losing sight of the enemy in a dense rain cloud. After he returned to base, he heard a report from the Royal Observer Corps at Norwich that the Dornier had actually been seen to crash into the sea off Cromer at the exact time he had delivered the attack. The 12 Group log recorded that morning: 'The Battle of Britain has now started.'

For 12 Group there followed an irritating five-day lull in activities, partly due to weather that was poor for this time of year. The total 12 Group patrols during July tallied 1,101, involving 2,668 operational flights. August was destined to be busier, but it would still be frustrating for Douglas and 242 Squadron until the thirtieth.

On its very first day, August was heralded with hostile raids and bombs near 12 Group airfields of Wattisham and Martlesham Heath. The enemy clearly knew their locations well. 242 Squadron were still on regular convoy patrol and F/O Christie, P/O Latta and Sgt Richardson flew over a convoy on the evening of 1 August. All three came in contact with enemy aircraft. Richardson saw a Junkers 88 at 1855 hours with the help of AA fire. Flying at only 700 feet above the North Sea, the bomber had black crosses on the side of the white fuselage. The Junkers tried to regain cloud cover. Richardson made two attacks, but even before he had started the second one, the enemy's starboard engine had stopped. Thick grey smoke trailed from the Junkers: a familiar sight in the weeks ahead. The bomber began a very shallow though inexorable dive and when just a few feet above the water its nose rose steeply so that the tail touched the sea first. The aircraft broke in two and sank within about thirty seconds. Richardson circled the scene and saw a rubber boat break surface on top of the wreckage – and drift slowly away from it. Only a single survivor was seen in the water and he vanished from view soon afterwards. No-one appeared to be in the rubber boat . . .

Raids increased over land, but 12 Group were only on the fringes of the activity and felt frustrated more and more. On 12 August hectic air action in the south was marked by German onslaughts on radar stations, shipping in the Thames Estuary, and similar targets around the areas of the Isle of Wight, Portsmouth and Southampton. On the night of 13–14 August, no contact could be recorded with the bombers, although the customary night patrols took off. Birmingham, Leamington and Wolverhampton were among the list of places attacked by the Luftwaffe.

The date of 15 August was a keynote, with tremendous enemy activity all around the English coast. 12 Group defended valiantly, but at Driffield aerodrome up to eighty bombs cratered the environs. Three main hangars were set on fire; the officers' mess was badly damaged; and the AA headquarters hit. Seven RAF aircraft were hit on the ground. The war was coming closer. Next day, Birmingham and Coventry were prime targets.

242 Squadron had their usual share of patrols over East Anglia, and on 21 August for instance, F/Lt Powell–Sheddon, P/O Latta and Sub Lt Gardner were all airborne intercepting strong enemy bombers on nuisance raids. Douglas got his eye in again within an hour of this patrol. Various R/T messages made him realise that there were enemy bombers in the vicinity, so although he had been detailed only for 'local flying' and was not ordered off, he rolled his Hurricane at 1300 hours and took it up to 9,000 feet. Quarter of an hour later, he was three miles north-west of Great Yarmouth and making a head-on quarter attack on a Dornier 17 from 250 yards, turning into a straight attack at 200 yards. He got in a couple of bursts before the Dornier scurried for cloud. He saw his tracer striking the enemy but nothing more definite than that.

The Dornier was coloured duck-egg blue underneath with black on top. It flew at 180–200 mph, he judged, and its tactics consisted of a straight and shallow dive for cover. As Douglas fired, it was only about 100 feet above the cloud, so things happened hurriedly. The enemy rear-gunner fired a machine-gun from above the fuselage – and weights attached to long wire were thrown out from under the fuselage. As Bader was almost on the same level as the bomber, these weights passed underneath him causing no damage to his precious Hurricane.

Before the Dornier disappeared, the rear-gunner only got in a single short sally at him, then seemed to have been hit. A lone bullet struck the Hurricane in the middle of the leading edge of the port wing. So ended a rather inconclusive exchange, but Bader would soon be in action on a more heroic scale. Meanwhile, 242 Squadron and all 12 Group read of the raids on the nights of 27–28, 28–29 and 29–30 August. A long list of cities as targets. They heard about it with mounting impatience – especially Douglas.

Chapter 5

Here at long last was the first of many memorable days for Douglas and 242 Squadron. Friday 30 August. But before it dawned, the operations of the night were divided into two parts. The first began at 2240 hours and was directed against west and north-west Midland industry. The second phase from 0200 concentrated on the East Coast. Lancashire industrial conurbations suffered during the first period – Liverpool, Warrington and Manchester. The Observer Corps were actually unable to plot raids for some time due to the holocaust around Warrington.

Throughout August Douglas and the other pilots of 12 Group were always being held in reserve, however impatient they became. They heard the growing number of reports on the gathering momentum of mass attacks in the South – and ached to join in the affray. True, they had been in action several times. Douglas much more than most of them. Douglas could now get in and out of his fighter more quickly with his artificial legs than most of the pilots with their real ones.

Now it was the sort of war where a German flyer fired at a Hurricane pilot parachuting down from a wrecked fighter – and killed him.

Early on 30 August, they got the orders: Take-off immediately for Duxford. Douglas was at last to lead his Hurricanes into action in some force.

'242 Squadron scramble – Angels fifteen. North Weald.'

They were off. At 1626 hours, 242 were ordered from Duxford to patrol North Weald at 15,000 feet on vector 190°. Just north of North Weald they received vector 340°. About then, too, Douglas's piercing eyes noticed three unidentified aeroplanes below and to the right of the squadron.

'Bandits to west. Blue Section investigate.'

So the squadron was depleted of three Hurricanes and had ten remaining. Green leader drew Bader's attention to a large Luftwaffe formation on their left. He turned with the other nine aircraft to witness what was undeniably an awe-inspiring sight – particularly to any of them who had not previously been in action. There were a vast number of twin-engined aeroplanes in front now, flying in an easterly direction. Bader counted fourteen blocks of six aircraft – all bombers – with thirty Me 110 fighters behind and above.

Altogether 242 Squadron's ten Hurricanes had more than 100 enemy to tackle. Odds of ten to one. The bombers, Heinkels with perhaps some Dornier 17s as well, flew in tight formation stepped up from about 12,000 feet. Then came a gap of 1,000 feet, with a swarm of fighters ranged from some 15,000–20,000 feet.

Bader could not see any friendly fighters near, so he ordered Green Section to attack the top of the lower formation of fighters, while his flight of Red and Yellow Sections went into line astern to go for the bombers. Immediately Bader had detailed F/O Christie to take his section of three to keep the Messerschmitts busy, this pilot from Calgary said 'OK, OK' with obvious relish, and away he streaked to deal with that vastly superior number of enemy fighters.

There was no point in trying to deliver any formation attack and Bader's only object was to break up the formation and start a dog-fight. The enemy bombers were flying at around 15,000 feet now, with the middle of the formation roughly west of the reservoirs at Enfield and heading east. When first sighted they looked just like a vast swarm of bees. With the sun at their backs and the advantage of greater height, conditions were ideal for a surprise attack and as soon as 242 were all in position they went straight down to the Germans. Bader did not adopt any set rules in attacking – he just worked on the axiom that the shortest distance between two points is a straight line.

So he dived straight into the middle of the tightly-packed formation, closely followed by the rest of his flight – Red 2 was P/O Willie McKnight and Red 3 P/O Denis Crowley-Milling. The enemy immediately broke up fanwise. He saw three Me 110s do climbing turns left and three to the right. Bader spotted McKnight veer left while he attacked the right-hand trio. Their tactics appeared to be climbing turns to a nearly stalled position to try to get on Bader's tail. He tried a short burst of nearly three seconds into the first Me 110 at nearly point blank range as he was at the top of his zoom. The aeroplane seemed to burst into flames and disintegrate.

Willie McKnight went for a section of Me 110s and two aircraft broke off specifically to attack him. He succeeded in getting behind one of them and opened fire at 100 yards. He hit it and it spun towards the Essex earth. He at once went for a Heinkel group, executing a neat beam attack on the one nearest to him. Its port engine paused and then stopped. A second or so later, the bomber rolled over on its back as if wounded and finally started to smoke. Then it conflagrated and crashed.

Meanwhile Douglas continued his zoom and found a second Messerschmitt below and to his right, just starting to dive after a stalled turn. So he turned in behind the German and got a very early shot at about 100–150 yards' range. Bader's first burst lasted two to four seconds. After this, the enemy's evasive action consisted in pushing his stick violently backwards and forwards. The second time he did this maneouvre, Douglas got in a burst as he was at the top of his short zoom. He saw pieces fly off the enemy's starboard wing near the engine and then the whole of the starboard wing went on fire. The aeroplane fell away to the right in a steep sort of spiral dive, well on fire. Bader did not see anyone bale out of either of the Me 110s, although it is possible that they did so. He was too busy looking around to worry once they had caught fire. There was just no time to stop and think of consequences.

Bader noticed in his mirror an Me 110 coming up behind him and he did a quick turn – to see five or six white streams coming out of the German's firing guns. It seemed as though the pilot were using tracer in all his guns. As soon as Bader turned, the Me 110 put its nose down and Douglas temporarily lost him. Eventually Douglas saw him travelling east far below. Bader tried to catch him but could not, so fired no more. Not once did an Me 110 get sights on Bader's Hurricane. Douglas saw nothing except Me 110s, though there were Heinkels and Dorniers in force as well.

One of those Me 110s was attacking Willie McKnight just about then, but the young Canadian pilot succeeded in getting behind. He followed the Me 110 from 10,000 feet right down to a mere 1,000 feet. The enemy used ultra steep turns to try and get clear, but eventually it had to straighten out or crash. McKnight opened fire at a range of thirty yards – the length and a third of a cricket pitch. The enemy's starboard engine stopped; the port one flamed. It crashed after having used a lot of rear fire at McKnight. He saw it go down alongside a large reservoir.

After Bader and McKnight had gone for the Me 110s broken off from the middle section originally, Denis Crowley-Milling flying Red 3 was left with a Heinkel open to himself. He attacked astern, giving the bomber a five-second burst. Tentative return rear fire soon stopped as the aircraft began an inexorable descent to earth. Crowley-Milling started to follow it, when tracer bullets from an Me 110 passed his starboard wing. He at once decided to nose away to port and in so doing lost sight of both his attacker and the Heinkel. But P/O Hart confirmed that the Heinkel went down in flames.

F/Lt Eric Ball led Yellow Section as Bader's own section broke up the enemy masses. He saw a single Heinkel circling, diving and turning all at once. Ball took it from behind. He closed to 100 yards, using one-third of his ammunition. Both enemy engines caught alight and the bomber force-landed on an aerodrome full of cars near North Weald. Ball then chased a straggler Me 110, which he finished off with a stern attack. The enemy engine stopped dead and the aircraft lost height rapidly. Ball had the sun behind him during both these attacks – as per Bader's dictum.

At 1705 hours, Sub Lt R.J. Cork, RN, was flying as Yellow 2 between North Weald and Hatfield when he attacked an Me 110 in company with several other enemy fighters. He saw the Me going down as he broke away left to go after another 110. Cork's beam attack hit its mark and the enemy executed a frantic stall turn with the port engine afire. There was no hope left for it as it reached the point of no return, and seconds later exploded on the ground. Cork swung back to the scene of combat and saw the first of these Me 110s burning in a field. Its swastikas still stood out against the dark green body. He could claim one of the enemy as destroyed personally, while the other counted as a probable. Six bursts of three seconds each had accounted for this damage.

Sgt R.V. Lonsdale flying as Yellow 3 sought a Heinkel which had become parted from its formation. He pressed the button to start a prolonged ten-second burst beginning 300 yards away and ending only fifty yards from the

Heinkel. The enemy circled like a wounded bird from this quarter attack and eventually crashed in the same area as the Me 110 attributed to Cork. A Hurricane could and did easily outfly and outrace an opponent like a Heinkel travelling at about 200 mph.

When Bader told Green Section to go for the top of the lower formation, F/O Christie as Green Leader launched a bull-like head-on charge for an Me 110 on top of the four layers. It arced off to starboard, diving as it went. Christie kept glued to its tail, spraying a burst from 50 yards astern. Something had to hit shortly and oil started spouting, gushing, from the starboard motor. The petrol tanks burst, the Me 110 took a vertical dive, and it travelled from 6,000 feet straight down into greenhouses about 500 yards from the reservoir at Ponder's End.

Green Section were flying behind Yellow Section when 242 Squadron saw the enemy originally. They received the orders to attack the fighters above them, but these quickly dispersed – things happened in seconds or even semi-seconds. So Green Section chose the bombers instead. Green 3, P/O N. Hart, stumbled on three in line – astern about 1,000 feet below his Hurricane. As he started to dive, he saw Yellow 1 attacking the last one of the trio. Hart took the second bomber and sent it into a steep dive. He was just about to follow it down when the first Heinkel made a steep right-hand turn. Hart turned inside it and used up all his ammunition on the bomber. It plunged into a field with all the crew still aboard. Hart did not dwell there, as three Me 110s began to chase him.

P/O Stansfield also attacked an enemy aircraft with Eric Ball. Stansfield first saw the straggler aiming eastwards. In the first of three attacks he silenced the rear gunner, who had opened fire at him with cannon. Both enemy engines were in trouble: smoke from the port, while the starboard stopped altogether. The Heinkel came down heavily on a civil aerodrome covered with wrecked cars, but three Germans staggered out of its remnants. Stansfield was Black 1 and Sgt G. W. Brimble Black 2.

Brimble followed Stansfield on to the Heinkel, firing from 250 yards. He saw Stansfield follow the bomber almost into the ground. Then Brimble broke away to find an Me 110 executing a gentle turn to port. He achieved a quarter attack from the same range as his previous one and had the definite sight of the enemy actually striking the ground.

As Brimble flew across to rejoin his section leader, the next thing he knew was an Me 110 aiming straight for him. He opened fire instinctively at 350 yards and saw all the glass splinter in front of the enemy aircraft. The machine took an a violent convulsive dive, as if in some fatal fever. Brimble did not see it crash as another Me 110 got on his tail. The rule was survival first.

Back to Bader and his advice about enemy aircraft on the tail of Hurricanes. As Douglas climbed back to 12,000 feet from 6,000, he could see no further enemy. He thought: 'Now, there's one curious thing about this air fighting. One minute you see hundreds of aeroplanes in the sky, and the next minute there's nothing. All you can do is to look through your sights at your particular target – and look in your mirror, too, if you are sensible, for any Messerschmitts which might be trying to get on your tail.'

Well, that particular battle lasted about five or ten minutes, and then, quite suddenly, the sky was clear of aircraft.

One pilot had sent a bomber crashing into a greenhouse. Another bomber had gone headlong into a field filled with derelict motor-cars; it hit one of the cars, turned over, and caught fire. Another of 242 Squadron had seen a twin-engined job of sorts go into a reservoir near Enfield. Yet another pilot saw his victim go down with his engine flat out; the plane dived into a field and disintegrated into little pieces. Incidentally, that particular pilot brought down three on this day.

242 Squadron had not shot them all down, of course. The enemy had not waited for that, but made off home in all directions at high speed. But, apart from the bag of twelve (eight Messerschmitt fighter-bombers, three Heinkel bombers, and a fourth Heinkel bomber already partly damaged by another squadron), there were a number of others which were badly shot up and probably never got home – like the one which went staggering out over Southend with one engine out of action.

As Douglas could spot no enemy despite his peeled eyes, he called Duxford by radio and was told to land. On the way he picked up Green Leader, F/O Christie, and also Blue Section. The infuriated Blue Section pilots had been sent off to investigate unidentified aircraft and missed the entire battle. They had not fired a single round between them and their language when they heard what they'd missed was unprintable!

One thing Douglas particularly noticed with surprise was that he received no rear gun fire from the Messerschmitt 110s and they appeared to be trying to fight with front guns only. This made the odds heavily in the Hurricane's favour, and not once did Me 110s get sights on Bader. Which was just as well because he admitted he saw nothing in this dog-fight except his own little personal battle.

So ten Hurricanes had fought and routed over a hundred of the enemy at odds of ten-to-one. Such was Douglas's leadership and strategic skill.

As a result of this successful engagement the notion of a larger formation than a squadron was conceived in the mind of Air Vice-Marshal Leigh-Mallory. On this particular occasion the squadron was called off the ground in time to meet a large enemy formation under favourable conditions south-west of Epping. They had position, height and sun in attacking an enemy bomber formation without Messerschmitt 109 escort. In the course of a congratulatory call from Leigh-Mallory that same evening, Douglas said to him.

'If I'd had more fighters, we would have shot down more of the enemy.'

Nightfall, 30 August. The raids began again on industrial areas and East Anglian aerodromes. Watnall was bombed for the first time, four delayed-action devices being dropped near the camp, killing two civilians. Watnall was the location of 12 Group Headquarters. Next morning 11 Group got a surfeit of enemy activity between 0800 and 0930. 12 Group were asked to try and help them, six squadrons being put on alert. The only squadron to make any contact was No 310. They hit an Me 110 but in so doing lost three fighters. One pilot was killed; one injured; and one baled out safely. In the afternoon, 310 Squadron met fifteen Dorniers and ten to twenty Me 109s escorting them. They lost one Hurricane, and others were hit, but could claim four Dornier 15s shot down and one Me 109.

All the Duxford squadrons flew sorties in those first few days of September. 310 had been in the thick of it. On 6 September, one flight of 310 and one flight of 19 Squadron plus 242 Squadron were all ordered to 11 Group but did not manage to contact the enemy. The same was *not* true on the next day. Meanwhile, throughout that first week of September, the idea of the Duxford or Bader Wing became converted from an abstract idea into a practical reality.

CHAPTER 6

After the customary recent pattern of night raids by the Luftwaffe on the north-west and Midlands, Saturday 7 September dawned. The afternoon was due to go down in aviation history as the first offensive patrol by the 12 Group Wing under Bader's leadership.

After the original idea and some discussion between Bader and the other two squadron leaders – Blackwood of 310 and Lane of 19 – they flew three or four practise sorties to test out the theory developed by Douglas. Then the Duxford Wing reported ready for action. The method of operation was uncomplicated. 242 and 310 Squadrons of Hurricanes took off from Duxford. At the same time, 19 Squadron of Spitfires unrolled from the satellite station of Fowlmere. There was no joining up over the airfield. Douglas turned straight on to course, climbing quickly, while the other squadrons took up position.

The Hurricane squadrons kept together, while the Spitfires flew 3,000–4,000 feet above, behind, and to one side. The intention was that the Spitfires, with their better performance, would guard the Hurricanes against interference by Me 109s while they attacked the enemy formations. If there were no enemy fighters, the Spitfires would come down on the bombers after the Hurricanes had broken them up. The Duxford Wing never took more than six minutes to get off the ground and on their way south – and frequently they did it in four minutes. The whole formation arrived over the Thames Estuary at 20,000 feet just twenty minutes after take-off. The Spitfires were then at 23,000–24,000 feet.

There was no more difficulty in the control of the Wing in the air than of a squadron. The three squadrons were all on the same R/T frequency. An occasional word from Douglas to the other two commanders and then finally his intentions when the enemy were sighted – that was all that was needed. Suggestions that the Big Wing was clumsy to operate are nonsense. Indeed they are disproved by the 1941 and subsequent fighter wing operations over France.

There was one fundamental problem, however, not only with the 12 Group Wing but with 12 Group squadrons and 11 Group squadrons; the frequent failure of the 11 Group operations room to get squadrons off the ground in time. Like everyone else, the 11 Group controllers were inexperienced when the Battle started. They did not appreciate that in order for a pilot to be successful, he needed height and position to dominate the battle. The vulnerable, indeed frequently fatal, position for a fighter pilot, was to be climbing with the enemy above him. The German formations used to assemble in the Calais area when the bombers were at 15,000–17,000 feet.

Short-range Me 109s joined them and the whole lot proceeded across the Channel towards the London area. This initially precluded a successful interception by any of the 11 Group squadrons based at Manston, Hawkinge, Detling, Gravesend and Redhill, because they were too *near* the coast. A single incident confirms and clarifies this situation: on its very first operational sortie out of Kenley, 616 Squadron lost five out of twelve fighters on the climb without touching the enemy.

So far as the 12 Group Wing was concerned, it seemed to them at Duxford that most times they were sent for as an afterthought, or to do what used to be termed 'the lunch-time patrol' when there was no single aeroplane either German or British in the air at all.

For some reason, the 11 Group controllers would not call squadrons off the ground, and more particularly the 12 Group Wing, until the enemy were at operational height and leaving the French coast. If you look at the map and measure the distance to the 11 Group stations mentioned, the error of this thinking is self-evident. On several occasions, while the Duxford Wing was at readiness, Douglas received telephone calls from the Duxford controller saying:

'Stand by, the Germans are building up over the Calais area.'

Every time Douglas asked:

'Can we take off *now*?'

Every time he received the inevitable answer:

'No, you must wait until 11 Group ask for you.'

Duxford to Tilbury is forty-three miles. If the Wing had taken off when the Germans were building up over the Pas de Calais area, Douglas and his team could have been in the Ashford/Tonbridge area under favourable conditions, to control a battle of their own seeking.

Laddie Lucas has summed up Douglas's views on this aspect of the Battle of Britain:

> 'Douglas's thinking was that he should be able to get these Wings into the air and into the right position to be able to attack the enemy aircraft as they were coming in to their targets, on the approaches to the targets. What he contended was that if you could get these aeroplanes up together, place them right, give them the right information, supply the right commentary, then it was up to Douglas as Wing leader to make the best use of it. His basic thinking was not only to get the aeroplanes off together and as quickly as possible, but that proper warning be given and proper decisions regarding control. The difficulty with the Duxford Wing was probably to get off the ground in time to discharge the tactics that Douglas believed to be necessary to fulfil his role. Too often he

found himself climbing up as hard as he could bloody well go, while the enemy were already coming in – so he would have lost all the advantage of height and sun and so on.'

Douglas disagreed with the attitude of fighting the Battle of Britain on a local level, rather as a private 11 Group affair, and an order from the AOC 11 Group subsequently available makes it clear that in his mind his fears were fully justified. This was Park's peculiar instruction in force from 19 August 1940, which went against so much of what Douglas felt to be the best approaches. It is worth quoting in full, so that Bader's reactions to it can be completely understood.

NO. 11 GROUP INSTRUCTIONS TO CONTROLLERS NO. 4
From: Air Officer Commanding, No 11 Group, Royal Air Force.
To: Group Controllers and Sector Commanders, for Sector Controllers.
Date: 19 August 1940

The German Air Force has begun a new phase in air attacks, which have been switched from coastal shipping and ports on to inland objectives. The bombing attacks have for several days been concentrated against aerodromes, and especially fighter aerodromes, on the coast and inland. The following instructions are issued to meet the changed conditions:

(a) Despatch fighters to engage large enemy formations over land or within gliding distance of the coast. During the next two or three weeks, we cannot afford to lose pilots through forced landings in the sea;
(b) Avoid sending fighters out over the sea to chase reconnaissance aircraft or small formations of enemy fighters;
(c) Despatch a pair of fighters to intercept single reconnaissance aircraft that come inland. If clouds are favourable, put a patrol of one or two fighters over an aerodrome which enemy aircraft are approaching in clouds;
(d) Against mass attacks coming inland, despatch a minimum number of squadrons to engage enemy fighters. Our main object is to engage enemy bombers, particularly those approaching under the lowest cloud cover;
(e) If all our squadrons around London are off the ground engaging enemy mass attacks, ask No 12 Group or Command Controller to provide squadrons to patrol aerodromes Debden, North Weald, Hornchurch;
(f) If heavy attacks have crossed the coast and are proceeding towards aerodromes, put a squadron, or even the sector training flight, to patrol under clouds over each sector aerodrome;

(g) No 303 (Polish) Squadron can provide two sections for patrol of inland aerodromes, especially while the older squadrons are on the ground refuelling, when enemy formation are flying over land;

(h) No 1 (Canadian) Squadron can be used in the same manner by day as other fighter squadrons.

NOTE: Protection of all convoys and shipping in the Thames Estuary are excluded from this instruction (paragraph (a)).

sgd. K R Park
Air Vice-Marshal Commanding,
No 11 Group
Royal Air Force

In Douglas's decided and considered view, these instructions revealed some serious errors of thinking in air warfare. Paragraph (e) was the fatal one, he maintained, as the best way to protect aerodromes was not to fly overhead waiting for an attack, but to go and intercept the enemy where he wanted. Stop them reaching our airfields. This same argument applied to paragraphs (c) and (f). Finally, paragraph (a) at one stroke precluded successful interception by any squadron south of the River Thames.

Lord Dowding made two vital contributions to the defeat of the Luftwaffe in the summer of 1940. During his pre-war command, he had laid down radar coverage of the south of England so that we had early warning of the Germans' intentions: secondly, he had persuaded the War Cabinet against sending more RAF fighters to a defeated France in May 1940.

Instead of assuming control and direction of the air defence of Britain, which was the C-in-C's job, Dowding left the conduct of the battle to a subordinate Group Commander, A.V-M. Park of No 11 Group. Dowding had already increased the number of squadrons in 11 Group, making it the strongest in Fighter Command. Keith Park fought the Battle of Britain, not Dowding. He fought it under the disadvantage of being too near the enemy to deploy the strength which Dowding had given him. His problem was compounded by his operations room displaying a map of 11 Group territory only. In other words, Park was fighting an 11 Group battle which should have been a Fighter Command battle.

A map of the whole of England lay on the plotters' table at Fighter Command. It showed every fighter airfield, with the location and state of readiness of every squadron on the board above it. The difference was paramount. A controller at the Fighter Command operations room would have seen the enemy position as it was plotted. With the whole picture spread out in front of him, he would instantly have realised the need to scramble squadrons from the further away airfields *first* against the enemy. First, not last.

This would have provided the classic air defence in depth so desperately needed to make life easier for controllers and less costly for pilots. 11 Group controllers with their limited operations room facilities would have given place to Fighter Command ones with the map of England in front of them. 11 Group controllers were being harassed by enemy raiders almost overhead, which they were trying to intercept with only 11 Group squadrons available. The Fighter Command controllers would have had time to see the problem in its entirety. It was in this context that the Duxford Wing came into being, indeed for these very reasons. Leigh-Mallory saw the whole situation with clarity from his 12 Group headquarters. So did Douglas. Easy for them, say the critics, they were not in the so-called front line. Quite right. But this highlights the great error: the front line should have embraced the whole of Fighter Command and not just 11 Group.

If ever Dowding should have seen the light it was at the end of August, when the changing pattern of the German assault became clear beyond doubt. Vast enemy formations were to be seen congregating over the Pas-de-Calais. London must be the target. Surely the Commander-in-Chief, with his great reputation and the full resources of his headquarters and operations room, would now take over control of the battle from his 11 Group Commander?

In the event, he did not. A tired man with neither the authority nor the full available resources was left to continue the struggle. It was as though General Montgomery left a Corps Commander to fight the Battle of Alamein and told him to call on other corps commanders for assistance if necessary. The Battle of Britain was won by the efforts of tired but resolute controllers and the immense courage of 11 Group pilots. Properly exploited, the 12 Group Wing could have provided the spearhead against the enemy formations, creating havoc amongst them and giving the 11 Group pilots time to gain height and position to continue the destruction. To stress the irony of the 11 Group situation, squadrons sometimes had to climb northwards *away* from the enemy, to try and gain tactical advantage. At the top level of Fighter Command, there seemed an inability to grasp the basic and proved rules of air fighting. This is what Douglas felt then and still felt three or four decades later.

12 Group introduced its report on the first five Wing patrols with the following comments, setting the scene in the context of 7 September 1940:

> 'Experience has shown that with the mass attacks on London and the South of England, the enemy has used not only larger formations of bombers but very considerably larger formations of protecting fighters. In view of this, when No 12 Group have been asked to protect North Weald and Hornchurch Aerodromes, it was considered wholly inadequate to send up single squadrons for this purpose and therefore a Wing has been employed. Up to the present, five such operations have taken place. Definite roles have been allotted to the squadrons on each occasion, with the

> general idea of having Spitfire Squadrons above the Hurricane Squadrons so that the former could attack enemy fighters and prevent their coming down to protect their bombers, whilst the remainder of the Wing break up and destroy the enemy bombers.'

Johnnie Johnson described the situation on 7 September rather more dramatically in his highly informed book *Full Circle*.

> 'On 7 September, following Hitler's declaration that London would suffer as reprisals for Bomber Command raids against Berlin, Goering switched his bombers from RAF sector stations, and other airfields, to London and its sprawling docks. Towards five o'clock on that evening, more than three hundred bombers, and many hundreds of fighters, arose from their airfields across the Channel, swarmed into a dozen formations and, without feint or decoy, crossed the straits in two broad waves and headed for the capital. Because of their height, above 20,000 feet, and a stiff headwind, the bombers took a long time to reach London, but although RAF controllers found it easier than usual to intercept, the enemy fighter escorts seemed bigger than ever. There were so many enemy fighters, layered up to 30,000 feet, that a Spitfire pilot said it was like looking up the escalator at Piccadilly Circus.
>
> Near Cambridge the Duxford Wing of two Hurricane and one Spitfire squadrons had been at readiness all day and Bader, anxious to lead thirty-six fighters into action for the first time, had been agitating for hours about getting into the air. At last they were scrambled . . .'

The Wing was ordered off from Duxford at about 1655 hours to patrol North Weald. The altitude quoted was 10,000 feet. Control told Bader: '100 bandits approaching you from the east.' Arriving at North Weald on the 15,000 feet level, they noticed AA fire to the east and saw a quantity of enemy aircraft at 20,000 feet. Bader immediately advised Duxford of the sighting and obtained permission to engage the enemy.

He took the decision to attack with 242, 310 and 19 Squadrons knowing that such a move must have been more successful had the Wing been at 25,000 feet. The element of surprise was lost to them and they endured the added disadvantage of attacking the bombers knowing that there were Messerschmitt 109s above them and in the sun so that while pressing home any attack they would have to try to keep an eye behind them at the same time – if they were to survive. No wonder Douglas and other pilots of the Wing grew impatient at a policy which put precious aircrew at so substantial a hazard from the outset.

Bader opened his Hurricane throttle to 6¾ boost and climbed for all he and the fighter were worth. The enemy aircraft were proceeding north over the Thames Estuary. The result of the full throttle climbing to get level with the enemy made the whole fighter force struggle out of necessity – so the attack could not be pressed home with the weight of the thirty-six aeroplanes at Bader's disposal. But he had to engage quickly or not at all.

He turned left to cut off the enemy and arrived on the beam slightly in front with only Red 2. Bader was flying Red 1, and Sub Lt Cork flew Red 2. Bader opened with a very short beam squirt from 100 yards, aimed at enemy aircraft flying in sections of three line astern in a large rectangle. He turned with Cork, who also fired with him, and sat under the tails of the back section at 50 yards, pulling up the nose and giving short squirts at the middle back aeroplane. This was an Me 110 and it started smoking, preparatory to catching fire.

Even before attacking the enemy and whilst actually still climbing to meet them, Cork and Bader received a lot of cross-fire from enemy bombers, which kept in perfect formation. At the same time, they were set on by enemy fighters, who had had the advantage of 3,000–4,000 feet in altitude. Cork broke away slightly to the right of Bader's section and fired at a Dornier 215 on the tail end of the group. It followed the usual destruction sequence of port engine afire and a vertical crash-dive.

Before Douglas could see the result of his opening action, he made out the warning outline of a yellow nose in his mirror. The Messerschmitt 109 was on his tail slightly above and as Bader turned there was suddenly a big bang in his cockpit from a bullet – presumably an explosive one. It came in through the right-hand side of the fuselage, touched the map case, knocked the corner off the under-carriage selector quadrant and finished up against the petrol priming pump.

Having executed a quick, steep, diving turn, Bader found an Me 110 alone just below him. He attacked this from dead astern and above. The enemy could not combat the accurate fire and went into a steepish straight dive, finishing up in flames in a field just north of a railway line west of Wickford and due north of Thameshaven. The first Me 110 attacked by Bader had been confirmed as diving down and crashing by another pilot, although Douglas himself had not witnessed it. So that made a couple of Messerschmitts to the Wing leader: an example to the rest of them. Apart from the bullet in the cockpit, Bader's Hurricane also sustained hits in several places by bomber fire and twice by escorting Me 109s.

Just after Cork had destroyed the Dornier, he was set on from the rear by an enemy fighter and hit in the starboard mainplane. So he broke away downwards and backwards – and nearly collided with an Me 110. This was always a danger, and collisions did happen with fatal results to both parties. Cork pressed for a brief burst before pulling away to avoid the collision and he saw the front of the Messerschmitt cabin break up and the aircraft take a vertical dive. Two of the crew baled out. Cork followed the machine down. It was stalling and then diving again alternately.

While Cork continued his vigil, an Me 109 went for his rear. One shot penetrated the side of his hood, hit the bottom of the reflector sight and then the bullet-proof windscreen. 'As I could not see very well, I broke away downwards in a half-roll and lost vision of the enemy machine.' Not really surprising with glass in his eyes . . . Somehow he kept on flying, having accounted for a Dornier 215 and an Me 110. When he landed, his Hurricane was so shattered with enemy fire that it was not considered flyable.

A great friend of Douglas Bader, Denis Crowley-Milling was flying as his Red 3. The time was between 1700 and 1715 now and they were still in the thick of this dog-fight, started from a poorly placed position.

Red 3 saw a lot of the cross-fire from other bombers as he flew in to meet a force just above the AA fire. But he had to snap off due to a rear thrust by an Me 110. Red 3 banked left sharply and then came in again at the bombers. He spotted an Me 110 just behind the last bomber. He hit its port engine with a four-second burst and saw the starboard one smoking, too. At that instant he was shot at from behind by an Me 109. His Hurricane received a shell in the radiator, another in the left aileron, and a third behind the pilot's seat. No-one could deny he was lucky to be alive. He piloted the Hurricane down from 18,000–20,000 feet to a crash-landing near Chelmsford. In fact he had destroyed the Me 110 which he attacked.

Irrespective of individual actions, the rest of the engagement continued its weirdly beautiful pattern, as if moving to some predetermined choreography in an aerial ballet.

After Bader had gone in originally, F/Lt Ball as Yellow I positioned himself a few thousand feet higher than nearby enemy aircraft, and opened against an Me 110. But Me 109s caught him by the tail and he realised that by now he was utterly alone, with no friendly fighters in immediate sight. He saw a second 110 and closed from 300 to eighty yards. It caught fire soon after his running attack from above and behind. He fired on three or four other aircraft but they were impossible to engage for long, owing to the horde of fighters buzzing around their bombers.

Ball actually followed the formation out to sea, picking off a 110 en route. Both engines of the enemy were smoking, but a 109 got on his tail and he had to give up further pursuit. Although the enemy fired on him sporadically, Ball found their aim very wild and he was not hit.

Sgt R. Lonsdale followed Ball in to the original affray. As he flew into the attack level with the enemy bombers, Me 110s came down and broke up their particular formation. The enemy fighters kept good grouping but for that very reason were fairly easily avoided. Three 110s dived for Lonsdale but again he twisted out of trouble.

Then he went for the bombers by himself. The sun was on his starboard side as he selected a Dornier 215 to attack from line astern. After a diminishing range from 350 to eighty yards, the Hurricane's fire stopped the port engine and smouldered the starboard one. While in the thick of this attack, Lonsdale suddenly found his Hurricane being bounced about a lot by the slipstream of the bomber. He carried on his attack from slightly below to get out of its line. The Dornier 215 gradually dropped back from the formation and started gliding down at about 120 mph.

Lonsdale had given it a full fifteen seconds of firing and at this stage ran out of ammunition. Despite this, he followed the bomber down for some distance until it disappeared from sight. Another Hurricane hit it as it glided on.

F/Lt Powell-Sheddon led Blue Section and estimated enemy forces at fifty bombers in tight grouping line astern with a strong guard of Me 110s and yellow-nosed Me 109s. The noses also had some silver on them as camouflage. He climbed to 22,000 feet to have a go at the fighters, having lost sight of Bader and the section in front. The other members of Blue Section had also become separated from him. But this was no more than typical of the style and pattern of such a dog-fight.

Powell-Sheddon chased several enemy aircraft but did not engage any for ten minutes. Volumes of jet black smoke were cascading up from Thameshaven oil refineries. Miles above, he saw a Hurricane being chased by an Me 109. They swerved right in front of him, a mere 100 yards ahead. He gave an instinctive deflection squirt at the Me 109 as it passed, and it then turned left and crossed his path at the same range. He repeated the squirt and got on its tail. As the Me 109 was firing at the Hurricane, Blue 1 was aiming at the German from a few feet above and only fifty yards. He could see his bullets finding their mark and saw pieces ripped from the Hurricane. He got in the enemy slipstream, ceased fire, eased slightly to one side, and fired again.

The Me 109 got the Hurricane, which went down with smoke streaming.

Then the Me 109 itself hung in the air for a few seconds before falling forward in a vertical dive. A tail of smoke etched its descent in the sky. It vanished into the dense blackness over Thameshaven. As it seemed to be in flames and out of control, the Me 109 could be claimed for Powell-Sheddon.

The speed with which the Wing went into action could be deduced from the time of these attacks: 1710–1715 hours. Only a quarter of an hour after actual take-off. Blue 2 was P/O P. Bush. He went for a Heinkel but had to break off because of rear attacks from an Me 110. He executed an astern attack on another Me 110, which he damaged badly. Two good bursts from 250 to fifty yards caused these hits.

A few minutes later, P/O H. Tamblyn as Blue 3 destroyed an Me 110 at 1720. It became a total conflagration. Tamblyn next went after a 109 at 150 yards. Evidence suggested he had hit it lethally as it veered gently to the right and began to go down. It was one of the special yellow-nosed squadron. Tamblyn felt an effect of slipstream from both these encounters but managed to control his Hurricane somehow.

Green 1 now – and P/O D. Turner. A favourite of Douglas Bader. He was in the last section to attack and as he approached he saw an Me 110 already in flames. This was the result of one of the Red Section hits. While hitting a 110 and watching his bullets tear at the fuselage, Turner was in turn fired at by a 109. He outmanoeuvred the fighter and got a good burst into it. The enemy flicked into a dive. Turner went for some bombers next, and before being driven off by 109s, he got in a snap shot or two. Nothing for it after that but to head for Duxford.

Still 1720: Gardner was the pilot of Green 4. He saw thirty Heinkels plus more bombers and many Me 109s. He noticed some Spitfures already in the fray. On entering the mêlée in sharp zig-zags, he found it very difficult – to distinguish friend from foe – certainly in the instants available for decisions. But he did recognise a Dornier which started to circle and dive. Gardner went too and discovered he had another Hurricane along with him.

At 5,000 feet Gardner got in three short bursts from 250 to fifty yards, stopping the port engine and bursting the oil tank. The crew baled out and the Dornier crashed in a field about three miles north-east of Shell Haven. Gardner got a hole in his wing and engine cowling but managed to land early at 1745.

A Dornier 215 singled out by Black 1, P/O M. Stansfield, loosed off about fifty rounds of machine-gun fire at him, but fortunately missed his Hurricane. Coming up from below it, he caught the bomber in the port beam. The enemy went into a roll and then attempted a second one – but this was too low to be executed.

It dived into the ground, the pilot having misjudged the altitude.

So much for 242 Squadron. They took off at 1655. They landed at 1755. An hour to remember. They lost two Hurricanes, force-landed in Essex, but both pilots were safe – that was the main thing. Five fighters became temporarily unserviceable through bullet holes.

The Czechs followed Douglas and 242 in line-astern. F/Lt G. Sinclair was leading 310 (Czech) Squadron, A Flight, and wheedled into an up-sun position. He put A Flight into line-astern to go for Me 110s behind the bombers. Having seen 242 attacking the bombers, Sinclair took as his target an Me 110 with full deflection shot. Another burst on another Me 110. He climbed into the sun and gave a third one prolonged attention. The port engine of this Me 110 ceased to function, but then Sinclair ran out of ammunition so had to call off further acts.

Sinclair was Red 1, P/Sgt B. Furst Red 2 and Sgt Seda Red 3. Furst fired at one of the Me 110s attacked by Sinclair. Seda did the same. But Furst failed to find Sinclair again. Furst next hit a 110 and left it smoking from the port engine over Whitstable. This was a far cry from the days of peace and the famous oysters. The enemy glided down in turns towards the east, with both his engines failing to function. But Furst could only claim a probable success.

He was more definite a few minutes afterwards. He trailed a group of enemy bombers north of Canterbury. Far below the cathedral made its cross as it had done in plan view over the centuries. Furst found himself fifty yards behind an Me 109. One burst hit the Messerschmitt. But not before the pilot somehow baled out. Furst was waylaid by two Me 110s and had to beat a hasty retreat.

Sgt Seda followed Sinclair as he led their section in a curve towards the enemy bombers. Next moment, he saw an Me 110 only fifty yards ahead. He fired. White smoke made parallel trails from the engines but Seda did not see the enemy crash. Hence: one damaged Me 110.

Again at the five-minute spell from 1715–1720, P/O S. Janouch was leading Yellow Section, A Flight, at 25,000 feet over Grays Thurrock. He took the section towards enemy fighters, level out of the sun. Then they had to transfer efforts to a bomber force. But the fighters wedged between the bombers and themselves. An Me 110 appeared just in front of Janouch's windscreen and tried desperately to escape by going into a glide. Janouch fired five bursts at 400 to fifty yards, the middle burst producing smoke from both engines. Yellow 2 and 3 also went for this 110, but only Yellow 3 got in a burst. These other two of Yellow Section saw two men bale out of the aircraft. Janouch climbed to regain an operational height and joined another squadron of Hurricanes, before being called on to land.

F/Lt J. Jeffries led B Flight of 310 Squadron. He climbed into the sun, fired all his rounds at one fighter, and saw scraps of metal careering off it. But he was slightly out of range and was just unable to get any closer – so could not clinch his attack. Jeffries was flying Blue 1. P/O V. Goth came in behind as Blue 2, with F/O J. F. Boulton as Blue 3. Goth had an adventurous few minutes, surviving to tell about it.

Jeffries told them to attack scattered enemy singly. An Me 110 selected by Goth joined the bombers and was insisting on orbiting above. Goth delivered his fire from the sun and the rear. He dived on the Me 110 from the port, opening fire at 200 yards. By fifty yards' range, the enemy was emitting a heavy smoke pall and Goth saw the cockpit break up in the air. The enemy went mechanically unconscious, falling vertically towards the Thames Estuary area between Southend and Foulness Island.

As Goth broke away, however, he felt that his Hurricane had been hit. Then another enemy was upon him. A dog fight broke out. Enemy fire ceased – and he saw that their port engine was badly struck. The enemy machine lurched right and then dramatically left, apparently set for a spin. Goth saw the air gunner hit as the port engine flamed. They were both over the sea by this stage.

Goth could not see anything more as his cockpit was oozing with oil.

His engine started cutting off. The glycol tank was pouring forth white smoke. Then the engine cut off completely. Goth shut the throttle and dived towards the coast. Somehow he saw through all the usual obstacles, set against an invasion. He landed with his under-carriage up about two miles south-east of Maldon in Essex. A lucky denouement.

Blue 3 had a less dramatic outcome. Boulton made his attacks between 1715 and 1735. He fired at an Me 110 over the Estuary from below and behind. No results. Then he espied a Heinkel heading in a south-easterly course over Kent. After crossing the coast, he carried out a couple of stern attacks at 15,000 feet. He fired all his remaining rounds at the Heinkel and the port engine smoked. It lost height remorselessly and never recovered any aeronautical composure, crashing into the Channel not far from the Goodwin Sands. Another Hurricane confirmed this gain.

Green 1 and 2 were the last two Czechs reporting. P/O E. Fechtner as Green 1 fired at a force of bombers from below. He caused the middle of a bomber engine to smoke. An Me 110 appeared and he fired at this one. The Messerschmitt gave a little climb, lurched into a wounded spin, and descended into the mass of dense smoke over the oil refineries. An enemy bullet hit Fechtner's main tank but luckily for him it did not explode, nor was he hurt.

While P/O S. Zimprich at Green 2 was en route for Dorniers, he diverted to an Me 110 below him. Firing from 300 to fifty yards, he hit the port engine and the Me 110 glided groundwards. He followed another Me 110 just above the beach-line, only 400 yards over the blackness rising from the bombed oil tanks. The aircraft folded up on the left, crumpled, and crashed into the inferno. An enemy bullet struck the 'footstep' of Zimprich's Hurricane, but he survived.

Eight Spitfires of 19 Squadron accompanied 242 and 310 Squadrons. They saw a force of twenty bombers escorted by fifty fighters flying east at 15,000 feet. 19 Squadron was the last of the trio to attack, being 5,000 feet lower than this enemy formation.

While still on the climb to attack, they met an Me 110 diving past them at a substantial speed – with Red Leader, A Flight, after it. Two Hurricanes were also in tow. All five members of A Flight fired at this enemy which met its end a mile or so east of Hornchurch and south of a railway line. The crew of two baled out but one parachute failed to open . . . The other man landed in a field and appeared to be taken prisoner by two women from a nearby house.

Sqn/Ldr Lane was Red 1, with Sgt Jennings Red 2 and F/Sgt Unwin Red 3. Red 1 and 2 plus Yellow 1 returned to base as the main combat had literally vanished.

Red 3 mislaid the others but on climbing to 25,000 feet found and joined a Hurricane squadron. He was led into a force of some sixty enemy machines, bombers and fighters mixed about equally. The Hurricanes were busy with the bombers, while Red 3 suddenly found himself surrounded by Me 109s. He fired at – and hit – five. Two went down. He then extricated his Spitfire, shadowing an enemy group from a great height. This force was at 20,000 feet and being attacked accurately by AA fire which scored two strikes. Red 3 used up his ammunition on a batch of unescorted bombers.

Yellow 2, P/O Cunningham, also lost the rest of the squadron and joined up with the Hurricanes. They flew east and aimed for twenty-four Heinkels. Yellow 2 selected and fired at one of them, set it ablaze, attacked again from below and finally saw it die some ten miles inland from Deal or Ramsgate – he was not sure which at that moment and it did not really matter.

B Flight of 19 Squadron were out of range of the enemy by the time they had staggered up to the level required and Blue 1 and 2 had to return to base without firing. Blue 3 cottoned on to another squadron and shot down an Me 110 into the sea off Margate. Blue 1, 2 and 3 were respectively F/Lt Clouston, F/Sgt Steere and P/O Dolezal.

So summarising the results of the first Wing patrol in adverse conditions, the three squadrons under Douglas Bader inflicted this claimed damage: twenty destroyed; five probables; six damaged. Our losses were four destroyed, one damaged, with one pilot killed or missing and one wounded. They heard later that P/O Benzie was in fact dead.

Analysed by squadrons, the results claimed were that 242 Squadron destroyed ten; probables two; damaged three. 310 Squadron destroyed five; probables three; damaged three. 19 Squadron destroyed five.

There was one day's respite before the next Wing action, probably due to showers and cloud conditions. Meanwhile the enemy restricted itself to night raids. As far as daytime attacks were concerned, it was almost as if they were licking their undoubted wounds of the previous day and considering the next move to make.

The Canadian fighter squadron led by Squadron Leader Douglas Bader had a brilliant record. In three engagements the squadron destroyed 33 enemy aircraft. The photograph *(above)* shows Bader *(centre)* with some of the Canadian pilots of No.242 (Canadian) Squadron RAF. *(Below)* Flight Lieutenant Ball DFC, Squadron Leader Bader DSO and P/O McKnight DFC show an unofficial emblem on one of their aircraft, Duxford, September 1940. ***(Imperial War Museum)***

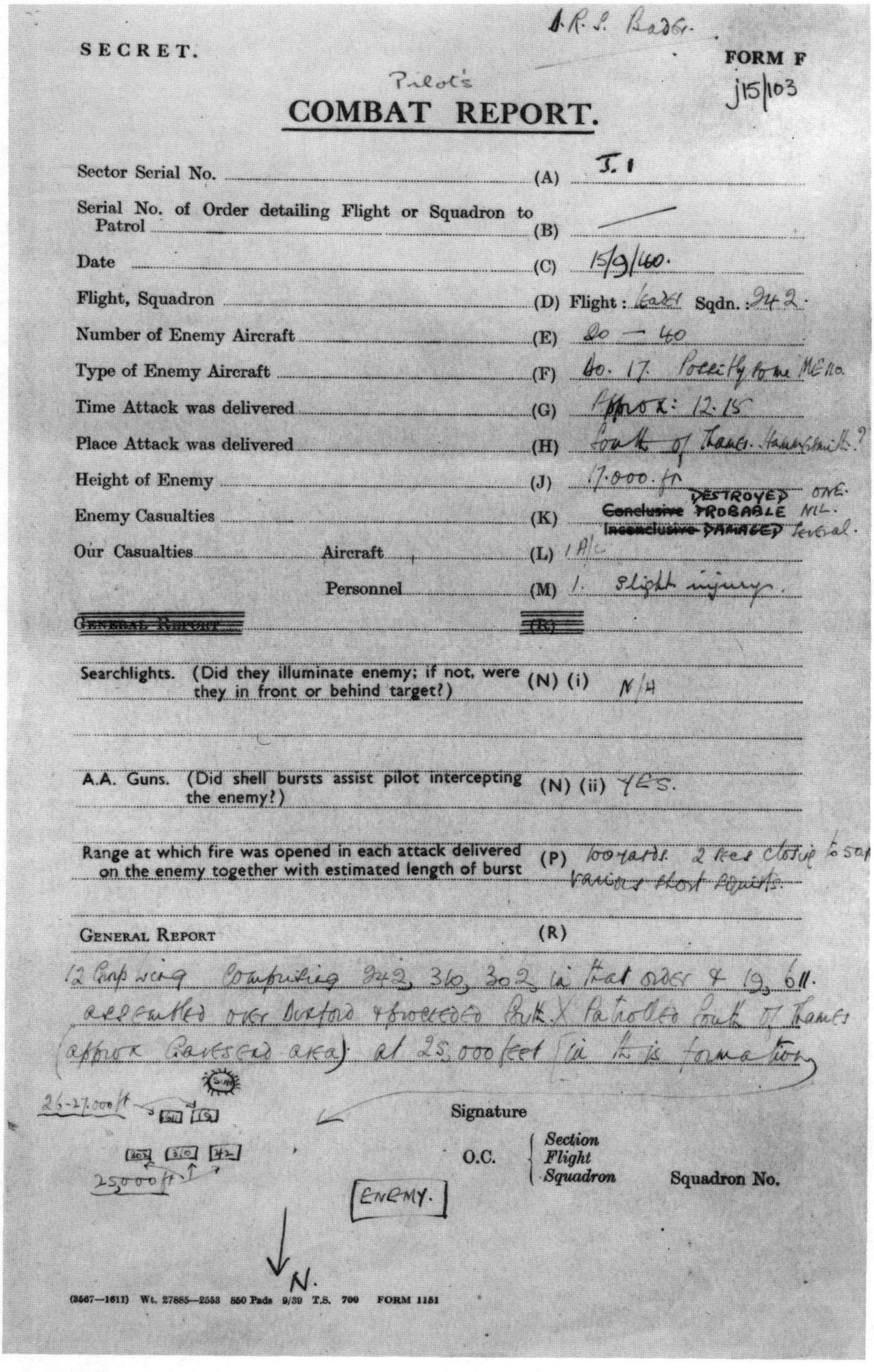

D.R.S. Bader.

SECRET.

FORM F

J15/103

Pilot's

COMBAT REPORT.

Sector Serial No. .... (A) J.1

Serial No. of Order detailing Flight or Squadron to Patrol .... (B) —

Date .... (C) 15/9/40.

Flight, Squadron .... (D) Flight: Leader Sqdn.: 242.

Number of Enemy Aircraft .... (E) 20 — 40

Type of Enemy Aircraft .... (F) Do. 17 Possibly some ME110

Time Attack was delivered .... (G) Approx: 12.15

Place Attack was delivered .... (H) South of Thames. Hammersmith?

Height of Enemy .... (J) 17.000. ft

Enemy Casualties .... (K) ~~Conclusive~~ DESTROYED ONE. PROBABLE NIL. ~~Inconclusive~~ DAMAGED Several.

Our Casualties .... Aircraft .... (L) 1 A/C

Personnel .... (M) 1. slight injury.

~~General Report~~ ~~(R)~~

Searchlights. (Did they illuminate enemy; if not, were they in front or behind target?) (N) (i) N/A

A.A. Guns. (Did shell bursts assist pilot intercepting the enemy?) (N) (ii) YES.

Range at which fire was opened in each attack delivered on the enemy together with estimated length of burst (P) 100 yards. 2 secs closing to 50 ~~various short squirts.~~

General Report (R)

12 Group Wing comprising 242, 310, 302 in that order & 19, 611. assembled over Duxford & proceeded South X patrolled South of Thames (approx Gravesend area) at 25,000 feet in this formation

26-27,000 ft 611 19

302 310 242

25,000 ft

ENEMY.

N.

Signature

O.C. Section / Flight / Squadron Squadron No.

(3567—1611) Wt. 27885—2553 850 Pads 9/39 T.S. 700 FORM 1151

A combat report of Wing Commander Douglas Bader, DSO and Bar, DFC and Bar, issued in 1943 when Bader was a prisoner of war. *(Imperial War Museum)*

Chapter 7

Slight night-time activity again, including a couple of raids around the Mersey, one of which dropped a stick of two bombs near Wrexham. Small-scale bombing sorties over East Anglia had objectives at St Ives and Mildenhall. Once more, Johnnie Johnson sets the scene for the second Duxford Wing action that afternoon:

> 'On 9 September the Luftwaffe repeated their tactics of the 7th, sending over two waves in quick succession, with fighter forces ranging ahead and on the flanks of the main formations. The Germans were after London and aeroplane factories at Brooklands, Weybridge, but had little success, for one raid was met, as Park intended, well forward, and the bombs were scattered through much cloud near Canterbury.'

As usual Bader ventilated his feelings to his sector commander, Wing Commander Woodhall, about getting into the air – or not getting into it. Woodhall pressed the 12 Group controller who, in turn, inquired of his opposite number at 11 Group whether the Duxford Wing was required.

Eventually they were scrambled, and once radio contact was established between controller and Wing Leader, Woodhall said: 'Will you patrol between North Weald and Hornchurch, Angels Twenty?' Never one at the best of times for blind obedience to orders, Woodhall's *Will you* was not lost on Bader, and this intimacy between the two men was important, because it had wide repercussions on the authority of Wing Leaders.

Woodhall, affectionately known as 'Woodie', was a veteran of the Kaiser's War, and was one of the best and most trusted controllers in Fighter Command. His calm and measured tones seemed full of confidence and assurance, and he was fully aware of the limitations of radar, which, at this time, was often distorted by enemy jamming. Woodhall knew that his Wing Leader was in the best position to judge how and when to attack, and therefore his controlling technique was to advise rather than to instruct.

Bader, climbing hard to the south, figured that once again the Germans would come out of the evening sun, so he forgot about Hornchurch and the height and climbed high over Staines, thirty miles from Hornchurch and well within 11 Group's preserves. He was just in time to position his Wing between the sun and two big shoals of bombers accompanied by the usual pack of 109s.

It was at about 1740 hours that Douglas saw the enemy coming from about fifteen miles south-west of them and at the same height of 22,000 feet. Leading the same three squadrons as two days earlier, thirty-three fighters this time instead of thirty-four, he turned to head the enemy off, while climbing all the time to gain advantage of altitude. The enemy were in two large rectangular formations; one of approximately sixty, then a space of about a quarter-mile of sky, followed by a further sixty, with a 500 feet step-up between the two groups.

Bader radioed Duxford to tell 19 Squadron of Spitfires to climb up and protect their tails and then he turned 242 and 310 in above the front bomber formation – nearly down-sun and 1,000 feet above them. Bader had told 242 to attack in loose line-astern and to try to break up the enemy formation. He was aiming at the leader, who was slightly in front of the first section.

As he turned 242 directly above the bombers, Bader noticed some fighters diving out of the sun between the twin enemy bomber forces, but he dismissed them as friendly fighters. Actually they turned out to be Me 109s, which went for 242 on its turn. The squadron retaliated though, so Bader was not really worried by them.

Bader followed his plan by diving on the leader with a two-seconds' burst at point-blank distance. Douglas continued his dive past the enemy, through and under the formation. He pulled up underneath them, intending to give his victim another squirt from below, but saw white smoke misting from both wings. Then he saw the machine roll over on its back in a dive. He did not bother to watch it further, but Sgt Brimble and P/O Bush both saw at least one person bale out as it descended in a flame-trail. Douglas could not be sure at that second whether it was a Dornier 215 or 17 – he admitted to finding it hard to tell the difference.

P/O Willie McKnight was Bader's faithful Red 2. At 1745 they were south of the Thames now. McKnight flew into the enemy from 1,000 feet above and on his left beam. He broke to the left to go for the protecting enemy fighters. He got behind one of them and send it up – or down – in flames. Next he got between two enemy attacking his Hurricane. He opened up at one and the machine shed metallic fragments as it dived to earth. But the German at Willie's rear also opened up and blew off his left aileron. He saw his second Me 109 quite out of control. McKnight survived with his missing aileron.

While Douglas manoeuvred into the sun and did his dive on the leading section, F/Lt Ball leading Yellow Section took his Hurricane at the second enemy section. He dived right through the enemy, pulled up, and did a frontal attack on the leading section, hoping to split them up. He saw no effect from his plan, but he did see an Me 109 buzzing on his tail. He wriggled around to reverse their relative positions and, firing from 300 to 100 yards, witnessed the spectacle of the 109 literally blowing up in mid-air. Satisfying yet sobering. Ball got only one enemy bullet in his Hurricane.

Blue Leader was by now a veteran of 242: F/Lt Powell-Sheddon. Even before the attack, the sections became open and irregular, with Bader still out in front. Powell-Sheddon, Blue 1, saw Bader drop his nose and head ramlike for the first thirty enemy aircraft. Blue 1 admitted to making a mess of his first attempt. He tried to get the leader but overshot and could not open fire.

Then he made a steep climb, turned swiftly, and roared at the bombers again – aiming this time at the second leader. Three seconds at fifty yards and he saw the bullets striking the engine nacelle and the wing. He passed over the enemy about twenty feet from it and broke away in another steep climb. Glancing back, he saw the port engine afire. The bomber lagged behind and fell out of the formation, like a runner dropping behind with cramp.

Powell-Sheddon then lost sight of it for a very good and immediate reason. He lost control of his Hurricane. His starboard aileron control cable had been shot clean through and broken. By a bit of superior piloting, he managed to regain some semblance of control and set his nose towards home, with the enemy lost amid the mixture of haze and cloud. But he was credited with the destruction of one Dornier 215. The dog-fight went on.

Bader remained under the formation he was attacking – some 300 feet below them. He pulled up periodically, squirting various aeroplanes at very close range. But although he damaged them, he saw no definite results. He did see another Dornier in the front diving slowly in a left-handed shallow spiral, obviously out of action and smoking. This was the second leader shot down by Powell-Sheddon.

Suddenly Douglas discovered salvoes of bombs falling all around his Hurricane, so he decided to ease his stick away to the side. The bomber formation veered to the right and made off south-east. They were still in formation, about twenty of them, but they had left a lot of stragglers all over the sky – some damaged and others going slowly, even for bombers.

It was obvious that their bombing was absolutely indiscriminate. London was covered by a 3,000-foot layer of broken cloud thick haze up to 9,000 feet, and clear above. They were bombing from 20,000 feet and so far as Douglas could see, south of the Thames, around London Bridge and in the Battersea area. Douglas went on with his plan of chasing the stragglers and firing close-range bursts at them to conserve ammunition. But finally it was all gone. Before he left, he saw a very large bomber with a single rudder flying home quite slowly and sedately. He attacked it by flying very close and then turning across it to put it off its stride. But it took no notice and did not even fire at him. There was nothing more he could do. His tally was one Dornier destroyed and several damaged.

Flying close to Powell-Sheddon as Blue 2, P/O R. Bush sighted the enemy first over the Thames near London Bridge. He took part in a line-astern attack from the sun on these bombers. Evading an Me 109, he found a 110 and shot it down, the aircraft breaking up like some miniature toy machine. But this was not child's play. Fire from behind by another 110 prompted Bush to execute a neat half-roll and call it a day.

Blue 3 was P/O F. Tamblyn. He saw some 200 enemy, a daunting sight. This was at 1735 now. As he approached, he observed five Me 110s detach themselves and turn in a right-hand circle towards the rear of the enemy formation. Their altitude measured 22,000 feet. Tamblyn turned into an astern assault and noticed a Hurricane set a 110 on fire. And in turn, on the tail of the Hurricane another 110 dogged it. A long burst at the Hurricane did not seem to do any damage. Tamblyn opened at the 110 whenever it straightened up – and after one of these bursts, both engines lit up. Meanwhile Tamblyn also noticed a Hurricane with its port wing folding up and another fighter in a similar predicament.

Tamblyn flew to the far side of the formation and climbed again. He saw a 110 making across at him in a steep turn, so gave a brief burst. From dead astern he then devoted seven seconds to the same aircraft which crumpled into a fairly steep dive. The Hurricane Blue 3 followed it down and watched it crash in front of a cricket clubhouse within a hundred yards or so of another crashed aircraft. There were many star-like spots on the ground, which could have been the results of incendiary bombs.

Sgt E. Richardson as Green 1 found a Dornier 215. He brought smoke to its starboard engine and main-plane. The sergeant pilot broke away at 200 yards. Regaining position 300 yards behind it, he closed to 100 yards, seeing smoke from the port engine after his second six-second burst. Richardson then experienced a long return fire from the Dornier. This seemed to be tracer but had no apparent effect on his Hurricane. After a third onslaught from 100 yards astern, flames sprang from the starboard main-plane. It was clear that the Dornier was doomed.

Both Green 1 and 2, P/O Latta, had already been singled out by a group of eight to ten Messerschmitt 109s. Green 2 engaged one and fired for six to eight seconds – a long time in terms of aerial combat. The only evasive tactic taken by the German was a steep climbing turn left. He then instantly lit up in the cockpit, like a struck match, and spun off the climb – and continued spinning. The fighter would not recover from such a situation.

Latta was then attacked and a bullet jammed his port aileron. He dived steeply to get a second to think. Luckily he was not followed and he got back to base. But it was a near thing, like everything else in the air.

As Bader had gone into his own attack, Sgt R. W. Lonsdale in Yellow 4 saw three Me 109s speeding towards the rear of 242 Squadron and about 1,000 feet below. He made a quick turn but could not catch them. Then he found himself on the tail of Dornier 215s. He attacked the rearmost one which swung across the rest. Lonsdale found he was virtually touching the tail of another Dornier, slightly to one side of it. His Hurricane was being hit by heavy cross-fire from the rear gunners of the bombers, but he managed to dispose of the balance of his ammunition into the Dornier.

While carrying out this second attack, he was being hit repeatedly in the engine and the controls. Smoke began to seep into his cockpit – as well as streams of glycol mixture and oil. His controls were practically useless except for the elevator. As he broke away from the attack, the enemy had smoke wisping from the fuselage and an engine stuttered to a halt.

Lonsdale baled out at about 19,000 feet and came to earth in a pine tree at Caterham.

His Hurricane took its own course down, crashing rather symbolically on Kenley aerodrome about 200 yards from the main guardroom. While he was dropping to ground, a Spitfire pilot flew around Lonsdale all the time to protect him till he touched down.

The time: 1740. The squadron 310. F/Lt G. L. Sinclair was Yellow Leader as he turned to attack the bombers. But he saw Me 109s hurtling down on them from port. The squadron was turning to starboard and he turned slightly to port to see what the Messerschmitts were doing. Without any further warning, Sinclair received a hard blow across the shoulders. This was accompanied by a loud noise and followed by three more distant bangs. He then found his Hurricane in an inverted spin. He was thrown hard against the roof of the cockpit. He was apparently without any starboard plane, though he found it very difficult to discern anything in that position. He had to think quickly. He decided to get out. He had much trouble in opening the canopy and undoing the straps, due to the pressure in the cockpit. But he knew he had to somehow – if he were to live. At last he did it and just shot out into space without any further effort on his part.

The parachute descent took nearly thirteen minutes and Sinclair landed in a wood just off the Purley Way at Coulsdon. He was picked up Lieutenant G. D. Cooper of the Irish Guards from Caterham. Cooper had been watching the whole action through his field glasses and told Sinclair what had happened. F/O Boulton, also flying a Hurricane, had collided with Sinclair and Boulton's machine had afterwards collided with a Dornier 215 – both machines crashing in flames. Boulton was lost. Sinclair survived. So a Dornier had been destroyed but at a cost of one pilot and two Hurricanes.

P/O Fejar flew as No 3 to Sinclair's section. After preliminary skirmishing, Fejar found an Me 110. It tried to wriggle free from him by a series of twists, turns, climbs and dives, but Fejar hit it with a trio of attacks. Smoke from the port engine encouraged him to make one more attempt and the whole port side of the Me 110 licked into fire.

But at that precise second in time 22,000 feet over south-west London, Fejar noticed the starboard leading edge fairings of his Hurricane were loosened. The fighter began to vibrate badly and head towards the ground. He slowly pulled up the nose. He reckoned that the Hurricane had been hit not by the enemy but by a splinter from an anti-aircraft shell. He left the battle and landed safely.

After the sight of the two Hurricanes colliding in front of him, P/O Bergman saw an Me 110 trailing another Hurricane. He increased the boost and followed the enemy. The Hurricane broke away safely. Bergman hit the Me 110 with a determined burst. Both engines blazed with a blackness that turned into a red glow. It was a victory for sure.

Sgt Hubacek also saw the collision. He had a brush with a Heinkel. Next he found a quartet of Me 110s and set about them from the side out of the sun.

The last one retaliated but Hubacek did likewise. The fuselage and rudder of the Me 110 were both fragmented and he saw several splinters fall away from the machine, wafting into airspace. It was to be hoped they did not hit anyone on the ground. The enemy dived into a cloud, and counted as a probable for Hubacek, who had fought hard from 20,000 feet right down to 8,000.

At 20,000 feet over east London, P/O Rypl made several turns. Above his head he saw enemy fighters not yet in action. When he saw that some of them were on to his section, flying below, he chased one. He got in a shot or two at this Me 109 and saw grey smoke gushing out of the engine. His altitude at this precise stage of the proceedings read as 23,208 feet! This must take any award as the most accurate height reading made during the entire Battle of Britain.

Rypl flew on. He chased bombers, eluded fighters, and at length saw that he was over a hilly and partly wooded countryside. As he was by then flying with the reserve petrol tank open, and had therefore not much time for orientation – and as he could find no aerodrome – he decided to make an emergency landing to save the aircraft. He did his very best and landed in a long field with the undercarriage down. Unfortunately, the field was obstructed with anti-invasion glider-wire fixed on wooden poles, which Rypl could not possibly see from above. So his Hurricane was damaged after all, though he was safe. Visibility by that time of the September evening had grown rather poor as well.

Back aloft, the battle was approaching its latter stages. Sgt Rechka had to cope with three Me 110s who all chose to fly at him. He gamely fired at the first one and hit its port engine. Diving away in distress, the Me 110 could easily have come to grief over the suburbs of south-east London. Rechka did not see.

P/O Zimprich wanted to make a really typical Czech dash at Dornier 215s with the leader of his section, but he lost his number 1 in a sharp turn. This was all too easy to do. So he tried to go for the first Dornier alone. Then he saw an Me 110 so transferred to this adversary. He scored on the port engine before having to evade other 110s seen in his mirror.

That was not the end of Zimprich's sortie. He picked up another Dornier 215 and decided to destroy it at any price. Closing from above and from starboard at 300 to fifty yards, he sent him spinning down. But Zimprich went round to the front and port this time from fifty yards, repeating it from starboard. He saw both engines stopped, the gunner cease firing, and the Dornier gliding. Then he espied things falling out of the aircraft, presumably bombs being jettisoned. The Dornier landed near Westerham in Kent without its undercarriage down. Zimprich circled and saw the Army approaching the Luftwaffe crew. He landed at Biggin Hill aerodrome. It should be remembered that the Czech pilots were not familiar with the general terrain of southern England.

Nine Spitfires of 19 Squadron saw the enemy initially as the Luftwaffe were flying north-west. The fighters wove and searched above the bombers.

It had been arranged by Bader for 19 Squadron to take the enemy fighters. F/Lt W. G. Clouston as Blue 1 put them in line-astern and clambered up to 23,000 feet for an attack on half a dozen Me 110s also on the climb. Just then a pair of 109s cut across their bows and Blue 1 caused a burst before them. The second started a downward glide.

The squadron went on to tackle the 110s. But Blue 1 had used all his ammunition so could not participate further. He had had his moment. Blue 2, F/Sgt H. Steere, cut across in front and Blue 3, F/Lt E. Burgoyne, took a full deflection shot, closing to fifty yards before breaking away underneath. The enemy was then slipping inwards and Blue 1 saw it fade into a left-hand spiral out of control. Blue 2 chased another Me 110 out over the Channel but failed to get in range. Blue 3 stayed with Blue 1 and so did not take part in the main attack: he preferred to protect his leader which he did successfully.

Red 1, F/Lt W. J. Lawson, opened fire on the tail of an Me 110 at 300 yards, scoring a starboard strike. With bits of wing blown off, the Messerschmitt finally crashed five miles east of Biggin Hill, Kent.

Red 2, S/Lt A. G. Blake, did not fire in the first dog-fight but followed the main enemy formation out to sea, and stumbled on a straggling Heinkel. He left it dropping, flaming, towards the water. Red 2's windscreen was pierced by a bullet which ended in his petrol tank. Red 3 got on to an Me 109. Some of the enemy's engine flew out in a rather surrealist manner and P/O W. Cunningham left the 109 flame-enveloped. Red 3 got a bullet in his mainspar.

Lastly, Yellow Section. Yellow 1 attacked one of two 109s with a deflection burst. No hits. He was F/O F. M. Brinsden and saw a Hurricane going for a Heinkel, so he joined in from dead astern until he could fire no more. By that time, around 1800, Red 3 had landed at Detling and the Heinkel was down to 1,000 feet, with both engines stopped and his flaps and undercarriage down. He was gliding east, aiming to make a forced landing a little south of Detling, too.

Yellow 2, P/O A. F. Vokes, dived to attack one of six Dornier 215s, straggling and with its wheels down. He fired all he had and then left it to another Spitfire. Yellow 3, Sgt D. G. Cox, shot down an Me 109. But Cox's Spitfire was hit during the exchange in the mainplane and airscrew. It also transpired later that he had a bullet through the petrol tank. He was lucky to live . . .

Douglas Bader could not see a single other British fighter in the sky by this time and he maintained that the fleeing Germans could have been broken up still more severely and savagely and shot down if two fresh squadrons had arrived – five instead of three. The enemy adopted tactics as with previous interceptions made by 242 Squadron. They had approached from the south, flying north over the west side of London, before turning south-east for home. 12 Group Wing were instructed to patrol North Weald and Hornchurch, a useless procedure in Bader's very experienced view, because he could see fifty to eighty miles to the east but no distance to the west – up-sun. In his considered opinion, quite unshaken and in fact substantiated by 9 September, they should have been patrolling many miles south-west, where they would have been up-sun from the enemy and could have attacked before the Germans got to the Thames. Bader was convinced that would have shot down at least twice the number. If Senior Controllers would have confined themselves to telling formation leaders where the enemy were supposed to be and left it to them to choose height and place to patrol, much better results would have been achieved.

Bader insisted with good evidence that if aerodromes like North Weald and Hornchurch wanted protection, the patrol line should have been somewhere west of the Thames in the evening and south-east in the morning, because of the sun. The Battle of Britain was being fought not at ground level or on some plotting table, but five miles high above the Thames Estuary, London, and Kent.

So what were the results claimed by the three-squadron Wing on 9 September? Twenty-one enemy aircraft destroyed, with five probables and two damaged. Our casualties were four aircraft destroyed or missing, three damaged and two pilots killed or missing. The individual squadron claims read as follows:- 242 Squadron, eleven destroyed, two probables; 310 Squadron, four destroyed, two probables, one damaged; 19 Squadron, six destroyed, one probable, one damaged.

Let us leave the postscript to 9 September once again to Johnnie Johnson:

> 'Fortunately for Bader neither North Weald nor Hornchurch was attacked, otherwise Park might have lodged an official complaint with Dowding who, however, would have taken into account the tremendous results of this engagement – twenty enemy aeroplanes destroyed before bombing, for the loss of four Hurricanes and two pilots. And Leigh-Mallory must have thought a bit of occasional poaching like this was well justified, for he was so delighted with the results that he offered Bader two more squadrons, making five in all, for the next show. So it was in 12 Group, if not in 11 Group, that a leader could interpret instructions from the ground as he thought fit.'

Perhaps it was just as well that 12 Group had a breather for twenty-four hours. During the night of 9–10 September, few raids reached recent targets. The 12 Group headquarters accounted for this respite in two ways. Firstly, the enemy were by now still concentrating their main attack against London. Secondly, the weather became very showery in the north-west and spread diagonally across to the south-east and on to the coast of France.

This could only be England. At the height of the Battle of Britain, Her Royal Highness the Duchess of Gloucester visited 12 Group Headquarters. Hitler and the Luftwaffe notwithstanding, sherry was served formally in the large ante-room before lunch on Wednesday 11 September. Leigh-Mallory was there too. The Duchess left camp at about 1410 hours.

Seventy minutes later a Wing took off from Duxford under the command of Squadron Leader Lane. This comprised half of 19 and 266 Squadrons and the whole of 74 and 611 Squadrons. For once, Douglas was not in the scrap.

The outcome of this third Wing patrol was that the thirty-six aircraft involved claimed twelve enemy destroyed with fourteen probables and seven damaged. RAF casualties included one pilot killed and one wounded.

After the first three Wing patrols, Air Vice-Marshal Leigh-Mallory reported on his tactical conclusions in an interim viewpoint on the Battle of Britain as at 11 September. He pressed for the use of five squadrons in the Wing – two Spitfire and three Hurricane. It did not take long for this submission to be implemented.

Meanwhile by 12 September many 12 Group aircrew had received awards for their flying, but no-one will mind if Douglas is singled out on this day, when it was announced that he had won the Distinguished Service Order. Next day there was literally no activity in 12 Group. Perhaps it was just as well, for the date was Friday 13 September . . .

It was almost as if with a sense of impending history that the Battle of Britain resumed its upward curve on 14 September, ready for the following day. Contrary to popular conception, the Big Wing of five squadrons did not fly on the offensive for the first time on 15 September. For on 14 September, Douglas Bader took up the following squadrons: 242, 310, 19 and 611. They left for the London area at about 1600 hours but made no contact with the Luftwaffe. Sgt Marek of 19 Squadron had to break away from the formation owing to oxygen trouble, and his aircraft crashed – killing him.

Then a couple of hours later, the Big Wing of five squadrons took off for the first time intending to intercept. The squadrons were 242, 310, 302, 19 and 611. Five squadrons as envisaged by Bader and Leigh-Mallory. Bader was told to patrol the Debden/North Weald/Hornchurch region, but they failed to sight the enemy. Not their fault of course. But at least the sortie had provided practice for the next round – on a date that has gone down into human history.

CHAPTER 8

Although no-one knew it then, Sunday 15 September was the day that the Battle of Britain was won. Over the south-east of England, the day dawned a little misty, but cleared by 0800 to disclose light cumulus cloud at 2,000 to 3,000 feet. The extent of the cloud varied, and in places it was heavy enough to produce light local showers. But visibility remained good on the whole, with a slight westerly wind shifting to north-west as the day advanced.

The first enemy patrols arrived soon after 0900. They were reported over the Straits of Dover, the Thames Estuary, off Harwich and between Lympne and Dungeness. At about 1130, Goering launched the first wave of the morning attack, consisting of 100 or more aircraft, soon followed by 150 more. These crossed the English coast at three main points, near Ramsgate, between Dover and Folkestone, and a mile or two north of Dungeness. Their goal: London.

This formidable force comprised Dornier 17s and 215s escorted by Messerschmitt 109s. They flew at various heights between 15,000 and 26,000 feet. From the ground the German aircraft looked like black dots at the head of long streamers of white vapour; from the air, like specks rapidly growing. They appeared first as model aeroplanes and then as the range closed, as full-size aircraft. One controller said:

'This looks like the biggest show yet.'

Battle was soon joined, and raged for about three-quarters of an hour over east Kent and London. Some one hundred bombers burst through our defences and reached the eastern and southern quarters of the capital. A number of them were intercepted above the centre of the city itself, just as Big Ben was striking the hour of noon.

To understand the nature of the combat, it must be remembered that the aircraft engaged in it were flying at speed of between 300 and 400 miles an hour. At those speeds, place names became almost meaningless. The enemy might have been intercepted over Maidstone, but not destroyed on the return route until within a few miles of Calais.

'Place attack was delivered – Hammersmith to Dungeness.'

'Place attack was delivered – London to the French Coast.'

These phrases forcibly illustrate the scale of the area over which the battle was being fought. In fact it took place roughly in a cuboid about eight miles long, thirty-eight miles broad, and from five to six miles high. It was in this space between noon and half-past-twelve that 150–200 individual combats were waged. Many of these developed into stern chases, only broken off within a mile or two of the French Coast.

Sixteen squadrons of 11 Group followed by five from 12 Group took-off to engage the enemy. No 10 Group was also utilised. All but one of the squadrons in the battle came face to face with the Luftwaffe very soon after taking to the sky. Five squadrons of Spitfires opened their attack against the oncoming hordes over the Maidstone/Canterbury/Dover/Dungeness area. These were in action slightly before the Hurricane squadrons, which intercepted further back, between Maidstone, Tunbridge Wells and south London.

The Few found the enemy flying in various types of formations. The bombers were usually some thousands of feet below the fighters, but sometimes this position was reversed. The bombers flew either in Vics of from five to seven aircraft, or in lines of five aircraft abreast, or in a diamond pattern. The Me 109s were usually in Vics. One pilot saw the enemy as attacking in little groups of nine, arranged in threes like a sergeant's stripes. Each group of nine was supported by nine Me 110 fighters with single-seat Me 109s or Heinkel 113s circling high above.

The enemy soon realised that our defence was awake and active, for the German pilots could be heard calling out to each other over their wireless: 'Achtung! Schpitfeuer.'

While Spitfires and Hurricanes were in action over Kent, other Hurricanes were dealing with those of the enemy which had broken through to the London outskirts by sheer strength of numbers. Fourteen squadrons of Hurricanes, almost at once reinforced by three more of Spitfires, took up this challenge, all of them coming into action between noon and 1220. Then followed an engagement extending all the way from London to the coast – and beyond.

It was precisely 1122 hours when 242 Squadron were ordered off. The Wing comprised 242, 310 and 302 in that order, plus 19 and 611 Spitfires. The five squadrons formed up according to plan over Duxford and at once proceeded south towards the action. For once they had been scrambled in time. They were speeding towards the Luftwaffe at height, at the very time the enemy were over the Channel. The Wing sped south to patrol a flexible area beyond the Thames in the Gravesend region. Bader made sure he had the sun behind them as 242, 310 and 302 reached Angels two five, with 19 and 611 stepped up behind them to an altitude varying between 26,000 and 27,000 feet. The Hurricanes had the task of harrying the bombers, while the Spitfires kept fighters at bay. So much for the theory. The practice was about to begin again.

Douglas saw two squadrons passing right underneath them in formation, flying north-west in purposeful manner. The enemy looked like Dornier 17s and Junkers 88s. AA bursts caused Bader to turn the Wing. He saw the enemy again now 3,000 feet below. He managed to perfect the approach with 19 and 611 Squadrons between the Hurricanes and the sun. The enemy were still below and down-sun. Next he noticed Me 109s diving out of the sun, so he warned the Spitfires to look out for these and also to watch for friendly fighters. The Me 109s broke away and climbed south-east.

Bader was about to attack the bombers which were turning left to west and south when he noticed Spitfires and Hurricanes of 11 Group presumably already engaging them. He was compelled to wait in case of a collision. Then he dived down with his leading section in formation on to the last section of three bombers.

'Leader calling – prepare to break – line-astern.'

As P/O N. N. Campbell took the left-hand Dornier 17, Bader went for the middle one, while Sub Lt R. J. Cork took the right-hand. Bader opened fire at 100 yards in a steep dive and saw a sudden large flash behind the starboard motor of the Dornier as its wing caught fire. The shots must have hit its petrol pipe or tank. Bader overshot and pulled up steeply. Then he carried on to attack another Dornier 17 but had to break away to avoid an oncoming Spitfire. The sky seemed full of both Spitfires and Hurricanes queueing up. They were metaphorically pushing and jostling each other out of the way to get at the Dorniers, which were for once really outnumbered.

Bader squirted at odd Dorniers from close range as they silhouetted into his sights, but he could not hold them there for long for fear of collision with the friendly fighters. Bader was flying as Red 1. He saw a collision between a Spitfire and a Dornier 17 which wrecked both aeroplanes instantaneously. He finally ran out of ammunition while chasing a crippled and smoking Dornier 17 into clouds. Bader realised even in the midst of the mêlée that for the first time the 12 Group Wing had position, height and numbers.

This is an extract from how Douglas Bader himself described those minutes around 1215 somewhere over Hammersmith:

> At one time you could see planes all over the place, and the sky seemed full of parachutes. It was sudden death that morning, for our fighters shot them to blazes.
>
> One unfortunate German rear-gunner baled out of the Dornier 17 I attacked, but his parachute caught on the tail. There he was swinging helplessly, with the aircraft swooping and diving and staggering all over the sky, being pulled about by the man hanging by his parachute from the tail. That bomber went crashing into the Thames Estuary, with the swinging gunner still there.
>
> About the same time, one of my boys saw a similar thing in another Dornier, though this time the gunner who tried to bale out had his parachute caught in the hood before it opened. Our pilot saw the other two members of the crew crawl up and struggle to set him free. He was swinging from his packed parachute until they pushed him clear. Then they jumped off after him, and their plane went into the water with a terrific smack.
>
> I've always thought it was a pretty stout effort on the part of those two Huns who refused to leave their pal fastened to the doomed aircraft.'

But Bader was only the leader of fifty-six aircraft. What happened to the other fifty-five? We left Sub Lt R. J. Cork nosing for the starboard Dornier 17 of the rear section. After the first sally, he dived to the right, climbed again, and saw the starboard engine of the bomber groaning and flaming. The Dornier did a steep diving turn to port and down. It was also being fired on by four other Hurricanes and a Spitfire, so Cork decided not to pursue. Instead he fired at another bomber. It was last seen steeply falling into the clouds and must have failed to recover. Cork contributed a completely unsolicited testimonial to the Wing Leader:

> 'The success of the whole attack was definitely due to the good positioning and perfect timing of the CO of 242 Squadron, who was leading the Wing formation.'

So even if Douglas did not account for more than one definite Dornier plus others damaged, the final figures soon to emerge would be because of his shrewd skill in the air.

P/O N. N. Campbell was Bader's Red 3, and he attacked a Dornier 17 from astern and below. The lower gun of the bomber fired close to his Hurricane, but ceased soon after Campbell fired back. Smoke billowed and blew from the lower part of the enemy fuselage, so he could claim one Dornier damaged.

Successful as this engagement was, the element of risk remained present for the RAF just as for the Luftwaffe. Yellow 1, F/Lt Ball, poured all his fire towards a Dornier 17 without noticeable result. But then he sustained a hit in his own fuel tank. The Hurricane caught fire quickly but Ball managed to lose height while still in control and bring down the fighter in a field a few miles from Detling.

Yellow 2 was P/O N. K. Stansfield. During an astern attack on another Dornier 17 the rear gunner fired at him steadily. But Stansfield silenced the enemy which dived for cloud protection with smoke streaming in ragged parallels from both engines. He followed it through the clouds to make sure of the outcome. The Dornier crashed directly on top of a house, but Stansfield had not time to wonder about either the Germans or the occupants of the house.

Blue 1 was to have an adventurous day, only he did not know it yet. F/Lt Powell-Sheddon made several stabs at Dornier 17s. While setting an engine on fire at one stage he nearly collided with a Hurricane, also after the same bomber. Three of the enemy aircrew baled out as the Dornier descended and crashed into a small wood near a house. The bomber exploded on impact and the whole tree area appeared enveloped in a sheet of flame. Powell-Sheddon landed at Duxford to find he had a bullet hole through his oil tank. But the afternoon was still to come . . .

Meanwhile, behind Blue 1 came P/O Tamblyn as Blue 2. He fired on a Dornier 17 at 150 yards and turned away till friendly fighters had completed their attacks. He remembered Bader's advice about watching for our own fighters. Next time at the Dornier, he noticed slight smoke from the enemy engines which decreased a little. The damage had been inflicted in company with five other friendly fighters. They followed the Dornier down to 2,000 feet when the crew baled out. The bomber crashed near West Malling in a field. Tamblyn thought one of the crew failed to survive. Blue 3, P/O Latta, for once could make no definite claims, though he did engage the enemy more than once. That was the way things went.

On to Green Section. Green 1, P/O P. S. Turner, chose a straggling Dornier to attack three times. The last close-range pressure hit home and burst the oil tanks. Three crew managed to get out before it began its final unpiloted plunge into the inevitable field, where it blew up. Turner thought there seemed to be an acceptance of their fate on the part of the Germans from the moment his Hurricane opened up.

Seeing that the enemy bombers were well engaged and on equal terms, P/O Hart at Green 3 veered to go for the next best thing – an Me 109. It was flying at 15,000 feet in the general direction of France. Hart proceeded to dive on him, forcing the enemy down to 11,000 feet. This put the Messerschmitt right on top of the cloud layer which had built up a little since early morning. Hart continued his gentle dive on the enemy till he was directly above it. Then he instigated a steep dive and opened fire. The bullets completely smashed the pilot's enclosure and the engine cowling. Flames spurted. Hart flew on after him and saw the Me 109 disturb the surface of the Channel some eight miles off the English coast.

All the 242 Squadron managed to get back to Duxford except Ball, but at least they had lost no pilots. Would the other four squadrons fare so well? How many men would survive this day? These questions of life and death still remained to be resolved.

F/Lt J. Jeffries was leading B Flight of 310 Squadron when they saw the enemy first. The Luftwaffe were west of London and flying north, but as the Wing turned south to attack, they also took a turn southwards. The B Flight dived on the enemy and Jeffries fastened his sights on one machine. He caused its port engine to catch fire, whereupon it was taken over by some other Hurricanes. That was a Dornier 215. Jeffries attacked another 215 and its occupants baled out almost at once. He did the same thing again and a second Dornier crew also baled out. A Spitfire then dived straight through the fuselage of this Dornier and the RAF fighter went down out of control.

P/Sgt Kominek started an attack with Jeffries, but at 15,000 feet he lost sight of his leader. Probably because Jeffries was four miles above Kingston on Thames while Kominek had by then reached Tunbridge Wells! Kominek and three other Hurricanes fought a Dornier 215 which made the clouds. The other Hurricanes went elsewhere but Kominek persevered with three more bursts. After the last one, some sheets started to fall off the bomber and smoke signals appeared. The crew just dumped their bombs over the Kent countryside and baled out not far behind the missiles. The Dornier ploughed into an already furrowed field three miles south-west of Tunbridge Wells.

P/Sgt Kaucky shared a Dornier 215. He delivered his effort over London at 1205–1210. Two other Hurricanes were also in this fight. Kaucky used up all his ammunition and between the three fighters they saw the Dornier going groundwards – minus its crew.

At about the same time and place, P/Sgt Hubacek had an exchange of fire with a Dornier 215. He made his run from the port and rear, and the enemy soon started to glide. Another Hurricane helped in the conflict. The enemy glide steepened to a dive as several more Hurricanes and Spitfires joined in to seal the agony of the stricken bomber. At 8,000 feet part of the Dornier's rudder broke off. Two men got out. One did not. The Dornier crashed somewhere south of London. As Bader had said:

'It was sudden death this morning.'

Finally in 310 Squadron, Sgt Puda challenged a pair of Dornier 215s. He opened fire and the aim must have been impeccable, for the bomber fell with both engines streaming. Puda broke away to prepare for a further finishing off. But just then a Spitfire did it for him from fifty yards.

The Poles followed the Czechs. P/O J. Chalupa of 302 Squadron saw the bombers through puffs of our anti-aircraft fire. He got in three bursts at the leader of the second vic in an enemy Dornier formation. The range was shortened from 250 to thirty yards. The bomber dived violently. Then Chalupa saw a second Dornier, attacking it from 100 yards. Smoke and flames from the port engine signified success. Two airmen jumped from the burning bomber which dived to earth. Meanwhile one of the other Polish pilots cut off the tail of this burning aircraft with his own wing – tearing it in the process.

The Poles were certainly going in irrespective of survival. F/Lt Chlopik went for the hindmost section of Dorniers. He hit one and saw its port engine smoking heavily, with blue smoke also emitting from the starboard. The Dornier dived on its back. The three crew jumped out in time and three parachutes brought them down safely. There were going to be a lot of Luftwaffe prisoners of war.

Chlopik was over south-east London now. He hit a Dornier from behind and above. With its port engine faltering, the bomber became the focus for a whole group of Hurricanes and a couple of Spitfires. The sun was on his beam during his first fight and later behind him. F/Lt Chlopik was flying at 14,000–17,000 feet over the southern suburbs of London. He had taken off at 1125 from Duxford.

The report ended with the poignant words:

'This pilot could not sign, as he was killed . . .'

The Poles knew what freedom meant – and the lack of it. They were willing to risk everything in their passionate nature to try to restore it to Europe. Bader did not forget Chlopik. Nor should we.

302 Squadron had height advantage as they flew their Hurricanes in at 300 mph. F/O Czerwinski met a Dornier above and in front of him. He went in alone with three bursts. The port engine sparked into fire and the bomber

dived. Three other Hurricanes also attacked this one, so that by the time Czerwinski had gone in again the bomber was written off by the crew, who had wisely jumped. More POWs.

F/Lt Jastrzebski flew down-sun, gave a Dornier some brief squirts and paused to consider the situation. The Dornier did not fire back, but wiggled sharply to left and then right. Another Hurricane went for it, too. The Pole turned 180° to the right of the Dornier and did not see it again. But on climbing he was confronted by five parachutists. Owing to loss of position he landed at Henlow and refuelled before returning to Duxford.

F/O Kowalski fired at the last Dornier of a group. Two bursts of two seconds each. The bomber took to the clouds, but Kowalski was sure it must have crashed. Below the clouds he saw two more Dorniers already being set on effectively by Hurricanes. After a few seconds, both enemy bombers plummeted.

F/O Palak was one of three Hurricanes sharing a Dornier 215. It crashed. Palak climbed again to notice a more formidable and perhaps worthier opponent – a Messerschmitt 109. It was diving towards another Hurricane, so Palak turned towards him at full throttle, squirting twice. Bits spun off the Me 109 as it took a vertical dive. Palak could only claim a probable, although the aspect of the enemy machine made it unlikely that any recovery would be possible. Palak landed at Maidstone at 1235.

Sgt Paterek encountered enemy bombers, probably Heinkel lll s, flying in formation of five close together at a measured speed of 270 mph. He made a beam attack. The enemy rear gunner of the bomber selected ceased to reply. That left Paterek free to aim a long burst at very short range. He could scarcely miss and the bomber took the inexorable course downwards, out of any semblance of control. There was no smoke. The altitude at the start of the dive was 5,000 feet. It never recovered and fell the remaining mile to earth. Paterek was not exactly familiar with England yet, and so he landed at the likeliest looking aerodrome he could find. It turned out to be Wattisham (from where I flew in my first Lightning a quarter of a century later!).

S/Ldr W. Satchell was leading 302 Squadron. As Douglas Bader had headed for the most westerly of the three formations of enemy bombers, Satchell took the middle group, flying in vics. He attacked the left leader and saw him go down straight. In this attack, Satchell followed Bader's advice and dived from above the enemy almost vertically, giving a full deflection shot which seemed effective. He went through with the dive before pulling up.

This strategy presents a fairly easy shot and does not give much of an aiming mark for any enemy gunners. But Satchell did in fact get scratches from a few stray bullets. His Hurricane got the scratches, not himself. Then as he commenced to attack another Dornier, he was hit by an Me 109 but survived. Next he spotted a dozen Dorniers east of London flying east-south-east. Satchell made a beam and quarter attack from either side and saw one of them falling. It might have landed between Rochester and the coast.

Sgt Wedzik got on the tail of a Dornier 17. At the end of his firing burst, he observed the bomber in dire distress. Smoke from the port engine, flames from the port mainplane. The bomber banked steeply to the left. He did not see the end of it, as he returned over London trying to find his leader. But being unable to do so, headed back to Duxford. One hour and ten minutes after take-off.

Last in the Polish squadron was Sgt Sindak. He paced a Dornier 17 at 240 mph before squirting at it. The usual black smoke, this time from the cockpit and port mainplane. The enemy rear gunners fired at him spiritedly. Sindak lost the machine-gun panel of his port mainplane, while the whole mainplane looked to be badly torn. The Dornier spun down, as a second Hurricane finished it off. A large piece flew off the underbelly of its fuselage. 302 Squadron had done well.

So to the two Spitfire squadrons ranged higher than the original 25,000 feet of the Hurricanes. F/Lt Lawson led 19 Squadron as they spotted a score of Dornier 17s escorted by Me 109s. The enemy were 10,000 feet lower down. He hurried on ahead of the bombers and turned to deliver frontal fire. He dived past the left-hand Dornier of the rear vic. Then he turned and attacked the same aircraft from its rear – 300 down to fifty yards. Fragments fell from the starboard wing and the starboard engine started streaming glycol. The enemy waffled away from the rest and glided down with glycol still streaming. The result: one probable Dornier 17.

'Tally ho! Tally ho! Bandits ahead and below me.'

The air rang with such typical pilot jargon. The RAF might be mixing its vocabulary. The quarry was human and in the present state of history, more justifiable than fox-hunting.

S/Ldr Lane, Sub Lt Blake and P/O Cunningham were flying in one section of Flight A. Cunningham attacked behind the other two but did not really get a chance to fire. Veering off on a solo he fired at a solitary Me 110. Its starboard engine was hit and stuttered after this attack. Cunningham turned in from the port to deliver another squirt from that side. The Me 110 was already as good as done for – when a pair of Hurricanes shot it from the sky. The three of them had shared this success at Angels 16.

F/Sgt Unwin took on an Me 109 with a yellow nose. This was at 20,000 feet over Westerham. The six-second burst proved enough and the German pilot baled out. His Messerschmitt came down between Redhill and Westerham – around the Surrey/Kent border country.

F/Sgt Steere too saw the 109s bearing on them. He fired one burst from a poor position, then chose a better angle to attack another one. His first deflection fire from 350 yards soon diminished to a mere fifty. As near as safety allowed – if there were such a thing as safety. Thick bluish smoke swirled around the Me 109 as it spiralled into the clouds. The steepness of the near-vertical fall signified destruction. Steere chased another Me 109, came into range, only to find that he had no ammunition left – so no point in hanging about longer.

F/O Haines was south of London near Biggin Hill when he attacked an Me 109. It half-rolled and dived to 12,000 feet but then straightened out again. Haines was flying faster than the 109, and had to pull away rapidly right to avoid a collision. The Me 109 really rolled. Smoke seemed to be pouring from underneath the pilot's seat.

He went down with it to 6,000 feet and had to be careful to recover from this drastic dive, as the enemy was by then touching 480 mph. Haines made his way more slowly through a bundle of low cloud and as he emerged he saw the wreckage of the Messerschmitt already burning on the ground. It had been painted yellow from spinner to cockpit. Haines climbed through clouds and narrowly missed hitting a Junkers 88. This bomber was actually on fire and was being pounded by other Hurricanes.

The locale: Tunbridge Wells. The height: 15,000 feet. Sgt D. G. Cox had one or two abortive brushes before finding an Me 109 about to attack him head on. As the enemy passed above Cox, the Spitfire pilot turned and climbed steeply. He came up underneath the 109 with a couple of bursts, stalling as he did so. The Messerschmitt hit earth five miles east of Crowborough.

Bader's strategy of five squadrons was working. The second Spitfire squadron was 611. Red 1 saw the bombers at about 18,000 feet with their screening Messerschmitts at 28,000 feet. But Bader's perspicacity had put the Spitfires almost up to them. Red 1 was 5,000 feet above and to one side of the main Wing Hurricanes. They were flying north-west with the sun more or less on their left. As the Wing went into the attack, the 611 Spitfires kept company with thirty Me 109s, who were further west and slightly higher. They did not descend. After the Wing had broken up, the bombers turned round through 180 degrees to south-east. Red 1 waited for five to seven minutes before he told Bader he was coming down.

Red 1: 'Echelon port.'

They were then going south-east, still up-sun of both the Wing and the enemy. They made a head-on ramrod thrust on to ten Dornier 215s and 17s. Red 1 took a Dornier 215 head-on. Next an Me 110. It turned over on its back and went down in a death-throe. Red 2 behind him could not follow. Red 1 tried to pick up any enemy lame ducks along the coast but saw none.

611 Squadron attacked in three sections of four Spitfires: Red, Yellow and Blue. Yellow 1 was around Angels 18 as he sped some ten miles west of Canterbury. He first tried a trio of Dornier 215s. Then he picked out a single one and fired all he had at this. Its port engine literally exploded. Red 2 saw the crew bale out. Other Spitfires seemed to be going for this same unfortunate Dornier but Yellow 1 got the credit and it crashed seven to ten miles south-east of Canterbury.

Yellow 2 was in the same area: a moving triangle that at the time of his main action was pinpointed by London/Rochester/Herne Bay. Rochester with its memories of Dickens and *Great Expectations* and the marshes. Another century. Another world.

'Bandits at Angels 18.'

Yellow 2 heard the phrase and acted on it. He dived on thirty Dorniers from about 4,000 feet above them. No luck. Next he chased a Dornier 215 towards Rochester. The enemy's altitude began to dwindle as it neared the Herne Bay zone. Smoke from port engine. Crew baled out. It was getting almost monotonous. The Dornier crashed on the edge of a wood or thicket some four or five miles south of Herne Bay. Four attacks had to be completed before this final chalk-up. Yellow 2 was not exactly unscathed or fully fuelled. He landed at Detling, owning up to being slightly lost by 1300 hours.

Last of the morning's sections in this mammoth Wing action was Blue Section 611 Squadron. Blue 4 caught a Dornier 215 by itself at 14,000 feet. Blue 4 rolled over and carried out an old astern attack by diving on to the bomber. One long burst and both enemy motors began to smoke. Blue 4 climbed and carried out the same drill again. By this time, though, the Dornier had both its engines obscured by smoke and fire. Fire tongued from both mainplanes behind the engines. The result: one more destroyed.

There was scarcely time for a snack, let alone to add up the morning's score. But this was what the Bader Wing had been credited with in a little over an hour. Fifty-six fighters had destroyed, twenty-six enemy aircraft; with eight probables and two damaged. These were the individual squadron scores as listed by 12 Group on that midday. 242 Squadron, five Dornier 17s and one Messerschmitt 109; 310 Squadron, four Dornier 215s; 302 Squadron, six Dornier 17s and two Dornier 215s; 19 Squadron, three Messerschmitt 109s and two Messerschmitt 110s; 611 Squadron, three Dornier 215s. Twenty-six enemy aircraft claimed.

Chapter 9

The climax was coming to the Battle of Britain. And Douglas was in the very thick of it. Hardly had the Wing landed and refuelled when they were ordered up again – and again vindicating the strategy conceived by Leigh-Mallory and Bader.

The take-off time: 1412 hours.

The clouds were eight-tenths at 5,000 feet. The Wing consisted of forty-nine fighters instead of the fifty-six in the morning/midday combat. But the same five squadrons were involved. The same men. Bader led them up through a gap in the clouds and hurried south still climbing. The three Hurricane squadrons – 242, 310, 302 – were in line-astern and the pair of Spitfire squadrons on the right.

The Hurricane formations climbed slightly more quickly of the two types of fighter. Douglas and 242 were at 16,000 feet and still rising when they sighted quantities of enemy bombers punctuated by the dark clusters of anti-aircraft shells. The enemy were at 20,000 feet, still three or four thousand feet higher. This was just the sort of situation that tended to annoy Bader. Those precious extra minutes of warning to get airborne might have enabled them to gain the additional altitude, so that they could have been plus 4,000 feet instead of minus it. And it could mean literally – life or death.

Bader endeavoured to climb and catch the enemy, but 242 were set on by Me 109s from above and behind. Douglas told the Spitfires to come on and get the bombers, while he and his fellow Hurricane pilots broke up and engaged the enemy fighters. Bader was nothing if not decisive. Then things started to happen all over that particular patch of sky between the Kenley/Maidstone ground area.

After ordering the break-up, Bader himself pulled up and around quite violently. Coming off his back, he partially blacked out and actually almost collided with Yellow 2, P/O Denis Crowley-Milling. That could have been the end of a glorious friendship. Bader spun off Yellow 2's slipstream and straightened out at only 5,000 feet. He had not fired a shot yet.

However, he climbed back into the fray and got in a brief burst at a twin-engined bomber flying westwards. He was just in the enemy's range and fired a three-second squirt from a completely stalled position. He then had to spin off again and lost still more height. Eventually he went through the clouds near Ashford, Kent, to try and trace enemy stragglers but it was no use. Bader was furious at the whole situation. They were all too low. They had to seize whatever opportunities they could. He had to admit that his lead was not as effective as it could have been in better circumstances. They were up-sun, too low, and he spun out of position.

He turned his mind once more to the inescapable truth: if they had managed to get off ten minutes earlier and reached their height, then the whole story could have been better. That was perfectionist thinking, of course, but had a distinct grain of truth and reason in it. The reality of the situation was rather different, at least in that the Wing did manage to do phenomenally well – given their abysmal location.

Douglas did not mind missing his personal victories on this occasion and was naturally pleased later to hear how well things had gone after all. The faithful Sub Lt Cork as Red 2 made height at the maximum speed – as per instructions. As soon as Douglas told them to break formation, Cork went sharply to the right accompanied closely by an Me 109. He was now in a dive and found himself flying right through the second squadron, thereby losing his quarry. But he spotted a Dornier 17 to the starboard.

Cork dived 6,000 feet into the attack and concentrated a long squirt at its port engine, which started to smoke. His next thrust was a beam one, large lumps of the Dornier tracing crazy angles in the sky as they tumbled away. The starboard wing also flushed with fire near its tip. The Dornier dived gallantly for cloud cover but Cork waited till it emerged. Then he simply put in a head-on assault and the Dornier 17 died. Cork climbed a thousand feet and was stung by a vicious pair of yellow-nosed Me 109s from above. Rather like twin insects. He steeply tilted to the left and got on the tail of one. But in the midst of a promising burst of firing he ran out of ammunition. The other fighter was then on his tail, so he put his stick into a virtually-vertical dive down to 2,000 feet and got away unscathed. Red 3, Campbell, fired a couple of thousand rounds at divers enemy but made no claim. 'You can't win them all.'

Yellow Section got up to 21,000 feet: nearer the height that Douglas would have preferred. P/O Stansfield saw a Heinkel flying below cloud and under attack from two other Hurricanes. He joined in and stopped the enemy port motor. By then both engines were in dire trouble. So the Heinkel was, too. Other aircraft also fired on this unfortunate Heinkel, which eventually pancaked on to an aerodrome south-east of London. The aircraft carried a crew of five. On its tailplane were painted three pinkish stripes, presumably to imitate similar markings being painted on RAF aircraft and so confuse any potential attackers.

Denis Crowley-Milling, having survived the near-miss with Douglas Bader, picked out an Me 109. The enemy performed a veritable series of barrel rolls and aileron turns before he finally hit it. No amount of writhing seemed to make any difference. The machine caught fire around the pilot's cockpit and Crowley-Milling followed it down according to instructions – seeing it crash several miles south of Maidstone. While the midday battle had been over London, this afternoon's encounter moved south-east into central Kent. P/O Hart engaged the enemy but modestly refused to make any claims for success.

The time was around 1500 now. Three-quarters of an hour and more since the slick take-off. Blue 1 was Bader's friend Powell-Sheddon. He reported 200 enemy aircraft. One other pilot had put it more succinctly:

'The whole bloody Luftwaffe!'

Powell-Sheddon saw swarms of 109s mostly higher than 242 Squadron, plus hordes of bombers. All approaching London. Two hundred plus. Me 109s flashed out of the teatime sun and from behind. One came head-on and he fired at it. Then he saw some thirty bombers flying north-west for the capital. They were not being attacked by any of our fighters – from 11 or 12 Group. Blue 1 broke away from the dog-fight after them. Before he caught up with them, these bombers had turned round and were heading SSE.

F/Lt Powell-Sheddon got between them and the sun – and 1,000 feet above. He picked off a Dornier 17 flying a few spans away from the rest and fired. Heavy smoke and fire followed his second and third attacks. All his efforts came from the sun. After the last one, he climbed back into position and saw the Dornier disappear into 7/10ths cloud in a tight spiral with volumes of smoke as signals of impending impact with the ground. He reckoned the Dornier was bound to crash somewhere near Rye on the Kent/Sussex borders.

Powell-Sheddon set off for Duxford in a gradual dive for low cloud at low speed to economise his dwindling fuel. Almost at once he was pounced on by an Me 109 which must have scored a crucial hit on his Hurricane. The fighter became uncontrollable. Powell-Sheddon felt shaken up and baled out. He landed safely though his left arm felt temporarily paralysed. The reason was that he had dislocated it. He was soon in Rye Hospital, and credited with one Dornier 17 destroyed.

The afternoon was turning into a slightly more golden tone. The time: 1515. P/O P. S. Turner in Blue 2 sent an Me 109 into an uncontrollable spin. He could not be sure that it crashed but he believed the pilot was dead – hence the lack of attempt to correct the spin. He could not cogitate about it for long.

A gun shell exploded in the side of his Hurricane under its tail and hurled Turner into a spin. He retained consciousness, however, and recovered control. He found he was below the clouds. The sortie went on. He was still airborne. It was still the Battle of Britain. He attacked a Dornier 215 and its starboard engine smouldered. The Dornier took a gentle dive and hit the ground, exploding between some houses near a river bank east of Hornchurch. None of the crew got out of it . . .

P/O Latta was another old chum of Bader's. As Blue 3 he was under attack from Me 109s. One of them overshot him, so that he was able to get in a burst at it from fifty to seventy-five yards dead astern. The enemy was still on fire as it entered cloud at 5,000 feet. Latta was over the Maidstone area at this phase and he could not visualise any recovery for the damaged Me 109.

As now usual, 310 Squadron followed Douglas and 242. F/Lt Jeffries was leading them when they sighted the black-bomber blocks above and ahead.

Then 310 was jumped on by Me 109s and the Wing as such broke up. Jeffries rose rapidly to 24,000 feet into the sun – as if by levitation. It was certainly as planned. The enemy fighters turned west. Jeffries waited till they had done this maneouvre to aim a head-on attack at them with the sun behind him. He started, dived straight through their first formation. They were east of London. He fired at one of the leading Me 109 section, whose starboard engine caught alight. It broke away in anguish and went down.

Behind Jeffries came in Sgt Rechka. He and two other Hurricanes took a Heinkel so utterly that Rechka saw it crash-land on the beach near Foulness. Impassively he watched two of the crew get out safely. P/Sgt Jan Kaucky was also in the vicinity at the equivalent battle time of 1440–1450–1500 hours. He and two Spitfires from another squadron shot down a Dornier 215.

S/Ldr Hess and P/O Fejfar plus three other Hurricanes and a pair of Spitfires encountered a dozen Dornier 17s. One aircraft attacked by Fejfar had a stream of what looked like petrol colouring its wake. Fejfar went back for more Dorniers. As one of them flew hide and seek in and out of the clouds, the 310 Squadron pilot fired at him twice very effectively. Fejfar followed it down to see it make an emergency landing near the Isle of Grain in the Thames Estuary zone. He flew over it until he was quite sure that civilians had approached it and taken the crew prisoners. Then he nosed back to Duxford. The Czechs had done well once more.

The day had yet to take its final toll of Allied airmen.

Seven of the Polish 302 Squadron were told to scramble at 1410 and gain Angels Twenty as soon as humanly possible. The instructions were to fly due south where enemy aircraft over a hundred strong were about to cross the coast at Dover.

'Will you patrol Canterbury?' The Controller Woodhall had 'asked' Bader. The rest was up to him.

302 Squadron were the rear of the trio of Hurricane formations. When the drones of Dorniers dotted into view, Me 109s were circling around them. Blue 1 veered to go for fifteen enemy aiming east. Just before getting into position, Blue 1 – S/Ldr Satchell – spied an Me 109 in his mirror, flying above him. He waited until the enemy dived to attack and then pulled up sharply, letting it pass below him. Satchell then got on its tail and pressed several long bursts. The Me 109 groaned on to its back with smoke issuing – and spun to the Kentish ground.

Seeing that Blue 1 was busy, Blue 2, P/O Pilch, dived for the bombers. He found that Red 1 had done the same thing. The enemy formation fanned out for cloud cover, so Blue 2 waited underneath until they emerged. Then he took a Dornier 17 from above and head-on. At the same second, a Spitfire attacked this Dornier too. Blue 2 made a double-quick turn and attacked from its tail, getting in a trio of bursts down to almost zero feet from it. Smoke signalled hits and the downward direction signified the rest. From 6,000 feet the Dornier turned towards the Thames Estuary, losing height the worse it burned.

Just then, Blue 2 saw a Dornier 215 taking a peep out of the clouds. He actually saw the rear-gunner take aim and fire briefly – but after Blue 2's response nothing more was seen or heard. Smoke had started from the Dornier's port engine but the usual end was interrupted by heavy AA fire bursting all around the Hurricane. He waited for it to stop and went in for the kill. The Dornier dived into shallow waters not far from Margate.

Blue 3, P/O Kaiwowski prepared an attack at about this same moment, but as he did so, his port machine-gun panel became loose. It did not fly off completely, but caused very strong drag and prevented proper control of the Hurricane. Blue 3 was uttering Polish curses, but he had no choice but to dive away and find a field safe for landing. His left undercarriage wheel got in a rut and broke away, the fighter finally coming to rest with a broken under carriage. But the pilot was safe. Blue 4 also had the misfortune to be forced to break off his intended attack owing to engine failure. He got back to Duxford all in one piece – pilot and plane. He was F/O Czerwinski.

Red Section of 302 Squadron had a tragic time.

F/Lt Chlopik was attacking enemy Dorniers before Blue 2 arrived on the scene. He caused one to break up. Chlopik was forced to bale out later during a particularly violent exchange with the Luftwaffe and for some reason unknown was not able to pull his parachute ripcord. He was killed.

P/O Lapka dived for a Dornier 17 from the beam. At this moment, his starboard machine-gun panel blew up, causing a heavy drag. Lapka was hit by firing from the Dornier 17 rear-gunner and smoke filled his cockpit. Then at an altitude of 15,000 feet he dived away and things looked bad for him. But after a few frantic instants he managed to bale out, pull the cord, and sail to earth. His total damage personally was a minor foot injury.

F/O Kowalski swooped down on a lone Dornier 17 from above and behind. He did not open fire till he was within thirty yards. He could actually discern the small lettering on the Dornier's tail flank. The tailplane disintegrated and chunks of wing also careered from the bomber. It dived at about forty-five degrees for the ground.

Kowalski then saw another Dornier ahead of him. He noticed its rear gunner calmly firing tracer at him. He shot this one down, too. When he finally landed, Kowalski found that his flap and undercarriage were not working properly and one of his wheels was punctured.

So to the Spitfires. S/Ldr Lane was leading 19 Squadron. Just as he sighted thirty Dornier 215s, he glimpsed higher up the fighter escort screen at about 30,000 feet. Three Me 109s dived on Lane and his men. Lane lunged to starboard and a loose dog-fight ensued, with more Me 109s coming down. Lane could not get near any of the immediate enemy, so climbed to take on a collection of Me 110s. No result, though, this time.

Suddenly his second sight became aware of a couple of Me 109s just above him. He maneouvred round on the tail of one and fired. The Me 109 seemed a determined type and took positive and violent evasive action. While screeching for cloud cover, the Me 109 received a burst of five seconds from Lane. The enemy flicked over, inverted, and entered a cloud doing a shallow inverted dive. It was to all intents beyond pilot control.

F/Sgt Unwin saw the German bombers in vics of three, line-astern. Above there seemed to Unwin to be 'thousands of Messerschmitt 109s.' He was somewhere over Kent at Angels 25 + . He engaged one of them at close range and it half-rolled into the clouds. He followed keenly but during the descent amid the cloud his windscreen froze up at 6,000 feet and he lost it.

Clambering back to 25,000 feet, Unwin saw another pair of Me 109s passing over his head. He chased and caught them up at Lydd. He shot down the first, which went into earth, beach or water near the coastline – he could not say for sure where it fell. The second attack was equally devastating. The other Me 109 took a vertical thrust waterwards and ended up just off the Kent coast.

F/Lt Clouston took both Blue and Green Sections into an assault on Dornier 17s. After setting the starboard engine of one afire, he made a beam attack on it and watched while some ten feet of the bomber's wing snapped off. This was many miles distant from Kent, between Southend and Burnham on Crouch. One of the Germans baled out over a convoy fifteen miles east of Burnham. Clouston continued pressing home his attack on the depleted plane until it went down towards the sea, rolling over and over to port. It had definitely been destroyed. As he had by then used all his aummunition, Clouston headed for the Essex coast. He reached this after flying for some nine minutes at 260 mph. So he reckoned he must have been about thirty miles out to sea.

F/Sgt Steere followed Clouston towards the Dornier 17s and singled one out. He closed to fifty yards, firing most of the time. Chunks and lumps flew off the Dornier, whose port engine caught fire. The crew baled out and then the bomber waffled into the clouds. Three bombs had been jettisoned before the crew had abandoned the aircraft – and in fact they dropped uncomfortably close to P/O Vokes, bringing up the rear of this particular scrap of the whole picture: one more piece in the jigsaw of the day.

Vokes confirmed that the Germans had baled out of that stricken Dornier. Vokes climbed back into the fray and was surprised by an Me 110 sneaking in from astern. Always remember to look in your mirror, Bader had said. Tracer fire flashed past the starboard wing of the Spitfire, one bullet hitting the main spar. Vokes climbed still more steeply and after two or three minutes of aerial ballet, he finished on its tail. Vokes 'gave him everything I had' down to fifty yards' range. The enemy's starboard engine was really streaming forth. It seemed out of control as it hit the clouds. What could be worse than being in an uncontrollable aeroplane diving vertically through blinding clouds? Equally awful for German or British alike.

F/O Haines had already claimed an Me 109 at midday. Now at 1440 hours over the Thames Estuary he noted a quintet of Me 109s forming a defensive ring. One rolled off so Haines peeled off too. He took remorseless aim as he closed to fifty yards. The Messerschmitt lasted only a few seconds.

Hained re-climbed to 25,000 feet and patrolled the coast near Beachy Head. He saw bombers being attacked by Hurricanes. He also saw numerous Me 110s, fired at one, and hit the starboard motor. Although he was on the receiving end of fire from other Me 110s, he followed the original one diving badly now. Bits were being hurled from it as it fell. Haines was the persistent type of pilot and followed it to the bitter end. The Messerschmitt managed to scrape through the air till it got to the French coast, where it crashed on the beach. Haines did not hang about there, but scampered for home!

F/Lt Lawson and P/O Cunningham were attacked by Me 109s. Then Sgt Roden was hit and Cunningham broke off to try and help him. After a dog-fight with an Me 109, Cunningham lost the main party but saw three other Me 109s. With a Hurricane for moral support he went for them. Cunningham attacked one through the altitude belt of 16,000–14,000 feet. He saw the enemy reeling ablaze into the clouds and claimed its destruction. He reckoned reasonably that it would have gone down somewhere towards Dover.

Red 1 leading 611 Squadron of Spitfires ran into groups of bombers before gaining enough height. They ignored these targets as they rose westwards to keep the Me 109s off the Wing. There were only eight Spitfires in 611 and they could not outclimb the Me 109s in time.

As twenty-five Dornier 17s seemed to be flying south unmolested, and the squadron had got away from the Wing anyway, Red 1 ordered sections 'Echelon Right' and they dived. Red 1 took the rear Dornier. It seemed all over in moments. Smoke from port engine. The enemy was on the descent leaving a smoky flame wake. Red 1 blacked-out badly in the clouds but survived.

P/O Williams found a Heinkel 111. But to his surprise, he did not hit it with a five-second burst. In fact the enemy had the temerity to be firing back! Williams was then at 18,000 feet to the south of London when he saw a score of Dornier 215s flying west. They turned north and he went for one. Following it through clouds, he was only 100 yards astern as he observed one of its engines stopped. He did a slight right-hand gliding turn in the haze, then 2,000 feet thick. He could not see the enemy aircraft but did spot one airman dropping by parachute. The German landed safely on the edge of a wood near Hawkshurst Golf Club some five or six miles north of Hastings – near where another battle had been waged a mere 874 years earlier.

F/Lt Heather followed Red 1 into the attack. He fired every single round of his ammunition at one Dornier, which bore all the evidence of numerous hits. Me 110s then swooped on Heather, but he swerved clear in time. The claim was one Dornier destroyed. Heather took off from Duxford at 1415 but landed at Croydon at 1540.

P/O Brown followed Red 1's attack on the Dornier which had put an engine out of action. But Brown had flown rather close to the scene of this activity and oil or glycol from the enemy aircraft spattered the intervening airspace and covered up his windscreen. He had to break off as the fluid oozed down the screen. But he was not finished with the fight. He caught a straggler and fired a deflection burst. The enemy spiralled. He noticed that the escape hatch above the pilot's seat was hanging and flapping open, due either to his firing or the crew escaping. He did not see anyone bale out, but this could have been because a swarm of Me 109s darkened a segment of sky and Brown decided it prudent to become scarce in the clouds. The aircraft he shot down was a Heinkel 111K.

P/O Lund took on twenty-five Dornier 215s. But especially one 'drop-out'. Flashes of fire. But three or four other Spitfires were also after this Dornier, so the damage caused could have been by them. Lund climbed to 19,000 feet. He was deterred by the presence of six Me 110s – not good odds. One of these was coming at him anyway, so he fired a brief burst head-on and then turned. The Me 110 flashed by on Lund's port side. He saw a smoke trail from an engine and Lund's own starboard wing was punctured by at least one bullet hole.

The extent of the battle can be gauged by the towns quoted. Having fruitlessly attacked an Me 109 and a crippled Dornier 215, Blue 3 found himself approaching Brooklands Aerodrome at 10,000 feet. Dorniers and Messerschmitts flew above him – all after the aerodrome as a prime target.

Blue 3 climbed with the sun behind him until he was 1,000 feet beneath them and 1,000 yards to the port and front. He opened fire and saw his stuff hitting the leading aircraft. The effect was that the leading vic of four broke away to port with white smoke in parallel lines from engines 1 and 2. Before the incident closed, Blue 3 glimpsed the banking of the old motor race track surrounding the aerodrome. Bader too had happy memories of those distant pre-war days and the countryside near Brooklands.

F/Lt Sadler made two attacks on a Dornier 215 over the London zone from 18,000 feet. A Hurricane also attacked the bomber from line-astern after Sadler had finished. Although Sadler did not see the Dornier go down, it was behaving in a very disabled manner, eventually fading below cloud at a mere 3,000 feet. Not a height from which to recover and return to the Continent. Sadler simply claimed it as sharing destruction. The time was 1445–1450. The clash was nearly over. By tea-time the Battle of Britain was won. Not quite true, perhaps. But it was won within a fortnight.

During that afternoon, the Bader Wing of forty-nine aircraft had claimed destruction of a further twenty-six enemy aircraft, with eight probables and one damaged. These were the individual squadron scores as listed by 12 Group:- 242 Squadron, two Messerschmitt 109s, two Dornier 17s, one Dornier 215, one Heinkel 111; 310 Squadron, one Messerschmitt 109, one Dornier 215, one Heinkel 111s; 302 Squadron, two Dornier 17s, one Dornier 215; 19 Squadron, five Messerschmitt 109s, two Dornier 17s, one Messerschmitt 110, one Heinkel 111; 611 Squadron, two Dornier 17s, two Dornier 215s.

But whereas the Wing had virtually no losses in the earlier sortie, the first signs showed RAF losses as follows:- aircraft destroyed three, aircraft damaged two; pilots killed or missing two, wounded three.

Yet summarising the claimed successes of the Bader Wing during these two sorties on 15 September, the remarkable results achieved showed that for an average of about fifty-two fighters (fifty-six and forty-nine respectively), they had claimed fifty-two enemy aircraft destroyed. An average of one enemy per fighter flying.

The five Wing patrols to date between 7 and 15 September had notched up the following formidable figures against the Luftwaffe, claims made immediately after the actual battle:-

Enemy aircraft destroyed	105
Enemy aircraft probables	40
Enemy aircraft damaged	18
So over one hundred enemy aircraft were claimed for the RAF losses of:-	
Pilots killed or missing	6
Pilots only wounded	5
RAF aircraft lost	14

A contemporary portrait of Douglas Bader drawn by Captain Cuthbert Orde who completed portraits of many fighter pilots. *(Imperial War Museum)*

Sir Archibald Sinclair, Secretary of State for Air, in conversation with Douglas Bader.
(Imperial War Museum)

RAF decorations for gallantry and devotion to duty in the execution of air operations. *Left to right* P/O W.L. McKnight, awarded the DFC, Acting Squadron Leader D.R.S. Bader and Acting Flight Lieutenant G.E. Ball, awarded the DSO and DFC respectively.
(Imperial War Museum)

Chapter 10

The Battle of Britain was not yet over. Like some symphonies whose climacteric is reached towards the end of the fourth movement, this fight may have reached its zenith on 15 September but the graph and the aerial decibels had some way to go before the final bars.

After slight activity involving bombs on Liverpool and Manchester, as well as mid-Wales, at 0745 next morning a Wing was ordered to patrol Debden–North Weald area. They consisted of 310, 302 and 19 Squadrons. They made no contact with the enemy. At 0845 they were relieved by the other two Squadrons 242 and 611. They in turn were told to land about 0915, having failed to make any sort of sightings.

Heavy wind and rain in the night of 16–17 September meant merely scattered bombing in the Midlands and Liverpool. The Wing consisting of the usual five squadrons were once more ordered or asked to patrol North Weald but they saw none of the Luftwaffe. So the Bader Wing had a two-day respite from actual combat, if not from flying. Then came 18 September.

The Wing was despatched twice to patrol the North Weald airspace on 18 September, once at 0900 and then again at 1250. But on neither time did they glimpse the Germans. Then came the third take-off at 1616. The usual five squadrons started to patrol the zone from the centre of London to Thameshaven. Their height was 24,000 feet. At 20,000 feet the cloud reading was 10/10ths, with a lower layer at 6,000 feet, 8/10ths upper. The higher level was spreading from the south. This top layer was only about 100 feet thick so Douglas decided it was no good patrolling above it and chose instead immediately below at 19,000 to 20,000 feet. Suddenly he saw AA bursts to the south-west, coming eerily through the clouds, so he proceeded north-west and found two enemy groups. There were about twenty to thirty in each and seemed to be entirely unescorted. Flying along at 15,000–17,000 feet the Germans were approaching the first bend of the Thames, west of the Estuary, near Gravesend. The enemy were actually south of the river when Bader went for them.

242 Squadron attacked in a dive from east to west, turning north on to the enemy. Conditions seemed rather favourable to the Wing, with their targets set against the white cloud base. Never one to try and hide his few errors, Bader insisted he rather misjudged the lead-in, owing to a desire to get at them before they crossed the river. As a result, he had to resort to diving into the middle to break them up.

He fired in the dive, a quarter attack turning astern at the leading three enemy aircraft – Junkers 88s. His bullets scored on the left-hand one of the leading section and as Bader arrived right in amongst them, this Junkers swung away in a leftish dive, its port engine hit. It zoomed down and out of the fight towards the north bank of the Estuary, somewhere west of Thameshaven. Sgt Brimble as Yellow 3 confirmed the crash.

Bader's initial dive broke up the front of the formation and he found himself shortly afterwards among another hostile group. He gave a couple of quick squirts and then got out of this collection. He nearly collided with two of the enemy before extricating himself – and also nearly collided with at least one other Hurricane. He spun off someone's slipstream and lost about 3,000 feet altitude in next to no time. Regaining control, he set for the south-east. Douglas discovered a Dornier 17 rather detached so he closed to shortest range and fired. The immediate result startled him. He got no return fire but the rear-gunner at once baled out and in so doing wrapped his parachute around the tailplane of the bomber. The Dornier started doing aerobatics in the shape of steep dives followed by zooms on to its back – and then repeating the process. It was losing height as Bader watched.

After the second or third performance, two members of the crew baled out from in front and the Dornier was left doing its aerobatics alone with the rear-gunner. Bader tried to kill him to put him out of his misery, but he was unsuccessful. The last Bader saw of this aircraft was in a vertical dive into cloud at 4,000–6,000 feet, where he decided to leave it. Bader thought it crashed either into the Estuary or south of it, not far from Sheerness.

The faithful P/O Willie McKnight was Bader's Red 2. South-east of Hornchurch about the 17,000 feet line, he scored a direct blow on a Dornier 17. The starboard engine blazed and the surest guide to the degree of damage was, as usual, that the crew baled out. McKnight plus a Spitfire found a Junkers 88 and left it without either engine running. The crew again baled out and McKnight actually saw the pilot land in a field a little north of the Thames. The bomber also crashed north of the river.

P/O Campbell, Red 3, followed 1 and 2 on the German group. Campbell overshot his target but then drew off to the left and sought a fresh one. A Junkers 88 had got left behind on the turn so he positioned himself astern and to the left of this bomber. Campbell could hardly miss it. A short burst. Short range. The Junkers fell out of the sky. Another Junkers 88. Another short-range attack. Both engines gave up.

By this time, the sky was spreadeagled with friend and foe. Some of the enemy were still grouped but well ahead of Campbell. At full throttle, he set out to overtake them. When he got in range he opened fire. He damaged a Junkers 88, but at this precise second he was caught in a nasty bout of crossfire from the enemy. One machine-gun bullet hit his port mainplane. As his position was not advantageous, he broke off. Later he saw a Spitfire cause wisps of smoke to gasp out of a Junkers' starboard engine. Red 3 went in and hit the other engine, so the Junkers fell with flames issuing from both.

F/Lt Ball was Yellow 1. The time was then shortly before 1715 and the general area ten miles south of London. Ball saw Junkers 88s in a box formation and also Dornier 17s. But no fighters. Ball followed Bader into a diving astern attack and only effected a very short burst – though the idea of breaking up the enemy box seemed to have worked. Ball broke away, gained height, and turned into a favourable position as the altimeter rose. He saw a Junkers 88 on its own and went for it from dead astern. He opened up at 300 yards and then at about 100 yards he was suddenly covered in oil. Breaking away he was naturally alarmed but saw the starboard engine of the Junkers afire. At the time Ball thought he must have collected a bullet in his oil tank, but on landing at Gravesend as quickly as he could, he discovered that the oil had come from the Junkers, as his own oil tank was quite undamaged. That is how near some of these combats were fought.

Yellow 2 engaged without much luck. Yellow 3, Sgt Brimble saw Bader's Junkers 88 go down. Brimble found a Dornier 17 out of its rightful place in the box. He despatched it with four bursts of three seconds each and saw it go down to earth a little north of the Thames.

F/O Stan Turner must have muttered some curses as engine trouble forced him to turn back to Duxford before sighting the enemy at all. He was Blue 1. P/O Tamblyn at Blue 2 found himself right in the middle of the enemy formation he had attacked! He shot at a Dornier 17 before turning to get out of this slight predicament. He did not notice any outcome of the firing, but Willie McKnight did. One Dornier shot down by a pilot who did not know he had done so.

P/O Hart at Blue 3 opened at a Junkers 88 and could clearly see the bits cascading off the pilot's enclosure. Hart pulled up to make another attack. As he flew in, he saw smoke from the enclosure. He gave another short burst, causing the enclosure to catch alight. The bomber dived down with all its crew. Hart followed it till the crash came on the north side of the Thames some fifty yards from a railway line.

Leaving that scene, Hart turned south to see another Junkers also southbound at only 5,000 feet. Very low. He saw that the enemy port motor was already dead, though otherwise it was all right. Hart stole up underneath it in a vertical climb, firing about thirty yards in front and hitting the wings and fuselage. The other motor gave out. The Junkers rolled over and crashed down the mile to earth.

Green Leader, Sub Lt Gardner, was already a veteran. He found a few stragglers and made a good quarter attack on one. Port wing and motor aflame, this Dornier 17 dived steeply to its doom somewhere in the Thames Estuary – graveyard of so many bombers.

Turning in pursuit of six or eight bombers heading for France, Gardner caught them up. One was flying 100 yards behind the rest, so he fired at its port engine. The propeller slowed to a halt and smoke signalled the hit. He pulled away and went for the other side. Its second engine also gave the fatal smoke signal. The Dornier glided down from about 10,000 feet over Canvey

Island. Bader confirmed the destruction of Gardner's first Dornier, and though the other one probably went down too it could not be claimed as more than that – a probable.

P/O Bush at Green 2 followed Gardner into the onslaught on the rear of twelve bombers. He got in a shot at one of them. But he did not see any more as he was set on by a Spitfire! The Spit did not actually fire at the Hurricane but would not get off his tail. A slight case of mistaken identity – very easy in the stratified emotions several miles over the Home Counties with cloud and evening both coming up fast. P/O Denis Crowley-Milling, at Green 3, for once could not claim anything.

F/Lt Jeffries was leading the Czechs. 310 Squadron saw fifteen Dorniers over London at about 19,000 feet. He drew level with them but they turned towards him, so he had to break away to avoid passing too close. Jeffries hit both engines of a Dornier 215 which went down. Sgt Kominek behind him saw it crash. The leader then followed the bombers out along the south bank of the Thames, attacking all the way. Fierce AA fire forced him to stop at one stage. As the enemy passed over the Kent coast, the Dornier he had just been firing at seemed to have engine trouble and Jeffries was doubtful if it would have reached France.

P/O Zimprich went after a Dornier 215. He hit and heavy smoke obscured much of the enemy. Zimprich was already well out over the sea, near North Foreland. The Dornier glided seawards and Zimprich fervently wanted to finish it off. But his ammunition was expended so he never actually saw it in contact with the sea. Claim: one probable.

P/O Janouch was leading Red Section. They were south of London at the 20,000 feet mark. An over-sharp turn brought them too close to the enemy on the first run-in. Next time, Janouch went in with two other Hurricanes. Two attacks on a Dornier and he saw the whole crew bale out. No doubt about that one. A Dornier could not be expected to find its own way back to base. P/O Fejfar at Red 2 was sharing the early attacks with Janouch. As another bomber started doing aerobatics, the reason became clear. The crew had left it. There was a strange visual sense about an aeroplane in its death throes with no human beings aboard. Uncanny.

P/Sgt Jirovdek at Red 3 hit both engines of a Dornier 215, which was in direst distress. Two other Hurricanes hit it as well, and P/Sgt Puda saw it crash and 'burn down' on the ground until there seemed nothing left of it at all. Jirovdek and Puda claimed a share of the bomber. Puda saw at least one of its crew bale out. From an angled turn the Dornier had dived and crashed not far from Stanford-le-Hope.

P/O Fechtner fired a burst at a Dornier 215 from 800 yards! No luck! He later hit it again and again. Both engines ended on fire. But before the final moments, the enemy gunner fired at his Hurricane and made a hole in a blade of his airscrew. Fechtner later found he had four bullet holes in his aircraft, the one in the propeller plus three in the elevator. But he was unhurt, that was the main thing. Pilots were precious.

P/O Bergman aimed for the whole lot of the Dornier 215s, then took one especially. The usual story. The usual end. One engine. Both engines. One bomber destroyed. No more to say, nor to do. P/Sgt Prchal accounted for another Dornier. The crew baled out; the aircraft spun down; and it drilled into the ground.

There was still time for some courtesy left, even amid this battle. An enemy pilot baled out. A Czech pilot reported: 'It is a matter of regret that his parachute did not open . . .'

The Poles had a field day that afternoon. Ordered to scramble at 1650, the instruction came over as 'Patrol Hornchurch Angels Twenty.' 302 was the third of the Hurricane squadrons as usual, with the Spitfires on flank above. Thirty-plus bombers were in vics of five. Red 1, S/Ldr Satchell made attacks and closed to eighty yards. His target bomber was then enveloped by a mixture of smoke and flame and was never seen again. Before breaking away, Red 1 had his Perspex covered with oil from the burning aircraft, showing just how near he was. This was happening more and more with these close combats – one extra hazard. Red 1 saw two enemy crash altogether, one in the sea off Sheerness, the other on the peninsula between the Medway and the Thames.

Red 2, Wg Cdr Mumler, chose a different bomber on the port side. He fired but then had to break away to make room for another aircraft attacking. As he did so, he saw flames from the turret of the enemy rear-gunner. Red 3, F/O Kowalski, went for one Dornier, then another. At his last burst, he saw a full-size parachute open from the rear-gunner's turret. It became entangled in the mainplane. Bits of the aircraft flew off this mainplane, causing Red 3 to break off the combat temporarily. He never saw what happened to the unfortunate rear-gunner. That seemed to be happening increasingly.

Yellow Section went in behind Red. F/Lt Farmer at Yellow 1 chased a Dornier 215 and then a Junkers 88. Pieces peeled off the Junkers before it vanished into a convenient cloud, by which time Farmer had used all his ammo. Yellow 2, F/Lt Laguna, had trouble in that he could not focus his sights properly and rather than risk hitting another Hurricane, he could do little but fly along for the ride. Sgt Wedzik, at Yellow 3, chased a Junkers 88 out to sea, forcing it down to a dangerous altitude of only 1,000 feet. He and another Hurricane attacked it alternately, with pieces flaking off it regularly.

P/O Pilch was leading Green Section, which caused a good break-up of an enemy group. Green 1 went right for the middle – Bader-like – and saw metal careering about the sky. Next he found a Junkers 88 whose rear-gunner fired at him the whole time he was making five attacks on it. By the fourth attack, the port engine was obviously out of action. At the fifth, the enemy bomber fired a red light, clearly a signal. One man at least jumped out of the fated Junkers.

Sgt Peterek was Green 2. He also had a Junkers 88 as target from 100 yards. With one engine afire, the Junkers was attacked again. The crew of three called it a day and jumped – their parachutes all opening at once. But as they did so, too, a few fragments of the Junkers flew off and hit Green 2's propeller, causing the Hurricane to flutter violently. Something hit his radiator – and his reserve petrol tank broke, spattering him with petrol. Green 2 wisely switched off his engine at once and glided southwards. He saw the enemy crash and then made a forced-landing himself, sustaining no further damage. Green 3 was P/O Karwowski. He destroyed a bomber very violently. One parachute emerged from it.

Blue Section now. F/Lt Riley as Blue 1 put paid to two Junkers 88s. They both dived away, doomed. Blue 2, F/Lt Jastrzebski, had shots at several enemy. Then he noticed that seven bombers were hurrying in formation across the Channel for France to lick their heavy wounds. They had already lost the other five or so of their formation. Or more.

P/O Wapniarek at Blue 3 was attacking for a second time. He saw that the rear-gunner jumped out of the Junkers 88, near Southend-on-Sea. He wondered momentarily what would happen to the man. He caught another Junkers about to be dimmed by cloud. The bomber fired at him from two of three guns, using tracer bullets. Blue 3 was not deterred and used all the rest of his ammunition on this bomber. He saw it break up utterly on striking the sea. Blue 3 flew for eight minutes over the water before reaching the coast again. By then he was virtually out of fuel so had to make a rapid landing at Rochford, Essex.

As there was a cloud-layer at 20,000 feet, the Spitfire squadrons 19 and 611 started their patrol above it. No enemy were encountered but the AA fire burst through the cloud with exciting if alarming effect. So 19 Squadron followed the Hurricanes below the cloud, where they met the enemy. 611 Squadron remained on patrol overhead. By the time that 19 Squadron commenced to attack, there seemed to be only one of the original two enemy groups left. This consisted of a score of bombers and some scattered Me 110s. The bombers were mainly Junkers 88s and Heinkel 111s.

F/Lt Clouston fired almost all his ammunition at a single Junkers 88 with devastating effect. The crew baled out even more urgently than usual and the bomber crashed behind some houses to the west of Deal in Kent. The indefatigable F/Sgt Steere closed with a Heinkel 111, hit it, and watched while it struck the waters at the mouth of the Thames. Steere then finished off a Junkers 88 already on the dive from a Green 1 attack. F/Sgt Unwin set an Me 110 on fire; the pilot got out; and the aeroplane came down near Eastchurch.

F/O Haines met two Me 109s and observed fire coming laterally from one of them. It seemed to be from a fixed gun below and behind the pilot's seat. Undeterred from this unusual occurrence, he closed to fifty yards and after his attack the Me 109 looked to be diving vertically.

P/O Dolezal was next to Haines. He took on a Heinkel. Jet black smoke. Spinning aircraft. The Czech saw the Heinkel spin right down into the sea. And the Spitfire next to Dolezal picked another Heinkel. By the end of his third attack, both enemy engines were stopped and the crew saw no reason to stay longer. They escaped. The Heinkel hit the ground near Gillingham, Kent.

F/Lt Lawson led the last section on nine Junkers 88s which turned desperately south-east. He fired at the rear one and looked set for a success when he got a bad glycol leak and had to land at Eastchurch. Lawson was Red 1. Red 2 attacked the same Junkers. Red 3 joined in until it was finally seen to crash at Sandwich, down on the Kent coast. They all shared the credit for this one, willingly, with P/O Cunningham and Sgt Lloyd.

These were the destroyed claims of the individual squadrons: 242 Squadron, five Dornier 17s and five Junkers 88s; 310 Squadron, five Dornier 215s; 302 Squadron, five Junkers 88s, one Dornier 215, one Dornier 17; 19 Squadron, three Junkers 88s, three Heinkel 111s, one Messerschmitt 110. Twenty-nine enemy aircraft claimed with scarcely a scratch. Bader had done it again!

After the devastating day success of the Wing, that night the enemy restricted their raids to several slight jabs around the Mersey area until 0230. A couple of bombs burst on Norwich, while some of the RAF aerodromes in East Anglia and Lincolnshire received some attention. Night and day the air war went on for a week or more without the Wing being in actual action. Several times they went up, but no sightings.

Then the date of 27 September was destined to be famous as the final large-scale Bader Wing battle in 12 Group. The Wing went up three times on that day. At 0900 they did not meet the enemy. But at 1142 they were ordered off from Duxford to patrol the London area. On this occasion the Wing comprised four squadrons: 242 and 310 of Hurricanes and 19 and 616 of Spitfires.

Bader heard over R/T:

'Bandits south-east of Estuary . . .'

When he could not find them, the Duxford Controller told him to return. Douglas said:

'I'll just have one more swing round.'

Turning the Wing southwards and flying at 23,000 feet, he eventually sighted enemy aircraft apparently circling around the Dover/Canterbury/Dungeness triangle at 18,000–20,000 feet. They were Me 109s just milling about – a strange sight indeed. Visibility was good with a cloud layer higher at 25,000 feet. The sun lay behind the Wing, so Douglas decided to dive into the attack. No formation or organised onslaught was either possible or desirable, so having manoeuvred himself into his up-sun position, he ordered the Wing to break up and attack as they liked.

Bader chose a 109 which was passing underneath him. He turned behind and above the enemy and got in a two-second strike with the instant result that the Messerschmitt dissolved into thick white smoke, turned over slowly, and took a vertical dive. Others of 242 confirmed this success.

A second 109 flew in front and below him, so Douglas turned in behind. After a typical Bader burst, the 109 took evasive action by rolling on to its back and diving. Bader did the same but pulled out short and cut it off on the climb. The Hurricane had a long chase, finally getting in a long distance squirt from 400 yards. A puff of white smoke slowed the 109 perceptibly. More bursts from the keen eye of Red 1. One missed completely but others hit. The last squirt produced black smoke from the port side of the enemy fuselage – and Bader's Hurricane had its windscreen covered with oil from the 109. The enemy propeller stopped dead. The last seen of the 109 was as it glided down under control but with engine dead at a shallow angle into the Channel.

As Douglas himself was on the edge of the coast and out of ammunition after all those squirts (his favourite word), he decided that discretion was required. He dived to ground level into the haze, went back to Gravesend and landed. This last combat finished somewhere off the coast between Dover and Ramsgate. Symbolic that Douglas should be protecting his country actually over the white cliffs of Dover. Bader rearmed, refuelled, and had lunch with 66 Squadron!

But back in the air much was still happening – or had already happened.

His Red 2 was P/O Stansfield who chased an Me 109 across Dover and then lost sight of it. A Junkers 88 crossed his sights so Red 2 fired at him from 200 yards. The enemy plodded on, smoking and turning now, flying parallel to the Kent coast eastwards. At about fifty feet from the bomber, Red 2 ran out of ammo. He did not see the Junkers crash, due to bad weather, but he felt convinced that it could not get home.

Red 3 was Sgt Lonsdale, who could make no definite claims.

By Bader's standards this was turning out to be rather an unpredictable patrol, although the results were coming in, nevertheless. This was because, in a complete 'shambles' with everyone manoeuvring in a confined air space and the enemy on the run, the chances of scoring were less than when a bomber group were being attacked further inland.

F/Lt Ball got Bader's original 'Break up and attack' message along with the rest of them. He was Yellow 1. It was noon, give or take a minute.

Ball seemed to have chosen an experienced adversary, but eventually he got on the 109's tail and opened fire from 200 yards. But he had difficulty in closing due to their relative speeds being virtually the same. He hit the cockpit of the Me 109. But Ball realised that he had been hit in the tank. He was in trouble. He tried to make an aerodrome but the engine of his Hurricane started to catch fire. A few quick mental calculations and he knew he had to get down somehow – in seconds. He force-landed with the wheels still up in a field somewhere between Deal and Manston – the latter had been his goal. Happy landing.

Neither Denis Crowley-Milling nor Sgt Brimble had anything to report.

F/O Stan Turner was Blue Leader. Behind him at Blue 2 came P/O Bush. He found he was not in the right position to fire during that initial dive on the Me 109s. Climbing to gain precious height again, he saw half a dozen of them about 3,000 feet above him. Not a nice sight. While Bush was still climbing to try for the rear one, their leader did a quick turn and dived on Bush.

The Hurricane pilot put his fighter into a spin and dived, only to find an Me 109 still after him. So he managed to conjure a quick turn and reverse their relative situations. He fired at the 109 and saw it plunge into the sea somewhere between Dover and Gravesend. Blue 3 was P/O Hart. It was a rare occasion when one of Bader's best men did not happen to get near enough to connect.

Green Section was the last one of 242 Squadron. P/O Tamblyn at Green 1 put his dog-fight at 'Dover to mid-Channel'. As Tamblyn picked one, it throttled back and made for the sea. He found it hard to stay with the Messerschmitt. The enemy evasive tactics consisted of skidding turns, porpoising, and violent climbing turns to 500 feet. The fight had descended all the way down from 12,000 feet to 100 feet! This called for some desperate precision flying. Tamblyn could see his shots hitting the Me 109 and eventually petrol or glycol was pouring out of the fighter. Tamblyn overshot on his last burst, so could not finally claim to have destroyed the enemy. He had 40 rounds left in one gun but a stoppage prevented him firing them. Visibility was down to a mile or even less and so, reluctantly, he turned for home.

F/O M. G. Homer at Green 2 was missing . . .

P/O Latta at Green 3 was 21,000 feet up when he caught an Me 109 at 18,000 feet. As Latta got within range, however, the German levelled off and received a burst from astern. A direct hit on the petrol tank. The Me 109 crashed five to ten miles inland from Dover. That was the first of two Me 109s which Latta destroyed on this sortie.

He spotted several making for the French coast in some disarray. Still having a height advantage, Latta was able to overtake one of them and close to fifty yards. Latta's aim appeared deadly, for once again the petrol tank sparked a general fire. The enemy maintained a fairly steep dive from 10,000 feet straight into the sea, five miles or more off Dover. Although he did not know it then, Latta's Hurricane had sustained some damage both to its tail and one wing. This must have been when he was firing at the first Me 109. Like Bader, he landed at Gravesend. The time, 1315.

310 Squadron of Hurricanes destroyed one Me 109. 616 Squadron of Spitfires did likewise.

19 Squadron had greater opportunities and took them. F/Lt Lawson at Red 1 led an attack on a large group of Me 109s. Lawson saw his tracer striking home on one of them. The enemy struggled to head for France but smoke started to be seen as it fell to an altitude of 3,000 feet. It dived into the sea about ten miles short of Cap Gris Nez. Lawson was close behind it all the way and only when he was satisfied it had crashed did he turn through 180 degrees and hurry home again.

Sgt Blake at Red 2 also fired at an Me 109 as it turned across his bows. Eventually the Messerschmitt hit the sea. Blake saw some other Me 109s speeding for home almost at sea level. He went on to attack one of these actually parallel to the surface of the sea – and in the confusion the enemy pilot flew into it. Red 3 was P/O Bradil. He claimed damaging an Me 109 but not destroying it.

A pair of Me 109s were going for Yellow Section from above. F/Sgt Unwin at Yellow I gave an Me 109 burst after burst. It writhed about trying to escape for ten minutes or more. At length, it stalled, seemed to hang in the air, and then spun into the sea. A worthy opponent.

At Yellow 2, Sgt Jennings flew in fearlessly at the leader of quintet of Me 109s. He hit one, causing smoke to envelop the whole aircraft. Yellow 2 could not follow it down further, as he was set on by the other four Messerschmitts.

Sgt Cox had a crash and was wounded. He was rushed to hospital . . .

Green 1 led an assault on eight Me 109s. F/Sgt Steere fired from 300 yards, but could not claim any successes on this day. Green 2, F/O Parrot, was about to follow Green 1 into the attack on the same aircraft when it burst into flames, so perhaps Steere should have had credit for it. Green 2 got another Me 109 which went down near the golf course at Sandwich.

Having lost the rest of his squadron, Parrot joined with 616 Squadron for a head-on charge at other Me 109s. Green 3, Sgt Plzak, fired at an Me 109 and followed it from 10,000 feet. From Folkestone, he saw it smoke, flame and dive. The end of yet another Messerschmitt 109.

S/Ldr Lane flew above the main formation and witnessed the small upper group of Me 109s preparing to attack. He went for two of them and pulled back his stick for a second attack. His Spitfire failed to respond and he was unable to pull out of the dive until he came down as low as 3,000 feet.

Green 4, P/O Burgoyne was missing . . .

So counting the cost on both sides, the Bader Wing claimed thirteen destroyed, five probables, three damaged. The individual squadron scores were as follows:- 242 Squadron, four Messerschmitt 109s destroyed; 19 Squadron, seven Messerschmitt 109s destroyed; 310 Squadron, one Messerschmitt 109 destroyed, 616 Squadron, one Messerschmitt 109 destroyed.

Our losses were five aircraft damaged or missing. The pilots lost or missing were three:- Homer, Smith and Burgoyne. Luckily these losses were subsequently reduced.

Duxford was delighted at the results achieved, but there was a sour postscript to these actions of 27 September.

They got a message from Air Vice-Marshal Park that they had been 'poaching' on 11 Group's preserves. Good for him, they thought – it was his way of congratulting them. But not long afterwards, Douglas discovered that this remark had been deadly serious and actually couched in the form of a complaint. Even so, Douglas was prepared to make excuses for Park. Bader was too big to worry about such pettiness.

A new artificial leg for Douglas Bader was dropped by parachute over an aerodrome in Northern France on 19 August 1941. This photograph shows the leg being dropped.
(Imperial War Museum)

A group of British prisoners in Colditz Castle, including Douglas Bader, front row centre.
(Imperial War Museum)

Group Captain D.R.S. Bader, DSO, DFC casting a Victory Bell at the Kent Alloys Ltd. Foundry, Strood, Kent, 7 September 1945. *(Imperial War Museum)*

Chapter 11

By October 1940, the night raids increased, the day raids diminished. Over the following month or so, the Bader Wing was ordered up about another dozen times. Yet the momentous days were already ending. Despite Douglas's strong views on the subject of aerial warfare, even then he thought it only fair to remember that Dowding may have been considerably preoccupied in his daily contacts with the Air Staff, the War Cabinet, and indeed possibly even the Prime Minister, Winston Churchill. Under such conditions of mental stress, it was reasonable and indeed excusable that he may have been unaware of the changing circumstances of the Battle of Britain. In this case, he failed in not appreciating the need for overall control from Fighter Command. He should have appointed a deputy, an Air Marshal, to co-ordinate and direct the Battle.

What has been built into the Big Wing controversy stemmed solely from mutterings in the Mess by the pilots of the Duxford Wing against the 11 Group habit of calling them off the ground too late, so that they arrived in the battle area at a disadvantage. This was coupled with the fact that 11 Group headquarters used to complain when they were late – which was duly passed to them by 12 Group headquarters. The result was a vicious circle, with 11 Group saying that 12 Group took so long to get off the ground. Towards the latter part of the Battle of Britain, matters did improve.

It should be remembered that the Duxford Wing went into action first as such on 7 September and that the big battles ceased after 21 September, so the period under discussion is only fourteen days. The difference of opinion had not been resolved by the end of the Battle of Britain. Park was opposed to the Big Wing ideas and to the general line adopted by Leigh-Mallory. Douglas found Leigh-Mallory had a quick, questing mind and a character of charm and understanding. He was tough, enthusiastic, and completely honest with his juniors. He cared about people. They mattered to him. Later Leigh-Mallory moved from Group Commander of 12 to 11 Group and subsequently Commander-in-Chief Fighter Command. Then as an Air Chief Marshal, he served as C-in-C Allied Air Forces Europe until he was killed with his wife in an air crash in 1944.

Douglas found him a great leader. Leigh-Mallory's career after the Battle of Britain certainly confirmed that his ideas on fighter tactics were received with considerable sympathy and agreement by the Air Council. A famous meeting held on 17 October 1940 proved that the weight of opinion was with both Leigh-Mallory and Bader in the Air Council. Leigh-Mallory caused a minor stir by bringing Douglas with him to such a high-level discussion in distinguished company. But the meeting vindicated them and their successful strategy of the Big Wing.

Although by then the Battle of Britain was assuredly won, neither the rest of the conflict nor the war in the air generally were over – and 12 Group suffered several tragic losses at this late phase of 1940. While Douglas was in London on that very day of 17 October, Red Section of 242 Squadron got orders to orbit base at 0840 hours. And though instructions were given to pancake, these were cancelled and at 0917 Red Section received a vector. Flying at a height of about 7,000 feet about 0915, they saw a Dornier 17 cruising on a course some 3,000 feet below. Visibility at 7,000 feet was good but at 3,000–4,000 feet there was 8/10ths cloud. When first sighted the Dornier was making for a cloud.

They were thirty miles north-east of Yarmouth as Red 3, P/O Rogers, attacked from above and to starboard of Red 2. Red 3 got in a good burst Then Red 2, P/O Brown, positioned himself dead astern of the enemy bomber and also got in a burst before experiencing fire from the enemy rear-gunner which connected with his throttle control. Red 2 was followed in line-astern by Red 1, P/O Campbell. Red 2 saw nothing further of Red 1 before breaking away. When he returned to attack, the enemy had vanished into the cloud and Red 2 made back to base.

Red 3 followed the Dornier through a succession of clouds, catching occasional glimpses of all or part of it. But he failed to close in for a further effective burst and finally lost it altogether. When last seen by Red 3, the Dornier was still proceeding at a fairly slow speed on an easterly course in no apparent difficulties. Red 2 landed at 0950. Red 3 landed at 1020. Red 1 failed to land. P/O Campbell was posted as missing . . .

On the next day, the Polish Squadron 302 suffered still more severely. Operating with 229 Squadron, they were told to scramble at 1500 in poor weather and patrol Maidstone line at Angels One Five. Twelve fighters were airborne by 1506. They joined up with 229 Squadron over the base, 302 leading. After one or two varied manoeuvres and various vectors, F/Lt Jathomson at Red 1 espied an enemy. He turned towards it and attacked three times. The first was from behind slightly above. The second and third followed vertically from above. During the first attack he met heavy enemy fire from machine-guns, two of them in the rear-gunner's turret. The other two guns were located in 'blisters'. Many Hurricanes were also attacking enemy aircraft at the same time so he broke off to avoid collision. His bandit scampered into the clouds pursued by several Hurricanes. Red 2 attacked unsuccessfully. Red 3 was unable to fire at any enemy as he could not manoeuvre into position.

Yellow 1 was likewise unsuccessful. Yellow 2, Sgt Nowakiewicz, closed on the enemy to a mere thirty yards. He broke away on a climbing turn after firing a burst. As he did so, he saw two men jump from the enemy aircraft and their parachutes open safely. The aeroplane dived rather gently towards earth. Yellow 3 could not position himself for an assault but confirmed the sight of the two parachutists.

No pilots in Blue or Green Sections who returned were able to attack.

After the initial attack, the squadron reformed and Yellow 2 said that he was the last aircraft in the squadron. He counted ten others besides himself. The leader asked for his position and was told he was thirty miles from base at 1626 hours.

The leader thinks he lost the last three sections when descending to Angels Five to investigate bandit reported at that altitude at 1630. At 1646 he asked for permission to land, as he had been up for one hour forty minutes. But he was told to orbit for two minutes as another bandit was nearby. Red Section eventually landed at Northolt at 1708 hours.

The fate of the other sections was as follows:-

Blue 1 landed at Cobham with one gallon of petrol left in his tank.

Blue 2, P/O Wapniarek, crashed at Cobham. An eye-witness said he saw four aircraft flying overhead very low in and out of cloud. One of these detached itself and seemed to shut off its engine. A moment later it came out of the cloud and crashed, catching fire immediately.

Blue 3, P/O Zukowski, crashed and was killed near Detling.

Green 1, F/O Carter, and Green 2, F/O Borowski, both crashed at Kempton Park Race Course, within 200 yards of each other.

Green 2 and Yellow 3 both landed safely.

So four pilots were killed: Carter, Wapniarek, Borowski and Zukowski.

Equally tragic to Douglas Bader were the later losses of pilots from his original Canadian 242 Squadron. On 5 November, P/O N. Hart, to be followed by two others, P/O J. B. Latta and P/O Willie McKnight. Douglas remembered these men always. They were the immortals of The Few. And a lot of other men remembered Douglas from those days – and to this day. Opinion is still mixed over the question of the Big Wing tactics and it may be interesting to quote three or four Battle of Britain pilots on this question, and also on their memories of Douglas as he was in 1940.

Johnnie Johnson:

> 'Douglas was a well-established figure and a squadron leader when I came in as a pilot officer. Everybody had heard about this almost legendary chap, even in those days. I first met him in August 1940. My own squadron 616 had been pulled out of the front line. Half the squadron had been lost or wounded. We went back to Coltishall to re-form. Douglas was there with his Canadian squadron. Here was this legendary chap with his tough Canadians. We had an invasion scare one Saturday evening. Everyone was getting in a terrible panic with rumours of impending German landings. Douglas just walked into the mess and said, "We'll give them the squirts – jolly good show" and calmed things down at once.

Douglas was all for the Big Wings to counter the German formation. I think there was room for both tactics – the Big Wings and the small squadrons. The size of the fighting unit in 11 Group was conditioned by the time to intercept before the bombing. It might well have been fatal had Park always tried to get his squadrons into "Balbos", for not only would they have taken longer to get to their height, but sixty or seventy packed climbing fighters could have been seen for miles and would have been sitting ducks for higher 109s. Also nothing would have pleased Goering more than for his 109s to pounce on large numbers of RAF fighters. Indeed Galland and Molders often complained about the elusiveness of Fighter Command and Park's brilliance was that by refusing to concentrate his force he preserved it throughout the Battle. This does not mean, as Bader pointed out at the time, that two or three Balbos from 10 and 12 Groups, gaining their height beyond the range of the 109s, would not have played a terrific part in the fighting. Park only had time to fight a defensive battle. The Balbos could have fought offensively. This was a matter for Fighter Command.'

Peter Townsend:

'Bader was a very great person, but of course he was involved in a highly controversial thing and in the judgement of many – and occasionally in my own judgement – he did infringe the rules. But I've let that be known in a very friendly way. He even visualised control of squadrons should have been handled from Fighter Command, even by Dowding himself. When I put this to Park, he said, "Well, I must say, that beats the band."

Sholto Douglas thought it "ideal" if Park's squadrons could attack the incoming bombers, with Leigh-Mallory's Wings harrying them as they retreated. Douglas Bader's idea was exactly the opposite: operating only from 12 Group or the flanks of 11 Group, Wings should take-off and gain height as the enemy was building up over France, and then advance in mass to attack them as they crossed the coast. Meanwhile, 11 Group squadrons climbing from forward airfields beneath the fray would tear into the retreating enemy. Bader never thought Wings could operate from 11 Group's forward airfields.'

Peter Brothers:

'There was a lot to be said for this Big Wing conception if they could be marshalled in time. But it obviously wouldn't work in 11 Group. But it could work in 12 Group. I flew in both Groups. Of course later on in the Battle, one was organised in Big

Wings. You had that little bit more time to play. There was something to be said on each side. Park was quite right that it wouldn't work in 11 Group – they were too far forward. There was certainly a case when you were further back for a large formation.'

Alan Deere:

'I first met Douglas during Dunkirk operations, when I was operating at Hornchurch and he came down. When I first met him, I didn't know about his legs. I walked into the mess. I can remember very distinctly. He was standing near the hatch where we got our drinks. He struck me at once in the way he attacked you, came at you. I met him and at that point I hadn't even heard of him before. He kept pumping me about tactics and shouting and all this sort of thing. Immediately he stood out as someone who was keen to get on with the job and wanted to find out all about it. That was in May 1940. I was shot down during those Dunkirk operations and don't recollect talking to him again at that time.

I heard about him during the Battle of Britain, because of these Wing tactics which are now so much in controversy. All I will say is that tactics will always remain a matter of opinion. But it is my opinion that the mass Wing formations of 12 Group could not have been successful in 11 Group. There just wasn't time to form up and get airborne. For example, when we were operating from Manston – the most forward airfield in 11 Group – we actually had to fly inland to get our height before we could go back to meet the raids.'

But of course Douglas never did advocate Big Wings from Kent or Surrey. But he did advocate an offensive attitude to the defence of Britain. No-one can prove him finally right or wrong, but he had certainly scored substantial successess – for the minimum losses. Then in the following spring and summer, he really went over to the offensive, and as Johnnie Johnson says: 'His greatest qualities came to the fore . . .'

Chapter 12

In March 1941 Douglas Bader was posted to Tangmere, Sussex, as Wing Leader of what soon became known as the Tangmere Wing. He was the RAF's very first Wing Leader and the three squadrons he commanded were 616, 610 and 145. Many of his lasting friendships dated from that spring and summer. The flavour of these days can be conveyed by the impressions of some of those friends – and then the sorties themselves. But first, the friends.

Johnnie Johnson:

> 'We went on to a Wing of three squadrons which was about right. The great thing was that previously we had been fighting a defensive battle. Then we began to reach out and take on the Luftwaffe over the Pas de Calais. There Douglas's greatest qualities came to the fore: leadership, the ability to inspire, and his great desire to get out and at them. It was quite extraordinary. Something I had never known before or have never known since. The qualities of moral courage, the ability to command, and the fact that he spoke the same language as these chaps. I was still a pilot officer. Douglas was a wing commander. I think I had reached the elevated rank of flying officer by August. We were all rather like his pupils. Like master and apprentice. He always went to great lengths to have a post-mortem afterwards and explain things to us. Everyone loved him.
>
> Tactically, because the enemy abreast formation was better than the astern pattern, Fighter Command lagged behind the German Fighter Arm. It was not until this spring that Douglas Bader copied the Schwarme, which he called the "Finger Four" because the relative positions of the fighters are similar to a plan view of one's outstretched fingertips. Bader's pilots were immediately impressed with their finger fours, for, unlike the line-astern pattern, all pilots were always covered, and all stood an equal chance of survival. Soon all fighter squadrons followed Bader's lead. It had taken a long time to relearn the doctrine of Oswald Boelcke.'

Laddie Lucas takes up this theme, as an observer rather than a participant in 1941.

> 'As I see it, every pilot in the RAF owed something to what went on in World War 1. These tactics were used again, by ourselves and by the Germans. But the actual line-abreast flying, the basic concept of a pair of aircraft, or four aeroplanes in the form of a finger four formation – these were fundamental tactics whether used in World War 1, by the Spaniards, or the Germans, or whoever else. The fact of it was that Douglas modernised it, brought it up-to-date, made it fresh and practical for flying in the 1940s. And don't forget, this was in direct conflict with a lot of the flying thinking that was being done in 11 Group, which was all line-astern.
>
> It was quite all right to climb a squadron or a Wing up in line-astern to battle height, but then so often they stayed together like that and never came into line-abreast. Terrible for the junior pilots at ass-end Charlie. Douglas started with the basic two aeroplanes then the finger four, then the fours in touch with one squadron, two squadrons, three. This was the basis, with two pilots looking inwards, so that the whole sky was covered right through 180 degrees. This was really fundamental to all his flying, both defensively and offensively, in the sweeps over the north of France from Tangmere. Douglas never claimed to have pioneered the technique.'

Some people have criticised these tactics as being old hat, but nothing could be further from the truth. Hugh Dundas takes it one stage further:

> 'Douglas was very much a pioneer in getting away from that line-astern formation. In fact he and I conducted an experiment together, following a long conversation in the mess. We tried a bit of finger four and adopted it. I certainly never flew anything else for the rest of the war. We were flying over France all the time now, instead of over England. We were doing sweep after sweep after sweep, all day, every day. We always flew in fours. I flew as the other leader, next to him. We did over sixty sweeps together that summer. He liked to have the same chaps with him. He was a hell of a help to me. I had a very nasty bit of being shot down in 1940. I was shot down and couldn't get out of the aeroplane. The hood stuck. The aeroplane stopped flying. I got out very low indeed at about three or four hundred feet. I was only on the end of a parachute for three or four seconds. That shook me considerably. I think if I hadn't come up against someone like Douglas, I might have found it very difficult to get going again. He was a great leader. He liked his wide circle of friends. We used to go to his house and we spent most of that spring and summer together, one way and another.'

Douglas and Thelma now lived near Bognor, in a modern house with a big window. Bay House was five or six miles from Tangmere and its doors remained always open to anyone at the station. Thelma's sister Jill lived with them at that time. Once or twice a week, Johnnie Johnson would drive over to Bay House, to find the hard core of the Tangmere Wing grouped about its leader. Stan Turner was invariably there. He had been with Douglas in 242, of course. Douglas sipped his lemonade, analysed their recent flights, and discoursed on the importance of straight shooting. Meanwhile the sorties were stepped up. It became a strange contrast between high summer, high clouds, the scent of clover, and even an odd game of golf at Goodwood – and then the sudden sweeps over France. The electric trains purred on: Chichester, Barnham, Ford, and so to Brighton. Thelma and Jill looked after Bay House and were always cheerful. And the Tangmere Wing flew on. As 'Cocky' Dundas said, sweep after sweep after sweep. The years of 1940 and 1941 called for greatness. Douglas supplied it.

If flying seems to dominate Douglas's life in this era, it is because it did just that. Flying *was* his life. And all that went with it. Nothing can completely recapture the flavour or strain of sixty, seventy Spitfire sorties in two or three months. So here are just ten typical combat reports from 21 June to 23 July told in Douglas's own words:-

'*21 June 1941*

I was leading Tangmere Wing which was milling around in and off the coast around Desvres. Saw the bombers and escort go out near Boulogne, followed by AA bursts. We stayed around above and behind the bombers and escort when I notice two Messerschmitt 109s in line-astern about to turn in behind my section of four. I told them to break left and twisted round quickly (metal ailerons) and fired a very close deflection burst at the first Messerschmitt 109E at about fifty yards' range, about half to one second. My bullets appeared to hit him as his glass hood dispersed in pieces and the aeroplane pulled up vertically, stalled and spun right-handed. I foolishly followed him down with my eyes and nearly collided with a cannon Spitfire of another squadron in the Wing and then reformed by section. I claim this as destroyed (a) because I know it was and (b) because F/O Marples 616 Squadron saw a Messerschmitt 109 spinning down at the time and place and S/Ldr Turner of 145 Squadron saw a pilot bale out of a Messerschmitt 109 at the time and place, as also did one of his pilots, (c) F/O Machatek of 145 Squadron saw a Messerschmitt 109 dive into the sea right alongside another Messerschmitt 109 which had been shot down by one of 145 Squadron, same time and place, and (d) no-one else claims the second 109 which I am sure was mine.

25 June 1941 (am)

I was the Tangmere Wing Leader flying with 616 Squadron and taking off from Westhampnett at 1158. Joined up with 145 and 610 Squadrons and proceeded up over Dungeness at 20,500 feet. Then flew on to a point opposite Gravelines and turned straight towards the coast, flying south. Noticed a number of Messerschmitt 109s from time to time above and what looked like a combat in the Gris-Nez/Boulogne area at 25,000 feet. When 145 Squadron informed me that they had found bombers and were escorting bombers back over Gravelines, I gave the order for the Wing to withdraw. As we crossed coast at Gravelines at about 18,000 feet my section ran into four to six Messerschmitt 109Fs milling around over Gravelines/Dunkirk area about 500 feet below. We flew into them and I gave one a short deflection shot and my No 2 (Sgt West) followed in with another burst of two seconds. Sgt West broke to port and lost sight of enemy aircraft but I broke to starboard and saw it half roll and dive down and followed it down – giving it half second burst – seeing pilot baling out about five miles off Gravelines in sea. Then vectored 280 degrees from this point, crossed over South Foreland and returned to Westhampnett at 1335. This Messerschmitt 109 was not visibly damaged although bullets were seen to strike: i.e. no smoke etc.

25 June 1941 (pm)

As Tangmere Wing Leader and flying with 616 Squadron, we took off from Westhampnett at 1549 and joined up with 610 and 145 Squadrons. Climbed up to 21,000 feet and crossed French coast at Hardelot (?). Joined up with bombers underneath and then flew east with them for a few minutes when numerous enemy aircraft were seen behind, below and to the north of us. Eventually was compelled to engage them and disregard the bombers, since they were all round us and we were flying down-sun. With the leading section I engaged eight to nine Messerschmitt 109Fs which were climbing east to west, i.e. towards Boulogne. We were then at 20,000 feet and the enemy aircraft between 16,000 and 17,000 feet. We dived on to them and F/O Dundas and his No 2 attacked two who turned north and climbed. I attacked four Messerschmitt 109Fs, with my No 2, who were climbing in a slightly left-hand turn. I gave a short burst at one at close range from inside the turn and saw white, black and orange-coloured smoke envelop the aircraft, which went down in an increasingly steep dive which finished up past the vertical. I did not follow the aircraft down and claim it as destroyed. I straightened up from turn just as some more Messerschmitt 109s (which were milling about some Spitfires) turned towards me. I gave a short head-on burst on one of them, who I don't think had seen me, but saw no apparent result of my fire. I then joined up with S/Ldr Holden of 610 Squadron with my No 2 and gave a short burst at another aircraft but saw no result. Landed Westhampnett at 1722.

2 July 1941

I was leading 616 Squadron's first section. Sighted approximately fifteen Messerschmitt 109Fs a few miles south-west of Lille so turned south and attacked them. They were in a sort of four formation climbing eastwards. They made no attempt to do anything but climb in formation so I turned the Squadron behind them and about 2,000 feet above and attacked from behind. I attacked a Messerschmitt 109F from quarter astern to astern and saw his hood come off – probably he jettisoned it – and the pilot started to climb out. Did not see him actually bale out as I nearly collided with another Messerschmitt 109 that was passing on my right in the middle of a half roll. Half-rolled with him and dived down on his tail firing at him with the result that glycol and oil came out of his machine. I left him at about 12,000 feet, as he appeared determined to continue diving, and pulled up again to 18,000 feet. My ASI showed rather more than 400 mph when I pulled out. Found the fight had taken me west a bit so picked up two (610 Squadron) Spitfires and flew out at Boulogne round Gris-Nez and up to Gravelines where we crossed the coast again and found a Messerschmitt 109E at 8,000 feet at which I fired from about 300 yards. No damage but this one is claimed as 'Frightened'! The first Messerschmitt 109 is claimed as destroyed since, although I did not actually see the pilot leave the aircraft, I saw him preparing to do so, and several pilots in 616 saw two parachutes going down, one of which was shot down by P/O Heppell. The second Messerschmitt 109 was seen by P/O Heppell and is claimed as damaged.

4 July 1941

Intercepted one Messerschmitt 109E some miles south of Gravelines at 14,000 feet, while with a section of four. Turned onto its tail and opened fire with a short one-second burst at about 150 yards. I found it very easy to keep inside him on the turn and I closed up quite quickly. I gave him three more short bursts, the final one at about twenty yards' range and as he slowed down very suddenly I nearly collided with him. I did not see the result except one puff of white smoke halfway through. S/Ldr Burton in my section watched the complete combat and saw the Messerschmitt 109's airscrew slow right down to ticking-over speed and as I broke away the Messerschmitt did not half-roll and dive – but just sort of fell away in a sloppy fashion, quite slowly, as though the pilot had been hit. Having broken away I did not again see the Messerschmitt 109 I attacked, since I was engaged in trying to collect my section. I am satisfied that I was hitting him and so is S/Ldr Burton from whose evidence the above report is written. This Messerschmitt 109 is claimed as a probable.

6 July 1941

During the withdrawal from Lille to Gravelines we were pestered by Messerschmitt 109s starting to attack and then half-rolling and diving away when we made to engage. Of an initial three bursts I fired at three Messerschmitt 109Es I claim three frightened (P/O Johnson subsequently destroyed No 3). Finally, two Messerschmitt 109Rs (I think) positioned themselves to attack from starboard quarter behind when my section was flying above and behind the bombers south of Dunkirk. These two were flying in line-astern and I broke my section round on to them when they were quite close (250 yards away). They both did a steeply banked turn, still in line-astern, and exposed their complete underside (plan view) to us. I gave one a short burst (no deflection) full in the stomach from 100–150 yards and it fell out of the sky in a shallow dive, steepening up with white and black smoke pouring from it, and finally flames as well. The pilot did not bale out while I was watching. This is confirmed by P/O Johnson and Sgt Smith in my section, and is claimed as destroyed.

9 July 1941

Just after crossing French coast (with bombers) at 18,000 feet I saw a Messerschmitt 109 behind and above me diving very steeply, obviously intending to get down below and behind bombers and attack from underneath and then zoom away. I instructed my section I was diving down, and dived straight through and under the escort Wing converging on this Messerschmitt 109 who had not seen me. He saw me as he was starting his zoom and turned right-handed, i.e. into me, and dived away. I was very close by then and aileroned behind him and gave him one to two second burst from 100–150 yards straight behind him. Glycol and heavy black smoke streamed out of his adroplane and he continued diving. I pulled out at approximately 10,000 feet and watched him continue downwards. When he was about 2,000 feet I lost him and then saw a large flash on the ground where he should have hit. I am sure it was him but I am claiming a probable only because when flying out over the same terrain I noticed sun flashes on glass in various directions, and as I did not actually see the 109 right into the ground these sun flashes must be recorded. Just after leaving the target area my section was attacked from above and behind and we turned into the attackers, Messerschmitt 109Fs, who started half-rolling. I got a good squirt at one and the glycol stream started. Did not follow him down and claim a damaged. Several others were frightened and I claim one badly frightened who did the quickest half-roll and dive I've ever seen when I fired at him.

10 July 1941

Was operating in a four over the Bethune area at 24,000 feet when we saw five Messerschmitt 109s below us in a wide loose vic. We attacked diving from above and I opened fire at one at 200 yards closing to 100, knocking pieces off it round the cockpit and pulling up over the top. I saw flashes as some of my bullets struck (presumably de Wilde). Was unable after pulling up to see it again, but saw and attacked without result three of the same five (so it is to be supposed that two were hit), immediately after pulling up and turning. My own aeroplane shielded my view immediately after the attack and I claim this one as a probable only, because of the incendiary strikes and the pieces coming off the cockpit.

Was flying with section of four northwards over 10/10ths between Calais–Dover. Sighted three Messerschmitt 109Es below flying south-west over the cloud. Turned and dived to catch them up which we did just over Calais. The three Messerschmitt 109s were in line-abreast and so were my section with one lagging behind. I closed in to 150 yards behind and under the left-hand one and fired a two-second burst into its belly under the cockpit. Pieces flew off the Messerschmitt 109 exactly under the cockpit and there was a flash of flame and black smoke, and then the whole aeroplane went up in flames. Time approximately 1250. Height 7,000 feet. Position, south of Calais or over Calais.

12 July 1941

When orbiting the wood at Bois De Dieppe about to proceed to St Omer at 26,000 feet, we saw approximately twelve to fifteen

Messerschmitt 109Fs climbing in line-astern from Dunkirk turning west and south. I told my section we would attack and told the two top squadrons to stay up as I thought I had seen more Messerschmitt 109s above. We turned so that the enemy – who were very close and climbing across our bows – were down-sun, and I fired a very close deflection shot at the second last one at 100–150 yards' range. I saw De Wilde flashes in front of his cockpit but no immediate result as I passed him and turned across him and fired a head-on burst at the last Messerschmitt 109 who had lagged a bit. A panel or some piece of his machine fell away and he put his nose down; as I passed over him I lost him. I then turned round 180 degrees to the same direction as the 109s had been going but could not see them. I called my section together and, after a little, made contact with them. I then saw the Bee Hive and bombers flying over the St Omer wood travelling south-east just below with a squadron of Spitfires above. I saw two Messerschmitt 109Fs above the Spitfires and dived down to attack. These two flew away south more or less level and I closed up quickly on one which I shot from 100 yards dead astern and produced black smoke and glycol.

The second one was banking to the left when I attacked the first and he dived a little after the first. I got in behind him with a good burst, followed him through 10/10ths cloud (about 100 feet thick) and gave him one more burst which set him on fire with a short quick flame under the cockpit, then black smoke, then the whole machine caught fire round the fuselage. The pilot did not bale out. I pulled away at 9,000 feet and I reckon this aeroplane crashed between St Omer and Bethune. I went up to 14,000 feet and called my section together, they were both above the cloud in the same area, and we had no more combat. I believe they had a fight at the same time. Of the four Messerschmitt 109Fs one was definitely destroyed and the other three are considered damaged. The one which disappeared through the cloud layer emitting black and white smoke I consider was more likely a probable.

23 July 1941

Took off from Manston with S/Ldr Burton at approximately 1340 after 242 Squadron on the expedition to bomb ship off Dunkirk. The weather was very hazy from about 1,000 feet upwards but clearer below. We flew from North Foreland and near Gravelines were attacked by a Messerschmitt 109 out of the sun. We countered and S/Ldr Burton had a shot at it. It flew low over the water to the French coast.

> We carried on up to Dunkirk and slightly past where we saw some flak and then a Spitfire (squadron markings XT) flying straight for home in a dive being attacked by a Messerschmitt 109. We immediately turned on the Messerschmitt 109 which saw us and did a left-hand climbing turn back to France, but I got a very close short burst (half second) at him from underneath and behind him. It definitely hit him and produced a puff of white smoke under his cockpit. I turned away immediately as I had no idea how many were about and did not want to lose S/Ldr Burton. I claim this Messerschmitt as damaged but would like information from 242 Squadron who told me on landing back at Manston that they had seen two Messerschmitt 109s go into the sea in that area. We flew back to Manston after this and landed amongst 242 Squadron, who arrived back at the same time. I claim a damaged aircraft just around Dunkirk out to sea, which may be a destroyed one. I never saw this Messerschmitt after breaking away but the visibility was poor.'

Although Douglas would have been the last to admit it, he must have been beginning to feel the strain by then. A year's operations and a century of sorties. In the final phase of July/August 1941, he led ten sweeps in seven days. Then came 9 August. He was leading the Tangmere Wing escorting RAF bombers on a raid on France. He was now flying a Spitfire Vb and the time was about 1100. First of all, Bader takes up the story of that morning:

> 'We crossed the French coast south of Le Touquet with bottom Squadron 616 at 26,000 feet and 610 Squadron above. The Wing had lost 41 Squadron after take-off. Attacked a climbing formation of about twenty Messerschmitt 109Fs. I told 610 Squadron to stay put, and dived with my section on to the leading four Messerschmitts. "Come on, boys, there are plenty for all. Pick one each." I nearly collided with the first one at whom I was firing, and had to go behind and under his tail. Continued downwards where I saw some more Messerschmitt 109s. I arrived among these who were evidently not on the look-out, as I expect they imagined the first formation we attacked were covering for them . . .'

Paul Brickhill told what happened next:

> 'He was suddenly surprised to see six more Messerschmitts ahead, splayed abreast in three parallel pairs line-astern, noses pointing the other way. More sitters! He knew he should pull up and leave them; repeatedly he'd drummed it into his pilots never to try things on their own. But the temptation! They

looked irresistible. A glance behind again. All clear. Greed swept discretion aside and he sneaked up behind the middle pair. None of them noticed. From a hundred yards he squirted at the trailing one and a thin blade of flame licked out behind it. Abruptly a flame flared like a huge match being struck and the aeroplane fell on one wing and dropped on fire all over. The other Germans flew placidly on. They must have been blind.

He aimed at the leader 150 yards in front and gave him a three-second burst. Bits flew off it and then it gushed volumes of white smoke as its nose dropped. The two fighters on the left were turning towards him, and crazily elated as though he had just pulled off a smash and grab raid, he wheeled violently right to break off, seeing the two on that side still flying ahead and that he would pass between them. In sheer bravado he held course to do so.

Something hit him. He felt the impact but the mind was curiously numb and could not assess it. No noise but something was holding his aeroplane by the tail, pulling it out of his hands and slewing it round. It lurched suddenly and then was pointing straight down, the cockpit floating with dust that had come up from the bottom. He pulled back on the stick but it fell inertly into his stomach like a broken neck. The aeroplane was diving into a steep spiral and confusedly he looked behind to see if anything were following.

First he was surprised and then terrifyingly shocked to see that the whole of the Spitfire behind the cockpit was missing: fuselage, tail, fin – all gone. Sheared off, he thought vaguely. The second 109 must have run into him and sliced it off with its propeller.

He knew it had happened but hoped desperately and foolishly that he was wrong. Only the little radio mast stuck up just behind his head. A corner of his brain saw that the altimeter was unwinding fast from 24,000 feet.

Thoughts crowded in. How stupid to be nice and warm in the closed cockpit and have to start getting out. The floundering mind sought a grip and sharply a gush of panic spurted.

"Christ! Get out!"

"Wait! No oxygen up here!"

"Get out! Get out!"

"Won't be able to soon. Must be doing over 400 already."

He tore his helmet and mask off and yanked the little rubber ball over his head – the hood ripped away and screaming noise battered at him. Out came the harness pin and he gripped the cockpit rim to lever himself up, wondering if he could get out without thrust from the helpless legs. He struggled madly to get his head above the windscreen and suddenly felt he was being sucked out as the tearing wind caught him.

Top half out. He was out. No, something had him, the leg holding him. (The rigid foot of the right leg hooked fast in some vice in the cockpit.) Then the nightmare took his exposed body and beat him and screamed and roared in his ears as the broken fighter dragging him by the leg plunged down and spun and battered him and the wind clawed at his flesh and the cringing sightless eyeballs. It went on and on into confusion, on and on, timeless, witless and helpless, with a little core of thought deep under the blind head fighting for life in the wilderness. It said he had a hand gripping the D-ring of the parachute and mustn't take it off, mustn't grip it because the wind wouldn't let him get it back again, and he mustn't pull it or the wind would split his parachute because they must be doing 500 miles an hour. On and on . . . till the steel and leather snapped.

He was floating, in peace. The noise and buffeting had stopped. Floating upwards? He thought, it is so quiet I must have a rest. I would like to go to sleep.

In a flash the brain cleared and he knew and pulled the D-ring, hearing a crack as the parachute opened. Then he was actually floating. High above, the sky was still blue, and right at his feet lay a veil of cloud. He sank into it. That was the cloud at 4,000 feet. Cutting it fine! In seconds he dropped easily under it and saw the earth, green and dappled where the sun struck through. Something flapped in his face and he saw it was his right trouser leg, split along the seam. High in the split gleamed indecently the white skin of his stump.

The right leg had gone.

How lucky, he thought, to lose one's legs and have detachable ones, otherwise he would have died a few seconds ago. He looked but saw no burning wreck below – probably not enough left to burn.

Lucky, too, not to be landing on the rigid metal leg like a post that would have split his loins. Odd it should happen like that. How convenient. But only half a leg was left to land on – he did not think of that.

He heard engine noises and turned in the harness. A Messerschmitt was flying straight at him, but the pilot did not shoot. He turned and roared by fifty yards away.

Grass and cornfields were lifting gently to meet him, stools of corn and fences. A vivid picture, not quite static, moving. Two peasants in blue smocks leaned against a gate looking up

> and he felt absurdly selfconscious. A woman carrying a pail in each hand stopped in a lane and stared up, frozen like a still. He thought – I must look comic with only one leg.
>
> The earth that was so remote suddenly rose fiercely. Hell! I'm landing on a gate! He fiddled with his shrouds to spill air and slip sideways and, still fumbling, hit, feeling nothing except vaguely some ribs buckle when a knee hit his chest as consciousness snapped.
>
> – Paul Brickhill

Meanwhile Tangmere had no idea of what had happened to Douglas. In the hectic moments of that fight, no-one had noticed his sudden disappearance, no-one saw the collision. Woodhall was the controller at Tangmere. At the end of the sortie, he called over the air:

'Douglas, are you receiving?'

There was no answer.

Johnnie Johnson called the group captain:

'We've had a stiff fight, sir. I last saw the wing commander on the tail of a 109.'

'Thank you, Johnnie,' the group captain replied courteously.

When they landed, they found that Douglas and Buck Casson were both missing. Johnnie Johnson and Cocky Dundas were two of the pilots who almost at once asked for permission to return and try to find them. They did so, but without trace.

It was about tea-time on that summer afternoon. Thelma and Jill were at Bay House, as they had been so often that summer, awaiting Douglas's return. Instead the intelligence officer arrived from Tangmere.

Thelma was sitting in a deck-chair in the garden. 'Hello, John, come for tea?' The name of the young officer was John Hunt. He thought that Thelma already knew about Douglas and became so embarrassed about it that he could not bring himself to tell her. Neither Thelma nor Jill could make head or tail of him. Then Woodhall arrived.

'Oh, look, here's Woodie,' Thelma said.

As soon as they met, she could tell by his face that something was wrong.

'I'm afraid I've got some bad news for you, Thelma. He hasn't come back from the morning sortie.'

Jill Lucas also felt the physical sensation of that moment. The sense of shock. As if one's heart had stopped. But Thelma and Jill had both been convinced that Douglas was absolutely invincible; that the Germans would never get him.

Thelma was quite calm about it. At least, externally. She sat down. She must have visualised the possibility of such a moment despite all her hopes.

Woodhall went on: 'Of course, we're looking for him and I hope we'll hear something very soon. We'll let you know the moment there's any news.'

Then he left. They were very quiet for a while. There was almost nothing to say. Then Jill noticed that for the only time she could ever recall, Thelma just could not cope with the cooking. The next few days were going to be bad.

Johnnie Johnson said:

> 'We, too, were silent when we drove to the mess, for we knew that even if our wing leader was still alive he would have little chance of evading capture with his tin legs. Before this, we had rarely thought of his artificial limbs, and it was only when we swam together and saw his stumps and how he thrashed his way out of the deep water with his powerful arms that we remembered his infirmity. At Tangmere we had simply judged him on his ability as a leader and a fighter pilot, and for us the high sky would never be the same. Gone was the confident, eager, often scornful voice. Exhorting us, sometimes cursing us, but always holding us together in the fight. Gone was the greatest tactician of them all. Today marked the end of an era that was rapidly becoming a legend.'

As soon as Douglas was taken to hospital, he asked his captors to search for his other artificial leg. He suggested that it would still be in, or near, the remains of the aircraft. In case it was not, he also asked if the Germans would signal to England requesting delivery of his spare right leg. This, in company with his spare left leg, was in his locker at Tangmere. To his surprise, the Germans acceded to both wishes. Within a day or two, the Germans retrieved and mended the missing leg.

Thelma thought Douglas was alive, but began to get more and more worried as she felt that the Germans would be bound to announce it if they had Douglas – as he was such a capture. Yet she still felt it was out of the question that he could be lost.

The boys from Tangmere told Thelma and Jill: 'You'll have to face it. He won't come back. One of us would have seen something.'

Jill had an absolute certain conviction that Douglas was still alive. He *felt* alive to her. She had never been so sure of anything. So she said to the boys:

'Well, I don't believe you.'

Jill used to lie awake at night thinking of Douglas and willing him to be alive. Thinking how lonely he must be out there. She wondered where he was. By then she thought that Thelma had really begun to believe he might be lost. The boys used to come down and try to take them out for a drink. It was awful trying to go on as if nothing had happened.

Days dragged by appallingly.

Eventually Woodhall was able to broadcast the welcome news on the Tangmere Tannoy: 'Attention all ranks. This is the station commander speaking. You will all be pleased to know that Wing Commander Bader is alive and well on the other side of the Channel. He is a prisoner of war.'

They had heard from the International Red Cross that Douglas was in hospital at St Omer and the Germans had offered safe conduct for a small aircraft to fly to France and take a spare set of legs.

The phone went in Bay House, telling Thelma and Jill that this message had been picked up on the radio. After they heard the news, they went out with the boys and had a tremendous party. Then the boys returned to war.

Douglas started to think about how he could get back to Britain. Obviously his only chance was to break out of the hospital before he was transferred to a prison camp. But the hospital was run by the Germans with only a small French kitchen staff, and patients were customarily sent to Germany as soon as they were strong enough to rise from their beds. If anything was to be done, it must be done quickly.

Seizing a moment when the German orderlies were not watching, Douglas soon put his fate in the hands of one of the French maids. The girl agreed to get in touch with English agents on her next day off at the weekend; and actually the following day she brought the injured pilot a letter from a French peasant couple who promised to shelter him outside St Omer until he could be passed along the line. When arrangements were perfected, their son would wait for him outside the hospital gates every evening after midnight, until the chance came for escape.

The next afternoon – Thursday – Douglas was suddenly informed that he was to leave for Germany the following morning. The girl had not yet been able to visit the 'agents' but it was obviously now or never. When she came up with supper, Douglas told her that he intended to get out that night, and asked that her helper should be waiting outside at 1.45 am.

There was now little time to perfect details. The corridors outside the small ward were under constant observation, and Douglas had already decided that he would have to climb through the window. The room was on the second floor, and for a man with no legs the difficulties were not inconsiderable. Letting his two comrades of the ward (both badly injured airmen) into his secret, Douglas waited until the hospital staff had completed their last round of the evening. He then collected all the sheets in the room, including those of his fellow-patriots. This was no easy task; for the two men were lying completely helpless, and Douglas, clattering round on his damaged artificial limbs, made an appalling noise. Eventually the job was done; the sheets were knotted together; one end was tied round the leg of the last bedstead; and the bed was pushed up against the wall. Throwing the coil of sheets underneath, Douglas returned to his own bed to await the appointed hour.

A few minutes before 1.45 am he rose, strapped on his legs and dressed. He then moved over to the window and threw out the sheets. It was pitch dark outside, and he was quite unable to see if they reached the ground. Trusting to luck, he heaved himself out of the window, bade farewell to his comrades, and lowered himself down his improvised rope. In a few seconds he touched earth, where he found to his amusement several yards of sheet.

He then made his way to the appointed spot outside. Across the road he could see the glow of a cigarette. He approached. A man moved forward out of the darkness. A word of recognition, and Douglas and his companion were making their way through the town.

The walk was long, and Douglas, besides the handicap of his damaged limb, was still dressed in his British uniform. The two men nevertheless proceeded unchallenged, and within an hour or so were safely at the peasants' house. There the elderly couple insisted that Douglas stayed until their son-in-law, an Englishman by birth, could come and talk things over. The peasants were Monsieur and Madame Hiecque.

The following morning the peasant's wife set off for town. She returned with what, to Douglas, seemed the very worst kind of news. A cordon had been thrown round the hospital and every house was being searched. The peasant and his wife, however, were only amused. Their house was well beyond the enemy ring and they repeatedly assured Douglas that the Germans would never look for him so far from the hospital.

Morning turned to afternoon and all seemed well. Suddenly a German staff car drew up outside the house. The escape plan had been betrayed by another girl worker in the hospital. Guided by the old peasant, Douglas at once bolted through the back door and into a garden shed, where he hid beneath some baskets and hay. He heard voices, first inside the house, then nearer at hand. A German soldier opened the door of the shed, rummaged about with the baskets, and went away. Douglas breathed out.

Then the door opened again, and another German entered. This one was more thorough than his predecessor. He systematically jabbed his bayonet through the hay until Douglas, suddenly realising what it was when it came within a few inches of his face, could bear it no longer. Doubtless his instinctive decision was not unconnected with thought for his hosts. Giving himself up, he denied that he had ever set eyes on the Hiecques, and he carefully explained that he had entered the garden from the side gate. His story did not convince the enemy, who in due course hauled off the peasant and his family, together with the helpful girl from the hospital, to forced labour in Germany.

Fortunately the Hiecques survived this, as we shall see later. After the war all were able to return home, while the informer, despite Douglas's representations, was sentenced to twenty years' imprisonment by the French.

Douglas was now placed under close guard, and any further attempt to escape was out of the question. He was taken to German headquarters in St Omer. There a surprise awaited him. While he was with his shelterers, a number of British aircraft in the course of a normal operation had swept across St Omer airfield. As the last of them had streaked away, a long yellow box had been seen floating down on a parachute, surviving the attention of the German gunners on its descent. It had reached the ground, where it was found to be addressed to the Commandant of the airfield for transmission to Wing Commander Douglas Bader, DSO, DFC. The box was now before him. It contained, of course, his spare right leg from Tangmere.

Leaving Douglas and his story for a moment, his example was helping to win the war. The Tangmere pilots remembered those sixty-odd sweeps; that calm, matter of fact leader; his complete control; the voice that never rose an octave higher, no matter what was happening all around him; and more than anything else, the tactics he taught them.

Laddie Lucas went out to Malta in the early part of 1942. He sailed out with Stan Turner of 242 Squadron and also from Tangmere. They got to Malta on a shimmering-blue Mediterranean morning. They were just going into the mess for breakfast when the air raid sirens started to sound. The place had been hammered to hell. At that moment, four Hurricanes flying in line-astern climbed away, like whiting eating their own tails. Stan Turner looked up and said:

'Jesus Christ! They're sure not going to fly like that with me.'

In the Tangmere Wing led by Douglas, Stan Turner was squadron commander. Douglas, Woodhall and Turner had developed the finger four into what was required in the early middle part of the war. Stan Turner became Wing Commander Flying at Malta. He came to fly with 249 Squadron, when Laddie Lucas was a flight commander. Stan Turner told them:

'Well, I don't know what you fellows have been flying. I saw four Hurricanes flying around yesterday morning line-astern. I don't like that. No-one's going to fly line-astern around here any more, because I'm interested in *living*. This is what we flew with Bader at Tangmere, and that's what we're going to fly here. And if there are any of you who don't like it – there are plenty of ways out.'

Some very quizzical faces looked back at the tough Canadian. But he was determined they would fly this way. The direction that Stan Turner gave them in the air, coupled with the first-class commentary and controlling from Woodhall combined to enable them to win the rest of the Battle of Malta – by a Tangmere team plus a few others.

Later on still, Laddie Lucas was posted to RAF Coltishall to command the fighter Wing there. SASO 12 Group told him on arrival: 'We've lost three wing commanders in three weeks, Lucas, and I want you to understand that you've been sent here to stop the rot. We can't have it.'

Lucas saw that they were flying line-astern, so he said at once, just as Stan Turner had done on Malta and Douglas had done at Tangmere:

'We're going to fly line-abreast here. We won the Battle of Malta that way.'

The casualty rate was substantially reduced and the wing commander survived.

So the practice of flying line-abreast was one of Douglas's achievements. It became fundamental to a great area of flying in the Royal Air Force. Strangely enough, Laddie Lucas and Douglas Bader had not yet met. Their paths were to cross in an unimaginable way . . .

The fighter tactics Douglas developed spread fast and far. And when Denis Crowley-Milling got his own squadron, he also modelled it on all he had learned from Douglas's squadron and wing. Crowley-Milling formed his first Typhoon squadron, fittingly at Duxford. Douglas would not have wanted any credit for all this, but he would be given it. Meanwhile, it was still 1941 and he was a prisoner-of-war.

Chapter 13

After his recapture the Germans decided to transfer Douglas to a prisoner-of-war camp immediately. An ambulance conveyed him from St Omer to Brussels, where a train eventually took him on to Frankfurt. His first destination was Dulag Luft, the centre where RAF prisoners were always questioned initially. All he gave them was his name, rank and number, ignoring any technical questions about aircraft. They did not press him unduly.

But before he had scarcely settled in Frankfurt he was abruptly told that he would be returned to Brussels to appear in front of an enemy court-martial. After a short while in the presence of three German generals, and from the gist of the questions they began to ask him, Douglas realised that *he* was not on trial there, but the hospital staff at St Omer for allowing him to escape.

When he 'twigged' this situation, the rest was straightforward. Douglas convinced them that the staff could not have known he would clamber down from the bedroom window, and that they had carried out their normal guarding duties efficiently. That was the end of the court-martial as far as Douglas was concerned.

Then it was back to Dulag Luft briefly, with Douglas alternating between being cantankerous to the Germans and then pulling their legs. Little things like refusing to salute German officers unless they were senior to himself. He had the backing of the Geneva Convention, for what it was worth. Next stop: Lübeck. Bound for Oflag VI B. Here at least and at last Douglas was cast among some four hundred British officers – where he thought he must find some kindred spirits. As it turned out, only a handful were Air Force, most being military from the 1940 era and the fall of France. Oflag VI B made Dulag Luft seem almost Ritz-like. Here the Red Cross did not reach; the commandant was a swine; and the food comprised black bread, potatoes and soup.

Douglas had philosophically accepted losing his legs, so could come to terms with the first four weeks of this chilling prison camp. The one possibility that gave him heart was escape. But before he could do more than tap longer prisoners for their escape experiences or ideas, the entire population of prisoners were moved to another 'cage', as the camps were nicknamed. This was near Cassel.

Warburg was its name and it marked an improvement on Oflag VI B. The Red Cross parcels percolated through and 3,000 British officers were all grouped here in thirty dirty huts. Simple arithmetic meant 100 per hut. The first letter from Thelma also percolated the enemy system. In it she mentioned that she had heard he had been awarded a Bar to his Distinguished Flying Cross. Douglas thus became only the third person to win a Bar to the Distinguished Service Order and the DFC.

Although Douglas was associated with escape plans, his lack of legs often made it impracticable for him to render help. So he indulged in Goon-baiting to sap up some of his pent energy and frustration. One day he refused to go out in the snow for a head-count, until threatened with a pistol – then he succumbed with bonhomie. The Germans never knew how to treat him and were often left fuming, frowning and frustrated.

Two RAF types, Gardner and Lubbock, went to Douglas with an escape plan. The two men had devised a ruse via the clothing store hut, where they had discovered an unused spare room. Under cover of a diversion from other prisoners, the trio plus a captain in the Commando got into this little room. After a few midwinter hours' wait, another prearranged diversion enabled them to slip out of the window of the room. The Commando, Keith Smith, got clear but the others ran straight into a German guard. The result for them was solitary confinement for ten days. The enemy caught Keith Smith, too, after four or five days.

Spring came and they were allowed to join another escape plan involving a tunnel already thirty to forty yards long – with all that meant in human labour. Douglas was among three dozen men hoping that the tunnel would mean their passport home. Half a dozen of them got away – at least from the camp – but next day the Germans found the hole and that was the end of that.

Douglas and fifty other RAF officers were moved at minimum notice from Warburg to Stalag Luft III at Sagan. Here Douglas met again some old chums, Bob Tuck and Harry Day: Tuck being the ultimate Battle of Britain fighter ace. They started tunnelling under the stove in the hut, but Douglas could only keep watch up above to warn of danger. Some of the prisoners were against Douglas's persistent Goon-baiting, which could jeopardise their privileges, and they wished only to keep the peace.

A word must be said in Douglas's defence. He considered an officer's duty on capture was to do two things. Firstly, to resist the enemy and make life as unpleasant as possible for them. Secondly, to try to escape if humanly feasible and head back for Britain to continue the struggle. He was at his most 'black and white' about both of these attitudes. It was not a matter of choice. The officer had an inalienable duty. Some fellow-POWs found him overbearing and irritating because of his behaviour towards the Germans. But this was to misunderstand the nature of Bader and his beliefs. For him, life anyway was a struggle to survive. So how much more laudable that he should follow his 'resist or escape' precept in the face of his other hardships. Perhaps there was an element, too, of Douglas having to continue his life of leadership and proving himself.

The escape committee turned down one or two plans involving Douglas, which they considered too dangerous in view of his infirmity. Meanwhile, his baiting and non-co-operation cost them things like Red Cross parcels. And then the Germans decided it was time for Douglas to be sent elsewhere – he was too inflammatory for their comfort.

Before he would agree to go quietly, Douglas had one last trick. When the time came for him to be moved from the camp, the prisoners watched while he walked to the main gate, looked at the enemy squad detailed to guard his departure, and then started to walk with calculation right along the line of German soldiers.

One of the watching prisoners said:

'My God. He's inspecting the bastards!'

Douglas chuckled deeply, as only he could. Then they put him on a train to the nearest stop for Stalag VIII B at Lamsdorf. The complement of prisoners here totalled 20,000 Allied soldiers. He refused to wait long for his next escape attempt. He learned that a few prisoners were sometimes detailed to do dirty work near an enemy aerodrome – though they did not know exactly where it was. Douglas entertained fantasy dreams of actually stealing an enemy aircraft and flying it to Sweden – some three or four hundred miles across the Baltic Sea!

The small detail of soldiers smuggled Douglas in as one of them on duty near this suspected aerodrome at Gleiwitz on the German–Polish border. Douglas had the job of cleaning the latrines. But once again before he could even find the aerodrome, his absence from Lamsdorf had been discovered and he was caught, along with his main conspirator, Johnny Palmer.

Another ten days' solitary confinement which seemed as though they would never end. But they did – or almost. Then the German Kommandant actually came to see Douglas on his bunk in the solitary cell. They had exchanged words before starting the sentence, about Douglas's protest at being in a non-officer camp. The Kommandant said to him:

'I have some good news for you, Wing Commander. Tomorrow you go to an Offizierslager.'

Douglas asked him where it would be.

'The Offizierslager IV C. Kolditz Castle.'

Douglas completed his tenth day in solitary and was escorted by train on the prolonged trip to Kolditz – or Colditz in its Anglicised form. The castle had the reputation of being proof against any escape attempts and was reserved for the worst offenders among prisoners-of-war. Those who had tried to escape or had made the Germans' life most inconvenient.

Douglas certainly qualified on both counts. Along the way, it must be admitted, he had collected quite a few opponents to his viewpoint. Some POWs did not have the stomach to do more than try to survive and lead a quiet existence until the war was over. But Douglas persisted that it was his duty – and theirs too, really – to continue the conflict even in captivity. In other words, to make things as difficult as possible for the enemy, even if it meant people getting punished in the process. Not everyone was as strong a character as himself – with or without legs.

Night had fallen when they finally reached the railway station for Colditz Castle. Douglas saw it floodlit for security as he somehow walked from the village up the steep hill towards the entrance. The castle even had the traditional drawbridge. He heard for the first time the sounds of bars closing on vast doors, guards' feet on the pervading cobbles, and the inevitable lock grinding and clanging a cell open ready to receive him.

But before his guard could usher him inside, a familiar voice greeted Douglas, making him feel a hundred times better:

'Douglas – there you are.'

It was one of his old chums, Geoffrey Stephenson, who reassured Bader that he would only be in the cell for that night, until the Germans had gone through the routine drill of getting all his particulars. This happened just as Stephenson had promised. Next day he reappeared and was given charge of Bader officially by their captors. Geoffrey led him to a room which he would be sharing with three Army officers. Douglas had been on the move intermittently for a year or more and the sight of a personal bunk, chairs, and the promise of Red Cross parcels seemed highly attractive. They even had the luxury of a bath – unknown to him since 9 August 1941. Not that Douglas could be bought by such things.

At that stage, some eighty British POWs were among the four hundred or so total complement of Colditz coming from up to half-a-dozen Allied nationalities. Douglas saw at first-hand the sheer drop of nearly 200 feet from the barred windows to their room.

Douglas did not wait long for his initial abrasive brush with the Germans. They used to hold two roll-calls or head-counts a day, but Bader insisted that he would not under any circumstances drag himself up and down dozens of stairs twice daily. In the end, the Germans agreed that if he could be seen at a window from below, that would be as good as being accounted present. Yet another miniature victory for Douglas in his personal battle against the enemy.

In the absence of immediate escape plans, Douglas resorted to Goon-baiting again, as he had done at each of his previous camps. It helped him to keep sane and in one way also exercised his sense of humour, as well as sense of spirit. He led the others in songs, featuring rude lyrics about the Germans generally.

Douglas and another badly-behaved prisoner, Peter Tunstall, devised a way of separating photos so that messages could be secreted on the back and then they could be sealed up together again. The Germans discovered one of these during a search and unluckily Douglas had written some gleaned information about the effect of the Allied bombing on the enemy. They took him off to Leipzig where they confronted him with two charges: inciting other prisoners to behave badly and secondly, and more serious, espionage.

'You can be shot for it,' said the German officer accusing him.

Douglas pointed out that he had been in their custody completely, so could not possibly have found out any actual facts of military value. But the officer said that he would be hearing more about it. On the way back to Colditz, some thirty miles from Leipzig, Douglas's mind returned to thoughts of escape – never far from his consideration.

He submitted one scheme to the escape committee at Colditz for him to try and get over the roof with a couple of others; drop into the German section of the old castle; somehow just get down the last 140 feet to the moat; evade fences and mines; and thus escape! Not surprisingly, the committee refused to help them in his desperate submission. They could not waste precious resources unless the scheme submitted appeared possible.

Douglas did link up with an equally ambitious and futile plan by some Polish prisoners. This one involved the Colditz sewers, but fizzled out when one of the Poles reported back that the pipes just got too small for a man to get through them.

Douglas finally gave up all idea of escaping. Having realised it was hopeless he felt more at ease with himself. Now he simply concentrated on annoying the Germans. And all the while, the prisoners heard how the war was progressing through a radio which had been rigged up out of bits and pieces acquired in Colditz. Douglas also heard that the Germans had dropped the idea of court-martialling him for espionage, as they realised that the officers involved on their side might look very foolish in front of Berlin officials. For as Douglas had asked them: How could he have been a spy while shut away in Colditz with a 200-foot drop between himself and the outside world? Even the Germans would not bring themselves to convict him in the face of such an absurdity.

Douglas and the other inmates let off some of their pent-up emotions and energies by playing a version of soccer and rugger combined – and called stoolball. He was one of the goalkeepers, who sat on stools at either end of the courtyard. The teams tried to score a goal or try by touching a stool with the ball: hence, stoolball. Douglas as a goalie got himself in the wars and bent his metal legs quite badly. As he had been experiencing some hardship with his legs, he had to give up the game in case of further mishaps.

The Germans actually took him into the village, where a workman riveted a plate over a crack in one knee. Eventually the Red Cross managed to convey a spare left leg to him in response to letters sent to Thelma by Douglas. It was about this stage that Douglas was finding the absence of proper exercise irksome, on a physical and mental level. The Germans allowed him to take walks out of Colditz, perhaps in the hope that he would be a little more occupied and thus less likely to trouble them. For quite a while, Douglas and Lieutenant-Colonel Peter Dollar were allowed out for walks past the fields, with an enemy escort at a distance to the rear.

1942 was the year when Douglas first saw Colditz. He endured 1943 and then they were all immensely cheered by the news, via the secret radio, of D-Day, 6 June 1944. Two sick officers were actually approved for repatriation by the Germans, who also offered Douglas a similar opportunity on the grounds of hardship through his legs.

Bader refused to accept the offer. He wanted to be released with the rest when the time finally came – and that would not be in the autumn of 1944. Meanwhile they clung to little scraps of comfort to break up their interminable months there. Like the first time that they saw Flying Fortresses on a daylight raid.

Douglas shouted to the Germans:

'Wo ist die Luftwaffe?'

The air opposition was nowhere to be seen in the skies around Colditz. But likewise the Red Cross food parcels were now nowhere to be found at the castle. They had been the bulwark against real food shortage and they had stopped. The situation was tantalising. The Allies advanced. So did winter. And at Colditz, nothing changed, at least not for the better.

This winter of 1944–1945 proved the worst which the prisoners there had sustained. To try to offset the chronic food shortage, Douglas and his walking companion, Peter Dollar, started to swap cigarette rations from the POWs for food from the local farmers. Dollar brought grain, hidden by his overcoat, and eggs beneath his cap! An officer made Douglas a pair of slim bags which would hang inside his trouser legs to provide additional space for food storage!

The Germans knew he looked a little strange around his legs anyway, so did not suspect anything was amiss. Douglas felt thrilled that at last he could contribute something materially for his fellow officer-prisoners. And heaven knows everyone needed it. It is on record that some of them shed three stones in weight over the awful winter months of food deprivation, so even small additions like the grain he concealed about him helped them all survive.

Douglas went on bravely with this self-appointed duty, hiding not only the grain from the Germans – but the pain his stumps were causing him. Yet his friends did catch him once or twice after these expeditions lying utterly worn out by the extreme effort of getting the grain back over snowy ground.

One day Douglas fell over on to his left metal leg. He saw that it seemed snapped at the ankle; the entire foot section had rotted away with corrosion. Douglas and Dollar asked their guard to go back for his spare left leg, but when he returned an officer was accompanying him. Douglas realised that he could not replace the leg without revealing the bags of grain, so he pleaded embarrassment at his missing leg and went behind some cover to change it. The end of another minor crisis. So the source of the extra food was safe for a little while longer anyway.

Arnhem had come and gone. So had the Battle of the Bulge. The war in Europe would not seem to end, though they knew it must eventually. Meanwhile . . . on 9 February 1945 Douglas had been in captivity for exactly three-and-a-half years. Quite soon after this on the Colditz secret radio came news of Allied advances. They crossed the Rhine, ready for the final inroads into Germany. The inmates of the castle knew roughly how far

– or how near – the advancing armies were day by day. Then on 13 April came word via the radio that the US vanguard were only a matter of miles from Colditz itself. For some POWs this was emotionally almost too much to take.

Early next morning, 14 April, Douglas heard strange sounds. He adjusted his legs and hurried over to the nearest window, in time to see American Thunderbolt aircraft attacking enemy emplacements quite near to them. Later on, too, came the equally sensational sound of Allied tanks perhaps a mere two or three miles beyond the river marking the Colditz boundary.

The name of the Senior British Officer at Colditz was Willie Tood. Suddenly they saw him standing there and warning them:

'The Kommandant has just ordered that we are to evacuate the castle by ten o'clock. He says we're to be marched back behind the German lines.'

This came as a real bolt from the blue. They had all thought about the impending time of liberation and yet none of them had visualised this as an actual possibility. Douglas as usual was first to react:

'We aren't going to move now.'

The S.B.O. reassured him:

'Don't worry – I'm going to tell him that, but I want you to be ready for anything if he brings up his Goons to winkle us out with guns.'

They learned that the Germans intended to use an adjacent ridge as a defensive position, and Colditz would be in the way between the two forces. Willie Tood warned the Kommandant that the Allies would be very displeased with him if the Colditz prisoners were moved. Although time was short for consideration, the Kommandant pondered his dilemma and then decided it would be safest for himself if he did not try to proceed with the plan to evacuate the prisoners. He agreed to let them stay, but he refused to accept responsibility for their safety. So they did not have to implement their last-ditch device of barricading themselves in their own rooms to resist being shifted.

Douglas and Dollar watched through the barred windows as the sights and sounds of war erupted all around Colditz. A shell suddenly hit one corner of the window and the next thing that Douglas knew was a flash in front of him, followed by a force of blast knocking him on to his back. Perhaps the thickness of those castle walls had protected him from worse injury, but even so, plaster was spattering all over him. He recovered quite quickly, as he did not intend to miss the next instalment of the battle.

Despite all the optimistic signs of Allied advance, they did not really know for sure what the day had meant in terms of their potential liberation. The Germans were still guarding Colditz, while exchanges of shell-fire criss-crossed overhead. This jousting between rival artillery went on whiningly far into the night. Douglas and his room-mates finally got some semblance of sleep – albeit troubled – but they were really too mixed up emotionally to do more than doze. Emotions of hope and fear. After all this time, the fear to hope too strongly for release from their ordeal. The fear that something might yet delay their dreams coming true.

Chapter 14

On the night of 14 April 1945, Thelma Bader was living with her parents at Ascot in Berkshire. She had not seen Douglas for three years, eight months and five days. Over at Colditz, morning finally filtered in. It was to be a day they had both awaited throughout those years.

Douglas awoke to the sound of soldiers' feet in the courtyard below. He strapped on his two artificial legs and followed other Allied prisoners-of-war downstairs. He saw the German guards surrendering their arms to American troops. He was free.

In no time at all, three American war correspondents started questioning Douglas, one of them a redheaded girl reporter in khaki battledress. An American officer and a GI offered to take Douglas out of Colditz in their jeep, together with the girl. The officer and girl took the rear seats, while Douglas sat next to the GI driver. Although he had waited so long to be released, now that it had happened, the suddenness took him almost by surprise. The first moment he really *felt* free was when he turned to the GI and asked him:

'I suppose you're the American Third Army, you chaps?'

The driver came from Brooklyn:

'Us the Toid? We're the Foist, not the Toid!'

It transpired that the US First Army under Courtney Hodges had liberated Colditz and they were now driving Douglas to their headquarters at Naunberg, near Leipzig. The countryside looked wild and curving, rather like Salisbury Plain, and Douglas saw symbolically an airfield of Messerschmitt 109s, all destroyed by the Germans themselves. On the way to the headquarters, another sign of the outside world passed them in the endless form of an American armoured division moving up to the retreating enemy.

They reached Naunberg towards evening and after an army meal, Douglas felt sufficiently better to ask a British liaison officer: 'Are there any Spitfires around here?' But the major told him they were all with the British forces up north. Douglas persisted, asking if he could get to them, but was advised to forget it and go home.

Two American officers escorted him through the shrouded streets, till they reached a house that had been requisitioned as sleeping quarters. The Americans went in with Douglas. It was a nice house which had obviously belonged to a civilised family. None of the valuables inside had been touched or removed by the family before they had left. One of the Americans turned and said:

'Ah, hell, Doug, if you want any of this stuff, just take it.'

Douglas said: 'No, I don't want it.'

'There's no need to feel sorry for these bastards' the American pressed.

But Douglas did feel some sense of sorrow. Certainly his hatred for the enemy seemed to have evaporated. Actually, it was partly that after all that time in captivity, he just felt uncomfortable being in this house at all: a home so recently occupied by its owners. Everything was still there, even to their clean linen on the bed. It was an odd sensation, difficult to define, of being intrusive in a home where he was not welcome. Perhaps a temporary reaction or anticlimax after the excitement of actual liberation. That night he lay in a feather bed, not really sleeping but making the mental transition from Colditz. He was a thirty-five-year-old wing commander in the Royal Air Force. Soon he would see England again, for the first time since that last day, 9 August 1941.

With daylight a sense of perspective returned, and after breakfast in the mess they drove him to a nearby American airfield. Douglas saw a whole succession of transport aeroplanes – Dakotas and others – landing and taking off again. They were shuttling supplies from the West and returning as quickly as they could to get more. He learned that they were not allowed to fly prisoners-of-war back yet, so he tried a personal approach. He asked an American officer:

'Look, are you going back to Paris? Would you mind taking me with you?'

'You'd better ask the commanding officer.'

Just as Douglas was beginning to feel this was slightly unreasonable, a small aeroplane landed and he button-holed the pilot.

'Paris? Sure. Do you want a lift?'

Soon Douglas was sitting in the co-pilot's seat of the little Beechcraft. The sight of Coblenz, bombed and in ruins, brought the effect of the intervening years home to Douglas. The aeroplane belonged to the American General Macdonald, and they landed on a small airstrip near the Palace of Versailles, where an American headquarters was located.

Once more the Americans made him very welcome, in their uniquely hospitable way, but when they toasted him in champagne he stuck to his customary soft drinks instead. However, he did accept their offer of a car to drive him into Paris next morning. After a trip round the liberated capital, Douglas got back to Versailles in the late afternoon. He was quite content but he just did not want to talk much or do anything at all. He simply wanted to sit around and gradually grow acclimatised. For forty-four months, he had not been by himself and now he wanted to be alone.

That same evening, someone came in and said to him in a studiously casual tone: 'Say, Doug, there's a phone call for you.' Before Douglas could think 'who the hell can be ringing me up here?' he had picked up the receiver.

'Douglas – it's Thelma.'

They were both a bit dazed and inarticulate. The call had come almost as much as a surprise to her as to Douglas.

'Where are you?' Thelma asked.

'I'm in Paris.'

'I thought you might be out – but a little later on. I didn't know they'd got to you yet.'

'Well, they have and I'm out! I'll be back as soon as I can.'

Apparently General Macdonald had told them to arrange the call. This was extremely kind of the Americans, Douglas thought, and typical of their consideration. They had taken the trouble to find out where Thelma was living, without any reference to Douglas, and got her on the line as a complete surprise.

Next day they drove Douglas to the RAF Provost Marshal's department in Paris, where he wanted to talk to them about the Hiecques. These were the old French couple who had shielded him when he escaped from the hospital in St Omer. Douglas discovered from an intelligence officer that the Germans had sentenced them to death, but this had been commuted to life imprisonment, according to a report received. They promised to let Douglas know of any further news and he heard they were safe soon afterwards. Meanwhile, he enquired about his RAF friends and learned that one of them, Tubby Mermagen was then at Rheims serving as an air commodore at RAF HQ.

'Hello, Tubby, have you got a Spitfire I can fly?' Douglas asked by phone.

'The C-in-C said you'd ask that. No, we haven't. But we've got an Anson that will take you back to Northolt. We'll send a car for you.'

'Bloody good show,' Douglas said in his typical vernacular.

Douglas actually still hankered after a final squirt in a Spitfire before he went home. But he realised it was no use arguing about it, and was put in a car and taken to an airfield. An Anson turned up with a Polish pilot and Douglas clambered aboard. France – The Channel – then England. By a quirk of fate, the route back crossed the Sussex coastline and took them almost over Tangmere. Douglas peered down and just recognised it in the distance through the spring haze. Tangmere, 9 August 1941 . . . The mist drained the colours from the green and brown landscape, but it did not matter. He was over England again.

They touched down at Northolt and from there Douglas went to the Air Ministry. Then he spent a day or two at the Provost Marshal's department near the Royal Albert Hall. Here the usual formalities had to be followed, while the RAF kept the press at bay. By then Douglas had become a celebrity, a unique war hero, but he felt very indisposed to coping with reporters.

In fact, he was still far from adjusted to the prospect of meeting friends. He rang up Thelma each of the two evenings he spent there, before finally being driven down to Ascot to meet her. The press had been literally picketing the house day and night, so that neither Thelma, her mother, nor her stepfather had had any peace since the moment Douglas had landed in England. The phone rang regularly too, and Thelma could not know whether it would be Douglas or another reporter.

At length Douglas was about to walk up the path to the house. As he stepped through the gate, two newspapermen appeared from the bushes and his meeting with Thelma was almost spoiled. They had not seen each other for all that time, yet for some reason at first there seemed little to say. Douglas wanted to tell her lots of things; he was thinking them; but somehow he was inarticulate. They both were. But it did not really matter.

After two or three days at Ascot, Douglas got hold of his old MG car again and they decided to get away from everything and everyone. The Air Ministry had handed him masses of petrol coupons, so he filled the tank and they set out for the West Country. They headed for Thurlestone Sands, in Devon, and stayed at the same hotel as they had done before the war. In the distance across the bay rose the little island used by Agatha Christie as the setting for her *Ten Little Niggers*. Here at Thurlestone, Thelma and Douglas got to know each other again. It had been a long time since pre-war times and it would take a while yet to resume their normal lives.

That spring seemed early and warm. And the special flavour they recalled a quarter of a century later came from the daffodils and crocuses and wild flowers sprouting in the high Devon hedgerows. Those lanes that are like topless tunnels cut through the coastal fields. The scent of the spring flowers lingered with them for the rest of their lives.

Even down in Devonshire, people started to recognise Douglas and ask him questions, but by then he was beginning to get used to it. By the time their three weeks was up, he felt much better. At least, as long as he was with Thelma.

When people asked Douglas later how long it took for him to get adjusted, he said 'I didn't need to at all, old boy! But my wife insists that I was a bit odd!' There were some grounds for maintaining this, as even after they returned to Ascot, whenever anyone came to call at the house, Douglas climbed out of a back window to avoid meeting them. He used to say 'I don't want to see them,' and vanish headfirst into the garden. He also had a temporary peculiarity about food. Thelma's mother nearly went demented. She tried to make dishes as attractive as she could, and all Douglas wanted were puddingy things made of the sort of powdered milk they had got in Colditz! He used to tease her, saying 'Oh, to get back to the Schloss and the good old food!' He simply seemed to want what he had been eating as a prisoner.

Douglas's version was that it took him several weeks to get back to the prospect of normal food again. He did fill his plate 'to the ceiling' several times, only to find that after one or two spoonfuls he could not stomach any more.

The other irritation for him was that he got tired of everyone asking him 'What was it like in prison? Did you have a terrible time with the awful Nazis?' Or someone would waylay him with 'You simply must meet my son. He was in prison camp too, and only came back last week.' At that time, the last thing Douglas – and indeed any prisoner-of-war – would want was to meet any other POW!

When Thelma and Douglas went down to Devonshire, the war in Europe was still being fought. By the time they came back, it was over. One of the first things Douglas did was to make a radio appeal for the Star and Garter Home at Richmond. This world-famous establishment was founded many years earlier and had looked after many 'unrepairable' men who had been wounded in the spine and elsewhere during World War One. Some of them had been in bed for twenty years or more. Douglas knew how it felt to be bedridden. He also knew how it felt to lose limbs. So he made what he described as an 'aggressive appeal' for these chaps because that was the way he felt for them: positively, pugnaciously sympathetic. The BBC were trying to tell him 'You must not say things like that because it will upset the people listening.' But Douglas and the BBC have always remained on very friendly terms. The result of that appeal for the Week's Good Cause was phenomenally successful, raising a record amount of £32,000.

Since that time, Douglas was often being asked to make appeals for disabled organisations or hospitals or other equally good causes. But he had to restrict these to one every three or four years. He said: 'I can't become a professional appealer, otherwise people might say "What on earth is old Bader beefing about now?"' And in the end, he might destroy the very causes he was trying to help.

In June 1945, Douglas was posted back to Tangmere as a group captain to run the Fighter Leader School there. It sounded a marvellous job, but it brought short, sharp disillusionment. The spirit seemed so very different from 1941, and so was the attitude and approach. Somehow he felt he did not fit into this fresh era and was happy to accept an alternative posting as commanding officer of the Eastern Sector of Fighter Command. This was based at North Weald and extended from north of the Thames Estuary right up to Norfolk. The sector embraced airfields like Bentwaters, Martlesham and Duxford. At the sight of Duxford, memories of 1940 and the Battle of Britain practically forced themselves on Douglas. He had already got back into flying condition and he found a Spitfire which he used almost continuously to travel from one station to another. By coincidence, Laddie Lucas was commanding Bentwaters after VE-Day. He later married Thelma's sister Jill, so they were all closely related after that event.

Lucas had only to watch Douglas in the air to know that none of the skill had been lost in those intervening four years. A lot of people might have regarded Douglas as an exceptional fighter pilot with a good deal of risk and devil-may-care about him. Laddie felt that although this was true as far as his wartime background was concerned, they might not realise the perfection and precision of that flying. With over-modesty, Laddie felt that to an 'amateur' like himself it was particularly noticeable. Those pilots like Laddie, with the perception to do so, really noticed how beautifully all the Cranwell-trained men flew – with a degree of pure precision that the amateurs professed they could not match.

Douglas used to ring up Laddie early in the morning sometimes and say he was coming over to Bentwaters for breakfast. An hour or so later, Laddie would look out and see the Spitfire, with D.B. painted on it, doing slow rolls and upward Charlies and all that sort of thing. Douglas did several circuits and landings, involving tight turns on the run-in and then he put the fighter down absolutely on the point of stall, perhaps taking no more than seventy to eighty yards of the runway. Laddie observed other pilots watching from the dispersal huts, absolutely electrified at the sheer skill.

One of the things Laddie always felt about Douglas's flying was that he was the master of the aeroplane. Laddie flew with people sometimes when he felt that the aeroplane was flying the pilot. Douglas regarded the aeroplane as his servant, but one he treated very well. And of course, Douglas may not have had any legs or feet, but he had wonderful hands. When he put down an aeroplane in these small areas with such delicacy, his hands were gentle, caressing, coaxing.

He soon had a suitable occasion to demonstrate his abilities. VJ-Day passed and on 1 September he was told to organise and lead the Victory Flypast arranged for 15 September. A symbolic date. He had to lead twelve Spitfires, which would be followed by Beaufighters, Mustangs, Meteors – and all the war's fighters. The date was of course significant as being just five years since the climax of the Battle of Britain. Clearly this would be nostalgic for The Few: men like Stan Turner, Denis Crowley-Milling, Bob Tuck, and Peter Brothers.

When they first considered the overall plan, Dermot Boyle had the good sense to come over to Bader. 'Look, Douglas, what's the form for this? What do you think about joining up?'

Douglas replied: 'Well, sir, there's only one way of joining up and that's by timing. It must make sense that as we're all coming from different directions, we all set our watches to the same time.'

Dermot Boyle agreed, so it was to be the first time that synchronisation had been used to control a flypast like this. Douglas always remembered the night before the 15th. There were all these aces, group captains, wing commanders and others, covered in decorations from 1940 onwards. Some of the chaps who had been leading formations for a long time were saying:

'Oh, hell, I can't fly on the right-hand side, I can only fly on the left.'

Someone else was saying: 'I *can't* fly on the left.'

Douglas said: 'I don't give a damn about that, because I'm flying in the middle. That's your problem, old boy!'

Next day dawned cloudy over London. Signals from 11 Group Fighter Command said that the formation would not take off unless there were 1,500 feet cloud base, or some such arbitrary figure. Dermot Boyle and Dowding were both at North Weald, and talked to the dozen Spitfire pilots. The weather was still marginal, raining with a bit of cloud. Finally, Dermot Boyle, who had himself been a pilot of considerable distinction, said: 'I reckon Douglas decides whether they fly or not'. Douglas very much appreciated that gesture, but replied, 'Let the chaps who are going to fly decide'.

It was a Saturday. Peter Brothers recalled that it was quite dangerous, as their squadron was composed wholly of all these aces: pretty tight and pretty hair-raising. They all reckoned they were just that little better than the next man. They staggered off the ground and gradually shuffled themselves into the sort of shape that looked like The Few who had borne the brunt in 1940. They passed over London below 1,000 feet in the end and it all went off with due success. It seemed to mark not only the end of the war, but for many of them, the end of a phase in their lives.

Douglas Bader, W.G. Glowton and Sir Keith Park with the Battle of Britain class locomotive *Fighter Pilot*. *(Hulton-Deutsch)*

On 15 September 1945, Battle of Britain pilots flew from North Weald for a fly-past over London to celebrate the fifth anniversary of the historic battle. Air Chief Marshal Lord Dowding is seen in conversation with Douglas Bader. *(Hulton-Deutsch)*

Douglas Bader climbing into his Spitfire, 1945. *(Hulton-Deutsch)*

Chapter 15

Douglas decided with some sadness to leave the Royal Air Force. He realised that he could not serve overseas in a hot climate for any length of time, and he was not going to stay on with restricted postings. He felt this would be unfair to the Service. He also knew he could not go on pretending one could live in the past, or on past achievements. That was never his outlook. So one Saturday in March 1946 he drove the MG from North Weald to Ascot. In June they moved back to the flat where they had lived before the war, in North End Road, Kensington. Then Douglas rejoined Shell, the company he had worked for throughout the far-off 1930s.

One of the best things about the job was that Douglas had his own Proctor monoplane to fly, and almost at once he was invited to take a trip in it with Lieutenant-General Jimmy Doolittle, a Shell Company vice-president in the USA. Doolittle was rather like Douglas, a man of pulverising dynamism. And like Douglas, he had a war record in the air, having led the famous first US carrier-borne raid on Tokyo early in the Far East war. In the following twelve months, Douglas flew practically all over Europe and Africa in his Proctor.

In March 1947 he found himself down Lagos way with the single-engine aeroplane. The Shell man in the area wore a monocle and spoke a number of languages fluently. Douglas was flying this gentleman over a particular part of West Africa, where the thick jungle below looked like endless bunches of parsley from four or five thousand feet. The vegetation was so dense that if anyone fell in, they would not come out – and even if they survived a crash, no-one would see or know where they had gone in. Douglas and his passenger were just between the end of Lagos lagoon and Benin City, cruising calmly over an especially jungly bit of terrain.

The single engine stopped.

Douglas fiddled about with things, but absolutely nothing happened. They started to glide down towards the trees. Douglas said to his companion:

'Put your hands against the front, because if we hit the trees, we'll go forward pretty sharply. I'll do my best.'

The Shell man turned to Douglas. He had a face with a fine Roman nose, and his monocle was still stuck securely in one eye. It had no attachment to it. Then he slowly took the eyeglass out, removed his handkerchief from his khaki jacket pocket, polished the monocle and then wrapped it in the handkerchief, which he replaced in his pocket. Only then did he take up the position Douglas had advised, with his hands on the coping. As far as Douglas was concerned, this did a lot to ease any gathering tension, and he had another go at the engine. By the time they had lost half their altitude, and the jungle was looking less like parsley and more like treetops, the engine started as suddenly as it had stopped. Douglas took advantage of this at once and a potentially dangerous situation was over.

When they got back to Lagos, he realised that there was fuel starvation somewhere. This was not the sort of thing Douglas wanted to happen again, as he was due to go down to South Africa by way of the Kalahari Desert. At the nearby RAF station, Corporal Williams and Douglas together took the carburettor to pieces, without result. Then they disconnected the pipes from the two fuel tanks. There was a union in the middle where the pipes came in, and the pilot switched to outer or inner. In the petrol pipe from one outer tank into the union, they found the union stuffed with khaki-coloured wool, which somehow must have got in during manufacture and assembly. That was the tank Douglas had been using when the engine failed. Not surprisingly. During this trip, the Nigerian heat caused rashes to form on the stumps of Douglas's legs, but talcum powder helped him.

Later on, Douglas was down in Lagos again, this time flying a twin-engine Gemini. A tall African called Joseph used to drive him out to the airport and back, and this man became a firm chum. One day Douglas asked him:

'Would you like a whizz round in the aeroplane, Joseph?'

'Oh, master, I would like that very much.'

So Douglas took him up very early one morning. A certain amount of the usual haze was gradually being burned off by the sun as it got up. They took-off from the airport, about twelve miles out of Lagos. At once they were in this cotton-woolly sort of stuff, and through it into bright sunshine by about 1,500 feet. Beneath them was no sign of the ground, which Douglas knew would appear in the end.

Joseph was obviously enjoying it all and looking at everything inside and outside. After they had been up for some ten minutes, he turned to Douglas and asked: 'Master, how you find your way? There are no signposts in the air'.

Douglas pointed to the radio compass. 'Look at this. Watch that arrow.' He turned it into the beacon and the arrow swung round accordingly, then stopped. He added: 'That's where the airport is. We will follow that arrow and we'll find ourselves over the airport'. Joseph glued his gaze to the radio compass. About ten miles off, Douglas went through the cloud, very wispy by now, and underneath were the trees. He said: 'Keep looking ahead and you will soon see the airport'. In a few minutes, there it was. Douglas pointed to the radio compass and chuckled, 'White man's ju-ju, Joseph'.

After landing, they got into the Humber Hawk. Douglas sat beside Joseph, who started to drive back to Lagos. The African was clearly contemplating all that had happened to him in the last hour or so. After a few miles in comparative silence, he turned to Douglas and said: 'Master, there is not so much foot palaver in the aeroplane'. Douglas thought this was an astute comment, because Joseph had three pedals in the car and he had not seen Douglas do much with his feet.

In fact, when Douglas used to fly up to the end of the war, the problem of his feet proved fairly simple. He did not have to use toes, like people do when driving. For the rudder bar was a bar pivoted in the middle – and Douglas put one foot on each end of it. To move the rudder to turn to the right, he pushed with his right foot, pressing that side of the bar. Similarly for the left.

When he first flew an aeroplane after he had lost his legs, he wondered whether he would have to adjust himself or the tin legs so that they would operate the rudder bar. He thought it was bound to feel different. But when he put his feet on the bar and took off with Peter Ross, to his gradual astonishment it seemed that Douglas had never flown any differently from how he was flying then. Nothing at all had changed. He could feel the rudder bar and he knew what he was doing with it. Later on, too, when he was being tested at the RAF Central Flying School, they could find no difference in his abilities.

Douglas said to a doctor at that time: 'I seem to be able to feel where my legs are'.

The doctor explained: 'This is something nature supplies you with, when you lose a limb. A sort of compensatory feeling'.

Then later again, neither the Spitfire nor Hurricane had foot brakes. This was lucky for Douglas, as if either had employed these, he could not have managed. Because, of course, he could not do what an ordinary person could do – bend his toes and the front of his feet. Their method of braking was by hand.

When Douglas got his own aeroplane after the war, all he had to do was arrange for the foot brakes to be taken off and fitted on the side of the cockpit as two hand brakes. So it all boiled down to what Douglas's Nigerian friend Joseph had observed when he got out of the aeroplane and into the car: 'There is not so much foot palaver in aeroplanes'.

One of the first trips under the umbrella of Shell was in 1947 when Jimmy Doolittle arranged a tour of the US to see some of the thousands of American veterans who had lost limbs in World War 2. This in fact marked almost the start of some thirty-three years of ceaseless travelling to help the disabled all over the world. For the rest of his life, in fact.

Strangely enough, however, it was the case of a little boy that Douglas remembered best from that entire US trip. He visited the Shriner Hospital in Chicago and met Dale Richey, who had lost both his legs in an accident. He found Dale quite bright and able to cope. Douglas told him: 'When you grow up, you'll be able to dance and lead a completely normal life, just like me'.

Dale said: 'But say, mister, I don't get it. I've got no legs – but you have'.

Douglas replied: 'No, I haven't, but anyone can get a pair like these. I'm in the same boat as you and everything will be easy. Think of this as a game that you can play quite well and you'll be all right. You believe me'.

This was true, because if a child loses his legs at an early age, he can almost put on artificial ones like a pair of skis. For a child is very adaptable and receptive and responsive and when young they do not really notice it fully. It may sound a severe thing to say, but Douglas firmly believed that if anyone had got to lose their legs, the earlier they lose them the better. But this was not the end of the Dale Richey incident.

Just as Douglas was leaving the boy, his father turned up and was introduced to Bader in the corridor. Douglas told him he thought Dale would be quite all right and that he seemed to be full of spirit. But then the father said:

'The trouble is, I'm afraid Dale doesn't realise yet how serious it is.'

Douglas felt strongly about this: 'Look, he must never realise that it is serious at all. This is the important thing. If he thinks it's serious, he'll have much more of a problem'. The concern of the father was natural and understandable, but Douglas never forgot that lesson from the early days of his experience with helping people. Sometimes it may be a child who needs help, but it can also be a parent that requires advice, even though they do not know it.

While on this American visit, Douglas saw New York for the first time. The miracle of Manhattan lay all around him. The long-awaited, legendary New York skyline loomed out of an early-afternoon haze. Then the first close-up: the downtown skyscrapers of Woolworth, Metropolitan Life and the rest, seen through the great vertical struts of Manhattan Bridge. And again, the fretted filigree of Brooklyn Bridge. On towards the Statue of Liberty – 'Give me your tired, your poor, your huddled masses yearning to breathe free . . .'

As Douglas said so often, it is people not places that come first. People made this city. While in New York on that visit, Douglas was invited to attend a Chamber of Commerce lunch and found himself to be the only 'Britisher' there. The host asked him to say a few words. Douglas agreed and discovered to his delight that the man who was introducing the guest of honour was none other than Courtney Hodges, the Commander of the US 'Foist Army, not the Toid.' Douglas naturally told that story in his best British Brooklyn combined accent, which also quite naturally brought the house down.

In fact, Douglas always felt that to retain a sense of humour was the best way to overcome 'a comparatively minor disability' like the loss of arms or legs. He deliberately used the word minor because he never regarded the loss of his legs as anything more than an inconvenience. His point was that paralysis, blindness, arthritis, or something else really crippling could be worse.

Douglas talked to a man in another Chicago hospital who had lost both legs below the knee and reckoned life was 'lousy'. Then he discovered that Douglas was minus two legs and actually worse off as Douglas had only one knee. In that short single visit, they became friends. The man recovered his sense of humour and in Douglas's own words was 'going great guns' when they parted.

It does not matter what language you talk, so long as you do communicate. That is the vital thing in life. Or so Douglas always maintained. When he had been in one of the POW camps in Germany, he was taken to a military hospital for an X-ray. While there the doctor asked him if he would care to visit some of the 'enemy' soldiers who had lost legs. Douglas did not refuse. They were human beings with whom he had something in common, so he helped them as much as he could.

Ironically, too, at the same time as Douglas was a prisoner, people used to write to Thelma for advice. The letters would come from men who had lost limbs or the relatives of them. Thelma would write back to them and give exactly the sort of forthright advice she thought Douglas would have given. She told them practical things like the usefulness of Johnson's baby powder and any other products Douglas had rubbed in or otherwise found good. Thelma found that if she ever had to say something about getting rid of sticks, they would tend to get hostile or at least be sceptical about it.

Back on the American trip in 1947, Douglas met Harold Russell in San Francisco. Both Russell's hands had been blown off while he was serving as a soldier during the war and he had been fitted with two metal hooks instead. He was the youngster who stole the post-war film *The Best Years of Our Lives*. Douglas met Russell and his wife while they were having a meal with a man called Walter McGonigle, who had lost his hands in World War One. So neither of the two men had a hand between them, yet each coped perfectly well with their metal hooks. With those mechanical extensions to their faculties, they grasped a knife and fork and they cut and ate a piece of steak just like anyone else. Douglas accepted these two Americans as normal to him in their present state, with hooks not hands. It was all part of their personality. Their lack of hands was utterly unimportant because they had made it so. They told Douglas that they both preferred hooks to artificial hands, which might look better but were not nearly so useful in operation as a hook.

Douglas did some definite, tangible good on this visit. He told one man 'You'll have to get rid of that stick, you know.' The man looked at him, as much as to say 'No, I won't.' Then the light gradually came into his eyes and he began to think 'I wonder if I could . . .' Just seeing Douglas striding down the aisle of a hospital ward was often enough to start this train of thought. And that was the important thing: sowing the seed of intention. The rest would follow.

While touring one hospital, Douglas noticed an American trying to walk in the type of parallel bars he had not seen since his own pre-war days at Roehampton Hospital. Without any preamble, Douglas went straight to the crux as usual.

'Come out of there.'

'What do you mean?'

'You'll never get anywhere fiddling about in those bars.'

They were trying to teach the man to gain confidence in walking, but Douglas always insisted that, wherever possible, people should have no sticks or crutches, and he told them so.

The American retorted: 'What do *you* know about it, anyway?'

Douglas said: 'Well, I do know – because I've got two artificial legs myself – and I've only got one knee:' He pulled up his trousers to show the man and then demonstrated how well he could walk.

'Well, Goddam', said the American. He came walking out from the false protection and comfort of the parallel bars.

Then taking the advice one stage further, Douglas met a man minus both legs in Toronto. He was walking well with the aid of a stick, but Douglas said: 'Chuck that stick away – you don't need it.' The man had simply required reassurance that he could manage without the stick, and he was quite ready to do so. Yet only someone in a similar condition would have been able to convince him: someone who had actually done it. Douglas certainly qualified as a man who had lost his legs and survived.

After the war, Douglas went back to his pre-war bone-setter Harold Langley. Douglas got various aches and pains, ranging from nerve spasms to sciatica. Langley was one of the original bone-setters and was not rough. He got his fingers and thumbs into wherever the pain was occurring and would gradually fiddle around. It could be soothing or painful but never violent. Coaxing a nerve from where it should not be was bound to hurt a bit. His fingers felt the place and found it instinctively. Then he put the part back where it ought to have been and told Douglas what to do to stop it happening again.

All through the years since the mid-1930s, Douglas occasionally had a sciatic nerve tied up somehow. All his leg nerves were tucked in anyway – they had to be. But when the sciatic nerve started, every few seconds for a night and even a day it was like an exposed nerve and physically jumped. The leg kicked and it just went on and on till Douglas could be treated. Thelma had seen him with the sweat dripping off his temples by the strain of it. The wet weather might bring it on, or something else. Then the pain was like excruciating tooth ache that would not stop. Once Thelma had to send for the doctor and told him over the phone: 'You'd better bring morphia with you.' Inoculations had been known to produce the nerve reaction, but there was really no way of telling where or when it might start. Yet outsiders would never know if Douglas was suffering any discomfort from this nerve trouble or from soreness of his stumps, which inevitably also occurred from time to time. He always hid the pain.

The next trip Douglas undertook for Shell was an extremely long flight in his Percival Proctor. This started early in October 1947 and his goal was South Africa, a great distance in a small aeroplane without any radio. In those days there was still some fun left in flying, before it had become hide-bound by the inevitable regulations created through the crowded sky of the subsequent decades. Then there were few if any controls and the light aeroplane landed where it intended to do, and went on the next leg when the pilot chose to.

It was a good idea to have two people on such a major trip as this, in case anything went wrong, and Douglas's companion was an ex-bomber pilot, Ian Debenham. Their first overnight stop was Biarritz, at a hotel devoid of residents. They came down to a meal in an empty dining room, completely surrounded with a panoply of wealth. They both ordered fish and for some reason changed plates. Ian's turned out to be bad and he was up all night. A small aeroplane with two people and all their luggage in the back is not the best location to have a stomach ache, but somehow they reached Lisbon and then Tangier. They decided not to go over the Sahara Desert from Agadir, so swung westwards to the Canary Islands, Dakar in French Senegal, Freetown and Lagos.

Douglas had been as far as this before, but did not know the country any further south. They headed for Leopoldville, capital of the Belgian Congo. The next place after that was some fifteen miles away from its position as indicated on the map; they were navigating with a map only sixteen miles to the inch, so the margin of error came to a whole inch. The night stop was Elizabethville, at the south end of the Congo, and from there they cruised on at a steady 120 mph to Broken Hill and Livingstone. They saw the Falls as they flew in, but the famous landmark was not falling very much, as it was the wrong time of year or something and the rains had not come. The total effect looked like a cold water tap dripping rather desultorily over an enormous sort of cavern.

While at Johannesburg, Douglas went to Pretoria, where a meeting had been arranged for him with Field Marshal Smuts. The elderly statesman was kind enough to receive Douglas in his room in the Parliament Building. From the window of that room, Douglas imprinted on his memory the view down an absolutely straight street, where the jacaranda trees were in profuse bloom.

'It is a privilege to see you', Douglas opened, and meant what he said. He remembered always that Smuts looked straight at him and replied:

'Not at all – I'm always delighted to see a *good* man.'

Douglas felt this to be one of the simplest and nicest compliments he had ever received. This was a historic room as far as South African affairs were concerned. Smuts pointed out to Douglas: 'There's the General's chair'.

Douglas said: 'Of course, sir, I had forgotten – you fought against us in the Boer War'.

'Indeed I did', Smuts said with no hesitation, apology or explanation.

It was not long after the meeting that Smuts died. Douglas felt lucky to have met him. So often in life, he thought, one wanted to see these great men and some stray chance robs you and then suddenly it was too late.

Douglas contracted malaria while at Johannesburg and quickly lost two stones. Despite this setback, he recovered with his customary resilience and was able to visit a hospital in the diamond city. Here he encouraged a Major Murray Kerr to throw down his sticks and called him to come on and walk without them. But Bader stressed later: 'I'm no miracle man. Please make that clear. I help, but it is only help. The boys do the work themselves.'

Then down to East London and more hospital visits. Douglas met a certain Corporal Burger, who had one leg off at the thigh and the other one below the knee, almost identical to Douglas's own situation. For half an hour, the soldier tried to walk, spurred on by the familiar Bader exhortations. By the end of that period, Burger had reduced his previous average time for hobbling a sixty-foot stretch from one minute to just a few seconds.

At Capetown, Douglas and Ian Debenham stayed for nearly a fortnight. There was a wonderful Scots chauffeur who worked for Shell at Capetown. Douglas swore that he virtually ran the company out there. If he took a dislike to anyone, he had a simple remedy: he refused to drive them. The classic case was of a rather autocratic man who had come out from London. Halfway from the airport to the general manager's house, the Scotsman stopped the car, took the visitor's luggage out of the boot, dumped it on the dusty South African road, and called to him in his best accent:

'You can bloody well walk the rest of the way!' Then he got back into the car and drove off.

Douglas asked this chauffeur if he would like a ride in the aeroplane.

'What? Fly with you, you mad bugger!' But after a few days, Douglas won him over and together they flew around Table Mountain.

On the return route from South Africa, Douglas decided to fly up the west coast, which took in the Kalahari Desert. 'There were no beacons or that sort of nonsense in those early days', Douglas recalled. They walked into the pilot's flight room and told the man where they were going and worked out the duration of the flight. As they walked out of the room, the chap behind the counter asked: 'When do you want overdue action taken?' Douglas thought this was a jolly cheerful thing to want to know.

'If I'm half an hour late, alert everyone instantly. I shall be within half a mile of this line I've drawn on my map.'

The chap said in the clipped Afrikaan accent: 'Don't worry, old boy. If you land in the Kalahari, police are there within five minutes to find out if you've got any illicit diamonds with you.'

Douglas and Thelma Bader in the garden of their home at Ascot with their Golden Retriever, Shaun. *(Hulton-Deutsch)*

Douglas and Thelma at home. *(Hulton-Deutsch)*

Douglas in his MG sports car. *(Hulton-Deutsch)*

Douglas Bader did a great deal to help the limbless and he is seen here at Queen Mary's Hospital, Roehampton. *(Hulton-Deutsch)*

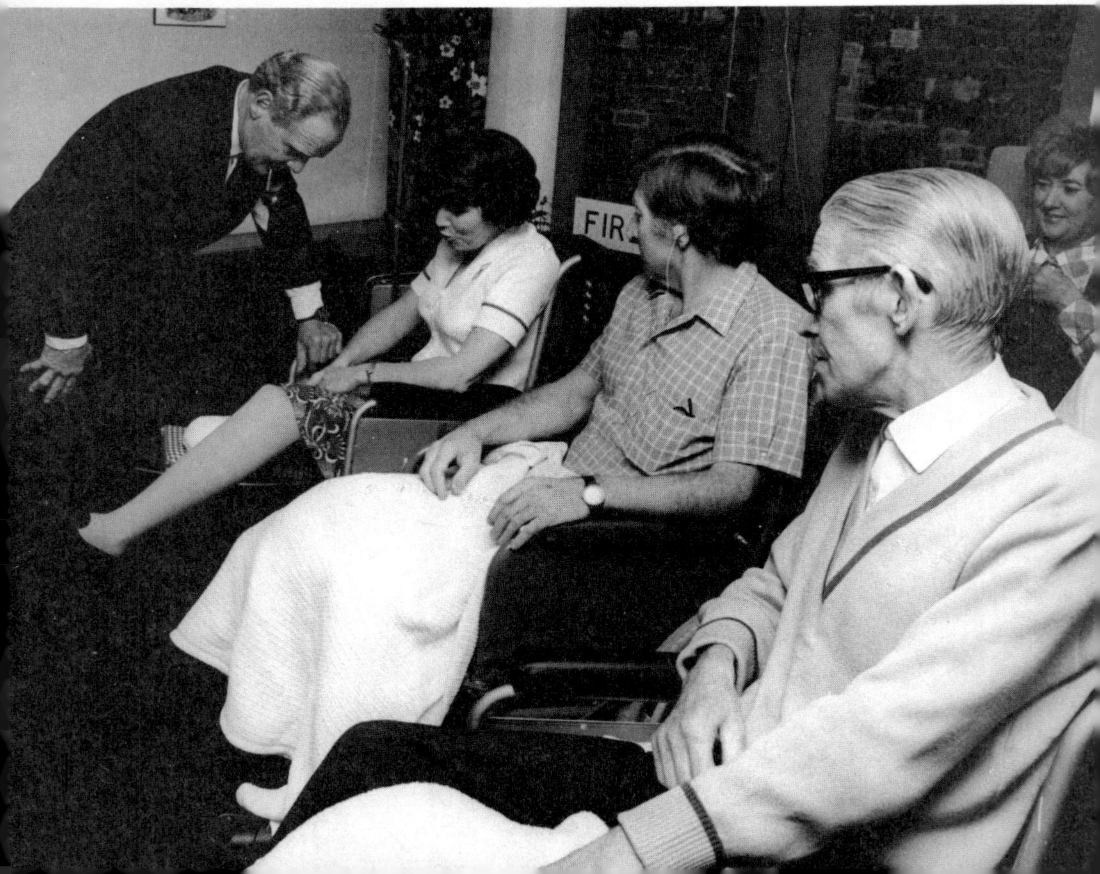

CHAPTER 16

Thelma told a friend at the end of the war in Europe: 'Peter Macdonald is very keen that Douglas should take the Blackpool seat – but it wouldn't work because he is not a conformer. He would only be there a month or two and they would have had enough of him!'

Once the General Election of 1945 was announced, Douglas got a phone call from Macdonald, his old adjutant back in the Battle of Britain days, and himself a Member of Parliament.

'Look, what about standing as a Conservative candidate?'

'Nothing would induce me to do such a thing', Douglas responded.

But Douglas did agree to go up to London to meet someone. Macdonald gave him the address of a large house in Hampstead quite near the Heath. It was the home of Roland Robinson, who seemed quite a pleasant chap and was the Member for Blackpool. This seat was being divided because of the increase in population, and as a result Blackpool South constituency would be created. They were very keen for Douglas to stand for this new seat, as it would be an absolute certainty for the Tories.

He was strongly pressed to accept the offer, but the trouble was that Douglas was never keen on politics as such. He had very definite views on politicians and the things they did – or didn't do – for the country, and he did not particularly fancy becoming one of them. Denis Crowley-Milling from 242 Squadron was there with his wife Lorna. It suddenly dawned on Douglas in the first few minutes that the politicians were collecting as many war heroes as they could to stand as Tory candidates, because they thought that the popular appeal of those officers in uniform would be irresistible. Douglas realised that he would get a safe seat but realised too that as soon as he opened his mouth to say something at all controversial, it would be rapidly shut for him. Thelma already knew Douglas sufficiently well to appreciate it would not have worked.

They were very pleasant about the whole thing, but Douglas still said NO. They asked him to think it over, but he added: 'No – I don't want to think about it. I'm quite certain in my mind'. At the same time, the Conservatives had been approaching other distinguished pilots like Max Aitken and Laddie Lucas.

Although Douglas was sure that politics were not for him, it did not stop him trying to help his friends where and when any practical assistance was wanted. Laddie Lucas was standing at West Fulham in that first election after VE-Day. Douglas was forthright: it was in his nature. He was not a compromiser. This could be a strength and a weakness, but his nature was such that he was a positive person. Douglas supported anyone who spoke for Britain, whether Conservative, Labour or Liberal. In fact he might equally have gone to speak for a Socialist, certainly a Liberal. He was a great patriot. He had good friends in all parties and he took a very broad view. That was what might make him so unorthodox among politicians of any persuasion.

So Douglas went down to support Lucas, who was standing against Edith Summerskill. The election proved to be acrimonious, one of the bitterest Lucas could recall. This meeting was in a school hall two or three days before the poll and was very crowded and quite a bit heated. Douglas got up to speak to a cheer for himself and his uniform. He let fly with some real pro-British feelings in tremendous vein, which raised the emotions. But there was a chap at the back of the hall who kept shouting out: 'Just a minute now. I've got it here. King's Regulations. It says here that officers in uniform are not allowed to address public meetings'.

They kept telling the man to shut up as they had special dispensation to speak in uniform, but he would not do so and this rather marred Douglas's debut. But there was no doubt about the public adulation for him. Altogether that was a strange time, with Laddie Lucas freely admitting that he could not know much about what was going on in the political world. Douglas chuckled about it afterwards and though Laddie got in, he reckoned that the chaps who came to speak in his support cost him several thousand votes! Douglas also spoke for Henry Longhurst and considered he cost him a few votes, too!

Douglas's next venture on to the political platform came early in 1948 when Air Vice-Marshal Don Bennett was contesting a Croydon seat for the Liberals. Bennett had commanded the Pathfinder force of Bomber Command during the war, so that was good enough for Douglas. He knew the man and liked him. When asked why he was supporting the Air Vice-Marshal, Douglas replied: 'No-one is trading on my disability. I have just come down to support a jolly good fellow. I would like to see him creating a row in Parliament. Never mind the political label – it's the man who matters.' Bennett did not get in. Douglas did not mind who he spoke for, as long as the man was a friend of his. The old loyalty question.

Then came the 1950 and 1951 elections. Laddie Lucas had a shot at Brentford and Chiswick, where the sitting member was Francis Noel-Baker. They got him out and Laddie in. But not without trials and tribulations. Douglas got on to the theme of Britain being firm in the world, and then in the middle of it an explosion engulfed the hall. The old ladies in the front rows leapt out of their genteel skins. Laddie Lucas recalls it as the only time he had actually heard a gun let off at a political meeting.

Then the fireworks started, too – real as well as verbal. Douglas was determined that people were not going to get him down, but as he pressed home a point, they let off fireworks to distract attention from what he was saying. This was all part of what he described as 'the further adventures of the legless ass'.

One thing Douglas did notice about Laddie Lucas was that in 1945 his stock answer had been 'I'm a Churchill man' to all the questions hurled at him. Then five or six years later, Laddie had time to do his homework and Douglas was amazed to hear this smooth, suave chap saying to some especially awkward customer's questions: 'Now that is exactly what I hoped you would ask me'.

Laddie's final memory of Douglas and politics came later. Lucas spoke first and had been delivering a powerful piece for the United Nations. Then Douglas got up on his behalf and the audience heard him develop a blistering onslaught on that organisation! Someone at the back called out: 'Hey! Which side is this chap on? Is he supposed to be supporting the candidate?'

What Douglas objected to about politics and politicians was that there was too much talk and too little practical action. Laddie Lucas always remembered his example. There was a boy called Derek Dimmer in Laddie's constituency who served as typical of literally hundreds of similar cases. He had been run over in a serious road accident and his left leg had to be amputated at once. He had thirty or more operation altogether, as his other foot had also been crushed. Derek was given an artificial left leg and began to walk with the aid of crutches. His parents wrote to Laddie asking if it would be possible to get Douglas to come and have a word with the boy when he was next near the district of Chiswick.

Laddie arranged the meeting and went into the house with Douglas. The lad was sitting there looking slightly sheepish. The first thing that Douglas said to him was:

'Where's your football, then?'

The boy looked at him as if he were a bit mad, so Douglas repeated the question, 'Where's your football? Don't you play football?' Then they went out into the street, borrowed a ball from someone, and Douglas started to kick it about with Derek. A few other boys soon joined in and before Laddie could believe his eyes, there was a football match in full swing. In a period of perhaps ten minutes, Douglas had transformed this boy from being in a passive state into a dawning of realising that things need not be as bad as he had feared.

'Never let that thing get you down – and never let it be an excuse', Douglas told him before leaving. 'You've got to live with it, but you can always master it. Don't listen to anyone who says you can't do this or that. That's all nonsense. And make up your mind you'll never use crutches or a stick. Then have a go at everything. Join in all the games you can. Go anywhere you want to go. Try anything.'

The effect was remarkable and the boy progressed steadily. He discarded his crutches for sticks and later put away those as well. Laddie kept in touch and as a further result of Douglas's visit, some wealthy businessman set up a trust fund for the boy, providing for his education and other needs. And all this was done anonymously. Incidentally, Douglas would never permit publicity unless it was to help someone or some cause.

Douglas's last word on politics was: 'I've been begged to go into politics, but I've always said no. I wouldn't touch it. I want to keep my integrity. I have said I'd be prime minister, but I wouldn't go into politics under any other condition. It was a good laugh, but it's not so silly as it sounds because your mind is clear. You know that you've got to *do* something, and you haven't got all tangled up in the intrigue and the corridors of power. You see, politicians these days think in such a complicated way. They don't think simply. My view of politics is that you're a Conservative, Labour, Democrat, Republican, or whatever you are. But once you become Government, your party allegiance stops or should stop. Because your allegiance goes to the country. It's as simple as that'.

But back in the spring of 1948 the Labour Government had inherited a host of shortages and problems from the war. Many things were still rationed and on coupons. To help meet shortages of clothes and other things, various organisation were started. Some ex-WAAFs, for instance, started a Nappy Service. There was also a place in Walton Street called Batman! Thelma used to say to Douglas: 'We must get hold of Batman' to do something or other. Then a chap would come round and press Douglas's suits – he only had about three anyway. Rather aptly the man's name was Taylor and he broke away from Batman and came round to see to Douglas's suits once a fortnight. The charge rose from ten shillings, to fifteen, to thirty shillings.

The Baders were not well off after the war and places like Batman gave Thelma and her cousin Sue the idea of launching a little service of their own to augment their incomes. The name was Bachelor Service and its purpose was to mend and renovate personal and household linens. Douglas was not keen on the idea at first, but relented a little. They used to take in socks, shirts, linen, anything, and farm it out to several helpers. Douglas used to come back to the North End Road flat sometimes and find Thelma mending strange socks.

'What the hell are you doing?' he would ask her.

'I'm mending socks.'

'Well, they're not *my* socks, that's sure!'

'No – I'm being *paid* for these!'

Young chaps used to call round with shirts needing buttons; socks with holes in them; and various other first-aid for clothing. Even sheets to be sewn up. Thelma and Sue did very well and could have made a lot of it if they had developed it. Sue acted as secretary, as she was working on *Harper's Bazaar* at the time. She used to take a mountain of mended stuff home at the weekends and they would dash round delivering it together. Douglas helped, too, by taking them in his car, although he never fully approved of the venture. He had to admit that it was good stuff while it lasted, but as things gradually came off coupons, the demand dropped, the moment passed, and the little service gradually died a natural death. It had served its purpose and belonged to the era of the late 1940s.

The Bader's golden retriever Shaun was also an integral part of the same post-war years. And when one thought of Douglas one also thought of the dog not far away. Thelma was loved by Shaun with equal devotion and it was Thelma herself who had arranged the marriage which produced the dog. Both his parents were in the Royal Air Force, Shaun's father belonging to Hugh Dundas. Shaun was born at Tangmere, but when Thelma moved to Ascot, he naturally went with her.

Then after the war when the Baders were reinstated in the London flat, Shaun went along too. The dog could do everything except speak and Thelma loved him very much. But he was no gun-dog. He had no idea about that at all. Laddie Lucas had their red setter called Red, who had been duly trained. The two families used to take them both to Windsor Park occasionally where there were lots of pheasants and birds. Red would be setting and pointing and doing all the right things. But Shaun, although lovable, had no notion of what it was all about! He would trundle up on the scene like a canine carthorse. As he bounded and thumped, Red used literally to look over his shoulder in apprehension. He knew from bitter experience that Shaun was going to do something like this and spoil things. And of course all the winged life within a mile radius would fly away quite happily. Red, with his exquisite russet coat, used to eye Shaun as if thinking 'I wonder if I will get any of them before this oaf comes along'.

Despite his apparent faults in this direction, his prowess really showed on golf courses. Douglas and Shaun were mad on each other from the moment they met. He went to golf with Douglas regularly. Shaun was terribly keen on golf. He really took an interest, and watched each shot. But he did put opponents off. He used to lie there just in front of the tee where the unfortunate player was about to drive. He crouched some twenty or thirty yards ahead of the tee, and then as the ball was struck, he veered round and bounded off, belting after its trajectory. One of Douglas's opponents used to dub Shaun 'the furry fucker!' Once on a fourth tee, Shaun was crouching down as usual in front, but as he turned, the drive hit him squarely. But he still went on to find the ball, often leaping in the air to register his protest over the poor quality of the mis-hit shot.

Then he had the extraordinary habit of circling over where the ball had gone. He used to find them but would not pick them up. He went over to the spot, and then sort of pawed the ground around so that Douglas would be able to find them. Douglas and Shaun were a couple of invincible buccaneers. Shaun could do no wrong. Like the friends of Douglas.

Shaun eventually developed athlete's heart. Thelma used to take him up to Kensington Gardens every day, but he took to walking so slowly that it became painful to watch. He put one foot in front of the other very laboriously, as if asking her why he had to go out at all. Then he could not get upstairs to their top floor flat.

Douglas phoned the office at Shell one Monday morning to tell his faithful secretary Joan Hargreaves:

'I shan't be in for a few days. Shaun's dying.'

They took him and buried him at the eighteenth hole of the Royal

Berkshire golf course. A day or two after Shaun had gone, Thelma and Douglas were both committed to attending an air race event. Thelma had to wear dark glasses all the time and even Douglas was insecure. They never had another dog. Douglas always kept a photograph of him on his desk at Shell, right up to the time of his retirement from the South Bank office.

Dogs seemed to love Douglas. Laddie Lucas swore that every time he and Thelma went there, Red used to smile at them. In return, Douglas loved dogs, and in fact all animals and nature generally. In view of the subsequent attention given to pollution, preservation, and the belated realisation that the quality of life is more important then the quantity of consumer goods obtainable, it is good to recall Douglas's words in support of the National Anti-Vivisection Society: 'If science conflicts with normal decent standards then to hell with the science and let the standards be preserved. I believe that if you are cruel to animals, you brutalise yourself. We saw this during the war when the Germans – who are quite reasonable people – brutalised themselves by cruelties in concentration camps.'

Douglas appreciated sooner than most people that factory farming and all the rest of the inhuman attitudes of man to animals does much more than condemn the creatures to existences below any acceptable levels. It also diminishes mankind far below the animals.

One of Douglas's earlier onslaughts was to join the battle raging about stag-hunting. In accepting an invitation to become a patron of the League Against Cruel Sports in Britain, he wrote: 'I would go even further than the few so-called blood sports you identify. If I had my way, I would abolish all zoos where animals are kept in cages'.

It was then no more than logical for Douglas to come out in strong support of Goldie the Eagle, whose twelve days of freedom in the Regent's Park area of London found an echo of admiration in the hearts of many lovers of freedom. Douglas expressed it well: 'I detest the thought of wild animals and birds being kept in cages unable to walk about at will or use the wings that God gave them. Surely it is time to abolish cages. The camera has replaced the gun. It is long overdue that the open air and green grass should replace the cage. Animals should not be frightened of human beings'.

Thelma and Douglas both had strong views on the subject of animals. This is an extract from an article he wrote, once again long before the fashion for conservation and preservation dawned on the world:

> 'We all remember the outcry over the export of horses from Eire for slaughter on the Continent. Despite all this, there is one ghastly and growing traffic in animals which should be stopped as soon as possible. Too frequently we read in the papers of monkeys dying in transit by air from Asia or Africa to Europe or America. Sometimes they have been suffocated through being crammed into space too small to accommodate them. Monkeys, mongooses and other species are trapped in

> their natural haunts and sold to the zoos and laboratories of Europe and the USA.
>
> In this day and age, it is hideous to contemplate the sufferings of these animals captured in a hot country; crammed together with barely adequate food and water; and put into an aeroplane and flown thousands of miles, terrified by the noise and unaccustomed feeling of being in the air; and landed in winter at the cold airports of Europe and America. And then they may lose their short lives in experiments by scientists. It is a shameful reflection on our human standards that this can be allowed to continue.
>
> We will kill animals for food; we kill them if they endanger human beings. This is inevitable. In any case they die quickly. Scientists say that they use animals in search of knowledge to benefit the human race. But the word science covers a wide field – from experiments on animals to nuclear weapons. Knowledge can be used for good or for evil and the record shows that science has no moral code. It is time this sacred word was put in its proper perspective. Being a so-called scientist does not exempt a man from the normal moral obligations of a civilised human being. Kindness to animals must form part of such a code.
>
> There are rules and regulations laid down by the International Air Traffic Associations, but there must be wide loopholes, since too often animals die in transit. The RSPCA are always vigilant, but it is clearly beyond their scope to deal with this ghastly trade effectively. If the air transport companies won't take a lead now, let us have a law prohibiting the transit through an airport or aircraft of any nationality carrying such cargoes.'

Perhaps Douglas felt so strongly about animals being caged because he recalled what it was like spending those years in captivity himself. I think that a psychologist would find that a reasonable assumption.

About this time Douglas's mother was left a widow, with the death of his step-father. For the remaining years of her life, Thelma and Douglas made sure she was cared for adequately. They were equally kind to Sue's mother, their aunt.

Douglas's name was liable to crop up at any time and place. Quite out of the blue, the War Crimes Tribunal at Nuremberg heard how Hermann Goering actually admired him. On being told of Douglas's escape from hospital in 1941, Goering was reported to have said: 'This Bader seems to be the very devil of a fellow. I must get to know him'. When Hitler and Goering heard of the escape for the first time, they both flew into their familiar rages, but it was on reflection that Goering had disclosed his feelings about Douglas. Presumably he admired Bader for his flying skill as well as overcoming the loss of legs.

CHAPTER 17

At the start of October 1948, the Baders started one of their most ambitious trips in Douglas's tiny Percival Proctor V. They set out from Croydon for New Guinea! Rather like one of those epic pre-war flights by aviation pioneers.

The route would take them to Rome, Athens, Baghdad, Basra, Karachi and Singapore. When asked about Thelma's role on the flight, Douglas said: 'She is coming to act as my air hostess. She'll pour out the tea en route'. They flew to many exotic places all over the world subsequently, but no trip was more memorable than this one. These were to be the most fruitful, most productive, most interesting, most fascinating years of their lives, when they were probably at their happiest.

The great thing was that it meant so much to be able to say 'our lives' as opposed to just Douglas's life. Because if a husband goes away and returns to tell his wife 'I met a most amusing chap over there', the whole thing is somehow different. It is not a shared experience. Whereas in later years they were able to sit at home – if they ever did – and say 'By Jove! That chap looks exactly like the bloke we saw in Djakarta in '48, do you remember?' It made their lives so very much fuller. The New Guinea trip was still in the happy days with no nonsense about airways and clearances. They had no radio and they simply bumbled along at their own pace.

Impressions remained of places and people; like the primitive granite-grey rock of the Hautes and Basses Alpes. Then a solitary lake showing turquoise amid the wildness. The Riviera erupting with colour and Monte Carlo strung in splendour at the sea's edge. Incredibly deep-green water fringed the Italian coastline as Elba loomed large, and white clouds puffed a delicate tracery across it.

The peaks of Corsica pointed starkly away to starboard, rising wild through more cloud-clusters. Point San Stefano and Monte Cristo Island with the first of three large blobs of lakes lying inland. Then Rome. On down the leg of Italy: blue sea, green shallows, white foam, brown breaches. Then their first glimpse of the Greek Islands, looming like legends out of a faint purple mist. Douglas was always attached and attracted to Greece: its heroes more than its places, perhaps. Places are merely identified because some people did some great act of gallantry or something there.

Then out of sight of anything for a few minutes: an endless elliptical horizon of sea and sky. Much later, on to Baghdad and Basra. On the fringes of the desert and almost within earshot of the surf breaking on bone-white beaches. Towards Karachi and to India. Specks in the sea, and away to the south some palm-fanned, emerald-and-coral isles set in a sapphire sea. Turquoise reefs etched only a few feet below the surface.

And eventually Thelma and Douglas found their way in the little Proctor right across India to Calcutta and then down the Burmese coast to Singapore. Here the scent of flowers drifted in through open doors and windows, from the brilliant purple bougainvillaeas, hibiscus and the wonderful white frangipani petals. While tall palms stood sculptured to the sky, the call of strange birds awoke them. A slight heat-haze blurred the distances, inviting them still further East. They were 8,000 miles from Britain. Thelma loved the flowers especially.

Douglas made many flights to the Near, Middle, and Far East. That first one with Thelma was the forerunner of them all. One day flying at 9,000 feet in a small aeroplane, he suddenly sighted Khartoum. This historic city lies a thousand air miles south from Cairo at the junction of the Blue and the White Nile. He had not realised before that one of them really was blue. He literally followed the course of the river for more than that distance from Cairo, as it wound its wriggling way through the parched desert flanking each side. He saw small towns and villages only on its very banks.

Three hundred miles up the Nile from Cairo lay Luxor, with its tombs of the Kings of Egypt. Tutankhamun and Rameses and the rest. The heat was 107 degrees when Douglas landed at Luxor, but dry and bearable. Intriguing statues piqued his curiosity, while he was amazed to find that the paintings on the walls of the monuments – hewn from the solid rock of the Valley of the Kings – were brilliant with the colours that time had been unable to dull.

As he flew on out of Egypt into the Sudan, stopping at Wadi Halfa, and spun off the final five hundred miles to Khartoum, some of the names seemed familiar to him. When he overflew Berber, his mind clicked. He had been flying down over the route taken by Lord Kitchener of Khartoum. The Army chief had taken his men out of Egypt by river and by march, building his communications behind him as he went, and he rehoisted the British flag over Khartoum. Douglas crossed the cataracts of the Nile 150 miles north of the city.

General Gordon had been killed on the steps of the palace by the Dervishes and the English had been driven out. People can see Omdurman, where the battle was fought, and go down the river to Gordon's Tree, where the flying boats used to alight. The whole of the area still had the strange flavour of British history. He mused on the fact that he found it tedious flying the route 9,000 feet up in the cool air at a speed of 140 mph. Kitchener and his men had done it by boat and on their flat feet and fought on the way, too. The temperature went up beyond 107 degrees, but he did not suppose they had any tropical clothing or iced water in those days.

At Khartoum the moon rose wanly, shedding a mysterious milky sheen on the clouds. Douglas felt he could have been there in the age of the Egyptians, yet as with the Greeks, it was the people rather the place that made most impact on him.

A month or two before he was due to do another trip to Singapore, Douglas received a letter from a judge's wife in India saying that there had been an accident to a Dakota aircraft at Nagpur. One of the pilots was in hospital, having lost a leg as a result of the crash. The letter asked if Douglas could find time to write to the pilot, who was down in the dumps about the future. Douglas replied to the request and the letter was read to the young pilot. He said: 'I'd like to meet Bader – if he can fly with no legs, there's some hope for me yet'. It transpired that this pilot, named Bhatt, had lost his leg below the knee after he had done some heroic work in extricating passengers from the burning Dakota.

Normally Douglas flew across India from Karachi via Delhi to Calcutta – and out down the Burmese coast as with Thelma on that first trip. He worked out that by diverting from near Bombay to Nagpur, he could stop and see the Indian pilot and then continue to Calcutta next day. This time he was flying a Dove aircraft and the month happened to be June. The heat in central India was almost unendurable for Europeans, and especially for Douglas with the discomfort of his artificial legs. He was flying actually to Sarawak via Rangoon and Singapore with an engineer and a radio operator, and as they came down to Nagpur, they spotted the wreck of the Dakota spread to one side of the runway. The airliner had misfired on a night landing. Nagpur was quite a large and crowded city. They stayed with the Shell man there and then Douglas went to see Bhatt in hospital. He still seemed rather depressed as he asked Douglas: 'Do you think I shall ever fly again?'

'Of course you will', Douglas reassured him. 'If you are keen on flying, no power on earth can stop you. You can do anything you want to do.'

This seemed to encourage the Indian. Douglas continued his flight to the Far East, but they subsequently corresponded, and Bhatt told Douglas that he had improved a lot and got a job as a link instructor at Calcutta.

Then a year or two later, Douglas stopped at Calcutta as usual. He was just sitting down in the Shell office writing up his log-book of the flight so far, when he noticed white trousers and legs just in front of his gaze off the edge of the table. Douglas noticed instinctively that one of the legs was a tin one. He could always recognise it. As it came to a halt in front of the table, he looked up and it was no real surprise to see that there was pilot Bhatt beaming back at him. They had a tremendous reunion and the Indian told him that the artificial leg was fine. He had heard that Douglas was due to stop in Calcutta en route, so he had walked across to see him and show him, in fact, how he could walk. Another satisfied customer:

On yet another flight through Pakistan and India, Thelma and Douglas happened to be in Karachi while the Duke of Edinburgh was on his way back to Britain. The British High Commissioner asked them to attend a reception for the Karachi residents to meet Prince Philip, but Douglas said, 'Look, you need not ask us, because I would hate to feel that just being passers-through we had forced our way in and kept someone else out, who might not have the same chance again'. But the High Commissioner assured them that they were additions, and would not be excluding anyone.

Douglas and Thelma both liked the Duke very much. They felt he was always at his ease and had got the touch of talking to anyone. Douglas noticed that he had an extraordinary way of making people feel comfortable in his presence.

'What on earth are you doing here?' Prince Philip asked Douglas.

'I'm flying back from Singapore actually.' The whole thing was natural and spontaneous.

Then Douglas observed a practical case of his putting people at their ease. The great thing was that he asked a question and then bothered to listen to the answer. That was one of the secrets of his success. The Duke came up to a fairly young couple next to Thelma and Douglas and asked:

'Tell me, how long have you been out here?'

'About seven or eight years, sir.'

'Now what made you come here? Did you answer an advert in a paper saying a chap was wanted in Karachi?'

At once the man and his wife became relaxed. Before the meeting they had been noticeably and understandably tense. The Duke gave the impression that he really wanted to know the answers to the questions he put to them. Which in fact he did.

Douglas was going down the Persian Gulf at one time and landed at Muscat. The Sultan had some armed levees, some of whom came from his own people and others were men from Baluchistan. When Douglas landed at this little airfield at the bottom of the Persian Gulf, he discovered that a friend of his, Colonel David Smiley, was commanding the Sultan's men. Smiley said to Douglas, 'Look, old boy, I wish you'd come and see three of my chaps. We had some trouble out here with bandits and they were lashing mines about the place. We went in to clear things up and these chaps stepped on them and lost legs. I think you ought to come and see them.'

Douglas could scarcely resist an invitation like that. When he talked to the men, they all seemed cheerful as they hopped about. But Douglas was very dissatisfied. He asked Smiley: 'What happens to these blokes? Do they get artificial legs? What goes on?'

Smiley said: 'No. What happens is that the Sultan will give them a handful of money and they'll leave and go back to Baluchistan'.

Douglas was incensed. 'Well, this is quite wrong. I think the British ought to do something about it. After all, you chaps are British officers.'

Smiley said: 'We've tried, but the War Office say it's nothing to do with them and entirely the Sultan's business'.

But Douglas was far from appeased. 'I'll bloody well go back home and raise a stink about this.'

When he got back to London, he did try to do something and told people what a disgrace he thought it was about these men and what could be done. But nothing helpful happened. As a last resort, Douglas appealed to his own organisation, the Shell Company. He got on to the men concerned and told them the situation. 'It will cost about £150 or perhaps £200 altogether to give these chaps a leg each and I think it would be a jolly good thing to do.' Shell agreed, saying they would be quite happy to do this and pay for it, but it would have to come as a gift from Douglas personally. They said, 'We don't want to start a welfare state down at Muscat and Oman'.

Sam Elworthy was the Royal Air Force Commander in Aden at that time. He later became Chief of the Air Staff. Douglas wrote to him, explaining the whole situation and asking if he would send one of his doctors up to Muscat to measure the three chaps. The Commander said certainly, and his group captain medical officer flew up there. Douglas had previously arranged for the measurement plans to be sent out from Roehampton. So the three Baluchis were measured for their legs and duly got them.

As must be clear by now, Douglas was often up and down the Persian Gulf in those days. About a year or so after the men received their legs, he happened to be out there again on oil business and thought to himself 'I must find out how they are'. He rang up the new colonel stationed there.

The colonel said: 'My dear chap, you must come up and see these fellows – they're delighted with their legs, and they're all as mobile as hell!'

Douglas asked: 'What do they do now?'

The colonel told him that one was a tailor, one worked in the orderly room, and the other one was a cook. Douglas hurried to meet the trio. They all said practically in chorus, 'Oh, Sahib, look my leg, very good, Sahib!' Common humanity had succeeded. The legs were pretty simple to manufacture, once all the measurements had been properly taken. Douglas chuckled over it. He thought, 'Shell pretend they're hard, tough business people – but they're not really at all!' In fact, as a result of Douglas's own efforts and the company's great generosity, amputees in *seventeen* countries throughout the world walked on artificial legs provided by Shell. So there must be something in private enterprise after all.

This time Douglas had a Gemini aircraft and his goal was the middle of the Sahara Desert! He and Roy Snodgrass, also of Shell, were going to find a survey party that was to survey and dig under the desert with a possibility of striking oil. They started from Algiers.

The vital thing about the Sahara is that you can only go there between October and March, when the weather is not too hot. During these months the midday temperature is in the seventies and there are no dangers from sandstorms. The sky is crystal clear and remains like it day and night. The only time people get into trouble is when they disobey the natural rules of the desert and come in at the south end, try to drive across it, and get tangled up in sandstorms. But if you obey the rules, flying in the Sahara presents no special problems.

Douglas and Roy found it amusing that there was certain equipment you had got to take, even though you may only have a small aeroplane. They had the small aeroplane and its capacity was either two persons plus some luggage, or four persons with no luggage and no petrol. The fuel was clearly desirable.

They went to see the French aviation authorities before they set out, and these enigmatic Frenchmen explained all the equipage they would be obliged to carry. Medical kit with anti-scorpion serum. That seemed sensible. Then two gallons of water or some such equivalent quantity in litres. To this was added as a necessary stipulation, a huge quantity of rusks, light pieces of toast which they had to stuff into the tiny Gemini in the best places they could. They also had to take a Very pistol with cartridges, so that they could signal with flares in case of accident. Finally came a rifle and a specified number of rounds of ammunition. When they eventually got all this stuff stuck in the aeroplane, with the rifle literally sticking out, Douglas said to the Frenchman: 'What in heaven's name do we want the rifle for? Are the natives unfriendly?' He was thinking of Beau Geste and so on. The Frenchman said: 'Non, non, mon ami. If you land, fire three shots every hour and the French Foreign Legion will find you, wherever you are.'

And off they went. Algiers sprawled peacefully, the runways of its airport looking like taut yellow ribbons as they climbed. For the first two hundred miles south of Algiers, they had the guidance of a tarmac surface below, before it swiftly changed. The great thing about flying across the Sahara is to remember to do what the French call 'Suivez la Piste' – follow the track. The piste in this case soon became a foot road which was in fact a furrow. Acknowledging the Atlas Mountains by a slight climb, they detected the transition to the Sahara, while white puffs of clouds cast shade-clusters on the barren ground. Moving shadows. The terrain turned to total desert, formless and a bit frightening. The surface tones ranged through biscuit to bronze, and from grey to black. Occasionally strange tracks rulered across the wastes, like string stretched over a vegetable garden.

They were really in the desert now, clinging to the piste as it threaded due south, angling off a bit to south-east or south-west. Despite the odd fork or two, they could not miss the main furrow, white across black rocky surface for a way and then back into the endless sand again. Douglas managed to keep a course, but the map was not very good. They reached the town where Douglas wanted to stay the night. From there the goal was 293 miles straight into the blue. He said to Roy Snodgrass: 'Look, old boy, will you go down by road tonight, because I don't want to arrive tomorrow and find there's nowhere to land – assuming I can find the place anyway.'

So Snodgrass set off in a desert truck made in France and specially adapted with tyres for driving across the desert. He averaged 50 mph and it took him six hours to cover the distance. He got there and radioed back late that night, telling Douglas they would put up smoke signals. At the moment the message came through, Douglas was sitting talking to the French transport manager of Shell, who was running the affair. He asked:

'Look, how do I find this blessed place in the morning?'

'No trouble at all.' The Frenchman got hold of a menu, which Douglas kept over the future years. Then using the dining table as support, the man started drawing. 'You go straight down la piste till you come to Fort Mirabelle.' He drew this on the side of the line as if to imprint it more clearly on Douglas's mind. 'Just past here is a fork. The left goes to . . .' and he spoke some unpronounceable nameplace. 'You take the right fork. You go on down that one. After you've gone a hundred miles or so, you will see a huge cairn of stores – you cannot miss them, they are at least fifteen metres high. You turn right and then just up that track you'll find the camp.'

Though he had never made such a casual flight plan and on the back of a menu, Douglas thanked him and felt that it seemed to be all right.

Douglas took-off fairly early next morning and positively boomed down the piste at about 3,000 feet. He soon saw Fort Mirabelle – a sort of Sahara Old Joe's Cafe. He went on again till he came to the fork. He took the right fork, thinking it was a pushover – and that he must do more flying by menu. He was timing himself on how long it would take to get to the various stages of the 293-mile flight. About the time he thought he must very soon turn to the right again, he came to quite a lot of little tracks, with the main route going on to the left. He contemplated rather idly whether he should descend and try to spot a signpost or something, and started circling down to have a look. At about 500 feet, he saw a plume of 'smoke' coming across the desert, obviously being made by a vehicle. It was a jeep and the plume was of course dusty sand. He thought that those chaps must know where they were going. They were up to the lot of little tracks, and after hesitating they turned off north towards the right. Where the hell is the camp? Douglas began to wonder. He overtook the jeep and had gone on about fifteen miles, when the camp of white caravans and things suddenly appeared as if a mirage. But the smoke flare was no imagination. Roy Snodgrass had laid it out well.

Douglas landed and they went in to lunch. They were just sitting down to start when the two chaps from the jeep burst in gratefully. They rushed up to Douglas saying:

'Merci, merci, you showed us the way to the camp!'

Then Douglas and Roy flew back and dined with the local head of French civil aviation. The two Englishmen were offered specially prepared and cooked pancakes as a savoury to the meal. Much to the Frenchman's disgust, Douglas added about half a pound of sugar to his own portion. Generally speaking Douglas preferred sweets to savouries.

He flew Thelma to the Sahara on yet another trip, just before they moved into their new home at Petersham Mews, off the Gloucester Road. It was a little house that I got to know well in later years . . .

CHAPTER 18

Thelma and Douglas decided they wanted a house as opposed to a flat. They were on the top floor of the block of flats in North End Road and one of the drawbacks had been the lack of a garage attached. Douglas had to put the car away about five minutes' walk away from the flats every night. In the flat, too, the bedrooms were on the same floor as the living rooms. Douglas always 'set great store by' going upstairs to bed. That always seemed right and proper to him and in the mews house they would be doing this. He was a great man for liking bed. At a reasonable hour of the evening Douglas was 'in bed' and at an early hour next day he was definitely up and about, having enjoyed his eight hours' sleep.

In fact, these regular habits helped to keep him fit through the years, like taking plenty of exercise; avoiding putting on weight, which was not good for him to carry; and not drinking. He was a teetotaller by inclination not ethical choice. He simply did not like any alcoholic drinks, so did not have them. As for food, he had definite likes and dislikes, too, as will emerge. He was a bacon and eggs man, if ever there was one, and loved straightforward British dishes – including sausages. Though in more recent years, the Baders created more exotic menus at their regular dinner parties which became a feature of life at Petersham Mews.

The mews house was being converted when they saw it first. The builders had pulled down practically the entire inside and had not then put it up again, so they were able to alter things as they wanted them. There were not even any stairs and you had to go up a ladder to get to the second storey. Originally it had been stables, like most London mews, and the people who lived opposite had actually been there with horses underneath them. They told Thelma that the clanking of hooves and shuffling about of horses was awful. The upstairs had of course been the hayloft area. The Baders had their own place converted comfortably into two rooms downstairs and two upstairs, plus kitchen and bathroom and dressing room – and the asset of a large garage opening right into the heart of the house. And all this in the centre of London. Here they would be living together for the following sixteen or more years.

Thelma had been part of Douglas's life, and a vital part of it, for twenty-three years before that, and she had supported and sustained him through the years with wonderful spirit. In fact they were completely complementary in every way, gaining from each other's strengths and weaknesses. Earlier on, every day was a struggle for Douglas. But in those earlier times, Thelma was very strong and used to cope with luggage and similar things.

She herself said:

> 'It's true that I've got a truculent nature, too, so I've never given in to him.
>
> Douglas was a domineering character. There's nothing derogatory in that. He wouldn't have been able to overcome his difficulties otherwise. In any case he has very definite views on almost every topic. One knows how to cope with this. You can't ever take him by surprise if you want him to do something that he is not going to want to do. You've got to give it time and sell him the idea first. Eventually he finds it agreeable. If he is told, we're off to do something, he'll dig his toes in and nothing on earth will make him do it. Occasionally one hasn't the time to lay the ground and it's always disastrous. Like going to see people he doesn't want to see.
>
> All my life I have been trying to prevent him doing more than he should. In the early days, he was very conscious of people attempting to be helpful. Some people make a fuss of moving chairs out of the way of him and this used to annoy him terrifically. Or people trying to help him up. One admires so many of his qualities. The kindness and the trouble he goes to on behalf of other people. They are fantastic journeys that he undertakes. And quite an expense, too. One would not think that someone who is such a strong character would necessarily have this quality of kindness as well. He can be quite brash to people. Somebody came up to him in dark glasses and said "You don't remember me, do you?" This is the sort of thing that drove Douglas mad. "Well, how the hell do you expect me to in those glasses?" he roared. They then recoiled embarrassed and discomforted. I told him he was rude and he said "Well, people are bloody fools to come up like that."
>
> He must have quite a lot of enemies as well as all his friends. Something else may have put him out before he has even got to these people and he is in a bad mood to begin with. I've seen people positively hostile at some reception or other. And then of course Douglas will suddenly realise it and turn on the charm. And then they absolutely melt and the whole thing is put right. He is a very fascinating character, there's no doubt about that. He is always prepared to change his views if he finds he is wrong. But he has to be thoroughly convinced first, though. Yet it is not everyone who is prepared to change and admit it. He will suddenly see the point and decide.'

Thelma had hit on a crucial clue to Douglas's make-up. She realised and so accepted the obvious truth that there can be no hard dividing lines between qualities present in people. Where does determination become aggression? And is aggression wrong if it is applied to ends that are positive and worthwhile? Douglas's character was still emerging and developing even at that stage, perhaps soon to show signs of mellowing!

Family and friends always meant everything to Douglas, and to Thelma as well. Thelma and her sister Jill were very close. Jill admired her very much. Thelma was very beautiful throughout her life and Jill remembers that as a child she used to press her evening dresses when she was going out. She always thought how tremendous Thelma looked, and regarded her as a best friend as well as a sister. Jill watched Thelma practising the Charleston in her grandmother's house. Thelma was living with Jill's grandmother when she went to the Pantiles and met Douglas. When Thelma first brought him home as her 'young man', Jill was about twelve. Jill and her brother had been told not to keep looking at Douglas's legs, so of course the minute he came into the living room and sat down, they did nothing *except* stare at his legs! He roared with laughter and made a great thing of it, knocking out his pipe on one of them to amuse the children.

Thelma's good looks must have been a boost to Douglas's ego – if he needed one. There Douglas was in the old days, with no legs, no money, and not many prospects apparently. It was amazing that he could get someone like Thelma and that she turned out to be precisely the right sort of person for him. Her parents were not keen on the idea of the marriage and her mother had told her: 'What a life you're going to have.' She thought it would be absolutely appalling and was often saying to Thelma: 'Of all the people you *could* have married . . .'

Douglas had little family of his own. Because Jill was younger, she was like a sister, or even a daughter to him. He used to take her out. He always loved young people and they always loved him, too. They felt an affinity. He could keep them in order, but always lightly.

Strangely enough, Jill did not meet Laddie Lucas through Douglas. A friend said to Jill: 'Do come to dinner on Saturday – I've got a great chum I'd like you to meet; Laddie Lucas.' She looked at a picture of him in a book of air aces before she met him that day, and had an extraordinary impression that he was the man she was going to marry. They were soon engaged. Then Douglas came back from prison camp and both being fighter pilots, he and Laddie took to each other at once.

So they were all very lucky, because Thelma and Jill were so intimate that neither would have liked it if either had married someone the other did not love. It was very cosy, in the nicest sense. Douglas gave Jill quite a generous sum for her to buy her trousseau. Incidentally some people have traded on Douglas's generosity, as he finds it very hard to refuse a favour for an old friend. So Jill and Laddie were married just after the war ended, and Douglas and Laddie started to play golf together. That was at the stage when Douglas was still restless and finding it hard to adjust.

Soon after the war, Jill can remember a man saying to people at large: 'Bader was just an absolute nuisance. He was always trying to escape when it was quite impossible. And then we had our privileges taken away. We all had to suffer for him'. The man was clearly upset by being a prisoner-of-war and his personality was not equal to Douglas's. For there was never any secret that Douglas took it literally as his duty to try to escape if humanly possible. Jill also heard people say that they were frightened of Douglas; their personalities could not contain his; they would be overpowered by him.

Being the sort of strong personality that Douglas was just did not go with pleasing everyone all the time and acting very gently. Yet he was so kind, generous, jolly, gay, that these more than made up for any difficult moments. He had plenty of pluses. Sometimes Douglas cancelled an arrangement and people got disappointed but they could never know why he had done so. Every hour of every day was an effort. They did not try to project themselves into his shoes, or rather, his legs.

Of course he could be a bit awkward! Douglas rang friends one day and said 'Thelma and I want to come and see you – now!'

They had to say, 'We're very sorry, Douglas, it is awful, but we've got somebody else here and we haven't any room.'

Douglas was put out and said so! 'Well, I want to come now.' Next weekend was no good. It had to be now. At once. The present was all. Though he thought of the past, and also looked ahead, this living instant was all-important, all-embracing. Yes, he might remember back, but he made a rule never to go back. He was always looking for new experiences, new ways to help.

Jill and Laddie had a son who became ill. While they were unable to be with him, Thelma and Douglas used to go. The boy was less than two at the time. Douglas used to take his hand and sit for hours with him. At that time, they thought the boy would never come out of hospital. The medical people told Jill not to keep going to the hospital as it would upset her too much, so that was when Douglas went instead. He talked to the nuns and admonished them for being depressing. They must be hopeful for the child, he insisted. You could do almost anything if you have the will and the nerve. It was his living philosophy.

He helped Jill through all that time, and so did Thelma, when Jill realised what a blow it was. It seemed more like forty years than the four it actually lasted. Just being close and in touch with someone having such a powerful and positive outlook helped Jill Lucas. And that identical philosophy has helped her many times over the years whenever she has felt depressed. If someone were feeling a bit sorry for themselves, they could suddenly think 'What have I got to complain about, compared with Douglas?' And he never did complain. Never.

Jill and Laddie could not have another child while he was alive, because he took all their time and money. Then they were very lucky because they had two boys. When they were young, Douglas told them in fun that if they were in a bunker on the golf course and wanted to throw the ball out – they must remember to take a bit of sand with it and wave their club about in the air, as if they had just played a stroke. They thought Uncle Douglas very funny indeed.

Later on, Douglas came down to David Lucas's prep school to watch the rugger. He was able to do that by then. When he arrived at the school, it was like the Pied Piper. From every window, heads began to appear. The word had got around. Boys came running down from every part of the place. They all stood around in the entrance, with Douglas joking with them all. Then he watched the match and went out at half-time to tell them that they had played like a lot of left-handed cripples. And they thought that was very funny. David gained a lot of prestige through having Douglas as an uncle.

Douglas did appeal to children. They just wanted to come and listen to him talking. Jill was watching on that rugger day, as they all stood there, absolutely transfixed. They came originally because he was Douglas Bader, but then they became mesmerised by himself. They responded to him naturally because he was childlike, too; not childish, but childlike. He had great innocence, and if someone said something pleasant to him, or wrote him a nice letter, or gave him a present unexpectedly, he was really and genuinely delighted.

He was very kind, though he could say cruel things. He could seem to be hard, when in fact he was very soft. He would speak honestly. He was impatient and restless. He had to be moving all the time. It was in his nature, and he had to go on or else he would not survive.

Later still, Douglas and Thelma were good to her father after her mother died. They used to take her father around with them, down to Sandwich or up to St Andrews. All over Scotland touring they went, and he enjoyed that. He used to say of those trips: 'I'm going touring with King Bader!' Because when they got to a hotel, they were received like royalty. People rushed to open doors to them. But things like that did not impress Douglas. Thelma and Jill and Laddie became his family, because he had not many of his own. But he and Thelma were also close with his cousin Sue Goodhew.

Victor and Sue Goodhew met and married about 1951. Douglas was then rather more caged-in than later on. At a party he looked tense and tended to put his head down and charge across the room to talk only to them. He did not then seem anxious to meet new people, unless he had something in common with them. Sue Goodhew thinks he found it difficult to meet new people, though no-one would ever have known it. She thinks he was full of contradictions. He had an innate shyness, yet he was one of the greatest extroverts possible to meet. How could these apparent anomalies exist? He could be outrageous or rude, having an inclination to shock people.

Sue Goodhew maintained fervently that Douglas was one of the greatest Christians alive. He came up to see a little girl in St Albans one day in the 1950s. Victor Goodhew was an MP and this was then his constituency. She had lost a leg and had cancer, so was not going to live. Douglas and Thelma both came. At once Douglas was able to get this little girl to walk, and then he said to her: 'Oh, look, they've made that leg too long for you. Tell them to take half an inch off it.'

Sue often felt that the pain Douglas suffered may have made him a bit out of humour at times, yet he would not refer to it. Sometimes when he and Thelma came to stay with the Goodhews, his stumps would be bleeding. He might have partly created this by overdoing it, but he felt he must drive himself on with exercise. He knew that if he were ever to become immobile, he would be very static indeed. The doctors told him a long time ago that once he let those muscles go, they would get flabby and he might not be able to walk.

No-one could really realise what it was like to lose one's legs, unless they had seen Douglas without his legs walking on his hands. Of course, he had great strength in his hands. He might take off his legs if he got an attack of the 'jumps' which he could not control. No-one would know if he were in bad pain, only from the greyness in his face. Sue Goodhew felt he ought to strike a balance between overdoing and underdoing things. But from Douglas's point of view, two rounds of golf a day were what he felt he had to do frequently to keep going. With Douglas the urges were magnified.

Laddie Lucas came out of the House of Commons eventually and Victor Goodhew was in. This was a signal for a typical Bader outburst. 'You bunglers don't know what you're up to.' If you accepted this without argument, he got even more annoyed. But if you turned round and said 'Well, what are you going to do about it?' he would react at once. He liked to be rough with you and for you to be rough back. Then he respected you for it, even though your ideas might be diametrically opposed to his own.

He could be irritated by people and things. Perhaps he behaved in a way that someone would not do normally. Sometimes he could not project into people's lives, just as they could not always imagine his. He could be incredibly sympathetic with a person who had lost a limb, knowing what they had got to suffer and face, yet over an everyday thing he could be intolerably abrupt. Usually he either loved you or loathed you.

Douglas never complained over the years and this attitude certainly rubbed off on Thelma – not that it needed to. So later on she never complained about her illness. Thelma had been terribly patient with Douglas. Living with someone as impatient of other opinions as Douglas could be, Thelma and her steadying influence were vital. She patched things up for him almost as they went along. Yet she was never a doormat at any time. She stood up to him and loved him. And he respected her opinion on everything and loved her, too.

Yet through any flaws, Douglas's most generous spirit shone through. He went to endless trouble getting some chap down on his luck a job. He gave people money and would do so to his last penny for an old friend.

Through it all, Thelma continued to look after Douglas ideally, shielding, sustaining, always in a discreet way. She virtually never went out socially for the forty-four months he was a prisoner-of-war. She thought it would be disloyal to him and might worry him if he heard. For someone with such a strong character and positive personality herself, Thelma led a very self-effacing, selfless life. Sue Goodhew used to say to him: 'I only hope you appreciate her, Douglas'. He would never have found anyone else like her, and Sue told Douglas that, too. Thelma always put Douglas first, always what was best for him and never for herself.

Completing the family circle in those earlier days was Thelma's step-brother, John Addison. During the 1930s, Thelma and Douglas used to come down to John's prep school to take him out. At that time, John rather hero-worshipped Douglas. Like the Lucas boys later on. John had found that Douglas possessed that boyish element about him. To John he stood for everything exciting and courageous right from the start. For instance, John considered himself to be not very brave, although he went into the Army at the beginning of the war. He was convinced that it was at least partly through the things he heard Douglas was doing that he got himself transferred to the Commandos. He would not have countenanced that normally. In fact he finally left them before they had been in action and went into something else, but the point remained valid.

When Douglas came back from the war, John's parents had the house in Ascot and he was demobilised and returned to studying at the Royal College of Music. It was then a nice family circle and they all used to meet at Ascot. Later on Thelma and Douglas found him a small flat in London's Thurloe Square. John remembers Douglas at that time as simply unique. He was someone they did not treat like anyone else. Douglas had his favourite kind of foods prepared by John's mother. When Douglas appeared, everything and everyone adjusted itself and themselves to him! Whatever he said or did seemed somehow acceptable, although it might well have been offensive from someone else! They were dealing with a man larger than life, and if anyone happened to find any of those things disagreeable, well, it was infinitely worth putting up with them for the rest of him. John Addison had learned quite gladly that he had to accept the whole man and he was powerless to do anything else. It was worth it.

When John's mother and father moved up to London, first to Prince's Gate and then to Melbury Road, their house became a sort of centre that kept the family in touch. A kind of Forsyte Change. Then John married in 1952. He was already becoming well known as a composer and was increasingly involved in the world of theatre, films and music. The result was that he began to see less of Thelma and Douglas than in the immediate post-war period. The Baders were always off abroad somewhere, and John used to be up half the night at work, so their paths just could not cross as frequently as before. But there was one coincidence that brought them together again, and this was when John Addison was invited to write the music for the film *Reach for the Sky*. John did this and found it strange writing love music for the scenes portraying his own sister Thelma, played by Muriel Pavlow. But before the film came the book. It changed the Baders' lives.

CHAPTER 19

Douglas and Thelma were asked many times what it was like having a book written about oneself. Douglas took the point from years earlier that the public interest in him and in them did not stem from his being a successful or well-known fighter pilot, because there were many men with equal ability as pilots. So it was nothing to do with his flying skill. What he realised, without any conceit and in fact in all humility, was that people were interested and inspired by the combination of his having lost his legs, having learnt to walk again on artificial ones, and then having gone on to fly in the war.

When the war started and Douglas shot down any enemy aircraft, the press were always concerned with 'the pilot with the tin legs'. The Air Ministry, too, referred to him in these terms: 'Legless pilot shoots down Dornier'. That was unique then, and Douglas was bound to get publicity for combats, where other pilots did not get it. The underlying thing was always the lack of legs.

Scarcely anyone minds being well-known, and Douglas thought that if a man said he did not like it, he was probably a liar. But it gradually dawned on Douglas that his disability was going to have the most profound repercussions in his life, not because it stopped him doing things but because he became 'an object of interest' to people – and especially to those who had lost legs or limbs themselves. It was this aspect that eventually reconciled Douglas to feeling that instead of being 'rather fed up' about losing his legs, he took it as a 'jolly good thing'. For having got beyond the stage of the problems, he could spend a lot of his time helping other people in similar circumstances, and others over the years who were going to continue to lose limbs. So there would always be new people for whom his experience and actually his name and address would be a help. This greatly expanded his outlook in the most worthwhile way he could imagine.

After the war, more and more of Douglas's friends said to him in these words or similar ones: 'You know, you really ought to write your story'.

Douglas's reply was usually couched in these phrases: 'No – the question of my writing the story simply is not on. Because apart from the fact that I can't read or write, a chap at the age of forty-odd could not, or should not, write his own biography. If he has any sense of proportion, that is to say.'

Douglas felt that for people like Winston Churchill at the age of seventy or so, it was different. He had a lot to write about and he had lived through a vital period of British and world history. But Douglas still said no to his friends. They wanted him to write about having been a good athlete, being in the England class at rugby, and then getting over the loss of his legs in a flying accident 'which was entirely my own fault', as Douglas freely admitted. So the next question was: 'Who is going to write this book, if we've agreed to have one?'

Both Thelma and Douglas had read *The Dam Busters* by Paul Brickhill. Douglas was enthralled by it. The thing that really struck him was that Brickhill had not known any of the men in that immortal 617 Squadron. Brickhill had a short career as a fighter pilot, went out to the Western Desert, was shot down, and became a prisoner-of-war, like Douglas himself. Douglas slapped his hand on the dust jacket of the book and said roundly to Thelma: 'If anyone writes our story, it must be Paul Brickhill'. Douglas felt quite rightly that he had a great flair for bringing things to life; to impart a sense of immediacy, actuality.

'And make no mistake', Douglas always insisted, 'It was *our* story, not only mine. Without Thelma I could not have survived.'

It was an interesting experience, having their story written by someone else. They decided from the outset to tell Brickhill the whole truth. As a result, quite a number of their friends who read the book later came up and said to them with wagging fingers: 'You might have told us you were secretly married in 1933 – when we all thought you were married – in 1937'.

As the book emerged, another thing that struck Thelma and Douglas was that an author tends to think that he has created the people he has written about! He may get so absorbed in his subjects that when Douglas said: 'Look, old boy, that isn't really quite right. That's not the way I behaved on that occasion', Paul Brickhill may have tended to think, 'Don't tell me what you did – I'm writing this book and this is my character'.

Then they would both realise that they had to get a resemblance to truth or an agreement on what they were saying. A normal human being is not so wholly predictable as a fictional character, and does not always react as might be expected – or hold views that might be anticipated. That certainly applied to Douglas. And as John Addison had always found, because Douglas expected loyalty, truth and honesty from people, he usually got them. There could be no double standards for Douglas with the people he encountered. Honesty meant honesty. Hence his suspicion of most politicians of all tones of the spectrum.

Brickhill had his usual flair for atmosphere. Douglas remembered his talking to them about Douglas's Canadian 242 Squadron and saying: 'Look, you obviously can't remember the exact words he used, but tell me the *sort* of thing he would have said'. This is where he got it so right. Douglas then found that Brickhill wrote very much what the man did in fact say. When the book was completed, they gave a proof copy to Jill Lucas to read. She had been with Thelma and Douglas during the war at Duxford, Coltishall and then Tangmere, so she had known all the chaps involved. When she read it, she said to Thelma: 'The extraordinary thing is that Brickhill never met any of those Canadians and yet he has got them so right'. Brickhill worked very hard on the book and got himself really drenched in the atmosphere of the first thirty-five years of the Baders' life. He spent two years researching before he wrote the book and Douglas had no quarrel with the result.

As far as the prisoner-of-war camp was concerned, he knew about this from his first-hand experience. Brickhill presented a general impression of Douglas as having to keep proving himself to go on living. Douglas thought that this was not really quite true, or else he was not aware of it. The only time he felt like that consciously was after his accident when he was trying to stay in the Royal Air Force. Then he admitted he was trying to show everyone that although he was operating on 'a metal under-carriage', he could in fact fulfil the normal duties of an officer. The emphasis in Brickhill's mind was on his trying to prove himself. But Douglas never regarded himself as disabled, and the word did not exist in his vocabulary. Douglas thought that the book pressed the point a bit too far, but conceded that this was only a very small criticism.

The book was an amazing success all over the world.

Douglas had always wanted to meet Winston Churchill, but he had never been able to do so. He was never at Biggin Hill when Churchill was living nearby at Chartwell and used to visit the RAF fighter station. Some of the other aces there had been lucky, including Sailor Malan. Then in 1954, Douglas's late squadron adjutant Sir Peter Macdonald, MP, said to him one day: 'You simply must meet the old boy – he would love to meet *you*'. Douglas said: 'Well, arrange it then, Peter, I'd love to see *him*'.

Peter came back and told Douglas: 'I've made a date for you to meet him in his room at the House of Commons. And I think you ought to give him a copy of your book'.

Douglas thought a bit before agreeing. He got hold of a copy and then wrote in it what he modestly considered to be rather an apt phrase: *To the Architect of Victory – from one of the Few*. And Douglas signed it.

Then they went along. Christopher Soames was Churchill's private secretary and he took Douglas and Peter into the sanctum. Churchill was getting a bit frail by then, but he was still in very good shape for his years – and acting as Prime Minister once again. He had a good gossip with them and his mind unfolded one or two things which he recalled from wartime days. Then eventually Douglas said: 'It's very kind of you to see me and meet me. I wonder if I could give you this. I really would like you to have it – it's my biography'.

Churchill took it, looked at it, read the fly-page with the 'reasonably sentimental' message on it, and then he said in his usual deep tones: 'Thank you. Thank you very much indeed. But you want to beware, because I can retaliate, you know!' Douglas thought that a marvellous remark right off the cuff. For of course he could – with dozens of his own books.

Douglas always referred to the book and the subsequent film as 'Reach for the Sticking Plaster'. Just as he was usually 'the legless ass'. As for the film, this started an eventful few months in the Baders' lives. Douglas was not exactly a shrinking violet about the possibility of this project; but he was most aware that if you had strangers making a film about your life, you were naturally sensitive to the fact that it must be as accurate as it humanly can be. The film people had to be allowed a little latitude, of course, although at the time Douglas did not fully appreciate this. He and Thelma were thinking of it from their viewpoint. Anyway the first script ended up with the hero escaping from a prison camp in Germany and getting home. Having read this with mounting amazement, Douglas said to them: 'Look, this last bit is entirely fictional, because I never escaped and got home. It's quite untrue'.

The film man looked him straight in the face and declared quite solemnly and seriously: 'Oh, I know that, but it makes a bloody good ending, don't you agree?'

The man clearly did not know Douglas or would not have said that: Douglas found that the thing about having a film made of himself was that when you see it actually portrayed on the screen, you think this:

> 'You see a chap staggering about over there who is supposed to be you. Your past is of no interest to you, because you know it all, you were there. You find people depicted, scenes and incidents you recall, words which were actually said – and the whole thing is done by strangers. Your wife is someone you have never seen before. It is not a nightmare but it is unreal. All the people saying things you remember are totally alien. Voices and appearances are all different. You know who they are supposed to be, because they are called by the names of your friends, many of whom in this particular case were dead. So it is impossible for you to view the film objectively. You see the supposed-to-be you, because he's got a pair of artificial legs, and the scene is a faithful reproduction of when you were trying to walk upright for the first time at Roehampton: one you can remember vividly in real life.'

Another difficulty Douglas encountered was that the film involved his loyalties. This proved hard to get across to people. For instance, in his accident, Dick Cruttenden had come to the aeroplane and got him out alone, carried him to the ambulance, and stayed with him – with his great hand over the right leg where the artery had been severed and the blood was spurting out like a tap. He saved Douglas's life. Without him there would have been no Bader story to write or to film. So it was actually of vital importance to Douglas that he should be portrayed in the accident scene and that his name should appear on the credit titles of characters – clearly identified as the man who took Douglas out of the crash. For some reason, this escaped the makers of the film and it was not done and Douglas felt angry as a result.

And again, there was a scene which the makers were intending to cut from the film. This was after Douglas escaped from hospital at St Omer and the Germans found him in the garden of the Hiecques. Douglas asked the makers: 'Have you ever had anyone condemned to death for you? They're bloody well going to be in the film', he insisted. And they were.

There were some brighter moments when it was being made. They did some of the shooting down at Kenley. Among Douglas's Canadian squadron were several Englishmen. And one of the chaps who was in fact English called in to see how things were going there. The actor representing him actually by name was talking with a very strong Canadian accent, and so this chap called the film man aside and said to him: 'Look, old boy, I'm not a Canadian, you know, and that fellow is talking with a Canadian accent'.

'Aren't you?' said the film man. 'That's funny – nor is he.'

But all these things were no criticism of the finished film, which was very distinguished. Eleven years later, Thelma and Douglas saw it complete for the first time together. This was on BBC Television. A lot of the immediate anxiety that surrounded its making and release had vanished with time and both of them watched it and thought it was 'jolly good.' There were some scenes that were so faithfully recorded that they could have been taken on the day that they had actually happened. Both the book and the film have done an enormous amount of good. People who have lost arms and legs have derived encouragement from it all over the world. And as this after all was the main reason for the story being told in the first place, Douglas was satisfied.

Right up to the time he died, Douglas still got letters about the film from Australia, America or other places, where it was shown, as well as some forwarded from the Columbia Broadcasting System. 'They don't realise that one is a thousand years old now, and round the bend and bent and wrinkled and everything else. They still think you're the dashing chap that Kenneth More was. But it's humbling and nice. An awful lot of the letters are from people who have lost legs – and this is a real reward.'

Thelma and Douglas did not go to the premiere of *Reach for the Sky* because they felt it was an occasion for the film people. But of course they had met Kenneth More before the film was made. Douglas said to him: 'Look, Ken, if I can be of any help, do let me know'. But More said: 'If I see too much of you, I shall caricature you'. And he was quite right, for once an actor gets all the movements and all the expressions, it is liable to become an impression or caricature. All he wanted to see was how Douglas played golf and to be able to feel 'That's the sort of character I'm going to portray'. And of course Kenneth More had read the original book, as well as the film script from it. They became great friends and played golf together sometimes. When they did, Douglas said: Look, old boy 'who is walking like who? We've got to sort this out and get it straight:' And then they both went off staggering down the fairway almost automatically.

Joan Hargreaves started working as Douglas's secretary in the early 1950s. Both of them had joined Shell in 1933 and both in fact retired from the company at the same time in 1969. Joan saw the Rattigan film *The Deep Blue Sea* in London before *Reach for the Sky* was even thought of as a book or a film. By a strange chance, it crossed her mind then that Kenneth More possessed Douglas's manner and also his mannerisms. Later of course came the book and film. Also strange, is how people still think of Kenneth More as Douglas Bader. In view of the importance to More of the role, it is interesting to trace the whole story of how he came to play Douglas on the screen and so helped to make the name of Bader more universally know than it already was from the Brickhill book. The presentiment of Joan Hargreaves was also to be echoed in a chance encounter More had at that time, too.

Vaguely Kenneth remembered those wartime illustrations of all the Battle of Britain pilots in the *Illustrated London News*. But Bader's actual existence was brought home to him when he was in the South of France one summer about that time. He was sitting on a rock about half a mile out from the general line of the coast. A man swam out to the rock and asked him: 'Do you know a man called Douglas Bader?'

Kenneth replied: 'Well, I know about him now – just recently because there's a marvellous book on him that's going to be filmed and Richard Burton is going to play the part'.

'Well, if that's true, it's a pity', the man said, 'because you are the only man who could play the part. I know you've done some acting and you're the only one I know who could fit this man. You see, I served with Bader in the Air Force.'

Kenneth said, 'Well, you're too late, old son, because Richard Burton has signed a contract to do it'.

When Kenneth got back to England after his holiday he was with his agent who had been looking after him well. Kenneth told him: 'You know, Harry, a strange thing happened to me on holiday'. Then he told the agent what the man had said to him on the rocks.

Harry said: 'Forget it, Kenny, Richard Burton's got the part already'.

Kenneth said, 'Well, I don't suppose they'd have me, anyway'. Harry was a great believer in fate and always used to say to Kenneth, 'Never mind if you lose a part, Kenny, another one will come along – probably a better one, too. What is to be, will be'.

They were talking about the Bader part in Harry's office. Kenneth had by then made several films: *The Deep Blue Sea, Genevieve,* and *Doctor in the House*. But *Reach for the Sky* was the one he felt could break all box-office records. At that very moment, Harry's phone rang and he answered it. He went quite white. He put his hand over the mouthpiece and motioned with his lips to Kenneth who was on the other end of the line. He said into the phone: 'Yes, what can I do for you then? Yes, he's available at present'. The caller was Danny Angel asking if Kenneth More could come and see him some time next day:

It was only when he learned that Richard Burton was not going to play the part and Kenneth had in fact signed the contract to do so that he knew he had to meet Douglas. Like Douglas, he believed that there was nothing like a game of golf for revealing quickly what a man's character was really like. They fixed up a golfing weekend at Gleneagles with the veteran actor Ronald Squires. Kenneth and Squires played Douglas and a friend on the Queen's Course there. It was quite obvious from the start that Douglas was determined to win. This had to happen – and he did win, of course. When Kenneth got back to the hotel, he asked Squires, 'What do you think of him?' Kenneth had already become very impressed by Douglas's performance and his character. Squires answered: 'I admire him, Kenny, but I don't know yet whether I like him. Time alone will tell. But he's a great man. A great personality. His integrity is beyond question. Whether I like him or not, I just don't know. That is for you to find out.'

That was Kenneth More's first introduction to Douglas Bader and he always remembered Ronald Squires' words.

Kenneth felt first of all that Douglas was not really keen on the film being made at all. If the film worked, he would become an international figure. But he also stood to lose a lot. If Kenneth had made a mess of it; or the producer had done so; or his role in the war had been misinterpreted, all these could have been fairly disastrous to Douglas.

At the end of the golfing weekend, Douglas paid Kenneth a half-compliment, conceding a bit grudgingly: 'Oh, well, I suppose somebody's got to play me – you'll do!' That was all Kenneth More got out of him.

They had their troubles during the making of the film. Douglas was worried about the way his walk would be depicted, and this presented Kenneth with a problem. He went up to Roehampton and told them that Douglas felt concerned by the fact that he had exaggerated the walk. The man there said, 'Mr More, all amputees think this. They all think they walk better than they really do. It's a common denominator'.

After Kenneth had shown him some shots from the film, the Roehampton man assured him: 'That's the nearest thing to a carbon copy I have ever seen. You're certainly not exaggerating the walk.'

As the story progressed, Kenneth made the Bader walk more stable through the years. But when they met later on, Douglas was still liable to protest to him: 'I suppose you're still making me walk like this' – and thrust out his leg horizontally:

Kenneth felt that Douglas could not fully appreciate at the time that they had to do certain things to make a film intelligible to a mass audience. Douglas objected because in one scene, Kenneth was supposed to say something like 'Get it airworthy again as soon as possible – there are a couple of holes in the wing.' Douglas interrupted: 'I said I've got a couple in the glycol tank.' Kenneth said that if they used that line, the audience might fall about laughing. Anyway, as films go, Kenneth was convinced there were fewer liberties in *Reach for the Sky* than in any other film he had ever seen. Perhaps due to Douglas's vigilance:

When Douglas was on the set, Kenneth took great care to ask him how he did a thing. They re-shot a scene of his climbing into a cockpit, when it did not seem right. Kenneth himself was a great stickler for accuracy but he had to remember not to give just an impersonation of Douglas. He realised he had a great deal in common with Bader. He was about the same build, and they shared the same sense of humour. He knew that he had Douglas well in his mind by the time they started shooting the film. Douglas was his generation, although a bit older than Kenneth. So he *knew* Bader. Douglas was the only man Kenneth could recall with an aggressive patriotism positively defying description. Kenneth saw him as believing in Britain, in its destiny, in its honour. Kipling was their God – Douglas was the living personification of all those qualities which Kenneth no longer saw in any other single living person in the post-war age.

When Winston Churchill was talking about a film of the life of he and his wife, he said: 'No-one could portray Clem – she's a light in the wilderness' And Kenneth More knew that Douglas felt that way about Thelma, too. At first Douglas wondered and worried who was going to play Thelma in the film. 'I'm not going to have any cheap little tart playing my wife'. As it happened, they managed to get Muriel Pavlow, who played the part so well – though she could perhaps never have conveyed all the strength Thelma imparted to Douglas over those years.

When Kenneth More went around the Royal Air Force in connection with the film, he found that quite a few people disliked Bader. He decide to try to discover why, and they turned out to be mostly men who had been in prison camps with him. Douglas, as we have said, believed in carrying out the Churchill dictum to hate the bloody enemy. They should never go along with them. They should always make life bloody awkward for them. Douglas carried out that belief and would not co-operate.

People told Kenneth that he made himself so aggressive to the Germans that one camp Kommandant, who wanted to make life easy for the Allied officers, said: 'How can I when this man stirs up trouble? Every time I say keep quiet, he tries to escape or something'. Then they had to stop the Red Cross parcels – that was why he was unpopular with some officers. So it was really because he was living up to what Churchill expected of them all, to prod and provoke the Nazis. In fact, Douglas was almost the only man Kenneth knew who did try to live up to that precept. He was a great patriot. When that is understood, it is realised too that he had no time for people who were not in the same mould. Kenneth pondered that Douglas was like Churchill in many ways – and Churchill had enemies, too. Douglas was inclined to go straight at things like a bulldozer. Kenneth found this a highly admirable quality, but a lot of people did not:

Some time after the film was finished and duly shown, Kenneth went to an RAF mess to open an air display to commemorate the Battle of Britain. All the service men were there with their wives in best clothes and hats. The group captain asked Kenneth over lunch: 'You're going to say a few words afterwards, aren't you?' Kenneth said: 'Yes, of course, if you want me to'.

The group captain said: 'What are you going to talk about, then?'

'I thought, Douglas Bader.'

'Oh, Christ, don't mention his name in this mess. You see those two fellows over there? They were both in POW camps with him and they don't want to know about him. He got all their Red Cross parcels stopped.'

So Kenneth's 'spontaneous' speech he had carefully prepared went right out of the window. The one he had got in mind extolling the varied virtues of Douglas. What those two officers presumably did not fully appreciate was that they had not been engaged in fighting a war simply to receive a flow of Red Cross food parcels.

To the public, Kenneth became their image of Bader, the great air hero. One of the later editions of *Reach for the Sky* even bore Kenneth More's face on the dust-jacket of the book. Kenneth got letters from all over the world as a result of the film, and letters from relatives of many incapacitated people. Some he passed to Douglas where applicable; others he dealt with himself. Kenneth More's career had been well established before the film, but did help to give him a certain financial security, because through his acting in it, he got a good contract.

Kenneth and Douglas remained good friends. They saw each other two or three times a year, usually on a golf course. Kenneth regarded Douglas as ageless. He was still the hero in an age of the anti-hero. Still the supreme patriot in a world where patriotism had become a dirty word. Kenneth More gave me his final word on Douglas as a character who became far more to him than just another part in just another film:

> 'If I was in a tight corner, I'd rather be in a tight corner with Douglas Bader – legs or no legs – than anyone else alive. He looks after people. He's a man of very superior intelligence. Unlike some aggressive patriots, he has a lot of grey matter. He has the courage of his convictions and also a lively and alert mind. To his friends, he is the most loyal man alive. As for his enemies, he would never do them a dirty trick. He would be more likely just to write them off and say: "Oh, I can't be bothered with them, let's go somewhere else". He would never do anything behind their backs. He has made enemies, but I think a lot of it is jealousy on the part of people. He is a glamorous, good-looking man and the fact that he has no legs actually enhances his glamour. People resent the publicity he gets, ignoring the fact that he never seeks it himself.'

CHAPTER 20

The capacity to care. Both Thelma and Douglas possessed this quality in abundance. Work for the disabled gathered more momentum year by year. They were active in innumerable ways on numberless occasions.

Douglas served on many committees and assisted official organisations. Alf Robens had first-hand knowledge of that and never saw Douglas's disposition change over twenty years. Like so many other people, Robens found it hard to think that Douglas had no legs when they were together. He had heard of some of the good work Douglas did, simply because Robens happened to be also interested in work for the disabled. Since 1951 he had been chairman of the training committee for the Queen Elizabeth Foundation for the Disabled, which had a residential college and trained people to be able to go out and work for themselves, earning their own living. This philosophy of self-help was very close to Douglas's heart as well. But Douglas never said anything about his own work; he would just laugh it off. Both men were adamant in believing that people do not want to feel dependent on either private or public charity.

Yet of course the various charities continued to do incredible good, even in the era of the Welfare State, through which they were living. Robens knew that Douglas would go into a place like the Star and Garter Home at Richmond and show chaps how he operated his legs. This was probably more valuable than anything else, because they knew that here was a man standing in front of them who had done it – so everything was possible. Yet he always did this quietly, almost surreptitiously. 'Come on, get out of bed, I'll show you', would be a typical Bader line.

One of the earliest organisations Douglas helped was BLESMA – British Limbless Ex-Servicemen's Association. All the driving spirits behind this had lost limbs, that was the remarkable thing. Sir Brunel Cohen, head of the British Legion, lost both his legs in World War One above the knee, but although he wore artificial legs he rarely used them. He was usually in a wheel chair. He did an enormous amount for the British Legion between the wars and Douglas first met him through BLESMA. Douglas was asked to join them in 1947 in an advisory capacity.

There he met some of the others who were associated with it and were ready to help the men from World War One who had lost legs. James, Earl of Ankaster was another. Charles Dunham, the Secretary, had only one leg. And the Hon. Richard Wood, also. While Douglas was a prisoner during the war, Thelma got a letter from this man. He had stepped on a mine in action and had both his legs knocked off. Thelma wrote to him with encouragement and then when Douglas got home he got in touch with Wood, too. He had lost both legs above the knee, became an MP, walked well, and did a lot of public good.

So these were the sort of men in BLESMA. They all decided to make the thing really work. And they argued or fought the various Governments and Ministers of Health to get more stuff for the men. As the years gathered, disabilities became more difficult for men to handle, so they tried to get things particularly for the men from World War One. They opened homes in various parts of the country and they went on doing it. The need was enormous – and still is.

Douglas opened an extension of a new home for BLESMA at Portsmouth. The Earl of Ankaster introduced Douglas by saying that 'After Nelson, he was the best known limbless ex-serviceman.' A good approach to a naval audience. Bader pointed out that the kindness shown to BLESMA people was much greater in Portsmouth than elsewhere. That was because the people of Portsmouth knew all about war. They had suffered themselves and they had seen their menfolk suffer, so they were more determined than some others to do something about it. King's Road, Elm Grove, Commercial Road – all these had been flattened in the Blitz on that famous naval city.

How vehemently Douglas agreed with the Duke of Edinburgh, who reminded people on one occasion that we should never patronise the disabled. That was the reverse of the policy to adopt. Practical aid was wanted.

Another committee Douglas helped for a while was a Ministry of Health one for the Government. He had been trying to get on it for ages and finally said to a friend: 'Look, it's absolute nonsense not having me on this committee'. He got on it and was the only one on it who had lost any limbs or anything at all! After three years, he got a polite letter saying 'Your time is up – thank you very much'. You must not have a chap who has ever done it himself, that was Douglas's translation!

As a member of the British Council for Rehabilitation, Douglas declared: 'Our first task is not to provide rehabilitation for disabled persons – but to educate employers in the advantage of using such persons'. Again, ahead of his time.

Affiliated Boys' Clubs was yet another of Douglas's interests. He went to one of David Westmorland's boy's clubs and watched some boxing, absorbed in what they were trying to do. If Douglas thought people were on the right lines, he would give all his support and considerable energy.

Westmorland first got to know Douglas through the Saints and Sinners Club. This club raised money for various children's charities. It was formed to bring together British and American people interested in this same subject and raised about £30,000 a year. Douglas was a leading light for a long time, and did so much for handicapped children.

Douglas went to make a speech for an appeal in Scotland on one occasion. When it came to the fund-raising part, he picked out one particularly prosperous-looking man and pinpointed him. He put the man right on the spot by saying: 'What the hell are *you* going to do about it?' The top table were rather embarrassed by this direct approach to one guest, but it certainly produced an electrifying effect. Not only did the man offer to make a large donation, but everyone else did, too! Only Douglas could get away with it – but he did because he said it with a twinkle.

He was a man without any side at all. Of course there were people who disliked him. Because there are always people who dislike men who speak their minds. Yet despite them, his public image was unique, supreme. He could not tolerate people who were not straight or sincere, hence his direct approach on that occasion. He took the offensive, but without being offensive. All this time, too, Shell were absolutely marvellous. They always accepted what Douglas wanted to do and gave him a very free hand. And it cannot be stressed too strongly that this was always done without publicity. Shell took their cue from Douglas and never cashed in on the publicity value. Neither needed to do so.

Douglas made many appeals on radio and television. Two of these were TV appeals for St Loye's College, Exeter – both extremely successful. Typically, he did not sit in a studio at Shepherd's Bush, he went down to Exeter for a day or so with a camera crew and talked to the people at St Loye's. So not only was he reaching the public but at the same time he encouraged the patients at the college.

Douglas got involved with people. While he was playing golf with Iain Stewart, he heard that one of Stewart's workers had a wife dying of cancer. She had always admired Douglas. The husband asked Stewart if he would get Douglas to drop her a postcard, as this would mean so much to her. But Douglas said 'No. Where does she live? Glasgow? Right, I'll fly up and see her'. Stewart met him at Prestwick and took him on to Glasgow. Douglas spent the afternoon with the woman and had tea with her. She could talk about nothing else for ages afterwards and they said that his visit prolonged her life by six months.

Iain Stewart had known Douglas since the early 1950s. He invited himself to one of the Baders' Tuesday evening dinner parties. The table accommodated only eight people, including Douglas and Thelma. Douglas had omitted to tell him that there would be eight present without Stewart! Douglas sat in a corner of the dining room on his golf stick! 'Those bloody people coming scrounging meals', he muttered in mock anger. It was all part of the patter. He did his best to make Iain Stewart embarrassed – and Thelma did her best to make him feel at home at the same time!

Sometimes the inspiration came by remote control. Sixteen-year-old Maurice Mitchell had worn callipers since he had been afflicted by infantile paralysis as a baby. He was so inspired by the Bader story that he threw away his callipers. When he received a special prize from Claremont Secondary School, it could be only one thing: a copy of *Reach for the Sky*.

Mrs Rose Orr was an Australian. She lost a leg and had an artificial one made, which enabled her to get about at home, 'though it felt like tugging the *Queen Mary* around'. Towards the end of 1954 she had her other leg amputated after some years of ill-health. So Mrs Orr faced a bleak prospect as she looked at her future from a hospital bed in Melbourne. The best she could envisage was a wheel chair. For Rose Orr was then seventy-five years old. But things did not work out quite like that. She was under the care of Mr S. F. Read, a leading surgeon in the city. Mr Read had also served with Douglas in the RAF.

'Read *Reach for the Sky*', he suggested. She did.

'I think what he did was wonderful. It has given me the determination to do my best, too. What Bader has done, I must try to do.'

After she had recovered from her second amputation, she thought she would take the plunge and see what sort of artificial legs Britain might have for her. So she set out with her husband by liner, first having bet her doctor that she would walk down Bond Street unaided and buy herself a new hat before her homecoming to Australia again.

During the long voyage to Britain, the Orrs shared a dining-table with a Mr Cave. Rose Orr happened to tell him one day that she admired Douglas Bader very much and hoped there might be a chance of meeting him. By an odd chance, Mr Cave was a friend of Douglas and also attached to the Shell Company, so he told Rose he would do his best to arrange a meeting. On arrival in Britain, Mrs Orr went to a nursing home in London, while Mr Cave presented himself at Douglas's office and said: 'I've just come off the ship from Australia. I've met the most wonderful woman and her husband'. He told Douglas that she was determined to get a couple of proper legs like his.

As usual, the Baders did things at once. They had an early supper and on the way to the clinic, Douglas said to Thelma: 'The old girl's seventy-five, and she's not going to last forever. So I suppose we had better be fairly careful what we say to her and not be too over-optimistic.' But when they went up in the lift and entered her room, they were amazed to find her quite strong and quite cantankerous. They had a good gossip, when Douglas admitted that they had intended to advise her to settle for life in a wheel chair, with someone to push her around. But after seeing that she had a lot of obstinate determination – rather like Douglas himself – the Baders decided to encourage her to get up and walk. She was obviously not really in need of sympathy.

Douglas got on to the people at Queen Mary's Hospital, Roehampton. He told them the problem: that she was seventy-five and wanted to walk. They took her in, fitted her up with legs, and started teaching her to walk. Douglas used to go there to see how she was getting on about once a week. One day when he arrived, she was sitting in her room. He said to her, 'Look here, my dear, what on earth do you want to walk for? You're seventy-five, so you don't want to play tennis or golf or anything like that.'

Rose Orr looked straight at Douglas. 'Look, Douglas, in Australia I've got a housekeeper. That woman talks, talks, talks. The whole bloody time. And I can't get away from her!' That was one of her reasons.

Each day she went to the gymnasium to do her exercises and a month later she was walking unaided, as she had said she would. One evening her husband rang up the Baders to tell them that Rose was out of Roehampton and they were going back to Australia the next evening and invited them to lunch.

Thelma and Douglas went to their table at the hotel to meet them. Rose Orr had a hat with a bird of paradise feather on top. She said to Thelma, as one woman to another, 'I said I was going to walk out and get a new hat and I've done it. And I'm going to walk on board that ship to go back home to Australia.'

After lunch, Rose said to Douglas: 'I'm going to take your arm and we're going to walk to the entrance hall'. The distance from the dining-room was quite a way, through a large lounge bar and then right to the end of a long deeply-carpeted hall. Rose hung on to Douglas's arm. Together they walked down to the entrance and Douglas said to her: 'For heaven's sake, don't fall down, because if you fall, we both will – and I don't know how the hell we would ever get up again!' In a minute or two the Orrs were in their taxi and away.

Thelma and Douglas saw her again later and used to correspond after the Orrs got back home. Rose Orr told them that she was really hotting up all the people over there without legs.

The Baders' trip to Australia in 1956 when they last met Rose Orr was memorable in many ways – for them and all the people they met there.

But before they left on what turned out to be almost a world tour, an envelope came through the little letter-box at Petersham Mews marked Prime Minister. Douglas had never seen one before, so he opened it with a jerk, thinking he was 'going to be arrested for treason at the very minimum!' Inside he found a letter from the Prime Minister's secretary saying that the Premier had it in his mind to put up Douglas for a Commander of the British Empire for services to the disabled. If this recommendation were made, would he accept it? This was a great surprise to Douglas.

Douglas had received all his war decorations from King George VI. So it was rather interesting that when he again received a decoration – a civilian one this time – it should be the Queen Mother who gave it to him, because the Queen was away on business elsewhere at the time of the investiture.

The Queen Mother was so sweet. When Douglas appeared in front of her, she said, 'It is nice to see you again. What are you doing now?' Douglas told her he was with an oil company in a job that involved flying.

'Oh well, you'll like that, won't you?' she said.

She had also taken the trouble to find out some background about his life. She was just as pleasant to everyone there, Douglas observed.

Chapter 21

The first, faint dawn-glimmer; a brilliant yellow-peach morning; sunrise in a vast void. Thelma and Douglas were heading east again, this time in an airliner. It was October 1956 and the start of a round-the-world trip. The story of aid for the disabled continued at once in Hong Kong.

Dick Frost was the Shell general manager in Hong Kong and he told Douglas soon after their arrival of a Chinese girl, twenty-two-year-old Dorcas Barr, who had lost both her legs below the knee in the air bombing of Canton during the Sino-Japanese war. Her Chinese name was Pak Toh Kah. Dorcas was working at a Salvation Army hostel which was run by a young Australian and his wife, so Dick Frost took Douglas to see her. She spoke English quite well and was a delightful girl.

Douglas found her wearing a pair of artificial legs which were rather ungainly and ill-fitting. She was getting around on these legs, but it was obvious to him they were not right.

'Where did you get these legs?' Douglas asked her.

'They were made by a man in the town.'

In fact, for this they were pretty good but not good enough. After a little further talk, he and Dick Frost got hold of the Chinese artisan who had made the legs and then they all met in Frost's office.

'How did you make these legs?' Douglas enquired.

'Oh I see in magazine. I copy.'

'Well, they're jolly good. Well done. But I think Dorcas deserves a pair still better.' It was phenomenal for the Chinese worker ever to have made the legs at all, and the fact that she could actually put them on without absolutely murderous results to her stumps was extraordinary and a tribute to his craftsmanship.

Douglas said to Dick Frost, 'It's an awful disgrace that we can't get this girl some decent legs. In London she would be walking quite differently. Anybody in Britain or Germany can make this girl a pair of legs and she would never notice she hadn't got her real ones.'

Frost asked: 'How much would a pair of British-made limbs cost?'

'They're about fifty pounds a leg. A hundred the pair', Douglas said. 'And I could easily get some measurement charts sent out. She has been on these things made by the Chinese chap, and her stumps have settled down – so we can easily do it by measurements.'

Frost said, 'We'll soon get that then. I'll take you to lunch at the club and we'll have a whip round. We'll get the money in no time flat.'

So they went to the businessmen's club and Frost saw the Dunlop man and one or two others. Between them, he and Douglas had the hundred pounds before lunch was over. They had only got to explain the cause and everyone was as helpful as they could be.

Douglas then wrote to Roehampton to send out measurement charts. 'When you get these, any orthopaedic chap out here will know what to do with them. I'll make sure we get full instructions sent out and then you can have her measured and send the charts back to be turned into legs.'

They did all this. In London, the firm of J.E. Haugh, who made Douglas's own limbs, got busy on Dorcas's pair of legs. When they were ready, BOAC flew them out to her free of all charge. Dorcas was quite overjoyed and put them on. Later Dick Frost sent Douglas a cutting from the local paper showing Dorcas Barr walking with her new legs. They were so good, she felt she ought to keep them just for Sundays, she said.

Long before this visit had been planned, Thelma and Douglas had received a letter from a matron in Australia telling them that there had been a bus accident involving boys from an orphanage in Perth, Western Australia. This was Clontarf Boys' Town. The accident had happened as some of the boys were travelling by the bus to people's homes for the Christmas holidays the previous year. As a result of the collision with another vehicle, four of the boys lost legs. Three had to have one leg amputated, while one of them lost both.

Douglas was asked if he would write to the boys, which he did. Then it happened that he got this trip to Australia in late 1956 and he said to Shell that he would like to fly from Djakarta, their previous place of call, to Perth instead of going to Sydney first. Shell as usual agreed. Douglas did not want these boys to think that he had come to Perth as an afterthought, just fitting them in between other arrangements. He could easily do the Australian part of the visit that way around.

Thelma and Douglas flew in from Djakarta and arrived at Perth Airport on the night of 3rd October. Word had got around of their visit, and they were really staggered to see a crowd of more than a thousand well-wishers to welcome them. The great excitement for Douglas was that for the first time in his life he had a real live police escort! It was something he had always wanted and it seemed just like a scene out of an American film. He maintained that the first time you were driven fast through a town with police sirens wailing and motorcycle outriders in uniform was the most tremendous excitement – and it would be a cold fish who would fail to be thrilled!

Thelma and Douglas stayed four or five days in Perth, a pleasant and expanding city not hemmed in by lack of space. They went along to the Clontarf home for children from broken families, as well as actual orphans. It was run by a Roman Catholic brotherhood. That first visit was an official one, with all the fanfare of press and publicity. Then they called back a day or two later and it turned out to be much more satisfactory in every way.

They talked again to the four boys, Desmond Mullins, Charles Gatt, and Tony and Joseph Bugeja. The boys varied from about eleven to thirteen, and they were on crutches. All of them were duly encouraged to get rid of them as soon as possible.

Douglas did not go back there until 1969; when he arrived on that later visit, two of the boys met him at the airport as a surprise for Douglas. They were the two Bugeja boys and both had their wives with them. One had two children, the other had one, and both were well established in business. One of them had been diffident as a boy after the accident, but had thrown off all that and was very bright. Both were extremely mobile on their artificial legs. Douglas asked them about the other two boys and learnt that they were both well, too.

Two of the priests whom Douglas saw in 1956 were still there thirteen years later. Perth had spread fast and was reaching quite near to Clontarf. Now a lot of people with children sent them to Clontarf, and their fees helped to pay for the boys' town. The boys who lived there also went and spent weekends at the homes of these outside pupils, so it all worked out well since those days of 1956.

Before Thelma and Douglas left Perth on that original trip, they went to the Trots. In Australia you go to the Gallops or the Trots. The Gallops are the ordinary races and the Trots are the two-wheel type of carriage racing. The horse is harnessed to the shaft and the jockey is behind. The Trots track in Perth was made of pure oyster shells and under the floodlights of a warm Southern Hemisphere evening, the magic of the setting had to be seen and smelled to be believed.

They were met by a chap looking like a Chicago gangster, with a large hat on his head and a cigar stuck in his mouth. He said out of the corner of that mouth free from the cigar 'Would yer like me to mark yer card?'

Douglas did not bet but was almost afraid to refuse! The man put a pencil mark against the number of a horse that was going to win each of the seven races, and then handed the card back to Douglas. 'The legless ass' was now in an awkward predicament. He felt he ought to act on this unsolicited advice, so he wandered down and found the chap who was acting as their chauffeur. He said: 'Look, old boy, you'd better take this card. It's marked – and I think you can rely on it.'

Thelma and Douglas watched several of the races, all followed by a judge in an open car. To their joy it was proposed that they might like to ride in this car behind one of the races, only a few yards from the actual trotters. When they finally got down to the chauffeur to be driven back to the hotel, he was tremendously excited.

'Do you know? Six of those horses won. Only one didn't come up.' And the one that lost broke a trace, so might well otherwise have done so. Douglas thought that if he could have gone back to the Trots and got that chap to mark his card again, he could have retired sooner from Shell!

The progress of their visit could be summed up by the incredible itinerary. They were with the Governor of South Australia, Sir Robert

George and his wife at Government House, Adelaide. Sir Robert had taught Douglas to fly at Cranwell in 1928. Then the President of the Limbless Soldiers' Association, Mr Albert Solomon, made Douglas an honorary member. At the Crippled Children's Home, Somerjoy, many took heart from Douglas's visit. After a quick trip to Tasmania, they went to Brisbane, where one of the many people they met was Gordon Mills, a double amputee and golf enthusiast. In no time, Douglas was deeply involved in a discussion on golf technique.

They also went to the outback near Charleville and stayed on a sheep station there. Everything was on a huge scale topographically. And the trip itself felt like a royal tour. Thelma had never known anything like it. Crowds lined the streets to see Douglas and would shout out 'Good on yer, Doug'. It quite took their breath away. They started at about nine each morning and went on till nine at night for a month or so. At one place they were short of space to hang their clothes, so the word went on ahead 'Give them cupboards:' And from then on, there were cupboards galore.

That colossal figure Bob Menzies invited them to a party and entertained them in the Houses of Parliament. The Prime Minister sent an Australian Air Force Dakota down to pick them up and fly up to Canberra. Douglas found Menzies a big man by any standards. Big in stature, thought, ideas. Rather like Roy Welensky. It was a quality he could not miss and he had not met many men like it.

The Baders loved the Australians and it was reciprocated. Douglas ran into the Aussies first as a bunch in prison camp. They had a wonderful pioneer background and spirit. They seemed to adapt themselves more easily and quickly to rough conditions than any other English-speaking men. If they had not got something needed, they jolly soon contrived to make it out of something else. They were a wonderfully generous people, always ready to help anyone.

Shell arranged for people to come and see Douglas, as well as for him to go and see them. One of his visitors turned out to be a marvellous little boy aged ten, called Tony Baker. He had come down from Canberra to see Douglas and arrived in the Shell office at Sydney. He said quite fearlessly 'I want to ask your advice, sir. I think I should have my second leg off. I've had one off and I've got an artificial one.'

'What's the matter with your other one, then?' Douglas asked. 'It seems to work all right to me.'

'No – it doesn't work at all.'

Douglas had known of the boy coming to see him, so he had taken the sensible precaution of getting a doctor friend of his more or less on attendance for when the boy arrived. This man Webster had been in prison camp with Douglas as well.

'I think you'd better see Dr Webster', Douglas told Tony. 'Because he is a good doctor and has got a nursing home just outside Sydney. He can probably tell you better than I can.'

'What's the trouble?' Webster asked Tony. 'Would you like me to have a look at it?' Webster saw that he had a foot with only one toe on it, the rest being a piece of flesh. It was bound to be a nuisance and require surgery of some sort to put it right. Webster said: 'I see your point, Tony, and I promise you we'll put it right. But you're only ten. Hang on to it for another year or two. I'll keep in touch with you and then we'll do something about it.'

Tony said: 'Thank you very much, sir, that's all I wanted to know. I thought I'd better have it off sometime'. The boy had fair hair and big blue eyes and was very much in command of himself.

'How did you come down from Canberra?' Douglas asked him.

'Flew down, sir.'

'Did your mother or father come with you?'

'Oh, no, my mother is busy. She's a school teacher – I came down by myself. And I'm going back by myself.'

Douglas went along to the end of the passage on that floor of the Shell building. He introduced Tony to two Shell girls and asked them to take him out to lunch and the cinema, and then put him on the airliner back to Canberra that evening. They did exactly that and gave him a day he did not forget. The day he met Douglas Bader.

While at Sydney, Douglas was given the title in a newspaper of Pied Piper of Crippled Children. He talked to some of them at a surf carnival along Long Reef, North Sydney, and wherever he went the children followed him. Douglas gave a boy called Bobby Finch a fountain pen inscribed 'To Bobby from D.R.S.B.' Douglas said that Bobby was his pin-up boy and more of an example to people than Douglas, because Bobby had lost not only both legs but an arm, too.

When Thelma and Douglas first arrived in Perth, they had not been there for twenty-four hours before telegrams kept coming to the hotel saying, 'Hiya, Doug, when can we meet?' So Douglas sent back the replies 'Six o'clock in Melbourne' on whatever date he had decided. Shell arranged a large cocktail party, with invitations to ministers of the Crown and various other VIPs. Douglas thought that would be the ideal and obvious place for him to meet his friends.

The only thing was that he had omitted to mention to Shell that he had invited a few of his own chums from all over Australia, as well as the official guest list. It turned out to be a very formal performance, with the guests lining up on arrival to meet the chairman and his wife, and Thelma and Douglas. The introductions were in full progress, when suddenly from the end of the line arose a great shout of 'Hiya, Doug!' A dozen or so of Douglas's chums had got there. The chairman looked mildly astonished but it all passed off hospitably in the end.

There was a very good public relations chap who tended to get all the Baders' arrangements wrong throughout the tour: Times and places became a bit jumbled. Anyway, on this very special night Douglas said to him, about the time that the guests finally departed, 'Get a table in the dining room will you for the rest of us and we'll have dinner'. They had just got rid of the guests, and Douglas's own chums started to make way for the dining-room at half past eight. 'Certainly, fine, Doug', the PRO said, 'but you know you're on the air at nine o'clock, don't you? You're the guest of honour, remember?'

Douglas said: 'No, I didn't know!' Then he added with considerable restraint for him, 'I don't mind, old boy, if we can get a car to take me to the studio'. In fact it had been mentioned to him in Perth but no-one had reminded him of it recently. He assumed it would be the usual sort of interview dialogue. Along the lines of 'How do you like Australia?' 'Jolly nice' and so on. It was bound to be made easy by the interviewer.

The car got Douglas to the studios and he was ushered up to a room, with the time then about ten minutes to nine! The interviewer said, 'How do you do. What are you going to talk about?'

'It's up to you, old boy, I don't care what you ask me. I'll either answer or tell you I don't know', Douglas said.

'No, no. You're on your own. It's nothing to do with me! You talk for fifteen minutes. All I've got to do is introduce you.'

Douglas thought an un-beautiful thought as the clock reached 8.55. Then he said quickly: 'Right. Tell me what you'd like to hear about, if you were listening on the radio. Your own radio at home.'

The chap mentioned list of things. How he felt when he lost his legs. What it was like being back in the Air Force. How the Germans treated him. And so on. Douglas jotted down seven or eight questions from losing his legs right through to his impressions of Australia. He simply glued his eyes to these points scribbled down and waited for the studio light to come on. He started talking. And he went on and on until the light eventually went off. From that day onwards, he had not the vaguest memory of what he actually said, only that he was in this sound studio with the awful little microphone in front of him and nothing, no-one, else. The minutes seemed to stretch into infinity. But he got through it somehow and next day people stopped him in the street or wherever he might be and said, 'Say, I sure liked that broadcast of yours, Doug!' It was one of the worst experiences he had ever had.

Now it was early November and Thelma and Douglas awoke in a Sydney hotel on the day they were due to travel over to Christchurch, New Zealand. The papers were pushed under the door of their room and in great headlines they read the one word – WAR. This was the Suez Campaign launched by Eden in conjunction with France. As they flew across the Tasman Sea later in the day, Douglas talked about it to Thelma and others on the aircraft. Douglas had decided his views, as usual, quickly but not without due consideration. 'I cannot feel that this is right – for the whole might of Britain and France to be directed against these people. After all, we've been to Egypt many times. We all know the country and although we have regarded the Egyptians as delighted if you kick them – this is carrying it too far. There's something wrong about this whole affair.'

But being British to the core and beyond, Douglas took even greater exception to the rude remarks about Britain which were at once made by certain of the Commonwealth countries. When he got to Christchurch and was talking to the Tin Hat Club there, he made a typical Baderism which was extensively quoted in the press. He said, 'If they don't want to stay in the Commonwealth then they can bloody well climb back up their trees – and we'll provide the trees'.

Then they went on to Wellington, first to the Houses of Parliament. Douglas was due to meet Mr Holland, the Prime Minister of New Zealand, and some of his ministers and members of the opposition. Thelma and Douglas had been invited to lunch there. Before Douglas reached the Premier, though, he had read in the papers that Wellington was the location of a meeting of the Columbo Powers who were visiting the city at that very moment, so when he was shown into the Premier's private room, his first words to Mr Holland were: 'Look, sir, I'm most frightfully sorry about what I said in Christchurch. It must have embarrassed you, as you've got the Columbo Powers here at present.'

Holland was sitting and Douglas was standing. He looked up at Douglas and said quite simply:

'That's all right, old boy, somebody's got to say it!'

The Baders attended an air display in New Zealand. Douglas treasured all his life a remark made to him there by a very small boy of five or six. He was with his mother in the crowd and she said to him, as mothers will, 'Say how do you do to Mr Bader.' The little lad did not raise his eyes above their normal level, but stared straight of Douglas's legs, saying, 'How are your wooden legs?'

Douglas always loved children, although he and Thelma never had any of their own. He liked the way they say exactly what they think, frequently with the most stimulating results. In this respect, Douglas could be said to resemble the childlike approach. He often felt that life would be much simpler if we could all retain that quality of the honest approach.

During the New Zealand stay, the Baders went to Rotorua, where all the gushers were duly performing. There they saw the girl head of the Maoris, who was a good public relations expert for her people. They watched the Maori dances and admired the dignified way in which this girl had everything arranged. They both loved this demonstration of the traditional native way of life. Douglas was not anti-black, and had many coloured friends all over the world. It was just that he was firmly and passionately pro-British and refused to apologise for being white.

Thelma and Douglas were due to leave New Zealand from Auckland in the north. When they got to the city the general manager of the Shell company there said to Douglas, 'Look, I've just had this telegram from London for you'. It came from the managing directors of Shell. It said in words to the effect that if what he had said in New Zealand had been correctly reported in New York, for Christ's sake keep your mouth shut when you're in America!

They went on a conducted tour of Pearl Harbor; to dinner at San Francisco; then to Denver and New York and down to Miami. The next stop was due to be Bogota, Colombia. Douglas knew it would be a tricky flight down there, as they would have to fly between mountains letting down into the capital, thousands of feet above sea level. They had the Shell man from Borneo with them, Jim Davis. Douglas and Jim talked about the flight and Douglas said 'I hope the chap up front knows what he's doing – because there are some bloody big hills in the way!' And there was only one way through, right down the middle.

They reached Bogota safely but were not enamoured of Colombia, mainly because it poured with rain all the time. Then they went on to Venezuela. An ironic touch on this South American leg of their mammoth tour was that Douglas was flown around locally by a German pilot who had been some sort of air ace in World War 2.

As a result of his South American travels down the years, Douglas developed a philosophy about the revolutions in that region of the world. The great thing was that the outgoing president never got killed. It was all part of the game. Because if you assassinated him, it started a nasty precedent and the next man would have *you* killed. So you did not do it. A great entourage waited for an ordinary commercial airliner. The retiring president was being seen off by the new power, complete with luggage and girl friends – bag and baggage, as Douglas put it. He saw all these people thronging the airport and thought 'They can't possibly all have come to meet *me*'. They hadn't.

On this trip, Thelma had fourteen suitcases. She had carried her hat in a hat box all the way out to Melbourne specifically for the Melbourne Cup. The box was then cossetted all round the rest of the world! After Trinidad, they spent Christmas in Bermuda at the Mid-Ocean Club where the golf professional was Douglas's old friend Archie Compston.

From Bermuda back to Britain. In those days, it was a flight by a piston-engine Boeing Stratocruiser. Passengers pulled down bunks from the ceiling and went to sleep for the night. They could undress, pull the curtains and it looked quite like home! Thelma went to sleep in no time, so Douglas took himself up front with the crew, drank coffee and gossiped. They were flying at about 16,000 feet and had reached a stage halfway on the 12-hour flight. The time was three in the morning, and all outside seemed peaceful. Some of the crew were resting in a little compartment just behind the flight deck, and Douglas sat beside the captain. A sliver of moon moved among the high cloud.

The captain was a mature man with a bald head and an aquiline nose. He had won a lot of gongs for bombing the Ruhr 'X number of times' and he simply oozed confidence. Douglas suddenly smelt burning. He sniffed a bit more and thought 'I'd better not say anything in case it looks as if I'm nervous!' Then he noticed the pilot sniffing, too.

'Do you smell it?' Douglas queried.

'Yes', the captain said calmly, 'but I don't suppose it's anything much!'

'What do we do about it?' Douglas persevered with a modicum of concern. He was not used to flying in an aeroplane on fire without at least trying to do something to put it out.

The Stratocruiser had an open sort of hatch behind the pilots' seats and the smell was originating from this area. Douglas wondered what on earth he was doing in the middle of the Atlantic at 16,000 feet with his wife asleep in the back of an aeroplane probably on fire. He looked across at the captain, who roused someone from the crew and said quietly:

'There's a smell down below of something hot. I expect it's the circulating fan.'

The crew member went as ordered, had a sniff and reported reassuringly, as if from the experience of several past occasions. 'Yes, that's all it is. I'll get the boy.' So the hatch was pulled up, 'the boy' stuffed down, and news awaited. After an indecent lapse of minutes, the boy came back and said, 'Yes, it was the circulating fan all right'. And the Stratocruiser flew on its merry way to bring the Baders back home.

Douglas and Thelma at Fort McMurray, Alta, 1957. *(Author)*

On a fishing trip with Shell pilot John Ebert at Marsh Lake, Yukon. *(Author)*

Douglas was a keen golfer and is seen here competing in the Open Mixed Foursome Competition of the British Limbless Ex-servicemen's Association, 1961. *(Hulton-Deutsch)*

CHAPTER 22

Golf is a game for life. It was the one game Douglas could play on equal terms with other people. Equal terms is perhaps an inaccurate phrase, for Douglas nearly always won. In the earliest days after his accident, Thelma used to watch him play; in that era when he fell flat on his face occasionally. Douglas also used to try squash and tennis but people had to play the ball to him. Anyone who knew Douglas would know that he would not play under those conditions; and after squash and tennis he used to come home with circles under his eyes, a reflection of the fantastic effort he had to expend. At squash, for instance, he had to hurl himself at the ball, and it is a strenuous game anyway.

Eventually he settled for golf. He had played every day for two or three months during his demobilisation leave with Archie Compston. One of the best golf teachers in this country told Laddie Lucas one day: 'I saw Douglas at Sunningdale and I was sure I could help him. It gives you great humility to watch him.' So Laddie arranged for Douglas to have a lesson from him.

This instructor told Douglas about the position of the ball, position of the body, and all the other things a professional can convey, and he got Douglas hitting the ball really well. Later he said to Laddie, 'It's a remarkable thing, you know. Here we are, we've been playing and teaching golf for years, always thinking in terms of people using their legs – underpinning. What this has brought out in my mind is to underline certain fundamentals in any golf swing and style'. The teacher had in fact learnt as much from Douglas as the other way around! From the end of the war onwards, Douglas really threw himself into golf. He started playing thirty-six holes a day, whereas pot-bellied old businessmen could only manage eighteen at the most!

So successful was the tuition from Archie Compston of Wentworth that Douglas got his handicap down to the phenomenal level of four. In April 1946, he was the first legless man ever to have competed in a national golf contest when he played in the Amateur Championship at the Royal Mid-Surrey course, Richmond. Then the following year Douglas entered the Swedish open golf championship and won the first round, beating his Swedish opponent on the last green.

Laddie Lucas went to the USA in 1949 as captain of the British golf team contesting the Walker Cup, and although they were well beaten, they were not disgraced. Soon after this, Douglas actually won the *Golf Illustrated* Challenge Cup at Camberley Heath with scores of 79 minus 5 and 82 minus 4.

Anecdotes about Douglas and golf are endless. For years he played regularly with Roy Snodgrass, his deputy at Shell. One typical occasion was a very hot spring day in the mid-1950s. Snodgrass won the first round in the morning. Douglas was determined to beat him in the afternoon, which he did. Over tea, Snodgrass was unwise enough to say that the evening was the best time to play, whereupon Douglas took that as a challenge and they went on for yet another nine holes. Douglas won, although he was completely exhausted and his stumps were badly blistered.

Douglas was always at his best when being watched by a crowd. He produced his best golf strokes before a gallery, whereas many players would go to pieces. Roy Snodgrass knew Douglas ever since the days immediately after his accident and used to play squash and tennis with him. As Thelma observed, his lack of mobility made him vulnerable at squash, but in tennis mixed doubles with Douglas up at the net and a good partner on the baseline, they were virtually unbeatable. Snodgrass said that Douglas was an exasperating man in some ways, because you could not compete with him – you knew he was going to win before you started. This took time to adjust to and it did not apply only to games, although there were times when Douglas would concede graciously that he had been wrong in the office. One other less known quality of Douglas's which Roy always recalled from those years was his power of mimicry. As he tells a story, or told a story, Douglas gave an impression of the man being described – both verbally and visually. He got all the characteristics of a man complete.

For years Peter Cadbury and Douglas played golf together because they both agreed that hardly anyone else would play with them! They both admitted to being fairly intolerant on a golf course. They liked to get around the Berkshire in a couple of hours or so. There are so many people with perfectly good legs who insist on loitering and fiddling and so holding everyone else up. Peter and Douglas wanted to plough on, and if anyone cared to join them, they did so at their own risk.

Once they were held up by a couple of men at Sandwich who had practically stopped altogether. Eventually these men let Peter and Douglas through. One of them was limping a little and said in a rather martyred tone, 'Sorry I'm so slow, but I've got my knee bandaged and I find it difficult to get along.'

Peter Cadbury said fairly tersely: 'My partner hasn't any legs at all – and he manages perfectly well. So I think you might try to move a bit faster with just a little bandage round one of yours!' As Peter Cadbury said, neither he nor Douglas suffered fools gladly.

Peter was playing with Douglas another day at Sandwich when someone who did not know him very well offered to give Bader a hand out of the bunker. The man unfortunately said 'Can I give you a leg up?' Douglas told him he did not want one. If he did want any help, he would ask for it. Sometimes he did need it when coming out of a steep bunker or up an equally steep hill.

Max Aitken had seen him fall flat on his back after getting an awkward ball out of a bunker. Douglas had collapsed and hit his head before then. Aitken had also seen his legs so sore that he had to take them off and go on to crutches until he had recovered. He thought that the reason Douglas was so fit was perhaps because his heart did not have to pump blood all around his legs. It was an interesting medical theory, anyway.

Harry Broadhurst was another of Douglas's many partners and opponents. He realised at an early stage that on or off the golf course you had to accept Douglas's sense of humour. Luckily Gus Walker did so. He had lost an arm during the war and on one occasion after a bad shot by Walker, Douglas called out 'Come on, Gus, try using your other arm'. Douglas knew just how far he could go and clearly Walker would take no offence from Douglas, but might have done from someone else.

One day Douglas asked Laddie Lucas 'Can you find a caddie for me?' There was one old boy who had always been a caddie at this particular course. The only snag was that he had one arm. He agreed to caddie for Douglas next day. They were playing a four-ball: Laddie, Douglas, Gus Walker and Lord Leicester. When Laddie and Douglas got to the club, there were Walker and the caddie already standing ready. Douglas had not seen the caddie previously.

'Good God! What the hell's the good of you coming and caddying for me? You've got one arm, the air marshal's got one arm, and I haven't got any legs! We're a fine bloody bunch. One complete lot of limbs missing between us!' Then when Walker pulled the ball, Douglas said he was getting too much right arm into it!

Gus Walker felt there was no comparison between their two disabilities. Generously he insisted that Douglas's was so much greater than his. He thought it was a feat of sheer endurance to live overtly in the way that Douglas did. It was a totally different order of disability. Just getting round a golf course without legs was an achievement. Walker admitted he had a handicap being minus one arm. Every process took so much longer, but it was only an inconvenience. Or so he said. He particularly liked the way Douglas struck the golf ball, with a very true attitude in character with the man. Douglas also took much less time than the average player to perform a putt, and he was a very good putter. He used a marvellous old metal putter with a wooden shaft.

Incidentally, every now and then Douglas heard from someone who had lost an arm and had written to him for help. He would say to Walker: 'Look here, I think it would be much more sensible if I throw this to you'. Douglas might tell the person who had lost one or both arms, 'I know a friend who has had this experience, and perhaps he would be better for you to deal with, or talk to, or write to, than me'.

There is a tremendous psychological effect just after the loss of a limb. This mental and psychological loss can be very serious, so reassurance can be of great value – showing the patients that they have not lost everything.

Because of course the shock to the system is very substantial. Nothing can be better than the words of someone who has suffered the same disability and who has made comparatively light of it. Walker felt strongly that Douglas made a great contribution to mankind in the most positive way possible. This was real mind-healing in acute circumstances.

Like Douglas, Gus Walker got a great shock in his own case but decided to try and make light of it. And he knew from the fairly few cases he had been concerned with helping, how much it meant to people. The great thing was to give them the sure realisation that life was not destroyed, that so much remains. So much of what Douglas did like this was purely as a matter of course, almost routine. But the inspiration was always there. He showed people their potential.

But back to golf. Johnnie Johnson was only an average golfer and consequently he got a lot of unsolicited advice from Douglas about what to do and where to hit the ball. Douglas still had the wing commander/pilot officer act, despite the fact that Johnson finished as an air vice-marshal – two ranks above Group Captain Douglas Bader!

Douglas used to play a lot with Alan Garrow, who died in 1970. Alan remembered him when he got into an unplayable line of bunkers. Douglas would be unperturbed, roar with one of his deep gruff Ha Ha's, and play an absolutely impossible shot out.

An old caddie who had done about fifty years on this course was with Douglas for the first time, so did not know what to expect. On the first and second holes, Douglas asked him about the greens for his putt: 'What's the line?' The caddie said 'A couple of inches to the left'. Douglas said: 'You silly bugger, it's two inches to the right!' This put off the caddie for the moment, but by the end of the round he was voicing what a great chap Bader was. Douglas could get away with anything.

Douglas played in literally any weather and never felt the cold. Alan Garrow was wearing a whole heap of clothes one freezing day, including an overcoat. Douglas appeared in his usual attire of a shirt and trousers. Alan simply could not keep his hands warm enough to grip his clubs, so he put them on Douglas's back to warm them up. When they had finished playing, it was pints of orange juice – Douglas could not stand delicate little glasses of liquid. Just as any elaborate food drove him mad. It was bangers and mash or eggs and bacon, and he was perfectly happy.

There was the delightful true story of the public relations man who was trying to soften him up for something. He took Douglas to the Caprice restaurant and presented the impressively large menu to him. 'Choose anything you like, old boy', he waved. 'Right, I'll have scrambled eggs and bacon, that will do me'. It was a carefully calculated response. Douglas's favours could not be purchased for any sum at all, certainly not for the price of a meal at the Caprice. He had also refused to go in the first place unless accompanied by Alan Garrow, who did in fact go with them.

Douglas played golf in Scotland as often as he could. He always tried to play in the September and May Medals with Iain Stewart and had done for years. One day they were going down the famous seventeenth fairway at St Andrews where a new hotel was being built. At that moment, the men were enjoying their lunch break and they were all leaning over the wall watching the golf. Iain and Douglas happened to have been talking about the inefficiency of industry, when suddenly Douglas shouted across to the men 'You lazy bastards! Get on with the bloody job! What the hell are you doing leaning over the wall?' One of them shouted back 'Okay, Bader, we know you.' Then Douglas went over to talk to them and found a couple of his mechanics from some RAF station where they had all served together. And before long, caps were being flung in the air. They found that the ruder he is, the friendlier he was really being.

Another day at St Andrew's with Iain, Douglas was playing at an incredibly low score. But every now and then, even in one of those rounds, Douglas got into trouble and instead of turning round and playing backwards, he had to try and get out the hard way straight ahead. He started off as follows: 3, 4, 3, 4, 5, 3, which is remarkable for any player, professional or otherwise. Then he took an 8, through getting caught in a bunker. Even so he finished at eighty-one, just one shot more than the medal winner. He had great potential and hit the ball long and hard. How he did it, Iain Stewart for one would never know. Presumably partly through his powerful arms. And he was 'as strong as an ox,' as someone remarked once.

Once hot, Douglas's joints creaked while he was playing. 'You want to use Shell oil' some wit shouted out to him. He chuckled gleefully.

The Berkshire was Douglas's club. He played a lot with the secretary, Walter Seabrook. Later he restricted his golf to a round a day, instead of two. Yet even then Douglas played in the foursomes and singles against Oxford University, and was as good in the latter as the former. The two rounds measured nine or ten miles in total.

One of Douglas's charms was the way in which he remained completely unabashed by anything, certainly by any eventuality associated with his legs. One day he had not got the adjustment quite right on one of his knees. Every time he moved it creaked badly, and as he walked round the course, they were accompanied by this enormous squeaking. People were looking across and wondering what the noise was, and Douglas could not have been more pleased about it!

One day he appeared wearing a very smart pair of golf shoes when it was wet. After the game, he came into the clubhouse and someone said to him 'Those are nice shoes, Douglas. Do they keep the water out?'

'How the hell would I know?' Douglas retorted.

Most Saturdays he played with Seabrook. He put a hand on a caddie's shoulder when going down steep slopes, otherwise he managed quite alone. He wore gloves between shots and carried his little wooden-legged leather stool to sit on at times. He still had a very good swing, yet obviously could not get the same degree of pivot as someone with legs. His power had to come from above the waist. His timing was perfect and although he could not follow through completely, he adapted his technique. It was told that he fell down forty times when he started to play golf, but Seabrook never saw him fall once. Douglas drove at least 200 yards and loved the Berkshire courses. They were probably the best pair of inland courses in the country, he thought. They were set in limelined country and at weekends they used one course for two-ball matches and the other for four-ball matches. Then they swapped over for the afternoons. It worked out pretty well.

Ian Collins was another of Douglas's partners when up north. When Douglas came to play at Troon, there was a queue of caddies to go out with him, as they adored him. They had one very old caddie up there who caddied for them in the morning. They told him to come back at four o'clock and they would take him back to Prestwick. At about five minutes to four, there was a tap at the side window of the clubhouse. The man had come back early. He had not come through the front door, and he tapped at this window so that he would not be noticed and disturb them. He said to Douglas 'I've got a watch that I had at Mons in the Great War and I would like you to have it in appreciation of the most enjoyable day's golf I've ever had'.

Golf is the game of a lifetime. It was certainly the game of Douglas's own life, at any rate since he was twenty-one. He successfully tried several others after the accident, but found that golf was the one game he could play through the years and the decades. In view of Douglas's absolutely overriding need to occupy himself physically, it would be impossible to stress too much how vital golf was for him: not only by helping to keep him fit, but also as a psychological means of showing him that he was still as good as, if not considerably better than, most other people when it came to proving himself competitively. And at times of crisis, too, golf was always there as a calming factor to help him restore things to their proper perspective.

CHAPTER 23

When Douglas had rejoined Shell in 1946, he went back to the aviation department. Quite a lot of things were cropping up in aviation as far as Shell were concerned. He found himself looking after not only commercial aspects like contracts with airlines in various parts of the world, but they also wanted him to fly in his own small aeroplane – which of course he did with joy. In oil territories like Borneo and Venezuela where they were flying, he became involved in the actual operations on the production side of the business, away from marketing. Then Douglas was transferred into the administration side of Shell. The range was very much wider than before. Shell had given him permission to take Thelma with him wherever he went abroad, so they flew all over the world, either in his own small or big aeroplanes, or in airliners.

Flying was almost like a drug for Douglas. He believed you could not play at flying; either you flew or stopped it altogether. It was no good saying, 'Well, I'll go up once or twice a year and fly around the airfield'. That was no good at all for him. As in other activities throughout his life, it was all or nothing. Fortunately age was no barrier to flying, so Douglas could go on indefinitely. Anyway, age was a point of view and a matter of physical health. Luckily he was strong and healthy, and his outlook was still young.

Joan Hargreaves started working with him at about the time he got his new assignment with Shell. When she first heard she was going to work with him, she was very pleased. She had a funny sort of feeling that this was the way her life had to go, so they stayed together for the next seventeen years. It was so successful because both of them were straightforward people. She was never frightened or overawed and she used to tell him exactly what she thought, which he liked and appreciated.

In the Shell Aviation offices, everything was always in an uproar whenever Douglas was around. They had two or three girl secretaries and Douglas would nobble the lot if he could. They would all be working for him. Joan never had five minutes to sit still when Douglas was there. Yet all the time she was working for him, she was nursing sick parents. Douglas was simply marvellous and said: 'Do what you have to do, but let me know first'. She could not have kept going without his understanding. But Douglas could be considerate one minute, and demanding the next; brilliant one moment, obtuse the next. Joan used to say that he was a mass of paradoxes, or apparent paradoxes.

Joan Hargreaves went to Douglas's osteopath, who said to her once about him, 'The most I can do is to relieve the discomfort for him'. But people would not know he had even discomfort, let alone pain.

One of the most moving things for Joan Hargreaves was to see Douglas on the odd occasions when he appeared in the office on crutches. Perhaps he had hurt his legs at golf or in some other way. That really used to bring her up with a jerk and she suddenly realised afresh what he had to go through. If he could not wear his legs for any reason, he had to come in on elbow crutches. He never made any bones about it and it did not happen very often, so perhaps that was why it seemed so noticeable when it did. It acted as a reminder that each day was still to be met and overcome, so much more than for ordinary people.

Joan Hargreaves was in the office one day in the 1950s when Douglas got a phone call from a friend in the Royal Air Force. They told him that Geoffrey Stephenson had been killed. Douglas went very quiet and was visibly upset. He did not talk, nor tell Joan about it, and she never asked him any directly personal questions. He just left the office and went home. She read about it later in the evening paper.

Douglas first met Geoffrey Stephenson in the RAF Medical Establishment in 1928, when they were both up for the same examination to go to Cranwell. They became friends and were in the same squadron at Cranwell. Then they were commissioned together and went to the same squadron as pilot officers in July 1930. Geoffrey was a wonderful rider, a good boxer, a long-distance runner, and he also swam well.

When Geoffrey was posted to Iraq, Douglas was held back because there had been that possibility of his playing rugby for England. Then he lost his legs. They kept in touch after Douglas left the RAF for the first time.

When the war loomed up and he wanted to get back into the RAF, Douglas had his first flight again with Geoffrey. He was a squadron leader then and did a lot of the preparatory work to get Douglas accepted back medically. When Douglas did get back and had successfully completed his refresher course on modern types of aeroplane, he was posted to 19 Squadron at Duxford, which was then commanded by Stephenson. Geoffrey was shot down at Dunkirk and finished up at Colditz, as we already know. Their paths continued to cross and after the war they met again while Douglas was at the Eastern Sector of Fighter Command.

Geoffrey Stephenson went over to America as an air commodore and was there flying the F100, which experienced control problems. Two or three other test pilots were killed as well as Geoffrey before they got it right. He was a very fine pilot. They always used to say that a chap who was good on a horse was good in an aeroplane, because it was the hands that mattered. In Geoffrey's case, this was certainly true. When he died, Douglas felt that a part of his own past had gone, too.

Douglas could be a blend of the very sensitive and the rather insensitive. He also had an extraordinary memory. At the drop of a hat, John Addison heard him quote whole excerpts of Shakespeare and other poetry. When Douglas was at school, he had a classics education. He acquired a very early appreciation of poetry and used to read it regularly at his prep school. When he was in the nursing home after his accident he used to read those masses of Swinburne. Douglas said to me once: 'Swinburne's Hymn to Prosepone – I can quote the whole bloody poem to you'.

His taste in poetry was not modern, though. He always loved the poems by the Canadian Robert W. Service about the Yukon. 'The goal you would strive for and win.' He knew that the thrill was in striving, not in the attainment. Douglas loved these four lines especially:

> 'There's gold, and it's haunting and haunting;
> It's luring me on as of old;
> Yet it isn't the gold that I'm wanting
> So much as just finding the gold.'

> 'There's another chap called Banjo Patterson from Australia. He writes about the Australian scene. It's all this rolling verse, the Kiplingesque style. The funny thing about poetry is that you hear Keats' *Ode to a Nightingale* and it all means something to you. Other things don't. A poet doesn't just reel off words. These chaps really had something to say. You must have read that one *Loxley Hall* by Tennyson. Go back and read it old chap. And that marvellous chap of World War One. Rupert Brooke, *Grantchester*, marvellous. I always wish I could write poetry. But I can't make two and two make four. Byron was a great chap and a great Greekophile – like me.'

As for music, Douglas used to love all the popular music of the 1930s which was evocative, and he was always keen on the music-hall and Max Miller. But as regards serious music, John Addison does not recall his ever having been to a concert, although Douglas did have an introduction to the ballet. He found Covent Garden intriguing and quite erotic!

About the 'Fifties era, John Addison did a musical show which turned out to be a disaster. It was called *Keep Your Hair On*. Family loyalty, however, was always a prime Bader virtue. Douglas and all the family went to the opening night. After the interval, the gallery started to boo, whereupon Douglas laughed and applauded all the more loudly and loyally, even though it may not have been his kind of show. So once more it came back to loyalty. For him there could be no double standards.

Tony Richardson asked Addison to write the music for *The Entertainer* by John Osborne. Addison found himself mixing with a group of people who were Socialists and who aimed to change the English theatre from pure drawing-room comedy into something that had social significance, and who also felt that they could play a part in changing society by this means. In such an atmosphere, many of the views that Douglas expressed in print were anathema to them and they would criticise him for them. On the whole, John Addison agreed with them about Douglas's views, but this had no effect at all on his feelings for Douglas, which had been formed for too long to be changed by external courses. Nothing could ever alter them. John did not care what Douglas's views were; he just thought he was marvellous!

John Addison had of course written the music for *Reach for the Sky*. The inspiration from the film was now in full spate and Thelma and Douglas received regular requests for their help. Ian Collins recalls several. They visited in Scotland a boy with a leg lost. Douglas went out of his way to the boy. About the same era they got a letter from a young father in Glasgow saying roughly: 'I wonder if you could help my wife and I? We are a young married couple. We have a little boy who has been run-over by a train and lost both his legs. We do not know quite how to handle this and we wonder if you would please advise us'.

Douglas wrote to say he would come and see them. They lived in a normal block of Glasgow flats, which were sandwiched between a steep bank going down to the railway and a canal. Thelma went with Douglas. The parents at once told them how sad it had been. They had always instilled into the boy not to go and play near the canal, in case he fell in and drowned. Of course the inevitable happened. He played on the railway side, fell down the slope and was run over by a train. Douglas said to them straight away: 'Don't worry or fret about that, because there's nothing you can do about it.' He was always a great believer in never saying 'If only I hadn't . . .' It was a waste of time and a negative attitude, so must be discouraged immediately.

The boy was still in hospital so Thelma and Douglas put the parents in the car and the four of them went to visit him. He was in a ward with a lot of adults and he seemed very silent. He had lost his legs below the knee which was better than higher up. One positive thing already. The boy was a bit tongue-tied and inclined simply to stare back at them. The shock had clearly been huge. So Douglas did not press too hard. He realised that it was the parents they had to worry about.

Driving back after the visit, he told them: 'You may not believe this now, but in fact about a year or sixteen months from today, you won't notice that the boy hasn't got any legs. Having it happen so young is better than later. He'll get around like nobody's business and you will be absolutely amazed, I promise you. He has been perfectly well amputated and there is nothing wrong with him. What you don't want to do is to be over-indulgent. Obviously you are going to spoil him a bit, but don't do everything for him, because as he gets better, he will be able to do it himself. Anyway write and let me know how things are going.' The parents were still doubtful but felt better than before seeing Douglas. For they could see personal proof of recovery in the very undeniable form of DB.

Douglas said goodbye with a last shot, 'If you're ever down in London, let us know and come and see us.'

The Baders heard nothing further from them for a year or so, then one day the phone rang at Petersham Mews. It was the boy's father. 'Can we come round and see you?' he asked Thelma. So Thelma in turn rang Douglas at Shell: 'You remember those people we saw in Scotland last year? Well, they're down in London visiting relations and I've asked them round to tea.'

Douglas saw the complete family group: father, mother and the boy, who was wearing a pair of jeans and a sweater. He stood upright, looking very pleased with himself. How much brighter than the last time he had seen the lad, thought Douglas. They all came in and almost at once the boy started galloping round the room. It was not long before he found the rather winding staircase in the Baders' home. He careered out of the connecting door and positively ran up and down them for most of the rest of the visit. All this was to show them just what he could do. Douglas had known he had it in his power and hoped that he could do it. No-one would have suspected that the boy had anything wrong with him at all.

Douglas said to the couple: 'What did I tell you? You didn't really believe me when I said he'd be doing this.'

The wife said: 'Of course we're very pleased. The only trouble now is that he's awful hard on his trews and his socks!'

Douglas replied: 'Surely that doesn't matter. You can always get him some leather trews!'

Apparently the boy was playing football with other young lads and doing everything normally. It really made Douglas feel a glow that the parents had taken the trouble to bring the boy round and show him that what he had hoped would happen had in fact come to pass.

One day Douglas was visiting Harry Broadhurst in France. It was summer time and Douglas noticed another guest, a blind girl, sitting on the edge of the swimming pool. He insisted on going over to talk to her and then spent the rest of the day with her. When the girl discovered who Douglas was, she felt marvellous and thrilled. He felt an instinctive sympathy for this girl with the great disability of blindness and was determined to do a little to help cheer her up.

Mike Kroge was engaged in Army bomb disposal on the Yorkshire moors when both his legs were shattered by an explosion. After he had them both amputated, he seemed to be losing heart, when an encouraging letter came from Douglas. Just this act alone did the trick, by implanting the will to recover. He actually put the letter under his pillow as a symbol of his goal and 'dragged himself back to life'. Four years later he could drive a car, play badminton, dance, cycle, box, and walk two or three miles. He achieved an ambition by meeting Douglas while learning to fly at Croydon Airport.

Stanley Coughtrey was a spastic with legs that 'felt like lead'. One day he was helped from his home in Romford, Essex, to see the film *Reach for the Sky*. It had a profound effect on him, and while riding home by bus, he started to think of how he could expand his life beyond his home and the hospital. When he got indoors, he unfastened the knee-lock on his callipers, the technical term for his steel legs. Then he started trying to walk every day, to use his legs. His mother said, 'He used to sit in his chair and didn't seem to bother until he saw that film. Now he wears his callipers all day'. After an effort, Stanley found he could climb the fourteen stairs up to his bedroom; he went on the bus by himself, through being able to unlock his leg; and he had games on the local putting green. He aimed to throw away his crutches altogether in time.

Another success for *Reach for the Sky* was Mrs Aileen Hockley. She lost a leg in South Africa. Then after reading the book, she wrote to Douglas for advice about her artificial legs, as she did not seem to be getting on well with them. He sent her his usually dynamic exhortation, and promised her that she would soon get used to the leg and find it a useful thing to have around the house. Heartened by his interest from so far away, she made rapid progress from crutches to a walking stick, finally managing to walk without any external aid whatever.

Case after case came along about this period. Douglas had always been the hero of a brown-haired, freckle-faced boy called Terry French. Then both his legs were severed by a train as he ran across the line near his Gateshead home. Terry's mother said that a letter from Douglas and his example kept her son alive. Terry fought back, learnt to wear his metal legs, began to think of football and swimming again. Later he was asked about how he had recovered. 'I want to say thank you to Group Captain Bader. I am going to write and tell him that I'm doing all right.'

A Pakistani woman wrote to say that her son had lost not only his legs but also the will to live. After seeing *Reach for the Sky*, he regained his spirit and started to walk. So it was a worldwide effect.

Terry Guiver was a twenty-six-year-old brunette who lost her legs in a car crash. For days she drifted between life and death, just as Douglas had done long before. 'All the time I just wanted to die'. Then the familiar DB letter reached her and it somehow tilted the scales. 'I cried when I read the letter. I re-read it until it came apart at the seams'. Terry Guiver was the first woman in Britain to be fitted with completely artificial legs. Soon she was wearing brocade shoes and nylon stockings again, having gone through the Roehampton rehabilitation process.

As a footnote to this *Reach for the Sky* era, when four hundred schoolboys were asked to name their favourite heroes, number one was Bader. Churchill came second, Lord Nelson and Stanley Matthews tied for third place. Elvis Presley was fourth and Tommy Steele sixth. What would the result be today? *Sic transit gloria.*

CHAPTER 24

At the start of 1957, Douglas received a letter from Canada on some splendidly headed notepaper. He was used to getting strange letters from all over the world, but this one was almost a record. The letterheading bore a Red Indian Chief's silhouette in full head-dress, and written across it were the words Kanai Chieftains. The communique came from the secretary of the Honorary Chiefs of the Black Foot Tribe and the gist of the letter was that they wanted Douglas to accept honorary chieftainship of the tribe at a place called Lethbridge in Alberta during that coming July. Would he accept it and let them know?

They also told him that a number of famous people were honorary chieftains, including the Duke of Windsor, various governors of Canada and other folk whose names he recognised. This was an honour because there were only a strictly limited number of chiefs and they could only elect another one when someone died. You had to wait for a vacancy. They were going to send out invitations to people all over the world to attend this ceremony. Douglas was quite excited at the prospect of this. As soon as he asked Shell about the question of getting to Canada and back with Thelma, they said it would be well worthwhile and he could go out and combine it with a business trip in the nearby oil territory.

Shell could not quite realise why the Baders wanted to leave Britain a week or so earlier than the date projected. The reason was simple. The Calgary Stampede was held in the first week of July each year and some of their friends out there had told them they must see the Stampede. So the schedule was the stampede, up to the Yukon for some Shell business, and finally to Lethbridge for the chieftainship.

Douglas and Thelma thought the Calgary Stampede was the finest show on earth. During the whole of that week in Calgary everyone wore a ten-gallon hat and all work was at a standstill. The show started at about noon each day in an enormous arena, like the stockade of one of the old pioneer forts but much larger. Activities were entirely to do with cowboys and what they did on the range – lassoing, herding, branding – and all in a competitive vein.

The bucking broncos were the real show. The horses usually came out kicking up their heels. One of them bucked so high that he actually toppled over backwards. They thought that the rider must have been hurt, but just before the horse hit the arena, the cowboy managed to slither out, with no saddle to hold him, and then he went back for a second shot.

There was one wonderful horse called Midnight, an all-black that had never been ridden successfully. In this bucking contest, they put a flanking rope around the horse, a strap that went right around up against his haunches and backside and hind legs. They tied it loosely and it was this strap that made the horse buck. The rider had to stay on for thirty seconds or some such duration to pass the test. The horse went on bucking for as long as the flanking rope was around it, bucking and prancing all the time. When a horse threw a rider, two redcoated riders officiating would ride up against the bucking horse and release the flank rope. At once the horse stopped his bucking and trotted out quite happily. It did not hurt them in any way, or Thelma and Douglas would not have approved.

The wild cow milking was a typical western amusement. Two cowboys on foot formed each team, several of which were in the arena at once. A herd of wild cows were then loosed into the arena, right in their midst. These cows looked less domesticated than the more familiar ones, rather rangy and generally more streamlined creatures. Each cowboy had an empty milk bottle in his hands and they had to fill the bottle from one of the cows. As soon as a cowboy got his hands near an udder, the cow would let fly with one rear leg or the other and the cowboys frequently turned a couple of somersaults.

The most exciting event of all was the chuck wagon racing in the evening. They were ordinary wagons with a canvas top, single central shaft, and a horse harnessed on each side and two more in front. Four horses drawing a four-wheel, two-axle wagon with a hood on top. At the back was an ordinary kitchen stove which fitted into a slot on the wagon. These were the feeding kitchens that went out on the range when the cowboys were out branding cattle.

The race was around a quarter-mile track. The line-up was two wagons often with someone's name on the hood. Beside the wagon at the rear were two riders with their own horses, while standing in front holding the lead horse was another rider. When the bugle blew, the two men picked up the stove and heaved it on to the wagon in the slots provided. The fellow in front set the horses off. To be successful they had to reach the winning post first with all three outriders complete as a team. The animals were almost racehorses, with their ears laid back raring to go and the whites of their eyes showing with anticipation.

After a week at Calgary, Thelma and Douglas were quite worn out. They had enjoyed perfect weather. They heard a lovely local story about the weather. One year the authorities decided to charge the Red Indians to see the stampede. They had always come in free, so did not take kindly to this innovation. Local legend has it that they put the ju-ju on that year's stampede and for the first time it rained much of the time. Ever since then, they have never charged the Indians again and it has always been fine. So – up to the Yukon and the land of Douglas's pet poet, Robert W. Service.

Eventually Thelma and Douglas got to Lethbridge for the real purpose of their Canadian journey: the investiture of Douglas as an honorary chief of the

Black Foot Tribe in their tribal reserve about forty miles south of Lethbridge. This initiation into the tribe had gone on for quite a long time and was due to take place at a spot rejoicing in the quaint name of Belly-Buttes.

When the Baders got to Lethbridge a day or so beforehand, Douglas immediately met one or two of his chums from former RAF days. A Royal Canadian Air Force officer, Don Donaldson, had started a tyre business in the region and asked Douglas to open it and have a chat on the radio, which he duly did. Next day, Thelma and Douglas had a look around Lethbridge early. There were kids wandering round the town with cattle, just as there had been in Calgary. The boys were busy getting breakfast in the open air from men cooking by the side of the street. It all looked like a Hollywood film set and Douglas expected to see two cowboys with their hands on holsters advancing from opposite ends of the main street. But all remained quiet.

Then they set out for Belly-Buttes. En route they passed Fort McLeod, one of the real old frontier-style forts with lookout posts and suchlike. The reserve stood right out in the incredible Alberta plains, about three thousand feet and more above sea level. Belly-Buttes itself lay in the midst of this wonderfully fresh, high veldt country. On arrival they met various people to do with the Indian councils and also other honorary chieftains, whose ranks Douglas would soon join. Crystal sunlight splayed over the scene.

The secretary of the Chieftains, a Mr McFarlane, had arranged a barbecue lunch there and to the Baders' delight they got their first real sight of some Mounties in their full kit. North-West Mounted Policemen normally wore a more drab uniform on duty, but here they were clad specially for the ceremonial to come, with scarlet tunics, dark blue trousers, boots, and their wide hats pinched in at the top. Piping down the trousers added just that finishing touch to these great tall men.

After lunch the Baders went off to the Red Indians' parade ground. This had been built as a large round dais, a proper platform, and all the other chiefs were already on the scene, from Canada, America, and other remoter regions. The Big Chief, too, had arrived, a fellow enjoying the unusual title of Jim Shot Both Sides. As well as the chiefs, a lot of other onlookers had gathered for the inauguration of Chief Bader – both Red Indians and white men. Palefaces.

Thelma and Douglas were waiting on the perimeter of this arena. From the open stretch of country, they could see for 'about a thousand miles in every direction' with nothing to mar the marvellous view. They were to be escorted inside by two Mounties and waited beside a fence with an opening in it.

Suddenly someone said: 'You can't come in yet, because they've got the Union Jack flying upside down.' Douglas looked at the flagpole and said to one of the Mounties: 'I can't tell if it's upside down or the right way up – it looks alright to me'. Anyway, they got it correct in the end and they proceeded on to the stage or dais. While certain incantations were being muttered by all and sundry, Douglas and Thelma just waited. He did exactly as they told him to do. He took off his tie and then took off his shirt. He was then left with just his trousers on and quite bare from the midriff up. He sat up as crossed-leg as it was possible for him to sit. But it was rather hard to sit crossed-leg when he had two artificial ones.

The witch-doctor in charge of the proceedings was a fine-looking man in his feathered head-dress. He started muttering more incantations and rubbing ochre on Douglas's face, chest and forehead. Some of it was yellow and some red. As he went on with his mutterings, and the others chanted their mysterious responses, Douglas happened to peep past the witch-doctor to beyond the dais where he was sitting. There he suddenly saw several heads he knew, looking back at him over the stage! One belonged to Gerry Wood, who had been in Colditz with him; another was Lieutenant-Colonel Charles Cecil Ingersoll Merritt, the Canadian who won the Victoria Cross at Dieppe and was also later in prison camp with Douglas. He spotted Ace Turner, from his 242 Squadron of Canadians, and Ian Arthur. They mostly lived in the Vancouver region and he thought it was extraordinary to find them all out here at Belly–Buttes, five or six hundred miles from the coast. Douglas had not the slightest idea they would be there, so it was a wonderful surprise which helped to make the day more memorable than ever.

Douglas supposed that the other Indians responding had been saying their own equivalent of 'Hear, Hear'. Anyway, having been finally daubed with paint fairly freely all over, he stood up. A head-dress was presented to the witch-doctor, who in turn conveyed it to Douglas. At last he had been installed as an honorary chief. Douglas made a strange sight with chest exposed and covered in various tones of chalk and ochre. At the crowning moment, he was christened Chief Morningbird. Thelma was also given an Indian name, but unfortunately the rites did not insist on her being daubed!

After the ceremonial came a dance. Douglas found himself paired off with the daughter of Big Chief Jim Shot Both Sides. Miss Shot Both Sides. She was extremely attractive and had recently won some beauty contest, so Douglas was quite happy as he had never been averse to a pretty face. Thelma was closeted on the dance floor with the Big Chief himself. She thought he spoke English freely, so started gabbling away at him. But she soon saw she was wasting her time, as his sole response seemed to be the classic Red Indian one of 'Humph!' This was merely interspersed with an occasional grunting noise. The daughter had been emancipated, but her father apparently had not. They all did a funny sort of shuffling, jogging dance around the stage. One, two, three, hop, variety. This did not last long – fortunately.

On these high plateau places, there was always a breeze blowing and that day it seemed very strong off the plains. The funny thing about Indian head-dress was that when wearing one it stuck up quite a long way above the forehead and stopped where the ears were. So there was a front and no back. Unless the wearer stood downwind, the breeze blew the whole outfit over the face. This was happening to the chiefs and to Douglas, so that they were all nearly taking off at times.

After it was all over, Thelma and Chief Morningbird went back to Lethbridge for tea. Douglas had a date to inspect the local Air Cadets and present certificates and prizes. The cadets looked amazed. Here was this Battle of Britain ace all the way from England. He was wearing an ordinary lounge suit with his face still completely covered in the paint that had been daubed on it. Because according to the rules and traditions of the Indians' ceremony, he was not allowed to wipe or wash it off until the whole day was over.

Douglas always kept his head-dress. He had it safely in his little dressing-room at Petersham Mews and he popped upstairs and put it on when he wanted to impress anyone unexpectedly!

His association with Canada and Canadians went back to 1940, of course. Soon they were great chums and always very loyal. When the war ended, a lot of those men had been killed, but a lot were left. Douglas went to Canada for the first time in his life at the end of the 1940s. The Shell Company out there decided to have a reunion dinner of 242 Squadron in Ottawa. Since then he visited the country many times, particularly on the western side. Most of his squadron came from that area, so he saw a number of parents of chaps who had been killed. Once he had established the connection, he always contacted the various people when over there. One evening in Calgary a pretty blonde girl came up to him and said 'You don't remember me'. He replied 'But of course I do'. She had been a very young WAAF in the Operations Room at Tangmere and she had married a young Canadian. Douglas liked this sort of link with the old country.

A number of the Canadians taken prisoner at Dieppe were with him in Germany. They became friends under wartime conditions in experiences they all shared. Ties forged in war made the bond that much stronger for Douglas.

One year he was talking to the Calgary Chamber of Commerce and told them that he really thought it was high time they had some streets or their new aerodrome named after some of their World War 2 citizens who had distinguished themselves. He suggested that they could call their new airfield McKnight Field, in memory of Willie McKnight, who died at the age of twenty towards the end of 1940 when he was with Douglas. Willie had been twice decorated with the DFC and he shot down a number of enemy aircraft. Some time later, Douglas saw someone from Calgary who happened to be visiting London. He told Douglas that it would please him to know that one of the roads leading to the airfield was now called McKnight Boulevard, which did indeed make Douglas feel glad.

Brian McDonald was the twenty-two-year-old son the Shell Aviation manager in Western Canada and he lost both his legs in the blades of a helicopter. Douglas heard about Brian on one of his Canadian visits and so went to see him. He found a jolly young chap full of beans and with a very attractive nurse looking after him. Douglas took one look at her and said to Brian, 'My dear chap, if I had that nurse looking after me, I'd know what to do! But the most important thing is to get off your backside and get moving as soon as possible'. Not long afterwards, Douglas got a letter saying that he probably would not be surprised to hear that Brian and his nurse were going to be married. Later Douglas saw them both again and he was delighted to find that Brian was walking well and they were very happy.

In 1970, Douglas had a letter from a girl in Yorkshire saying that her brother had had an accident in an aeroplane and was now detained at Vancouver General Hospital. He was minus one leg and had the possibility of losing the other one. She asked if Douglas would write and cheer-up her brother. Douglas wrote to a close friend of his over in Canada and asked him to contact Brian McDonald. He asked that Brian should go in his place to the Vancouver hospital and talk to this man. Douglas was completely confident that Brian would know what to say and do to help. So the chain of help was continued and extended via fresh cases and new people. Douglas wanted to develop his ideas of encouragement and self-help as widely as he could.

CHAPTER 25

When one thinks of Thelma Bader, a kaleidoscope of colourful impressions brighten the mind. For as someone said: 'Thelma's life cannot be described by a catalogue of achievements: indeed, any such approach would be to belittle her whole attitude to life itself'.

Douglas's thoughts of Thelma went back, in fact, to times before he met her. Jill and the others told him about the family scene in the 1920s. There was a wonderful old family house down at Windlesham in Surrey, where various relations lived or came and went according to their duties. Several of the girls had husbands in the Services or the Colonial Service, so they used to arrive from all points of the compass for odd lengths of stay. From rubber plantations in Malaya they would come to the seclusion of Hatton Hall, as it was called. But perhaps seclusion is scarcely the word, for this constantly changing pattern of people made for lively and happy times.

When Thelma was quite a young girl, she seemed to have mainly boys there as companions. They all played their childish games together, and Thelma used to complain in retrospect that as she was a girl 'I always played the Germans.'

Before she met Douglas, she had been engaged for a short time to an Australian naval officer whom she met in Malta.

Jill and John were a bit jealous of Thelma paying attention to this gentleman instead of them. They decided to try and do something about it and so told her that they had seen him kicking her dog down the stairs and into the garden. This was quite untrue, of course, but at that she broke off the engagement. Douglas was later deeply indebted to them for this!

Then in the 1930s, when Jill and John were in their teens, Thelma and Douglas used to enjoy tennis on a wonderful grass court at Hatton Hall. They played doubles, with Douglas up at the net being quite deadly towards anything in his reach, and Thelma used to indulge in the most unladylike language when she missed a shot. Among many partners and opponents in those far off summers were Alan Garrow and Henry Longhurst.

Thelma was also a strong swimmer and she and Douglas liked one pool particularly, at a house near Haslemere.

Throughout her life, Thelma retained a rare, distinguished beauty. She had high cheeks that were frequently broken by a smile. A naturally gay and vital personality, she possessed an attractive slight drawl to her voice, which somehow seemed to fit in with the elegance of the rest of her aura. She was utterly devoid of jealousy of any kind and took the greatest pleasure in someone else achieving something, and someone looking nice. She liked people to be happy and successful in the true meaning of success, and she got real enjoyment out of people's happiness.

Thelma had a great sense of humour and was always having tremendous chuckles. She never had any children, yet like Douglas, the young found her very easy to talk to. There was no generation gap or any of that nonsense. Later on, Laddie and Jill's two boys both said 'We wish we had known her better, because she never made a remark that was a typical grown-up's comment. She never said a banal thing'.

Thelma always took the trouble to do things for people. She used to say 'If you really want something enough, you can make it happen. If you haven't any money, you don't just sit there and moan about it. You go out and do something'. She did not believe in Jill's mother's philosophy of accepting the station to which you had been called. Thelma believed in doing things, not complaining about anything.

Right through the years, since she accepted her life with Douglas, Thelma helped other people with disabilities – as well as helping him when he wanted it. She was the one who was available to help Richard Wood after he had walked on to a mine in the Western Desert during the war. The mine blew both his legs off. He had lost his legs above the knee. Thelma told Douglas about him in a letter to prison camp, and then when the war was over, Douglas saw him, too. But Thelma had started it and kept it going. Douglas insisted that she kept him up to scratch in answering all the letters and requests that constantly came their way over the decades.

At some stage there was a girl from the north of England who appealed to them for guidance. She had one leg in a calliper. Whenever she visited London, she came in to talk about her leg and how she wanted to work on a farm. Thelma was genuinely concerned as usual, and did more for her than Douglas could. In fact, Douglas says that although all sorts of things like this started via him, after people had come to the house and met Thelma, they all went to her. He claims she gave them more strength that he could in many cases.

Thelma's passion was for everything beautiful in life. Flowers and plants of course. Clothes. Animals, she adored – especially dogs. She loved gardening. The minute she arrived at a friend's house, almost before she had said hello, she would be weeding or dead-heading. It was quite remarkable. She loved making things grow and needless to say had very green fingers. People only had to look at the profusion of plants in front of the mews house, exuding life and vitality. The facade was, significantly, pale green.

And because Thelma loved beauty, she collected some really exquisite antiques and other objects from all over the world. One of the nicest thoughts she had was to make a point of bringing back charms from all the places she and Douglas visited. These added up to so many that they filled no fewer than four bracelets. Every single charm represented somewhere they had shared and bought wherever they happened to be. They reminded her of happy years and tens of thousands of miles flown together. There was the limbo charm from the West Indies; the Taj Mahal from India; and even a little bag of golf clubs from St Andrews.

Over in one corner of the drawing-room stood a pair of scales which Thelma acquired in Dawson City during their visit to the Yukon. These scales were the actual ones used by the assayer. The prospector would bring in his little bag of gold dust, shake it on to the scales, and then the assayer would weigh it and dish out the dollars in exchange.

A place that Thelma loved was Muscat in the Trucial Oman. She was fascinated by this old medieval sort of rocky fortress right on the coast of the Indian Ocean at the foot of the Persian Gulf.

On the opposite wall to the gold scales hung a pair of old bellows. Like so many other little pieces in the home, there was a story attached to these. Thelma and Douglas were driving down from the north one day and decided to stop for the night in the Bell at Barnby, an old coaching house made famous in a pre war film called *The Great North Road*. They remembered the film and its star, Edmund Gwenn.

Around a huge iron fireplace in the hall stood an old chimney-piece. On one side of this chimney, the pair of bellows hung, looking rather dirty and tatty. They noticed these and were attracted to them, despite or perhaps because of their apparent age.

Douglas asked the landlord: 'Look, how much will you sell us those bellows for?'

'Oh, I'll give 'ee those. I've had the bloody things there for years.'

'No', said Douglas, 'I don't want you to give them to us, but I would like to buy them. How much?'

'Take the bloody things', the man said.

Douglas asked Thelma, 'How much do you think they're worth?'

'About ten pounds, I should think.'

Douglas turned to the man: 'My wife reckons they're worth ten pounds. So I'll accept them if I can give you a cheque for ten pounds to pass on to the local RAF fund'.

'That's reet enough', the man said.

Thelma always had little men who mended things for her, so when they got home, they took the bellows round to one of these ubiquitous chaps. The bellows needed repairing and polishing. She asked him: 'Are these Cornish?'

'No, they're Dutch', he told her.

'How do you know?'

'You can always tell Cornish bellows, because Cornishmen used to make them while sitting beside Customs men waiting for smugglers. They used to sketch the faces of these men. You'll always find sketches inside old Cornish bellows – but there are none inside these'.

'How much do you reckon they are worth?' Thelma asked.

'About ten pounds', he said after a little thought.

So she had got their value exactly right. Thelma always got her values right – usually though they had nothing to do with money.

Apart from the people and the places, perhaps the times that Thelma and Douglas remembered best of all were the hundreds of hours spent together in the air. Douglas would be flying either his Proctor, Gemini or Beechcraft. Twenty-two years of flying throughout most of the world. An enviable memory.

On their very first long-distance trip in the early Proctor, they landed in Rome. They were en route to the Far East in those halcyon days. But even then there was the inevitable Italian official who simply could not appreciate how Thelma could be a passenger and yet not be fare-paying. He seemed unable to grasp that as the aeroplane was a private one, a passenger manifest was not needed. After half-an-hour, Douglas was still saying But this is my wife and this is my aeroplane and she doesn't pay. They had become quite hysterical by that time and felt they would never leave Rome – not that that would be such a terrible fate.

Something had to happen. Suddenly a great grin creased the Latin face and he said: 'Ah! I know, she is the hostess.' So they were all right in the end. No mail, no disease, no animals, and no passengers. Just the captain and his hostess.

That was a tip they always recalled, for it saved them much form-filling later on. They never carried 'passengers' as such. Once they picked up the daughter of the Shell general manager in Karachi, who wanted to go to Calcutta. She also had a friend who asked to be put off at the Taj Mahal. On the manifest, Douglas wrote Captain, Douglas Bader; Air Hostess, Mrs Bader; Hostesses under instruction Nos. 1 and 2. Henceforth, any passengers were either co-pilot, navigator, radio operator or air hostess.

While in Calcutta early on, Douglas sought the advice of an experienced pilot who had been flying up and down the coast between there and Rangoon for years. They were due to meet the monsoon in southern Burma and it would be new to Douglas. This man gave him advice he always followed: 'The monsoon is mainly heavy rain with a cloud base seldom lower than 500 feet. You can follow the coastline even in the heaviest rain. Its intensity will vary continually. There are three sorts of monsoon raincloud: white, black and brown. White is heavy rain and presents no problem. Black is line squall stuff and best avoided by flying along it and round it. Never go into the brown'.

If you are flying a little aeroplane, particularly over sea, it is much more natural and sensible to fly underneath the weather. People talk nonsense about Inter-Tropical Fronts and things. But Douglas found very little trouble then or later. Most of the storms were actually inland, and you did not get them over the sea so much.

The airstrip of Robertsport was called Robert's Field and lay amid rubber plantations. It was not quite on the coast, but just up a creeky river. The rains were falling very fiercely just then and at *le moment critique* Douglas was still searching for the field through the rain, when Thelma said in her customary cool tone: 'We're right over the field now, if that's what you're looking for'.

It was still bouncing off the ground as they landed at the field 'to get some gravy'. After they had filled up the tanks, a black boy in shorts and carrying an umbrella walked out with a can of oil. The umbrella kept him fairly dry, but not the oil. So Douglas had to tell him to bring a new can and keep it under the umbrella. They took off from Robert's Field still in this warm, sheeting, tropical rain.

After Monrovia, the port and capital city of Liberia, they flew on still south-east towards Cape Palmas, where that great bulge of African coast turns left to face east-north-east. The rain accompanied them on and off all the way till they rounded the Cape, and then almost instantly they flew straight into an aquamarine sky with marvellous visibility. They had flown the entire route at the incredible altitude of 100 feet, cocking an eye inland to port at the drenched palms quite a few feet higher than the Gemini. Later they graduated from the Gemini to the sophisticated Beechcraft.

And what of Thelma through the eyes of one of the Baders' longest-standing friends? Denis Crowley-Milling first met Thelma and Douglas in 1940. He of course was one of 242 Squadron when it was in a pretty poor state of morale after returning from France. He was a close friend of both the Baders. Here he concentrates on his memories of Thelma:

> 'Thelma went everywhere with him. She was always there and has always been a tremendous prop to him. Yet it was never noticeable, obtrusive. Wherever she was, there was never a panic. Or if there were, she would be simply sitting there and letting it sail around her. She was very serene and complementary to Douglas. Yet you really felt she had a strong character.
>
> I was twenty-one. They were about thirty. Thelma was chuckling even then. In the mess at Martlesham over the winter of 1940–41, we were all in the ladies' room one evening singing *The Muffin Man*. You put a pint of beer on your head and bobbed up and down going round the room. I remember that with Thelma there, one of the chaps did it and took off his trousers at the same time: The point was that he felt he could do this although she was there . . .
>
> Then in 1941, I remember all of us going to a party at the night-fighter base of Ford in Sussex. There was Cocky Dundas, Johnnie Johnson, the Baders and the rest. We were all in no pain whatsoever by the end of the evening. We started singing over the station intercom the usual squadron songs and we were all chucked out. Thelma commiserated with us about it and had one of her chuckles. She was really one of us.

I was shot down about a week after Douglas. I was lucky in escaping and got through Spain to Gibraltar. When I reached home, I got in touch with Thelma again. Then I did not see much of her for a while, until I came across a chap who had been with Douglas in prison camp and had escaped and got home. He was a Norwegian. I arranged for Thelma to meet him and we all had lunch at the Dorchester together in the middle of the war. This was to give her first-hand news of Douglas. Lorna and I were married in 1943 and then we used to see Thelma in 1944, while I was at the Army Staff College in Camberley, quite near Ascot. She was marvellous throughout the whole time Douglas was away.

Then after the war we were all in touch again. I went to the Middle East in 1947 until 1950. During that time, Douglas flew out from Cairo to see me in his Proctor.

When I got back home, Thelma and Douglas used to come to dinner or else to our station Balls. We also met when Douglas gave a dinner party for General Galland. Thelma was there, too.

In the film of *Reach for the Sky* I thought Muriel Pavlow was not right for the part of Thelma. She was a nice English girl, but Thelma was so much more than that. She was never a clinging type of wife, yet she still devoted her life to Douglas. She had a strength of will certainly equal to his own.

When our second daughter, Gillian, was born, we invited Thelma to become her Godmother. If we had a boy, we were going to ask Douglas to be Godfather. Over the years, they have often come to spend week-ends with us. They flew up to West Raynham in the little Gemini. We have a good photo of Thelma with Gillian. Thelma is sitting in the garden. Gillian is leaning over her. Thelma at her tapestry work which she did so beautifully. She would sit there at it quite serene yet very much in touch with everyone and everything that was going on.

Thelma was so good, too, at bringing people out: at talking and getting them to talk. She was a very good listener for the simple reason she was vitally interested in people and in life.'

Chapter 26

In May 1958, Thelma and Douglas had one of the greatest thrills of their lives when they received an invitation, or a command, to dine with the Queen and the Duke of Edinburgh at Buckingham Palace. They felt excited and began to wonder and worry about what to wear and do. They need not have fretted though, for they received complete instructions as to attire: dinner jacket for Douglas and a long dress for Thelma. They were also told where to report and at what time and who to ask for on arrival. There would be some other guests as well, so they did not feel as nervous as they might possibly have done. In fact, once the arrangements had been formalised, the actual evening turned out to be quite informal – if that is not a contradiction in terms.

The Baders arrived promptly at the Palace and were ushered into a reception room, where they found one of the Royal Household whom they happened to know. That was a good start. They were then told that it would be an entirely informal dinner party just as they might have at home, and that Her Majesty wanted them to talk as freely as they liked – and not just to wait for her to speak to them, and then answer yes or no.

To Douglas's joy he found two friends were among the small company of other guests. They were Bobby George and his wife Betty. Air Marshal Sir Robert George had been Governor of Victoria when the Baders made that memorable visit to Australia, but Douglas had known them when they were courting at Cranwell in 1928: Thelma had also known them for years. Among the other guests were Alec Guinness and his wife and that legendary figure A. P. Herbert, who obviously knew the Royal couple well. The Princess of Athlone was also there.

Thelma and Douglas were presented to the Queen and Prince Philip early on and they chatted with the Baders for a few minutes. Then someone opened large doors and they all went in to dinner. There was a man standing behind each chair. The food was just how Douglas liked it, very simple and very good. Despite the occasion, the talk was perfectly normal and relaxed; at least apparently so. Douglas was sitting next to Mrs Alec Guinness, who told him that her husband had been extremely nervous before coming. Douglas said that he found that hard to believe in view of all the acting ordeals he had faced and overcome with ease.

After the meal, the Queen took the ladies, leaving the men sitting around gossiping. Then they joined them in the Queen's picture gallery on the same floor. Charles Wheeler was another guest and he accompanied the Queen on a short tour of the gallery, discussing various pictures which had been cleaned recently.

Douglas watched her talking to A. P. Herbert. He was old enough to be her father and she obviously liked him. He was blinking away as he always did so characteristically. The Queen came round and talked to each of them in turn. She moved down the gallery towards Thelma and Douglas and the first thing she said to Douglas was: 'Have you grown a beard?' It was rather a startler for an opening, but Douglas told her that he had once when in hospital many years earlier. Never one to be overawed by a moment like this, Douglas added 'My mother was delighted and thought I looked like one of the Apostles'. As Douglas's mother had been a religious woman, the beard had appealed to her sense of biblical atmosphere. The reason why the Queen had put the question was that Alec Guinness had told her he had grown a beard for his last film.

The Queen herself appeared to be a fraction nervous, too, fingering an evening bag in her hand. As Douglas pointed out afterwards: 'Perhaps wondering what this oaf Bader was going to say next'. Thelma was impressed by her bearing and felt that she had done her homework well, having a broad knowledge of all the subjects that cropped up during the rest of the evening.

Thelma and Douglas always insisted that they left the Royal invitation on their Adam mantelpiece for a long time afterwards so that all their friends would be sure to see it and be suitably jealous. They celebrated their silver wedding on 5 October 1958, so this was proving to be quite a year in their eventful lives.

Perhaps the most outstanding tribute to Douglas, among the many hundreds that have been paid over the last half century, came on 25 April 1961, when the National Sporting Club gave a dinner in his honour. Everyone who was there on that night remembered it years later: men like Harry Broadhurst, Gus Walker, Vivien Fuchs, Alan Deere, Dermot Boyle and dozens of others. Much of the credit for organising this event went to Charles Forte, who had been a supporter of the Bader image over years. Forte sat in the centre of the top table, with Douglas near him. Douglas's own specially invited friends occupied a table at right-angles to the top one, abutting it. When the actual meal was over, a silver box of expensive cigars was offered around to the guests at the top table. The moment Douglas saw and assimilated that they were not going to be extended to the other table, he grabbed a handful and scattered them to his friends. It was a typically spontaneous Bader gesture and its meaning was clear for anyone who cared to construe it.

Proposing the toast to Douglas Bader was his life long friend from the earliest Royal Air Force days, Dermot Boyle. This is what he said:

> I think that no speaker could have a finer or a more awkward subject: Fine – because few if any can in their

lifetime have established a world reputation for courage, fortitude and achievement greater than has Douglas Bader. Awkward – because through the medium of a book and a film called *Reach for the Sky* each and every one of you here probably know more about Douglas Bader than I do. Even though I've known him for thirty years.

Douglas Bader during his last year at his Prep school was captain of cricket, rugger and soccer. And in the athletic sports, he ran in every race in which he was allowed to run – the 100, 220, 440, 880 yards and hurdles and he won every one of them. While he was cooling off, he broke the school record for throwing the cricket ball.

He then went on to St Edward's where he represented his school at fives, shooting and rugger, and was captain of cricket. Then we had the anxiety of having him at Cranwell. I was there as an instructor at the time and the anxiety was considerable. There he got his rugger, boxing and hockey colours and again was captain of cricket.

At the age of twenty-one, he had played rugger for the Royal Air Force on no fewer than eleven occasions. He played regularly for the Harlequins. He had been selected to represent the Combined Services and everyone generally believed that that would lead to an English trial. At the same time, he was playing cricket for the Royal Air Force during two seasons. His most sparkling performance was I think at the Oval. The Air Force were playing the Army and he scored sixty-five runs in thirty minutes; those runs were made up of one six, one five, and twelve fours: this was at a time of day when all the experts said that bad light should have stopped play.

These achievements, great as they were, have been complete eclipsed by his subsequent struggle with adversity and the way he has overcome it. You will know about his crash, the loss of his legs, his struggle for life, his struggle to get back into the Royal Air Force on flying duty, his retirement and his subsequent rejoining of the Service when war was imminent.

You may feel that at times he was a bit unjustly critical of the Air Force, almost disloyal. Anyone who thinks that must underestimate the man; underestimate the enormity of the personal problem with which he was faced at that time. Douglas Bader outspoken, yes. Blood enthusiastic, yes. Terribly determined, yes. But disloyal – never. In fact I think his loyalty to his friends, his school, his service, and above all, to his country – for which he was prepared to die at any time during the war and jolly nearly did at least three times – his loyalty is one of the most endearing and lovable aspects of his character.

It is now history that he became not only one of our greatest fighter pilots, but one of the greatest fighter leaders and fighter tacticians of our time. His tactics he stole a little from the past. Instead of the modern gimmick of saying 'What's new?' he said 'What's old that matters?'. He found in the history of the First World War two things that are terribly important for modern fighter pilots. The sun and height. They were always valued in the First World War and they were much more valuable in the Second.

As for his powers of leadership, he had got whatever it takes to make a magnificent leader. A great understanding of human nature; absolutely fearless; unbounded enthusiasm; irrepressible energy; and a selfless devotion to his unit and to everything that that unit was fighting for.

On 9 August 1941, in the height of an air battle, he collided with an enemy which he had hoped to shoot down. He baled out and was taken prisoner of war. He already had a record of confirmed enemy aircraft destroyed. Then we all know the fantastic stories of being a prisoner of war. He was always either escaping, or planning an escape, or goon-baiting. After nearly four years of turbulent captivity, came his release, his repatriation and peace.

Then we came to the first Battle of Britain fly-past after the war, which he led – and I was responsible for. We had a great collection of these fighter aces who had been destroying all they could see in front of them for years. And this was rather a difficult problem – to arrive at the right time and to go through the haze of London. We were wondering whether you should do this flying business by looking where you were going or looking at a watch. I had a secret feeling that the time had come to look at the watch. There were two schools of thought. I thought it would be an appropriate thing to turn to Douglas Bader, and I asked him. He said, 'It's quite clear, the watch is the only thing'. Since then, that has been the way the Royal Air Force has always done its big formation fly pasts.

One tends to forget that all these things were done without his own legs. You can hardly imagine that he hasn't got any legs. In fact, if you stay long in his company, you get almost alarmingly aware of the great advantages which artificial legs bestow on the wearers: no sprained ankles, no knee-caps or cartilage trouble, no stiffening of the joints that can't be cured with an oil-can, and you need only change your socks when they wear out. And as you get on in life, no varicose veins, no gout, no housemaid's knee.

Douglas was the first man in the world to lose both legs, to walk without a stick, and to lead a normal life. It is a great triumph of mind over matter. In the past doctors used to spend all their time trying to condition patients to the handicap that they had got to accept, the psychological handicap. But that is all changed now. And it has all changed because of one man, Douglas Bader. I think Douglas has given the doctors just what they wanted. They wanted someone who had the guts and moral and physical strength. Doctors now encourage their patients quite differently. Douglas is an example of what you can do, thereby bringing hope and encouragement to thousands of people throughout the world. Douglas keeps up an almost continuous correspondence with people who have to suffer in this way. He is always visiting them, helping them, encouraging them.

He has excelled in a great many fields: as a sportsman, a fighter pilot, and as a loyal supporter of everything that we in this country hold dear. Above all, as a man who, by his example and courage, has brought hope and comfort to many thousands of people, regardless of country, creed, colour or class.

In the RAF we have a splendid motto. It is in four simple Latin words and I think it epitomises the life and struggle and the achievement of Douglas Bader:

PER ARDUA AD ASTRA.'

Douglas made one of his most profound responses. He said this:

'It is manifestly impossible to expect me to answer such a speech by a Marshal of the Royal Air Force, who has just told you that I'm a decent chap. If I were to try, it is possible that I might be emotional. And judging by the amount of alcohol that most of you have consumed, it's reasonable to suppose that you too might become emotional. The result would be a disaster.

When the National Sporting Club first invited me to this dinner, with great kindness and courtesy they asked me if I had any friends. And if so, would I like them invited.

As a result, some of you may find yourselves sitting alongside some disreputable characters whom you do not know. Indeed you may have already made a mental reservation that you do not wish to know them. Gentlemen – those are my friends. I have worked with them, played with them, I have been in prison with them – prisoner of war camp with them – I have nearly been court-martialled with them or because of them. In fact, over the years they have always been around. I thank God for them, particularly for their presence here tonight.

I like people. I love the warmth that friendship brings. As the years roll on, we find the pattern of our lives change. The violence, the vigour and the impatience of youth give place to more tranquil state of mind and body. Our memories multiply with the years and we have more time to enjoy them.

Amongst our memories, we treasure many firsts. The first time, for instance, as a boy at school we see our name on the notice-board to play for the first-fifteen or the first-eleven. The first time we made 100 runs at cricket, or broke 80 strokes in a medal round of golf. The first time we climbed into a boxing ring and won an important fight. The first time a Messerschmitt 109 shot us up the ass. Memories like these linger as the years gather. They stimulate our minds and give us a lot of laughs.

Mr Chairman and gentlemen. May I raise my glass to you all and wish you happy days. Thank you for coming here tonight and supporting this dinner. For bringing into this room for this short space of time, the warmth of your friendship. By your presence here tonight, you have made this a tremendous occasion for me. You have given me a magnificent first to add to my store of memories – and one which I shall recall many times in the future. And which will bring me much warmth and happiness as the years unwind.'

A complex amalgam of human qualities. How can a man's true self be conveyed? By what he says and does. But also by what other people say about him and would do for him. This is how people saw Douglas. Some, friends; others, not. From so many minds, perhaps the true portrait begins to take form:

'Douglas is forthright, it's in his nature, he's not a compromiser. It can be a strength and a weakness. His nature is such that he's a positive person and positive people are bound to pick up a thorn or two on the way.'

'I believe Douglas is one of the greatest Christians alive. He has never complained over the years and this has rubbed off on Thelma, too.'

'Douglas has a tremendous love of young people . . . he feels they don't mix so well with our generation, so he has them on their own.'

'Douglas doesn't like things foreign. He thinks the wogs start at Dover. Doesn't like the French. Doesn't like Spanish food. And all his friends are here. He's very gregarious.'

'Douglas was very thoughtful and considerate as a husband. He would drive Thelma wherever she wanted to go. He would drive to Scotland and back by Mini. He has fantastically fast reflexes.'

'A lot of people don't understand him when they first meet him. They may think he is rude or boorish. It's probably due to they way they approach him. Any sympathy is like a red rag to a bull . . . The more you know him, the more you understand him. You may make allowances for him because he's difficult . . . There is his opinion and the wrong one. It's unusual to persuade Douglas to change his mind. He is a great decision-maker. There are compromises on matters like Apartheid, but he's got his own cut-and-dried views and they are based on what he calls loyalty to his chums . . .'

'If a man is a prick he calls him a prick. In the peacetime Air Force you daren't do that, especially if he's a senior chap. You've got to say yes sir, no sir, three bags full. And he would never have done it. Especially after achieving the recognition he did during the war. At Shell he was virtually his own boss and his own master and he could come and go as he pleased. It gave him full scope for everything. All the time for his good deeds for the disabled.'

'He has strong views on people and personalities. And he doesn't take many words to define or express them. He sees a desired line of action and goes straight that way. He doesn't go by half-measures. This is part of his make-up and reflects his resolution of character. He has an enormous amount of commonsense. He can be a bit insensitive to the feelings of other people, but this is Douglas . . .'

'Douglas is a great person for self-discipline, which goes with fair-play. He has never harboured a grudge against life, though he has had great cause for complaint. It's no good looking at what might have been. He lives in the present, for the joy of the day alone.'

'Bader is not everyone's cup of tea.'

'He's such a remarkable person, one must allow him everything. He's terrific. For me he's a regular guy . . . What he has done is without parallel in the annals of flying. He has done a lot to become an example to young people. He's a good man. I love that man. He has steely-blue clear eyes. He says exactly what he thinks. If only one could always say what one thinks. He's a funny man, too; he makes me laugh. I knew someone who was in a POW camp with him. He was a pilot and a journalist. What they didn't like Bader for was that he always wanted to be in on the escaping things and they got fed-up with it as of course he could not run if necessary. When the prisoners were being harangued by the Kommandant at a camp, using fairly tough language, at the end of it Bader hobbled out of the ranks, advanced on the Kommandant, put his arms round him and said 'You're the most lovely boy!'

'No doubt about it. His personality has been influenced, moulded, to some extent by the fact that he lost his legs. The fact that he lost them gave him something extra. He's still not an easy chap. Let's be fair about it. I like him, but we argue. He's probably got nearly as many enemies as he has friends. But then all great men have – and he's a great man in his own way. There is a certain amount of egoism in his make-up. I don't say this unkindly and I would say it to his face. He always likes to be first. He's a showman. He's got minus two legs to be a showman with. The disability and the fame. He wasn't any better than a number of other fighter pilots. He's be the first to acknowledge that, if you pinned him down . . .'

'Bader is dynamic. Two hours in his company and one is worn out!'

'It was really an extraordinary thing. When that chap came into the room, the lights seemed to go dim. As if his electric quality caused that to happen. Such dynamism.'

'He trusts, wants to trust, people. But his judgement is not always infallible. Once he said what a good chap some African seemed to be, and the next he knew was shortly afterwards when the man had some of his opposition shot. He trusts people unless they trigger-off some alarm bell. One of his tenets is: you expect to be treated badly by your enemies, but when you've got friends and they do that to you, you're powerless.'

'He's a very forthright fellow. He's not frightened of what people think. He says what he thinks. He sees things very clearly. He is irritated by complications. He is very much on the side of people who fought for King and Country . . . He feels that if people are getting a raw deal, he has to talk about it.

There are fewer men like this nowadays – a great tragedy. He doesn't tolerate stupidity.'

'You could say that politically Bader would always leap to the defence of good things, as he saw them, and vigorously attack those things he thought were wrong.'

'Communications? It's inborn in him . . . He could take a public office because of his ability to handle people. He has technical and mental ability. He can sit down and make the right judgements. I knew him to have an extremely good business brain. He has a yen to do something in the public interest, because he's a great patriot. This comes as natural to him, to serve his country . . .'

'He has a mind that is flexible and receptive to industrial problems. He is pretty worldly in his outlook on business and what makes people tick. If it is a job he's really interested in, his staying power is enormous. He's as strong as an ox. As a speaker, he takes a good deal of trouble to make whatever impact he is trying to make – one or two vital points – and the rest is amusing rubbish. Any good cause he thinks he can make a contribution to – he'll be there. No matter how big or small. He's very quick to assess people and he's usually right. But if he's going to condemn somebody or something, he'll do his homework first. If you're a friend, he can see no wrong in you . . . Anyone who criticises a friend of his gets a real basinful. Ian Smith is a friend. Douglas knows him and reckons he has assessed his value. Hence his views on Rhodesia.'

'Douglas is a chap who is apt to have a rather dramatic effect on people when they first meet him. It's all part of Douglas. He's an ebullient sort of chap, an extrovert.'

'He does an enormous amount of charitable work which people don't know anything about. If you asked him about it, you wouldn't get a reply. He has given back to life everything that anybody has given him. I've never known any trace of bitterness in him . . . He's got a very nice sense of humour, but you've got to understand it.'

'I get on pretty well with Douglas. Strictly between ourselves, he's a bit of a bully. If you shout back at him, he's all right. I remember on one occasion, we had a slight contretemps. I told him to go and jump in the lake and from then on we became very friendly . . . He's very much an assertive personality. But you wouldn't get on with him if you kowtowed to him.'

'Our friendship stems from flying. There's a bigger sympathy between people who fly or flew than any others, I think.'

'Bader is loved by the young and is a great inspiration. He is pro-England, pro-RAF, pro all the right things. His great achievement was his continued stability after his accident. He would have had every reason for going peculiar, but he didn't.'

'Douglas can deal with all layers of people. After the war he advised Shell on technical aspects of aircraft and reported on whether chartered companies were working well. On his trips he made observations about conditions within the organisation. He told Shell about top staff, the sort of comment they would never get to hear.'

'I remember having dinner with Douglas one night at his house and the telephone rang. A man he had never heard of in his life before said that he was with his daughter in Great Ormond Street Hospital and she had lost one of her legs. She had always admired Douglas. The father said: "I don't suppose there's any possibility of you talking to her on the phone or writing her a note or something". Douglas went straight to the hospital and he sat with this little girl. Apparently, according to the doctor, the effect was magical. She suddenly got the will to live again. She had lost it due to the loss of her leg.'

'There are many great things about Douglas. He is an absolutely marvellous friend . . . He is the sort of linchpin of people, many of whom wouldn't have kept in touch with each other if it hadn't been for him.'

Chapter 27

In the early 1960s, Douglas received a request to visit HM Prisons and talk to the inmates. Douglas read the letter to Thelma and said, 'Well, I don't know. I've never been to prison yet, so I might as well have a go.' The result was that Douglas found himself one day on his way to Wandsworth. He had no preconceived ideas about what happened when one visited a prison. As soon as he had passed through the ominous-looking gates, he was shown into the governor's office.

From there Douglas was led into what appeared to be a theatre crowded with about four hundred prisoners, guarded at the back of the hall by warders in their buttoned uniforms. The warders, he soon found out, were known by one and all as the screws. The prisoners all seemed to be wearing some sort of off-blue battledress uniform. At that moment as Douglas made his way to the stage, he had literally no notion of what he would be saying to them. He relied on the inspiration of the moment, as so often, and it had never deserted him in the past. There was always a first time, of course.

'I've come here to gossip with you chaps. Not to talk *to* you, but to talk *with* you. I'm going to speak for about two minutes flat, and then I'll stop and I'll expect you to ask me any questions. I'll do my best to answer them. Looking around, I must ask you first of all, is there anyone here who served in the Royal Air Force?' A ripple of laughter rose and fell. No-one stood up, until a chap near the front said to him, 'I wasn't in the RAF, but I've often served you in the mess of the Shell Company'. This at least started the ball rolling. They soon got the message that Douglas was not some pompous welfare bore who would be lecturing them. He went on:

> 'I've come here because I know what it's like to be inside! I was inside under slightly different circumstances. But I imagine that you've got an escaping committee. We had some good ones when we were at Colditz – and some bloody good plans, too. Incidentally, I see that the warders at the back are wearing belts with their keys on them. The Germans used to do that when I was in prison camp. They sometimes used to lose quite a few keys like that.'

Douglas visited Wandsworth many times and then went to Wormwood Scrubs as well. Just after the time of the Great Train Robbery, one fellow said to him, 'Do you think it's right that a man should get thirty years for a bit of good honest thieving, when a murderer can get out in nine or ten years?' There was no answer to that and Douglas said that as far as he was concerned, he would hang the murderer or shoot him.

One chap in the front row said to him: 'Tell me, Mr Bader, how is it that I'm in here and you are outside? Why has it happened like that?'

'My dear chap, but for the grace of God, I'd be in there with you. It's just a matter of luck.'

Another man asked him pointblank: 'Why have you come here to talk to us?'

Douglas said: 'Apart from the fact that I know what it's like to have my liberty taken from me – which I had for over three and a half years – if you want me to come here, who am I to refuse? If you don't want me, you can bloody well tell me and I won't come again!'

Douglas deplored conscious do-gooders who said 'These poor chaps, they should have anything they like, all the television they want, and knock all the warders on the head if they like. All they need is a bit of psychiatric treatment; they must have had difficult lives', and so on. Douglas looked on the prisoners as human beings like himself, but he did not go along with the do-gooders' liberal attitudes. If he could talk to a man, make him laugh, make him think, or even perhaps stop him going to prison again – then obviously his visits were worthwhile.

One of Douglas's non-successes was a lad of about twenty-three. He looked very smartly turned out, even in his prison garb, and he was generally alert and alive. 'I'm not going to work from nine to five. I'd rather go and knock something off and have a jolly good time and then, if I'm caught, come back here for a spell.' Nothing Douglas said convinced this chap, although DB went on for half-an-hour in the attempt. At the end, he felt very, very sad and extremely irritated.

Although Douglas had a lot of genuine sympathy for the prisoners in Wandsworth and elsewhere, this in no way affected his unequivocal views on capital punishment. These he had expressed freely over the years and he felt strongly about the subject. The question of capital punishment he believed to be completely straightforward. It had no connection with religion or ethics. He had no inhibitions at all about it. He felt no doubt that as a result of the abolition of capital punishment in Britain, coupled with the introduction of legalised betting shops and the seamy gaming establishments, organised crime was created in this country.

It is almost our daily diet to read in the papers that somebody has been killed in a bank robbery; a child is missing and subsequently found dead; or a policeman has been shot and killed or at least injured in the course of his duty. Douglas maintained that these are now all so commonplace as scarcely to cause a raised eyebrow. It was no use the do-gooders talking about these poor murderers being just a bunch of mixed-up misunderstood kids. That was not good enough any longer.

To Douglas the answer was a simple one. We live in a man-made society, a so-called civilised society, and we wish it to remain so. There are certain rules. So if you live in a community, you obey the laws of that community. And if the laws are written up so that everyone can read them, there is no excuse for anyone to misunderstand them, or plead ignorance of them. If you kill, you die. That should be the law. Let us keep it simple. There is no such thing as a better or worse murder – there is just murder. Murderers like Haigh, Christie, Heath and Manual killed several times before they were finally caught. Douglas would have made virtually all murder a capital offence, including the so-called guilty but insane one. He would have made life imprisonment mean what it says, and there would be no remission for good behaviour.

If you stole, you got so many years' imprisonment, with no excuses for not understanding the law. Violence breeds murder and the public is sick of it. Douglas was adamant that if we want to live in a decent, civilised society, then we must have the courage to make and enforce laws to protect it. Liberty must be nurtured. Bader thought that the only murder he would have absolved from capital punishment was the crime passionel where a man may come in and find another one laying violent hands on his wife.

He thought that the man who must be firmly dealt with was the one who attacked an old lady alone in her cottage because he wanted to steal her savings. He hits her on the head and as she had a thin skull he kills her. Then he says to the police that he is frightfully sorry but he did not mean to kill her. Douglas also felt really strongly that anyone who walked about with a potentially lethal weapon like a knife or a cosh or a gun should be sentenced to certain imprisonment if he were caught with it. Because if he had it, he was almost bound to use it in the end or there would be no point in carrying it about with him.

In Douglas's eyes, a lot of people confused the issue by getting tied up with the method of disposing of a killer, all the macabre ritual surrounding it. The noose and the drop or the electric chair. A murderer should be killed humanely, as he has forfeited his life. It would not have cost Douglas a second's loss of sleep personally to kill the perpetrators of the Moor's Murders. The death penalty must be a penalty or it is nothing. According to present British law, these murderers would be out in a decade or some such period. Douglas cited the case of the murderer who was let out of Broadmoor and killed another child within the week. The psychiatrist cannot ever prove a man is all right until he has been let out – and then it may well be too late. Douglas was very annoyed when Parliament permitted the capital punishment law to be brought as a private member's bill. Anything as important as that should have been in the election manifesto of either party or both. They allowed it through and lowered the standard of Parliamentary conduct accordingly.

One evening Douglas got into a long argument with Alan Garrow's son about capital punishment. They were still hard at it after half-past three in the morning! Alan Garrow had to get someone to break it up. Douglas was expounding his views that if someone beats an old woman over the head with an iron bar, then they ought to be put down, and he personally would do it without losing any sleep. Garrow's son favoured giving the criminal another chance. The thing in favour of Douglas was that although he held such strong views on this topic, he took the time to argue his case. He did not just dismiss the teenage boy as a 'silly twit' but treated him as a responsible person.

Douglas's views were nothing if not decisive about many things. About this era, too, he came out roundly against the Committee of 100, declaring 'Deport this rabble'. And his opinion on Rhodesia would soon be crystallising and coming to a head.

Another of Douglas's more unusual activities was his association with the Knights of the Road. As well as Douglas, other people connected with this body included Alf Robens and Frederick Richmond. It was started a long time earlier by William Carr of the *News of the World*. Douglas of course used to write regularly on aviation on that newspaper, hence his being asked to join the club. The basic idea of Knights of the Road was that most problems and accidents on the road occurred through bad manners, lack of courtesy and general human failings. It was sponsored to try and change this outlook. People could write to it and recommend drivers for an award. Those approved for awards were put on registers, and the whole thing built up into quite a force in motoring. It was amazing to see the number of cases that were submitted for consideration by the council, who met about once a month.

Each of the people on the council took a turn at doing officer of the month duty, to sift out all the nominations. Having read all the bad manners on the road, it was a relief to read a bit of good news. People even put up complete strangers for the night; this sort of unsolicited help really did restore faith in human nature.

The awards were graded and there was even a badge for accident-free drivers. All these things did much to inculcate a sense of consideration on the road, a human quality so sorely needed then and now. What a pity the Knights of the Road no longer exists as an organisation. Gallantry seems to have once more became a casualty of the chronic power complex that seems to have assumed control of drivers' minds.

For the twenty years or more that the Knights existed, it did nothing but good. At Christmas they invited people who had received major awards to a lunch party. They also got some motoring VIPs to these affairs. At the usual monthly meetings, too, the council had guests like Macmillan, Heath and Wilson.

Douglas was a great believer in the practical aspects of safety on the road. The things that drove him mad were notices saying such fatuous exhortations as 'A little care gets you there', 'Can you stop if I stop?' and 'Fresh strawberries'. While reading these signs, you could quite easily take your eyes off the road for an instant and have an accident.

Douglas's own driving was absolutely extraordinary, an experience which cannot be adequately described. With his instant reflexes, he could squeeze among traffic with only an inch to spare. As one of his friends said: 'He's not unsafe – but I often shut my eyes.'

Meanwhile, Douglas went on driving all over the country to see anyone who appealed to him for help. This is perhaps an appropriate moment to record an account of a representative of the next generation of amputees, to show how the original inspiration of Bader was kept alive, nourished and developed. And how it will go on being a source of strength to succeeding generations. This is from the life of David Butler:

> 'I was injured by a bomb in 1956, and I was in hospital for just over two years. I was twelve at the time. Douglas came to see me at Mount Vernon, Northwood, when I was having plastic surgery. They took away part of my right thigh and chest skin and they transplanted it on to my knee. My legs are off inch-for-inch exactly the same as Douglas's. But he has two hands and my left hand is off at the wrist . . . The first letter I wrote to him, I asked if I could see him. I wrote the letter with my right hand because I was left-handed and I had lost that.
>
> When they showed the film *Reach for the Sky* locally, the nurses at Mount Vernon arranged for an ambulance to take me down to the cinema to see it. When he came to see me again, I asked him what the artificial legs were like to wear and how they worked. He told me all about them and how to use them. He also told me that I would get quite a bit of pain to start with. This was about six to nine months after my accident. Douglas told me not to let things beat me. I hadn't seen artificial legs and did not know how they worked, or what it was like wearing them. It was a great help to talk to someone like Douglas, to learn all about the legs, how they are fixed on, what sort of difficulties you are likely to meet.
>
> The sister warned me that when I left Mount Vernon I wouldn't be able to walk for about five or six months. In fact I was walking four weeks later, but I was in hospital for two years altogether.
>
> When I came out of hospital, I learnt to dance, drive and swim, and they had a programme on me, *This Is Your Life*. Douglas came on to this and presented me with a medal from the RSPCA. I had gone on the ice at the local canal and tried to crawl out in the middle to rescue a dog that had fallen in. But the ice gave way and I went through. A policeman grabbed me and pulled me out, but I didn't save the poor dog.
>
> Next time I came in contact with Douglas, I rang him at Shell. I was trying to get a motor racing licence and so I asked him if he could write something for me. I was coming up against a brick wall. The rules stated that you must only have

"one main disability". But what do you call one main disability? I had a row with someone over it. By then I had done over a hundred events. I told them that my car was built specially for me. Now I have a left-hand drive car. I sit on the left side. I use my hands, my legs, and one knee. For steering, I have a knot on the wheel for my left hand. I had a lot of good top-line drivers who wrote to me to say they would have no objection to starting on the grid with me. But it was no use. I am allowed to do auto-cross, racing on grass. It's the mass grid I can't do. But I hope to try and get a competition licence for motor racing unlimited one day.

I'm a chartered accountant now. I'm working for an accountant, but I also have a practice of my own at home . . . I was married two and a half years ago. We were courting for about six years before then, though.

We bought the land for this house six years ago with the idea in the back of my mind that when I qualified we would build a house here. We've got a garage and workshop. At the moment, I'm trying to build up my own practice. I still work full-time for the firm and work evenings and weekends at home. My wife does all my typing. She works part-time at a job as well.

I have come to terms with life and how I have to live now. The only thing I can't do is to run! It's not so much being well-adjusted or anything. It's something that you've got to do, so you go on and do it.

I've done most things. I've tried sailing, gliding and swimming. And water-skiing. I did about a mile with an instructor on either side holding me up. Then I decided one of the legs wasn't much use, so I took it off and tried on one ski. I did about fifty yards on my own. I had a hook on my arm, hanging on to the bar. Then the leg came out of the socket and fell apart. I went into the water and the two instructors fell in, too. The funny thing was that the water pressure pulled my leg off and pulled my bathing trunks off as well: I was going along with my pink bottom bobbing up and down in the water.

I also like fishing, it's very relaxing. I'm treasurer of the local fishing club. I also went up in a glider. There are no rules and regulations at all concerning gliding and the disabled – not like powered flying.

We have more or less finished building this house and I hope to take up motor racing again. The first car I built was rather like a Lotus 7. I took it onto Brand's Hatch and was pulling about 110 on the straight. Suddenly the gearbox gave out. I spun round once or twice and hit a concrete wall. If I had had ordinary legs, it would have smashed one of them, because it bent the side of my artificial leg. We bought a Mini with a lid on after that. Then we packed it in, when we got married. My wife used to race, too.

Disabled people are too ready and willing to sit back and be pushed around. They allow people with bad disabilities not to pay road tax. But petrol tax is always going up. Disabled people simply cannot rely on public transport; they've got to have their own. As the cost of running a car goes up, we should be allowed to claim. Why not give us a straight allowance per year?

I would like to see disabled people really given the chance to do things, the support to do things. If they can see someone else doing something, it spurs them on to doing it, too.

I very much admire Bader. When you see what he has been able to achieve, you go and try to do it yourself. It inspires you to do it. I'd like to do with motor racing the sort of thing Bader did in flying. To show people what can be done. When people say "You can't do it," you say to them, "I can and I will".'

Later, Bader got a letter from Eamonn Andrews, asking if he would appear on one of his series of programmes *This Is Your Life*. At that time Bader disapproved of this and he had been tried out as a victim at least twice. Both occasions he had been told about it in advance, once by Thelma and another time by a friend. Thelma knew how he would feel if he had been caught.

But when he was asked to appear on behalf of David Butler, he did agree, simply as a guest which was a different matter. Douglas thought it might help to do him some good in some way. Because he had buckets of courage, as he put it. Much later in life, Douglas did acquiesce and appear as the subject of a memorable edition of *This Is Your Life*.

CHAPTER 28

A fascinating friendship developed between Thelma and Douglas Bader and Mary and Harold Wilson. Perhaps it never really had an opportunity to deepen as much as it might, but it did throw light on both the Baders and the Wilsons.

Although it did not start until 1964, there was a brief prologue as far back as 1951. Thelma and Douglas went over to Canada early in that year under the aegis of Shell. Douglas opened the British Motor Show held in Montreal and they both had a busy but marvellous time. When Douglas got back to Britain, he received a letter from the then President of the Board of Trade, Harold Wilson. The young Mr Wilson was in the Labour Government which went out of office very soon afterwards for a long spell in the Westminster wilderness. The letter said:

9th April 1951

My dear Mr Bader

The United Kingdom Trade Commissioner at Montreal has sent me a report telling me of the outstanding success of the recent British Motor Show there. 23,000 Canadians saw the fifty-five British vehicles and at the same time contributed substantially to the funds of the Canadian Legion. This satisfactory result was due in large measure to the unstinted help that you and Mrs Bader gave; your cheerful acceptance of a large number of functions results in considerable publicity for the British products. I should like to thank you both most sincerely on behalf of us all for all that you did.

Yours sincerely,
Harold Wilson.

Douglas was never one to be a political pedant, and he thought 'that's pretty civil of him'. So he wrote a note thanking him for the letter and that was that. This left no particular impression in Douglas's mind except that Harold Wilson was a polite minister. Mr Wilson was then of course still in his early thirties.

Thirteen years later in 1964, Douglas was at a private lunch of about a dozen men. Harold Wilson and George Brown had been invited as well, while Labour was still in opposition. This lunch was held in a private room of the Cote D'Or. They were all standing about in a room next to the dining room, when the host introduced Mr Wilson to the rest of the guests. He came up to Douglas and said, 'I mustn't leave without getting your autograph, because my son Giles would never forgive me'. So Douglas signed a menu while they were actually still talking and gave it to Mr Wilson.

In the autumn of 1964, Mr Wilson became Prime Minister. He had not been in Downing Street more than a few months when the Baders got an invitation to attend a reception party in honour of the Prime Minister of Norway, who was in Britain at that time. Douglas said to Thelma: 'Well, we've never been asked to Downing Street before in our lives, so let's go along and see what it looks like'.

They turned up at the appointed time after dinner. There were a number of politicians already there and one or two chums Douglas and Thelma knew. The Baders were both greeted by the Prime Minister and his wife Mary with great courtesy, bordering on enthusiasm.

While Thelma and Douglas were busy gossiping with someone, Mary Wilson came up and said, 'Would you think it awfully wrong of me if we got Giles down, because he'd never forgive us if he didn't see you as you're in the house'.

Douglas said: 'Not at all, but why don't we go up and see him?'

So Thelma and Douglas got into the lift and went up to the flat where the Wilsons lived, at the top of No. 10 Downing Street. They went into Giles's room, which was enlivened by a lot of model aeroplanes and similar adornments. Thelma and Douglas proceeded to have an enormous gossip with Giles about aeroplanes – what else? They were really happier up there than in the crush downstairs, and before parting, Douglas promised to give Giles a flight in his aeroplane.

Douglas returned to Downing Street a few Saturdays later, when the weather was reasonable, to pick up Giles and take him for his flight. Douglas rang the front door bell and said to the man who appeared:

'Look, will you just tell Master Giles I'm here and get him to come along and don't disturb anyone else'.

In a minute or two, Giles came downstairs with both his parents. They said, 'It's jolly nice of you to give him a flight. We're so sorry we won't be here when you get back, but we're going down to Chequers.' The Wilsons waved Douglas and Giles away from the front door, just as any ordinary parents would do.

When Douglas's various Conservative friends first heard that Thelma and he had gone to Downing Street, they said, 'Oh yes, we heard you were there. I suppose you're a friend of this ghastly chap'.

Douglas countered: 'Look, all my friends who are supposed to be Conservatives have been in power for God knows how long and nobody has ever asked us to Downing Street. Now a Labour Prime Minister gets in and within three months, he has asked me there. So, as far as you chaps are concerned, I think you're a bunch of buggers'.

Douglas always felt that because of the friendly way that Mr Wilson had behaved, he was quite a reasonable bloke. And both the Baders thought Mary Wilson was an absolute sweetheart, really very nice.

The next time they saw Mr Wilson was when the Government gave a Battle of Britain party in the Guildhall for the twenty-fifth anniversary. This was 1965. Everyone was asked and the Baders went as well. Of course they had numerous friends there, dating back to 1940 and even earlier.

Mr Wilson was there with Mary. At some stage in the affair, a man came along and had a word in Douglas's ear:

'The Prime Minister's compliments and could you come over to his table?'

Douglas thought in fun, 'Well, this is good social climbing stuff, so I'll go and talk to the Prime Minister'. He went over to Mary and Harold Wilson, who were with an air commodore. He was the president of the Battle of Britain Fighter Association. Douglas was welcomed with enormous enthusiasm and was asked to stay with them at their table. He said he could not really, because he had his friends elsewhere and it would be rude. But once again he sensed this tremendous friendship and warmth from Mr Wilson. The interesting thing was that Douglas did not really know him much, but every time they met there was this awareness that the Prime Minister seemed so affable, friendly and pleasant to him. That was in September 1965, and almost the high point of their relationship.

In October, Douglas had Mr Wilson's private telephone number at Downing Street. Douglas was due to go to Rhodesia and then on to South Africa on Shell business shortly, so in view of the impending situation on Rhodesia he rang up Mr Wilson and asked him:

'I'm going to Rhodesia next week is there anything I can do out there?'

Mr Wilson said: 'I'll drop you a line. I'll send you the recent speech of the President of Tanzania. If you see Ian Smith, will you tell him from me to do nothing and go on doing nothing for as long as he can'.

Douglas confirmed to Mr Wilson that he would be seeing Ian Smith, another fighter pilot veteran of the Royal Air Force. Douglas duly went off to Rhodesia and saw Mr Smith. Douglas gave him Mr Wilson's message. Mr Smith said to Douglas:

'I don't understand these people. In 1963, when they destroyed the Central African Federation, they gave Northern Rhodesia and Zambia their independence. They gave Nyasaland and Malawi their independence. We asked for ours and RAB Butler said to us "Don't press us now. Time is on your side, so wait". Now Wilson is saying exactly the same thing. I just don't understand these people. Should we have taken it then or not?'

Douglas tried to mediate with him. 'Look, old boy, what you've got to remember is that these blokes are professionals and you're an amateur. So whatever you do, it's bound to be wrong. So for God's sake, don't do it.' They both had a good laugh at that exercise in Bader logic! Douglas had already seen the Governor of Rhodesia, Humphrey Gibbs, whom he knew anyway. Douglas told him what Mr Wilson had said. It was the Governor who had urged him to see Mr Smith and in fact arranged it.

At the stage when Douglas gave Ian Smith Mr Wilson's message, there was still no hint that the British Prime Minister was coming out to Rhodesia, but suddenly he decided to do so. Douglas wrote a letter to him in London, reporting that the feeling out there was one of perfectly goodwill towards him and the Government. Douglas ended by reminding Mr Wilson that he had said that this was a British affair and he would not brook outside interference. Douglas advised him that if he continued like that and said to the Rhodesians 'We'll go on arguing till the cows come home, but we won't put it to the United Nations – then the door will stay open forever'. He begged Mr Wilson to think of this. The Prime Minister got the letter on the Friday, delivered by hand to Downing Street, and he left for Rhodesia on the Sunday.

Thelma was with Douglas on the Rhodesian trip. When Mr Wilson came out, they were in Salisbury together. The Chief of the Air Staff, Harold Hawkins, was also over there. Another friend of Douglas's in Salisbury was Bill Harper, who was Minister of the Interior. Harper had been a pilot in 17 Squadron at Martlesham in 1940: the same station as Douglas at the time.

Douglas thought that Mr Wilson made one or two errors. He said that the Prime Minister insisted on seeing two African Nationalists. Dr Sitole was one of them. He saw the Governor, but he did not leave Salisbury. Douglas considered that a mistake. If Mr Wilson had gone down to Bulawayo and one or two other places and seen some of the African villages, he would have got a different impression. If he had seen the tribal system, he would have realised that the point of Rhodesia policy was that the Africans had lived in this tribal system for generations and wanted to go on living like it. This was Douglas's opinion. And if Mr Wilson had seen what was given to them and the way they were looked after and taught farming, things might have been different.

When Mr Wilson left, Douglas and Thelma were having lunch with Bill Harper. It was a Saturday. Bill had just seen the Prime Minister off. 'How has it gone, then?' Douglas asked. Bill said, 'It has gone jolly well and we think he has come a hell of a way round to seeing our point of view. Harper went on, 'Anyway, you'll see it all on television tonight on the news'.

Douglas watched the recording and remembered almost verbatim what Mr Wilson said, 'I'm leaving to go back to London now. The Rhodesian Prime Minister and I have had a very considerable conversation and have covered all the points. We have reached a large measure of agreement except for the constitution of the Royal Commission and its terms of reference. I am leaving behind staff to sort out these terms of reference. Then they will recommend to the Government what to do. There are some things I must say. I've been here only five days. I have interviewed a lot of people and I must say this. One man, one vote, is not today; it is not tomorrow; it is not within measurable time by the clock or the calendar. And if anyone thinks that the Royal Air Force will come here like a thunderbolt, that will not happen.' Douglas turned to Thelma and said, 'This chap is speaking like an Englishman'.

Mr Wilson left Salisbury. He landed at Livingstone, Victoria Falls, where he had a session with Kenneth Kaunda, head of Zambia. Then he went on to Nigeria, where he saw the Premier who was assassinated immediately afterwards. He stayed with Nkrumah in Ghana, before returning to London. Douglas maintained that Mr Wilson changed his mind. He said he was not going to abide by the recommendations of a Royal Commission and it would be subject to discussion in the British Parliament.

Douglas was down in Pretoria at the time, and had been there only a day or so. He was talking to a South African Air Force Association lunch there. The news came through that Rhodesia had made a Unilateral Declaration of Independence, that the British Government had imposed sanctions, and they would take the matter to the United Nations. Douglas said actually at the lunch: 'I'm ashamed of being British, the way the British Government have treated Rhodesia. And I've a good mind to take out a Rhodesian passport.'

This naturally got fairly wide publicity. Douglas received a large number of letters about it from places as scattered as Australia and America. One was from a Jim Flaherty in Great Falls, Montana. He said: 'Dear Doug – I don't know what the situation is in Rhodesia, but I sure agree with you about the white man falling over backwards apologising for being white'.

Douglas would have to be known and understood very well for someone to appreciate how this attitude could be squared with his liking for Nkrumah: Douglas knew him well, found he had a mind like quicksilver, and thought he ran the country well. Under Nkrumah the people had a sense of purpose. Douglas found it hard to avoid the conclusion that Nkrumah did a lot to give his country some form of national feeling and pride. Thelma and Douglas both saw it and sensed it. Yet that made no difference to Douglas's views on the Rhodesia situation.

When Douglas reached Durban, a party had been laid on for Douglas, but the British Consul refused to come. Obviously because of his recent remarks about the British Government.

On the way home, the aeroplane stopped for refuelling at Salisbury, and Douglas took the opportunity to ring up and try to speak of Ian Smith. He got Bill Harper instead. The Rhodesians had imposed a press censorship in those very early days of UDI and it was not doing them any good as far as world publicity was concerned. Douglas said to Bill Harper, 'For God's sake, tell your chaps to lift this silly press censorship, because it doing you an enormous amount of harm. There can be no point in it. It's never a good thing'. Harper said he would pass on the message to the appropriate quarter, but it was not long afterwards that the Rhodesian press censorship came off in any case.

When Douglas got back to London, he was still in a state about the situation out there. He rang up a Conservative MP friend of his and said: 'Get on to your leader and tell him to stand up and shout at the top of his voice that the Tories do not agree with this business of sanctions and everything else – and let it echo down Africa'. But the MP could not really get hold of anyone effective. Mr Heath was in Paris and Mr Maudling in Gibraltar. Later on Douglas went to see Mr Heath at the House of Commons to tell the Leader of the Opposition how he felt about the whole affair.

After he got back to London, Douglas also rang up Downing Street. A male secretary answered the phone. Douglas told him, 'If it's the smallest interest, you might tell the Prime Minister that I am back in London'. They both had a good guffaw over that.

Douglas did feel sorry about it all, though, because he thought that Harold Wilson was a man who might want to make a friend of him, and Douglas hoped he might have been able to influence him to see things outside the strictly political spectrum. He knew that throughout their relationship Mr Wilson had made the running, even though it was not then of very long duration. Douglas felt that perhaps the PM liked him and wanted to be friends, which was of course at least partly true. Mr Wilson must have known that Douglas was never interested in patronage or honours lists or any other nonsense like that. Douglas thought on reflection that men get so isolated in power and are surrounded by yes-men, that they do not take kindly to a no-man, one saying no I think you are wrong. This sheltered existence gets them right away from reality.

Douglas's summing up of Mr Wilson was that when on television in Rhodesia, he meant what he said. Douglas decided that this was to be the trouble with Mr Wilson, that he had 'some bloody good ideas' including trade union reform. He started them but he never carried them through. They got at him. He was a man of indecision. He had some good intentions, but he did not do what he was going to do. He was overtaken by events.' This was what Douglas thought later, anyway, in the light of Mr Wilson's years as Prime Minister. Perhaps a harsh judgement, some people might say, in view of his achievements in getting Britain into a straight state economically with some considerable courage and at the sacrifice of some personal and political popularity. But Douglas could not forgive his handling of the Rhodesia question. To Douglas, it was reduced to simple terms: you do not fight your friends.

After UDI, Douglas felt that it just became a personal vendetta between the two men, Wilson and Smith. In the House of Commons, various people got up and started pro-Rhodesian attitudes. But in the later debate on sanctions, one solitary Conservative MP, and a new one at that, got up and said he disagreed with sanctions. The majority of Tories abstained and some of them like Nigel Fisher and Tufton Beamish voted with the Government. So Douglas did not think any better of the Tories than Labour, for he had not forgotten that both parties made things go wrong in Rhodesia.

Douglas recorded his strong views on Rhodesia a fortnight or so after UDI and his sentiments did not really change with time.

Roy Welensky became one of Douglas's friends from Rhodesia. Douglas admired this great man and Welensky recognised that Douglas had many potent qualities, too. At one stage of the protracted problem of Rhodesia, he and the Baders were all sitting around a Braavleis at the swimming pool of Roy Welensky's home in Salisbury. This is the Afrikaans term for roasting meat on an open fire, so perhaps translatable into a barbecue. The subject occupying their minds was mostly the possibility of a Rhodesia settlement.

Welensky got Douglas's point that if two men really want a settlement, there is no reason why they should not find one. He realised that Douglas could not have a very detailed knowledge of the intricate constitutional difficulties involved in the Rhodesian situation, but he also saw that Douglas's instincts indicated that a settlement was in the best interests of everyone and that was what Douglas fervently hoped would be achieved. Welensky got the impression that Douglas's sympathy lay with Rhodesia, as if it were a case of coming to the support of the smaller chap in any kind of quarrel. But that was only Welensky's conclusion. Douglas felt it to be a family quarrel and as such it should be settled within the family. Although Welensky rated Douglas's intelligence very highly, he felt that Douglas did not take enough trouble to get down to detail; to him it remained a matter of basic principles irrespective of any difficulties in thrashing out the finer points. Douglas probably would not have disputed that view of his Rhodesian attitude.

The friendship of Roy Welensky and the Baders just grew from those days, and was closely associated with the problems. They met many times, both in Salisbury and also in London, whenever Welensky was there. Welensky liked Douglas because he was not only courageous but also for his sensitivity and his odd mixture of leg-pulling and 'jogging along'. And Douglas of course found Welensky one of that small select Bader band of big men with big ideas.

Douglas and Thelma both felt that a potential friendship with the Wilsons had been cut short by the Rhodesian business. Their final episode with Harold Wilson came when a lot of people in the Royal Air Force Association, including Douglas, had been thinking for a long time that Vera Lynn ought to have had some decoration. She was 'the sweetheart of the Forces' during the war. Then after the war, she always attended any RAF Benevolent Fund dance or other RAFA shows. She would always sing whenever requested and never charged a fee. They felt strongly that she should receive some recognition. The RAFA said to Douglas: 'You are a chum of Harold Wilson!' Douglas said, 'Well, I *was*!'

So they asked Douglas if he would write to Mr Wilson and put in a word for Vera Lynn. Douglas wrote to him, 'My dear Prime Minister'. He gave the facts and asked if he could please consider her for some decoration suitable to her services in the New Years' Honours List. That was in August. Douglas got a very civil letter back from Mr Wilson, saying 'Thank you for bringing her name to my notice and I will certainly see that her name is submitted on the next list for consideration'. Vera Lynn got the OBE in the New Year's Honours List. Later she was made a Dame. But as far as I know, neither Thelma nor Douglas ever met the Wilsons again. Sad.

CHAPTER 29

When Winston Churchill died, Douglas got a phone call from ITV that evening asking him if he would go along and record an appreciation of Churchill from the viewpoint of a Battle of Britain pilot. They asked if he could manage it that same evening in an hour or two. This was rather short notice and Douglas did not have time to gather his thoughts sufficiently. However, he went round to the studios and did it straight off the bat, but did not feel he had acquitted himself as well as he might.

'Can I do this again, please? he asked them.

'Yes, that will be perfectly all right.'

'Right. Then I'll come in again tomorrow afternoon.'

Douglas drove down to Nettlebed, Oxon, to see Alan Garrow and play golf with him. Alan could tell that Douglas seemed a bit upset and preoccupied and only felt like playing nine holes. This was extremely unusual for him. As they talked together, Douglas gradually clarified his thoughts on Churchill and eventually he tried out what he wanted to say on Alan Garrow. They wandered round the course on that Saturday morning until Douglas felt happy about what he would finally say. When he got back, Douglas rang ITV and told them he would be there at about three or four o'clock. He went in for the second time, did it straight off again, and this time it went perfectly, without any faltering or thinking. It almost said itself. The press reviewed it as the best of all the tributes to Churchill, and as he heard and saw it being transmitted, Alan Garrow wept. Douglas was clearly completely sincere, utterly convinced, with every word he spoke.

Douglas was pleased to be asked to go to St Paul's for the Churchill funeral service. He was driving in a large car with some Shell friends through streets kept free of traffic, other cars or buses. The procession of cars was threading along in two lanes, with Douglas's on the outside. The pavements were lined with Royal Marines and police – the silent crowd standing behind them.

The gun carriage had lined up outside Westminster Abbey, where it had lain in state. There were various companies and contingents of men waiting to join in the procession. One of these sections with a special place was for Battle of Britain pilots. It was composed of actual Service officers who had fought in the Battle, most of whom were group captain or senior rank. The Shell car happened to draw up right alongside this distinguished contingent, which had Alan Deere standing in front, and included Peter Brothers and many others Douglas knew so well. They were all wearing greatcoats and carrying swords as the car slowed and drew up alongside. Douglas opened the window and called across to them, 'For God's sake, straighten up and look as though you bore the brunt in 1940!'

While sitting in St Paul's during that service, Douglas remembered Winston Churchill and the meeting they had had in the House of Commons. Then his mind turned naturally to the war and the Blitz, particularly to the night of 29 December 1940 when the City and the East End of London lay burning after a merciless bombing raid by the German Luftwaffe. St Paul's Cathedral had been damaged, but against the night sky bright with flames, the great dome was silhouetted – defiant and untouched. Appropriately in that great church, the world was gathered to pay final tribute to Churchill. Douglas recalled his courage and firm resolve, which lifted Britain to a pattern of behaviour and a stoutness of heart that made victory inevitable. Douglas's memory was kaleidoscopic. He recalled the miracle of Dunkirk in late-May, early-June, 1940. Then the high summer of that year with a blue sky criss-crossed by the vapour trails of Hurricanes and Spitfires.

The black and orange plume of a mortally-wounded German bomber staining the sky as it plummeted to destruction. The dark brown smoke of the burning oil tanks of Shell Haven, into which plunged a broken Messerschmitt. The tobacconist shop on the corner of Victoria Street demolished by an enemy bomb – with a grinning Londoner standing on the pavement beside a trestle table on which lay some salvaged wares and a cardboard sign 'Business as Usual'. The morning after a night-long raid and the sight of Winston Churchill among the smoking ruins dressed in his siren suit, walking and talking.

As Douglas watched the cortège leave St Paul's, carrying Churchill on his last journey up the River Thames to Bladon, memories like those flooded his mind. Then he looked up to see the red, white and blue roundels of the Royal Air Force passing overhead in final salute to Churchill, that great man who rallied his countrymen in their finest hour. He was a man after Douglas's heart.

Douglas went on with his help for the disabled. Ever since Kenneth Gordon lost his legs as a small boy, he had found inspiration in Douglas's life and example. One day Kenneth went with his mother from their home at Norton-in-the-Moors, Staffs, to Stone Hospital to see a television set being presented there. Kenneth did not know that Douglas was to perform this ceremony and he was thrilled to meet him in the flesh. For so many people, Douglas was already a legend. He asked to see Kenneth walk and then took away the supporting sticks. Five times Kenneth managed to cross the ward, to Douglas's wholehearted approval.

Douglas also set an example to twenty-two-year-old model, Gloria Alesbury. She lost a leg in a crash and when in Croydon Hospital was visited by Douglas. Later on when she walked and put on dancing slippers again, Douglas was one of the callers at her Crawley home.

Perhaps the most memorable case of the mid-1960s was that of Randel Ferraioli. He lost his legs as a boy of only five and a half in 1953. Soon afterwards, a friend of the family wrote to Douglas about him, and Randel received quite a few letters from him over the years. This encouragement helped Randel when he was fitted with his artificial legs.

Douglas had sent Randel a photograph of himself in an aeroplane and promised that one day he would come and see him. While Randel was a young boy, he used to rush out every time he saw or heard an aeroplane, thinking it might be Douglas. Meanwhile he cherished the picture very much and drew comfort from it. As he grew up, he gradually did more and more, swimming and even riding a bicycle. This latter ranks as one of the most unusual of all accomplishments of a legless person.

Finally in September 1965, Randel met Douglas on a day he had been awaiting for twelve years. He attended the James Little Training College for physically handicapped students at High Blantyre. This had just been built by the Roosevelt Memorial Fund for the Handicapped. Randel was going through a course of typing and accountancy and eventually received five certificates for them. When he had been interviewed for acceptance at the College, the rector asked him all about himself and Randel mentioned Douglas Bader having written to him several times. So when it became time for an official opening ceremony, Douglas was asked to do it, and Randel's mother, Mrs Elizabeth Ferraioli, was also invited to be there. This College in Lanarkshire, Scotland, teaches students in both engineering and commercial subjects.

The rector, Mrs Morris, had designated each of the students a certain job for the occasion. Randel's was to man the car park, and guide the visitors' vehicles into position. He had been having a little trouble with one rather rude man, who would not park where he was supposed to do, and paused to recover from this. Then he turned round to see a large car parked in the middle of the driveway. Not thinking who might be inside, Randel started off towards it to tell the driver that he would have to move on, but as he approached he suddenly saw an arm stuck firmly out of the window and at the end of it, the thumbs up sign!

Douglas said: 'Hello, Randel, nice to see you – I just had to stop and see you before I go inside. See you again later'.

Randel was flabbergasted. He forgot all about his car park duties, so that when he eventually recovered, a lot of cars were strewn all over the place. The reporters came over to ask Randel about his encounter with Douglas. About an hour later, they both came to the front of the College where they had dozens of pictures taken by the Press. As they strolled up the pathway of this big old converted house, Douglas turned to Randel and said:

'Wouldn't we both look damned silly if we fell on our behinds just now.'

They both laughed at that, but Randel could not really think of anything to say to Douglas. He found it exciting but nerve-racking, too, with the combination of all the reporters and meeting Douglas. Yet beforehand he had so much he wanted to tell him. Randel felt more than ever that Douglas was a truly great man, for even though they met for only a matter of minutes, in that time Douglas revealed all the qualities that had inspired Randel. It had been a long time since Randel had watched to see if an aeroplane would land in the local farmer's field and bring Douglas to see him. When the meeting finally came, it was worth all the years of waiting and he would never forget it. Douglas said of him: 'He's got guts. He made it entirely on his own.'

To commemorate that day, they gave Douglas a silver goose putter with crossed British and American flags – the Union Jack with the Stars and Stripes – as it was an American fund which had provided the College.

Johnnie Johnson summed up Douglas's real contribution to the countless disabled:

> 'When I was commanding RAF Cottesmore years ago, he called up my wife and said, Can I have a bed for the night? He was coming down from the north and just wanted to arrive about nine o'clock that evening, after driving right up to Yorkshire. He cheered her up, turned straight round, and broke his journey by staying the night with us. All he wanted was a glass or orange juice and a poached egg in the morning and then he was off again. This was typical of literally hundreds of days spent by Douglas Bader.'

Before Churchill died, Douglas had received a letter from a Monsieur Rocourt, who was the mayor of St Omer, together with an explanatory newspaper cutting. This showed a picture old Madame Hiecque, who was due to be presented with the Legion of Honour for her efforts on Douglas's behalf in 1941. On being told of this and asked what she would like, the lady said she just wanted 'the legless ass britannique' to be alongside her when she received the decoration. The official letter explained all the details to Douglas, and he wrote back and pledged, 'Nothing will stop me from being there.' Mme. Hiecque had been sentenced to death for her part in helping Douglas, hence his determination to be there when she was decorated.

In the event, though, something did stop Douglas from going over there on the date arranged. The funeral of Winston Churchill. Douglas told the mayor of St Omer. 'It is of no concern', said the Frenchman, 'the whole of France will be at the funeral, so we have put off the ceremony'.

Later in the spring of that year, they honoured the Quiet Mother of the French Resistance. Monsieur Hiecque had died in the 1950s, so only his widow was left. Thelma and Douglas flew over to Calais in his little aeroplane. The British Consul met them and drove them on to St Omer. Douglas returned to the little place twenty-four years after that momentous time he had been there first.

The central square of the little French town looked gay with flags hanging out on the facades and over the actual window-sills. All the ex-Resistance people were there, together with an Air Attaché, Archie Winskill, who had been a pilot officer with Douglas at Tangmere in 1941. The old liberation feeling seemed to come alive again for a brief spell, as if it were being re-enacted for a film. *Entente Cordiale*.

Then Thelma and Douglas saw this little old lady, perfectly *compos mentis*, and brown as a nut. After lots of hugs and kisses all round, the band struck up a strident tune and a general pinned the Legion of Honour on her chest. Then more kisses and tears. To Douglas's intense delight, another roll of drums prefaced a further announcement. They had decided to make Douglas Bader an honorary citizen of St Omer and presented a scroll to him to mark the memory of that day.

In peace as in war, Douglas went on flying and flying. Perhaps contrary to the general concept of Douglas Bader as a great fighter pilot of World War 2, his civil flying was conducted with a great deal of forward planning. He never went on a flight without doing all the drill and having thought it all out first. Obviously all his life he took risks, but they were calculated carefully. Everything was very properly planned. He took Thelma, Jill Lucas and Laddie Lucas over to stay with Gus Walker in Holland once. This was a flight of a couple of hours or so. The weather was very poor, with low icing levels. He absolutely astonished Laddie by the care and precision with which he conducted that flight. Even in these days of correct procedures and stringent requirements, ordinary pilots would have taken only about half the trouble Douglas did. Perhaps that was why he always survived.

Another thing about Douglas's flying and his general aeronautical appreciation was his engineering sense. This was something few people could realise. He could produce a first-class critique of an aeroplane. He possessed an ability to assess the merits or otherwise of an airframe, and he also seemed to have an inbuilt engineering awareness of all its characteristics, good and bad. Douglas would have made a marvellous test pilot. He had not only the flying ability but also the knowledge and the desire for further knowledge.

He treated his Beechcraft aeroplane, for instance, with something much more than mere care. He handled it as if it were a precious jewel in his grasp – a diamond or an amethyst. Which to him of course it was.

Laddie Lucas's children were the Baders' two nephews. At Christmas or birthday time, the boys would get some sort of frightfully intricate toy Laddie could never comprehend, even after he had read the instructions several times! Douglas would come in, the boys would turn to him with an appealing look, and he would proceed to get hold of it and sort it all out at once. Or if he could not sort it out, he would take it to pieces and put it together again. This all stemmed from those early Cranwell days when he built and rebuilt his motor bikes. It was a background to his flying experience that was not widely known.

On that same trip to Holland, Gus Walker observed how strict Douglas was about weighting and loading. Passengers almost had to take their toothbrushes and nothing more! He weighed everything and everyone, even more carefully than usual perhaps, since he was flying his three closest relations in the world: wife, sister-in-law and brother-in-law. Gus Walker agreed completely with his attitude; it was so wrong when people got into casual habits in aviation, and Douglas complied with all traffic and other regulations perfectly. He was always highly disciplined. And being a teetotaller helped keep him fit for flying. He settled instead of drink for sweet things – chocolates and other goodies. And all those gallons of fruit juices he consumed incessantly.

One might have imagined that Douglas had done all there was to do in the air, but in 1967 he added to his experience. He had always had a secret interest in gliding and some years earlier had in fact flown or glided as a passenger once or twice. A friend said to him when he was in Shanklin, Isle of Wight, 'Let's go over to the gliding club and have a go'. In no time, Douglas was alongside a glider pilot in the open cockpit. From a hook under the nose ran a long wire hawser which snaked slightly till it disappeared down the airfield in front of them. The instructor gave a signal, the winch was wound up, and the hawser dragged the glider bumpily over the grass for a few yards. Sooner than Douglas had expected, the glider rose steeply into rather a vertical climb, still attached by the hawser to the strange device on the ground. Up and up to about 1,000 feet.

Suddenly Douglas heard a big bang and thought instantly: 'My God, they've got me at last! And in a glider, too. What an ignominious end!' But the instructor said reassuringly, 'It's all right, we've just cast off.' It was merely the hook releasing them with a sharp snap. The sound had been accentuated by contrast to the unaccustomed silence surrounding Douglas in the air.

This was an authentic new experience. They were sitting there at 1,000 feet with an airspeed of some 35–40 knots, idling around in the blue sky. Douglas could detect no noise, no vibration, and he found it fascinating to be talking in a normal voice to the pilot beside him. He was told that it was wise to talk rather quietly in the cockpit of a glider because if you shout, people on the ground might hear what you say. Which in Douglas's case could have proved embarrassing to all concerned. His language could occasionally verge on ripeness! They kept within the airfield perimeter and then pointed it downwards and put it on the ground.

Douglas's second experience in a glider was with a more luxurious model. This one had a closed cockpit, with the instructor sitting behind him. But on the whole he preferred the open cockpit, in fine weather anyway. Douglas still knew nothing about gliding except for these two flights, but they were plenty to convince him that he would like to try more. He likened it to the feeling of a sailor who goes to sea in a battleship or a destroyer, and then wants to spend his leisure time in sailing with a small yacht.

Over ten years elapsed before Douglas found the opportunity to take his fascination for gliding any further. He had always meant to find time to convert to solo, but when it did happen it was almost by chance. In 1967 he went to Royal Air Force Swanton Morley to present some air cadets with their gliding certificates.

The gliding instructor there was Flight Lieutenant Ronald Page, also a Shell man. He asked Douglas if he would like to go up again and of course the answer was yes. They had three short flights with Page instructing Douglas. The lack of throttle was a little disconcerting to an aeroplane pilot like Douglas, but the air brakes lever proved useful to give his spare hand something to do. This seemed to be a fairly easy performance. Then they had another go and a third. Page said to Douglas 'Right – you can go by yourself if you like'. So after only three check-out instruction flights with the pilot, he said 'Thank you very much' and set off on a couple of circuits. He qualified for his gliding wings on the same day as he had received his initial instruction. Needless to say, they were earned in record time. He received the wings from Page, who commented, 'This must be the quickest that anyone has ever qualified!'

But Douglas was more modest about it. He thought that anyone at all who had learnt to fly an aeroplane when he did would qualify in gliding very quickly. There is a great similarity in the judgment required for gliding as for flying a powered aircraft. And as he flew those first glider circuits, he was at once reminded of when he first went solo in an Avro 504 back in 1928. In those days, engines were apt to stop unceremoniously and you had to decide on a field underneath you for emergency landing. That was all part of a pilot's instructional technique.

When he came in to land an aeroplane then, he closed the throttle completely. The propeller just circled slowly and he made very sure he got into the airfield. When he was about 200 feet over the perimeter hedge, he used to side-slip off his surplus height and thus land in the airfield or emergency field. There was no problem at all in that procedure.

If a pilot undershot, he had to tickle the throttle. This was called 'doing a rumble' and he would be fined half-a-crown. As a result, they all learned to land properly. For every field was a potential forced-landing site, and although people said you could not side-slip with a low-wing monoplane, you certainly could.

With gliding it is the same as in flying. It is always best to overshoot. Flying accidents occur from trying to skim the near hedge of the airfield and almost never from overshooting the available distance. Students have this problem, but gliding represents no additional landing difficulties. Except that if you do happen to undershoot, you have not got an engine to rumble, which could be a bit awkward at times.

As a tailpiece to the mid-1960s, Douglas was interviewed about this time and said he would love to be Prime Minister for a year. He would:- (1) Settle Rhodesia by removing sanctions so that negotiations could take place without pressure. (2) Stop immigration into Britain immediately 'until the situation has been thoroughly examined'. (3) Reintroduce capital punishment for all forms of murder. (4) Strengthen the police force by putting up pay to the highest possible standard 'so that we had a strong, volunteer service'. (5) Ban betting shops and gambling places. 'They breed protection rackets. That's why we're getting like Chicago in the '20s'. (6) Cut Government expenditure. 'What's the point of being £900 million in debt and then nationalising steel? It's crazy'.

Sir Douglas and Lady Bader after his investiture at Buckingham Palace on 28 July 1976.
(Hulton-Deutsch)

A gathering of 'The Few' at the RAF Museum, Hendon. This group includes Czech, Polish and British pilots. *(Hulton-Deutsch)*

Group Captain Sir Douglas Bader with his old adversary, the former German fighter pilot General Adolph Galland. *(Hulton-Deutsch)*

Chapter 30

Thelma went to the doctor for the first time about her bronchial trouble in 1965. She had always had a smoker's cough, but she had scarcely ever been ill. Her first serious illness, however, did not occur until two years later. One of Douglas's most endearing traits was his deep concern for Thelma and her health. They went everywhere together whenever it was possible, and if Douglas were away anywhere alone, he would always phone her in the evening to see how she was.

Similarly, Thelma felt it impossible for her to leave him for very long. Douglas never once complained about his hardship over the years. This rubbed off on Thelma to a remarkable degree, so that when she did become ill she never complained either. Throughout the years she was completely well, Thelma had been an ideal wife to Douglas. Home always meant everything to him, and by home he meant Thelma. She was always there or else with him on one of their trips. No-one stood up for the family like they did. The family always came first for Douglas, just like the squadron or the country. And this attitude to the real values in life also meant that both of them always treated people who helped them – servants, caddies, everyone – in an exemplary way. Thelma loved flowers and gardens and was glad to get away into the country at weekends whenever they could. Douglas always brought her up to Scotland with him if he could, to see Ian Collins or Iain Stewart, or whoever it might be. Because if he were going to enjoy a day, he wanted her to share it with him. All through the years, Douglas was aware of what he owed to Thelma; how he could never have done it without her.

About a week before Christmas 1967, Thelma was taken extremely ill, so that she could hardly breathe. When they examined her, the doctors said she must go straight down to the hospital in Midhurst, Sussex, as she had a serious infection of the lungs. She had to be given regular oxygen to pull her through. They also told her that if she did not stop smoking, she would die. So she stopped smoking altogether. It was a terrible wrench for her, as she had been a heavy addict. During the war, Jill Lucas and Sue Goodhew used to save up all their coupons for Thelma, as she said she would go mad without cigarettes. But from that first illness of Christmas 1967, she never smoked again.

Thelma had to spend some two or three months at Midhurst. Douglas used to drive down there from London every single day to see her, all through those dreary January and February days. Of course both of them retained their usual incredible spirits. They had seen enough suffering to know that the only way to overcome it was to fight hard and try to live as completely normal a life as possible – ignoring any minor handicaps like loss of legs or trouble with lungs. Sometimes their sense of humour concealed a greater worry, but only close friends would be able to recognise this. At this particular period, and later ones, at Midhurst, Douglas used to stay with the Duke of Richmond some of the time. Frederick Richmond always liked to see people's reactions to Douglas who had never met him before. When Thelma was in hospital during that first spell, Douglas came over to Goodwood House, where the Duke lived.

The first thing that happened was that the boiler broke down, despite all the efforts of the poor little man who was the heating engineer at Goodwood. He stood practically buried in debris at the foot of the stairs. The Duke thought, 'As it's Christmas, we'll try to cheer him up'. So he gave the man a large glass of sherry and told him he had an even bigger surprise for him. He said he was going to introduce him to the great Douglas Bader. Douglas waded in with his best provocative style saying, 'Well, you'd better get on with it and get it finished or we'll all freeze to death!' The poor man sat there with his eyebrows raised not knowing quite what to make of all this, or of Douglas. But eventually things were all right again with the boiler.

A long time passed. Thelma had to go back into Midhurst in July 1969. Douglas had not been with the Richmonds since that Christmas a year-and-a-half earlier. When he arrived the Duke said: 'I've got a house full of guests, but you can go and stay with my son'. His son, Charles, had done a marvellous conversion on the house and brought it all up to date, including the central heating and hot water. But this had caused much trouble. Anyway, Douglas went to stay in the house that thereafter he christened the 'schloss!' He woke up the following morning, only to find the water stone cold for his bath.

Douglas thumped downstairs, opened the swing doors on his way to breakfast, and went straight into the arms of – Mr Paine, the heating engineer! Douglas exploded: 'My God, haven't you put it right yet?' Mr Paine was slightly stunned but, on the other hand, quite appreciative of being recognised by Douglas after so long a gap.

During that second spell in July 1969, Douglas drove to and fro every day as before. He had got around to the idea that he must insist on taking the greatest care of Thelma and he did so. Although it was not in his nature to cosset people generally, certainly not himself, he became increasingly domesticated and looked after Thelma more and more. Since her first illness, he always drove her around as she could not use public transport. It was touching to see the way that they both tried to do things for each other. To Thelma it came hard to take life more easily, as she had always been so strong and healthy. Now she could not lift cases or walk very far.

Douglas spent a lot of time with Peter Cadbury or at his home near Windsor throughout that summer. He sometimes slept there, left about nine in the morning, drove down to Midhurst for midday and stayed with Thelma until she went to sleep. He was very unhappy and desperately worried during those days. This was the softer side of Douglas's character, the more emotional face that only emerged when forced out by circumstances, and then it was only shown to his closest friends. The days began to form a pattern. He would always have a room and a meal waiting at Peter Cadbury's at any time. Or he might have the occasional game of golf to occupy his mind and body. But most of the time he spent with Thelma at Midhurst.

After her first illness, Thelma had acquired a portable oxygen cylinder which went with them on all their trips from then on. Gus Walker noticed how good Douglas was with Thelma, and how the oxygen went with them in the aeroplane or anywhere else. Thelma was determined that her condition was not going to make more difference to their lives than it absolutely had to. She was an intensely practical person. When they used to go off on their flights, even in these late years, she normally carried the map to see where they were going. Navigator and tea-maker combined were her roles in those 1950s and 1960s flights.

The cause of relapse in 1969 was influenza. At these times, she felt unable to breathe, looking puffed in the face, and rather ashen. She seemed to catch a cold or other infection, which would bring it on badly. Cold winds affected her and so did wetness. But the Midhurst people were marvellous and nursed her back for the second time. They told the Baders that with great care she could live for another five to ten years, but stressed the need for such care.

Fortunately Douglas retired from Shell before this second illness. During those last fews days at the office, Douglas drove Joan Hargreaves nearly to her limit. Roy Snodgrass noticed how he wanted work done almost before he had given it to her. Then, when he realised he had reached the brink, he swept over and kissed her – the first time for twenty years. She blushed and relented. He knew he had gone far enough, just as he had known when he had driven the Germans far enough in taunting them – and then suddenly changed his whole tune.

At the retirement party of Douglas Bader and Joan Hargreaves, he invited not only directors, managers and staff of Shell, but the chauffeurs, messengers and stewards, too. He went out of his way to talk to them all – not to show off or as a conspicuous gesture, but because he genuinely liked them all and felt glad they were all there with him.

Douglas had a great desire to be with friends, increasingly as he grew older and more mature. Sometimes people of his ability are loners, but he hated being alone. And when Thelma came out of Midhurst for the second time, they were determined to carry on entertaining as they had always done, but on a much more restricted scale. The dinner parties every Tuesday evening had been a feature of the Baders' lives for a long time. There one met an extraordinary cross-section of people – politicians, Service people, businessmen, anyone with a real contribution to make. Now they still went on entertaining, but less frequently so as to tire Thelma as little as possible. Yet it was her decision that her condition should not interfere with their lives. She insisted on it.

Douglas was still very worried about Thelma, even after she had recovered from the 1969 illness. He raised the question of her going to the Bahamas to live and for him to commute to Britain or come out as often as he could. But Thelma did not want that. She knew that Douglas would not be happy, so nor would she.

So life went on much as normal. Douglas went down to visit the set while the film *Battle of Britain* was being shot. He met Peter Townsend while there and also one of the stars of the film, Robert Shaw. Someone told Douglas that Shaw was playing a part strongly suggesting that he was the famous South African ace Sailor Malan. Shaw was immaculately attired in an RAF tunic and white polo-neck jersey, creating a really romantic image. Douglas went up to him and said:

'I hear you're taking the part of Sailor Malan.'

'Yes, that's right,' replied Robert Shaw with due pride.

'Well,' retorted Douglas, 'All I can tell you is that he was a bloody sight better looking than you are!'

In September 1969 the film was finally ready for viewing. Douglas was invited to tour Australia to coincide with the various premieres in that country during the following month. Thelma was better than she had been at Midhurst and had made her by now usual remarkable recovery. She knew Douglas would love to go on this trip but would not leave her behind, so she insisted on accompanying him. They went out at the expense of the makers of the film and virtually repeated that legendary trip of 1956. The primary purpose was to be in Sydney for the actual Australian premiére, where they had a fine time with the Australians. They renewed old friendships and formed new ones and as far as both of them were concerned, it was 'one hell of a place'.

Thelma was still not quite over her last bout, so Douglas had her driven to a place in New South Wales where she stayed for ten days with a cousin of hers who had married an Australian sheep farmer. Meanwhile it had been arranged for Douglas to do the circuit of the film wherever it was being shown.

Douglas was interviewed by all the various State television, radio and press people in connection with the film. At Adelaide, a television interviewer asked him 'Tell me, Doug, is *Battle of Britain* the best air film you have ever seen?'

Douglas said without thinking: 'Good God, no. *Those Magnificent Men in Their Flying Machines* was far better'. Then he suddenly realised what he had said. It had gone out on live TV, and got a great laugh from the Australian viewers and public as a whole. Actually, too, it did *Battle of Britain* a lot of good, because this is exactly the sort of thing that appealed to the Australians.

Thelma and Douglas accepted an invitation to a dinner at the Grosvenor House Hotel in London that same year. It was a very large function sponsored jointly by the US Air Force Association together with the Royal Air Force Association – those two superb benevolent organisations which have done so much to help ex-servicemen of both countries. During the evening, Douglas received a precious document from the Americans which read as follows: –

Citation of Honor
Air Force Association
pays tribute to
Group Captain Douglas Robert Steuart Bader, CBE, DSO, DFC

for sustained valor and heroism during World War II who, defiant of physical handicaps that would have thwarted ordinary men, became one of the legendary air aces of the Allied Forces and an inspiration to free men everywhere for all time to come.

The dinner was held in the great ballroom of the Grosvenor House, located one floor below ground level. By about eleven o'clock, Douglas thought it was time he took Thelma home. She was not strong after her illness and could not walk upstairs at all easily.

They bade goodnight to their guests and then found that no lift was available up to the ground floor. It was quite a long climb up the stairs from there to the street, and Douglas was not going to let Thelma attempt it. Resourceful as ever, he noticed the bandstand where the Royal Air Force band had been playing. At that stage, they were standing down and having a well-earned drink. Douglas had a word with the sergeant there, saying to him:

'Get hold of two of your chaps, will you sergeant, and carry my wife up to the street.'

'Certainly, sir.'

The men put their hands down to make a chair for Thelma and they carried her up the stairs, on to the street, and set her standing on the pavement right alongside the car! Nobody even noticed it at all.

Before Douglas received yet another American presentation that year, he had the interlude of the Lighthouse Club Dinner also at Grosvenor House. A friend of his asked him to come to this affair, so he duly appeared there at the appointed time. Douglas went in, saw a programme for the evening, and found for the first time that Douglas Bader was proposing the toast of the Lighthouse Club. They had omitted the detail of asking him if he would do it. So Douglas found himself sitting at the top table looking at about a thousand chaps, and alongside him his friend Charles Newman. He started his speech:

> 'When I came to the Lighthouse Club, I imagined sou'-westers and oilskins and 'for those in peril on the sea' and all that sort of thing! But what do I find? I find that this is a club that's got nothing to do with the sea. You're all a bunch of drunken mechanical engineers!

Douglas had discovered that these engineers had held a convention some years previously at Whitby, on the Yorkshire coast, and they were so drunk every evening that they could only find their way back to their hotel by the flashing of St Mary's Light – which came straight down the road and guided them towards their beds. Hence the name of the club.

The other American presentation to Douglas at that time was highly unusual and highly treasured by him. Some Americans were coming over to Britain and anticipated seeing Douglas, so they took advantage of the prerogative of any US citizens and wrote direct to the American President, Richard Nixon. They explained that they would be meeting Bader and wanted to give him a token from the people of the United States.

As a direct result of this request, the President's Office offered a wonderful album of colour photographs of all the American astronauts. More than this, the album was circulated among the men concerned and they either autographed their individual photos or in some cases added personal messages to Douglas. So when the album was finally presented to him in London, he read these greetings from some of the most courageous men in the post-war world. As usual, Douglas felt a sense of both pride and humility.

> 'To Group Captain Douglas Bader. Best wishes to one of the world's greatest fighter pilots – Thomas P. Stafford.
>
> To Douglas Bader. With warmest regards – your standards of airmanship and courage are an inspiration to pilots everywhere, particularly space pilots – David R. Scott.
>
> To Group Captain Douglas Bader. I have long admired the example you have set for the entire world – James A. McDivitt.

This is the complete list of signatories to the space album which must rank as one of the most remarkable of all tributes to Douglas and what he has meant to people of all nations. And to him, this meant so much, coming as it did from pilots, men of his own kind, men he could understand.

Alan B. Shepard, Jr.
Richard F. Gordon, Jr.
Thomas P. Stafford
James A. Lovell, Jr.
Edwin E. Aldrin, Jr.
Walter M. Schirra, Jr.
Neil A. Cernan.
David R. Scott
John W. Young
L. Gordon Cooper, Jr.

Charles Conrad, Jr.
Michael Collins
Eugene A. Cernan
Frank Borman
James A. McDivitt

When William Carr was ill in 1969, Douglas went to see him as soon as he was allowed any visitors. He did not just come in to say hello and goodbye, but he was willing to stay as long as he was wanted. Eventually a nurse would come in and say to him quietly: 'Look, do you mind, Sir William should rest now'. Carr of course was connected with the *News of the World* when Douglas used to write his regular features for the newspaper. When any of the editors would say to Douglas, as they did periodically, 'Look, there's a personal story here about someone who has lost his legs. Can't you write about what it feels like to have lost yours?' Douglas would always say 'No – I can't'.

Thelma had to go back into Midhurst in January 1970, with possibly the worst of her relapses so far. Douglas was desperately worried. And again he commuted by car every single day, either to and from Peter Cadbury's home or his own. Sometimes, too, he called in to see us at Guildford on his way there or back. All he wanted was to talk to someone and eat enough to keep going. The crisis came. Douglas was determined that Thelma should survive it. The chances were evenly balanced, but he tried to will her to go on. Strength was eveything and he did his best to instil it into her through himself. But Thelma had quite a lot of her own, as she had demonstrated over the thirty-seven years and more that they had known each other.

Douglas sat with her. She remained more or less unconscious. He did not know if she could hear him or not, but spoke quietly but firmly: 'You can't die – because I can't live without you.'

Whether or not this had any effect cannot be known, but the crisis passed and slowly she began to make headway. After the very worst, Thelma recalled some strange moments to me:

> 'I was virtually unconscious at the worst time. Soon after, for some reason, they kept putting friends through on the phone and I was having the most extraordinary conversations with people as though I were tight. They said 'She must be under tremendous sedation or something, because she's making no sense at all.' I was having lots of medicines then and was very confused. With this particular thing, you tend to poison yourself. You don't breathe out enough and so you breathe stale air which is carbon dioxide. They teach you how to breathe and I do it twice or three times a day.'

So for the third time Thelma recovered and left the peace of Midhurst. Douglas drove her back through its broad country street, and she resumed her struggle to survive.

Life proceeded and Thelma and Douglas both remained wholly outward-looking when either or both could so easily have become introverted. But the discipline of the years had strengthened them still more than in the earlier times. Not long before this, Douglas had said:

> 'You must intend a marriage to stick. And you must both be tolerant. I think a wife needs to be more tolerant. She mustn't think it important if the husband suddenly pinches a girl's bottom. I think a marriage gets easier as it goes on. You grow more sensible and you grow with each other. When you're young, you're emotional and then it's hard to be so tolerant.'

Douglas certainly looked after Thelma very closely. It was quite moving to watch them. She had always been used to taking some of the load off Douglas, without hurting his feelings. Now he had to assert himself to prevent her doing this, and it was his turn to look after her.

Douglas was partly responsible for Peter Cadbury taking the decision when he did to marry his wife Jennifer. He had known her for some time. The day before Peter was leaving for Nassau, Douglas said to him, 'You're so stupid. Why are you taking your daughter Felicity? Why aren't you marrying Jennifer and taking her? I want to be your best man.' It was the little nudge Peter needed at that moment in his life. Once you have been married and it has failed, it takes a lot to get married again, thought Cadbury. Douglas had been pushing for weeks for him to marry Jennifer.

Another typical case of Douglas's spontaneous friendship came about that same time, too. Cadbury had a row with Westward Television and in his absence they removed him from the board. Douglas was the first person to ring him up and say that he hoped Peter would give them hell! He said, 'I thought you'd just like someone to ring up and say so'. Douglas simply wanted Cadbury to know that all his friends were behind him.

Thelma survived over a year after her last illness at Midhurst in January 1970. After a difficult day on Saturday 16 January 1971, she was admitted to the London Clinic on Sunday morning. Her heart actually stopped at one stage during that day, but they were able to restart it. Her condition was described as critical, not surprisingly.

Another old friend of Douglas and Thelma, John Perkins, was told one day that he had 'this cancer bug' in his throat. Thelma was the first person outside his doctors who knew about it. He had been teaching at a preparatory school near Basingstoke. The evening that he heard, he had to stop teaching there and then; he felt in a complete turmoil. He went round to see Thelma. He came into the friendly familiarity of the drawing-room and they sat down alone together.

She asked how he was. 'Fine, fine,' he said at first. Then he blurted out: 'Thelma, I must ask for your advice. I don't know what the hell to do.'

She said, 'Look, I can see there's something wrong, so if you'd like to talk about it, please do'.

John explained exactly what the doctors had told him; that it entailed cobalt treatment, and that he was 'scared stiff'. The very act of talking to someone about it made things a bit better for him. And since the someone was Thelma, he did begin to gain some strength from her. In fact, he could not have talked to anyone else in the world.

Over the next seven or eight months, John came up to London every week for treatment and very often he went straight to the Mews from hospital. Thelma did not seem to know the meaning of fear for herself. She used to make John feel less frightened because she herself was not afraid. In some extraordinary way, she was able to help John through these months. She had a calming effect, though she could also urge him to fight when necessary. Thelma knew the depressing effect of the cobalt treatment, and she used to 'de-depress' him. She would tell him:

'You're not to give up, spiritually or physically. You've got to go on.'

Pain and depression were what frightened him. But gradually Thelma was able to help him, purely by sitting there and talking to him: just by *being*. John would think to himself, 'It's Thelma we should be concerned about, not me'. But she insisted on deflecting talk to other things than herself.

There were several times during these visits when John put his head in his hands and wept. Then a few minutes later, as a result of her understanding, he felt: 'My God, what a bloody fool I am. There's more to life than this'.

Then in December 1970, John went to Gibraltar for an operation on his throat. It was about a fortnight before Christmas. He decided it would be better to have the operation there, as he would be unable to speak for ten days or so afterwards and he wanted to spare his family unnecessary worry. A Swiss surgeon performed the operation and he came back to England on Christmas Eve, home to Norfolk where he was then living. Douglas and Thelma were staying with friends nearby and John saw them over the holidays. Thelma was determined that everything was to be normal for this Christmas, though John had a feeling that things were not as good with her as he hoped. She was having oxygen quite a bit, but played it down all the time.

Douglas would say 'You'd better have a whiff of the old gas'. Thelma objected at first, 'I don't really need it'. Then he would insist, 'Yes, you do'. Once when they were protesting at her insisting on washing up, Thelma said 'No, no. I like doing this. Leave me be!' She was not going to sit with her feet up as an invalid.

The last time John Perkins saw Thelma was early in the week of 11th January. He just dropped in to see her. Douglas was not yet home. Her nephews, the Addison boys, were due to come for a children's tea party the next day. John was standing and talking to her in the kitchen, while she was busy preparing things.

'Do stay and have supper', she said.

'No – I just wanted to come in and see you. Having seen you, it's always so much better. I can go away and feel fine.'

'That's wonderful', Thelma said.

'As long as you're here, Thelma, things are fine. Because we'll both go on.'

'Now, look, John', she said slowly. 'I'm not going to be here much longer. But you are to promise me that you're not going to stop now.' John's back was then giving him trouble which needed treatment. He knew that Thelma was very ill, but dare not believe it could be so close. Yet she knew and she told him for his own sake. It was something he could never forget. Because then when his 'leg goes stiff or the back goes funny' it was Thelma who kept saying: 'No matter what, you've got to go on. You must not stop. It'll be all right'.

In the evening of Tuesday 19th January, Thelma was unconscious and Douglas stayed at the London Clinic until further notice.

The next day he was more worried than before. Until now, she had had that 'brassed off' look on her face which Douglas took to indicate an irritation and consequently a will to fight back. Now it seemed to be replaced by more passive resignation and he was deeply disturbed. But being Douglas, he still hoped for a miracle.

That evening the Clinic said there had been 'a slight pupil reaction' to Thelma's eyes.

On Sunday 24th January, I saw Douglas. He looked tired but still had not abandoned hope, although it was now only a matter of time for Thelma. The January air was crisp and the sun strong. The traffic moved like some endless conveyor belt on the Marylebone Road, oblivious to Thelma and Douglas, the Clinic and everything else.

In the London Clinic, Douglas was sitting with Thelma, the fingers of his hand threaded through hers. She had been unconscious for a week. At about five o'clock, she suddenly squeezed his fingers tightly, and ten minutes later she died.

Next morning at the Mews, the phone started ringing and every time Douglas or Jill Lucas answered it, they were liable to dissolve into tears. Fortunately Denis Crowley-Milling arrived early and took over from them for the rest of the day. After that, Douglas turned to Jill and Laddie Lucas as his closest relatives. They were both wonderful.

Douglas did not sleep. The thought suddenly struck him during one of those first nights 'I must have something of hers'. Thelma's wedding ring was recovered and he had it threaded on to a chain, which he wore around his neck.

Almost at once he decided not to move from Petersham Mews. This was where he and Thelma had lived for the last sixteen years. If Thelma were anywhere, she would be here. Douglas felt close to her in these familiar surroundings. It helped him survive those first days and weeks to keep everything there just as she had done. The flowers were fresh. Her plants still bloomed, inside the house and outside the windows.

Douglas fastened on these things as symbolising their lives together. He was going to need all the memories he could summon, for just below the surface there was a sense of desperation, as the realisation of the loss returned to him. In fact he was phenomenally resilient. Some day he supposed he would laugh again, and only a fortnight later he was forcing himself to make a few jokes. 'I've got to keep things neat and tidy because she's watching me.' And for a fortnight nearly, he hardly slept. Then he played a round of golf, and slept through sheer exhaustion.

Many messages reached him, despite requests for no flowers or letters. One card could be said to sum up them all: 'From a fan – with deepest sympathy'.

'How are you?' I asked.

'Life goes on.'

'Are you keeping busy?'

'But of course.'

Douglas told me that he would have exchanged the rest of his life for one more month with Thelma. Now although she was gone, she would always be with him. He felt her near. He had the memories of their shared lives. Thirty-eight precious years. He knew he must live through the pain of the present; adjust to the future. Don't go back, he had said so often. He must face his own future.

Hugh Dundas wrote in *The Times*: 'Thelma Bader was an adorable person. More than that, she had courage which fully matched that of her remarkable husband, Douglas'.

The Royal Air Force held a memorial service for Thelma in St Clement Dane Church, London, on Friday 5 March 1971. In the midst of London, sudden complete peace. The church glowed in an aura of amber. Before four hundred Bader friends, Denis Crowley-Milling read the lesson. Then Dermot Boyle gave the address in moving terms:

> 'We are assembled appropriately in this beautiful Royal Air Force Church to pay tribute to a gallant and much-loved lady whose father was an airman, whose husband was an airman and who herself became involved in the human drama inseparable from the lives of those who fought in the great air battles of the last war.
>
> Thelma's life cannot be described by a catalogue of achievements; indeed, any such approach would be to belittle her whole attitude to life. Instead, we must realise that at an early age she acquired the qualities which enabled her to lead the life of a true Christian – generosity, courage, unselfishness, loyalty; intelligent interest in the things that mattered and a happy chuckle for those that didn't. It was the way she applied these gifts to the turmoil of living that endeared her to everyone. There are several examples of her strength and wisdom. When

she met Douglas, she was quite clear that he was the man for her; she was equally clear that there were difficulties, indeed, very great difficulties. From these she did not shrink but, instead, solved them by a mutual bond of unselfishness, wisdom and devotion, with the result, as we all know, that these two strong-minded people had the happiest of married lives.

Again, during the war when Thelma was inevitably, because of Douglas's activities, living amongst those engaged in the critical air battles of the time, she became a continuous source of comfort and encouragement to everyone. Many of the young pilots were a long way from their homeland, some of them were tired and saddened and even disillusioned by the futility of war. She gave so generously of her help and affection at this time, the fact that her anxieties were much greater than theirs tended to be overlooked – and when Douglas went missing for five long anxious days she devoted herself so wholeheartedly to comforting the pilots who had lost their Wing Leader that it was hard to realise that it was she who had lost a husband to whom she was utterly devoted. Thelma's life was a shining example that to give is better than to receive.

And then, in the final stages of her life, when she knew better than anyone how ill she was, Thelma continued to live to the limit of her physical endurance; continued to give those charming dinner parties in her happy home, and remained gay and interested in the affairs of others – always giving out help and encouragement to the exclusion of any idea that it was she who needed help. In fact, triumphantly, Thelma did not need much help because she did not fear death.

To those who were nearest and dearest to her, we extend our deepest sympathy at their great loss but I would hope that this lovely service in this friendly historic church – with its majestic music, and in the presence of so many warm-hearted friends, will prove to be, as well as a memorial to Thelma, a source of strength to those who mourn her.

It would be wrong for us to go forth from here in the belief that this is in any way a final tribute. The last tribute to Thelma Bader will not have been paid until time has removed from this earth all those privileged to have known her.'

We sang Parry's *Jerusalem*, with Blake's words so dear to Douglas's heart. The service ended with the exquisite *Elegy* by John Addison and Faure's *In Paradisum*. Douglas must have felt his friends all around him; sensed their love for him and for Thelma.

CHAPTER 31

I first met Douglas in 1969 during the decade when I was responsible for Royal Air Force publicity. I had written an article about him in an RAF magazine to commemorate the fiftieth anniversary of the Service in 1968. I had the idea of a book about Douglas and wrote to him suggesting it – and enclosing a copy of the article. He thought it was a good idea and we became close friends over the remaining thirteen years of his life. He rather liked the fact that I had done a lot of flying – routine and test. And that I had flown in a fighter at twice the speed of sound – which Douglas never did!

I saw him almost every week from 1969 to 1971, when Thelma died. I used to go to Petersham Mews after work, taking the tube to Gloucester Road and walking from there with my tape-recorder fully loaded. Sometimes, the three of us had dinner; at other times, just Douglas and I. Once or twice my wife Joyce and I were invited together. One evening near the end of Thelma's life, she had a sudden seizure of breathing difficulty and Douglas calmly handed her the oxygen cylinder until she recovered. Then we all went on with our meal as if nothing had happened. After dinner, Douglas and I used to record our talks, which were intended as the basis for the future book together.

At about half-past-nine, Douglas was usually getting tired, and I had to get home to Guildford. He always drove me from Petersham Mews – near the Albert Hall in Kensington – to Waterloo Station several miles off. And he always did it in approximately five minutes! That was including negotiating such traffic hazards as Parliament Square, which he hurtled round in mere seconds. Naturally after Thelma died, Douglas lost interest in our joint project and I agreed to put it in abeyance.

Somehow Douglas got through 1971. He clung to Petersham Mews as some sort of haven and we went on seeing each other at times. Gradually his staunch love of life and people reasserted itself and the following year he was offered a part-time post as a member of the Civil Aviation Authority. This proved a valuable help in his return to normality and it was an appointment he held from 1972 until 1978. This period covered years of dramatic increase in airline development with all the contingent problems. His office was, at first, at the top of Kingsway in London, and later on in the new rotund building set back just behind Kingsway. He was in the world of the air and aeroplanes once again.

It came as no great surprise when on 3 January 1973 Douglas married Mrs Joan Eileen Murray, a widow and daughter of the steel-mill owner

Horace Hipkiss. Thelma would not have wanted him to live alone, just as Joan's husband would presumably have felt similarly. So Douglas and Joan entered and embarked upon their marriage at a mature age. They lived in the country near Newbury, but Douglas kept on Petersham Mews as a London base, which was useful at times for work or if they happened to stay overnight in the Capital.

That same year as their marriage, Douglas and I collaborated on a book, *Fight for the Sky*, the story of the Spitfire and Hurricane. I supplied the written research for this, while Douglas and friends – a few of The Few – added their own colourful personal impressions of the aeroplanes in action. The project proved to be a happy one, and included a cache of colour photographs unearthed from wartime sources which had never been seen before then – 1973. William Armstrong of Sidgwick & Jackson was the guiding hand behind the book, which was a comparative best-seller. Later on, Douglas was kind enough to write an introduction to my own book on British Aircraft of World War 2. Later still, he got cross when I called a book on the activities of 12 Group in 1940–41 *The Bader Wing*. I thought he was being a bit unreasonable, especially when it was intended only as a compliment to him.

Meanwhile, Douglas kept busy. The Civil Aviation Authority post occupied him part of the week. At various spells, he also accepted several non-executive directorships; maintained his long connections with Fleet Street; and continued his public speaking engagements.

In 1974 he was appointed chairman of the Flight Limitation Board at the CAA. This lasted for about four years until 1978, when he ceased to be a member of the CAA. Douglas worked tirelessly on behalf of airline pilots and air crew and always kept safety in the forefront of his mind. He believed that it must come first at all costs, above profit or anything. So pilot fatigue and associated subjects were among the things considered by the Flight Limitation Board.

I used to have lunch with him at the Civil Aviation Authority and occasionally at the Royal Air Force Club. One day while at the latter, I saw at first-hand the kind of affection he inspired. We were sitting quietly talking when an Australian lady visitor came over to us.

'May I please just say how much I have always admired you, Group Captain?'

'Thank you very much, my dear,' Douglas managed graciously.

They exchanged a few further words and she returned to her friends, thrilled at having met the legendary Douglas Bader.

Better late than never . . . Douglas was knighted in 1976 for his services to public and disabled. No-one could have done more and at last this had been duly recognised at an official level. Douglas was pleased about it and took the honour on behalf of all the disabled whom he had tried to help.

For some reason, there came quite a flurry of honours in 1976 and 1977. He was made a Fellow of the Royal Aeronautical Society; received an honorary

Doctorate of Science from Queen's University, Belfast; and a DL of Greater London. His wife, of course, became Lady Joan Bader to his Sir Douglas.

Latterly, Douglas's main business interest was as consultant to Aircraft Equipment International based at Ascot. This was quite convenient to their home near Newbury.

The first time that I knew anything about his having any sort of heart trouble was when he told me that he had failed his medical to have his pilot's licence renewed. I suppose it was to be expected, given the tremendous strain on his heart over the decades since 1931. Nevertheless the news came as a jolt for Douglas, as he knew it meant that a major part of his life was at an end. I continued to see him regularly during these late years. He seemed very content with this phase and together Douglas and Joan continued their active concern for the disabled. They certainly both deserved their happiness together.

On 4 September 1982, Douglas spoke at a dinner in Guildhall, at the historic heart of the City of London. While being driven home through Chiswick after this dinner, Douglas died suddenly. I shall never forget him. He wrote his own epitaph for me – and more eloquently than anyone else could have done. We will give him the last word: –

> 'I can still remember, at the age of eleven, living in a Yorkshire village where my stepfather was the rector. There was a badly lighted country road entering the village from a bus stop about a mile away. This road ran round a hairpin bend following the contour of a wood. It was shorter to walk through the trees, because it cut out the bend. But it was spooky in the dark and I did not like it. The route ran down a steep, narrow path and was dark because the trees overlapped at the top. As I approached the dreaded place, I tried to talk myself out of it. It did not save much time. But always in the back of my mind, there was that nasty little voice saying 'You daren't!' The voice was quite right. So I always had to go through the wood. I never got used to it until I was older. Yet the shame of taking the long way round would have been far worse than those few moments of fear in the wood.
>
> Later in life when I was in action, I didn't think about fear or the possibility of death. It was only afterwards I had time to think of things like that.
>
> How do I want to be remembered when I die? As a fighter pilot? Look, I want to be remembered so that other people, when they talk about me, smile. That's how I want to be remembered. I don't give a damn about being a fighter pilot. The thing is this: I want to leave warmth behind. You know the sort of person you remember. It might have been an uncle or it

might have been a chum. But when you think of him, you smile. You say "If only old so-and-so were here – he'd have loved this." Something like that. Or some recollection you have. But it's warmth – that's what you want to leave behind you. You don't want to leave any other nonsense. You want people to say, "Look, he was a chap, this fellow. He wasn't a what not." I'm sure I'm right.

I certainly think I've mellowed with age. Perhaps you miss things. Or perhaps you present them a bit differently, instead of rushing straight in. But I'll never not feel strongly about things. The things I feel matter – I feel strongly about. You don't change. You can't change. People don't change. Basically you're the same as you were at your prep school. And if some little boy was a sneak then, he retains that unattractive characteristic all his life. He may become immensely successful, but you know.

Remember that one bit of advice I give to schools. Whatever you do in life, make sure you can look yourself in the face after you've done it. It's a very simple and worthwhile slogan because we've all felt it. We've all not quite spoken the truth on some occasion or avoided it by silence – that is even worse. You haven't got the guts to stand up and say "Look here, I'm sorry, but I don't agree". So you keep quiet and that is just as bad as physically putting your hand up to agree with something you dislike.

One must speak the truth. The few regrets I've had were over times I should have done something but didn't do it. The funny thing is that because you felt like that, it stays with you always. Another thing I regret is to part from someone in anger. Which brings me back to how I want to be remembered. I want to be remembered so that other people, when they talk about me, *smile*.

But although one's characteristics may be settled, one's philosophy of life isn't a fixed idea. Instead, it is a code of thought and action based on experience and assimilated through the years. I don't believe anyone can acquire a complete philosophy till he can look back on his traditional three score years and ten. So I'm getting near it now!

Even then it isn't a philosophy as we've come to understand the term from reading the classics or old philosophers. As the years roll on, you discover the things in life that are real. You also find out that you often chased the shadow for the substance. Your values change with the years, which is only to be expected. As a youngster growing to manhood, the things that matter are mainly and fortunately of passing interest. You don't appreciate until later that while attainment is so satisfying, the real thrill is in striving for the goal.

There's no touch-stone that can be called a recipe for happiness – we all look at life from a different angle. Few of us have the same needs or ambitions. Often we think how happy someone else is. Yet if we were to take over his life, we would have to take over his character and personality as well. He might even be looking at us and wishing that he could change places with us!

I think the greatest of all human virtues is loyalty. It embraces all the best of the human character: courage, faith, love and charity. Down through mythology and history, tales of loyalty have been told again and again. Loyalty to a friend, a cause, a country. I like the epitaph to the three hundred Spartans who died at Thermopylae:

"Go tell in Sparta thou who passest by, that here obedient to her laws we lie."

That was written over two thousand years ago. To this day, you can go and see the place and the Pass of Thermopylae. Or you can go down to the Plain of Marathon and stand on the mound where the Athenian dead lie buried from the Battle of Marathon. You can stand, as Thelma and I stood, and view the horseshoe plain. You can see the Persian ships coming round the corner between the mainland and the island of Euboea – and into the bay where the Athenians awaited them. You can recreate the scene. Your mind becomes saturated with it as you stand on the historic ground. The people have left the imprint of their personality. History is made by people, not places.'

INDEX